The Sound of Seduction

MIRACLES ON HARLEY STREET, BOOK 4

SARA ADRIEN

© Copyright 2025 by Sara Adrien
Text by Sara Adrien
Cover by Kim Killion Designs

Dragonblade Publishing, Inc. is an imprint of Kathryn Le Veque Novels, Inc.
P.O. Box 23
Moreno Valley, CA 92556
ceo@dragonbladepublishing.com

Produced in the United States of America

First Edition August 2025
Trade Paperback Edition

Reproduction of any kind except where it pertains to short quotes in relation to advertising or promotion is strictly prohibited.

All Rights Reserved.

The characters and events portrayed in this book are fictitious. Any similarity to real persons, living or dead, is purely coincidental and not intended by the author.

ARE YOU SIGNED UP FOR DRAGONBLADE'S BLOG?

You'll get the latest news and information on exclusive giveaways, exclusive excerpts, coming releases, sales, free books, cover reveals and more.

Check out our complete list of authors, too!

No spam, no junk. That's a promise!

Sign Up Here

www.dragonbladepublishing.com

Dearest Reader;

Thank you for your support of a small press. At Dragonblade Publishing, we strive to bring you the highest quality Historical Romance from some of the best authors in the business. Without your support, there is no 'us', so we sincerely hope you adore these stories and find some new favorite authors along the way.

Happy Reading!

CEO, Dragonblade Publishing

ADDITIONAL DRAGONBLADE BOOKS BY AUTHOR SARA ADRIEN

Wedding Fever Series (with Tanya Wilde)
Dare to Tempt an Earl This Spring (Book 1)
How to Lose a Prince This Summer (Book 2)

Miracles on Harley Street Series
A Sight to Behold (Book 1)
The Scent of Intuition (Book 2)
A Touch of Charm (Book 3)
The Sound of Seduction (Book 4)

The Lyon's Den Series
Don't Wake a Sleeping Lyon
The Lyon's First Choice
The Lyon's Golden Touch
The Lyon's Legacy

Dedication

For Terri—who reminds us what true care looks like.

For Jo—whose heart is as generous as it is kind.

For Dominique—to bring a smile and a little light when it's needed most.

For Lyn—for extra strength and all the healing yet to come.

And for every single one of my dear readers who draws strength from healing—as much as from being healed.

Preface

Welcome to Harley Street!

Prince Stan, Nurse Wendy, and the other doctors and characters you'll meet in this story are part of my beloved Miracles on Harley Street series. While their tales are inspired by history and my imagination, they are works of fiction crafted to transport you to another time.

The international conflicts and events you'll encounter are rooted in historical inspiration, though I've taken creative liberties to weave a compelling narrative—including creating fictional ancestors for the Hohenzollern-Sigmaringen royals. The medical techniques and tools featured have been carefully researched to reflect the innovations of their time, staying true to a three-to-five-year historical window.

If you're curious about the historical details and where I've added my own artistic flair, be sure to check out the "Author's Note" at the end of the book.

Now, let the adventure begin! Step into a world where history and romance intertwine, and enjoy the journey.

And if you are new to the *Doctors on Harley Street* and this is your first story, keep the following short overview handy so you already know who is coming back from other books. Think of the doctors on Harley Street as a group of friends, almost like in television shows such as *Grey's Anatomy* or *Friends*, in which the stories bring everyone back, even though the focus may only be one person and his or her love interest.

Philippa "Pippa" Mae Pemberton in book 1 is the cousin of the heroine in book 2, Lady Beatrice Wetherby "Bea." In book 1, *A Sight to Behold*, Pippa fell in love with Dr. Nicholas Folsham, "Nick," who is one of the doctors at 87 Harley Street. Bea lived with Pippa at Cloverdale House, a large estate surrounded by parks with an abutting orangery, which belongs to Pippa's family and is being converted into a rehabilitation center in the book you are about to read.

Dr. Nicholas "Nick" Folsham is an oculist at 87 Harley Street, and the best eye surgeon in London. He studied in Vienna with Alfie Collins and some of the others, including Felix. Nick's story is book 1, *A Sight to Behold*. He's Wendy Folsham's older brother and, with his wife Pippa, moved to a townhouse close to the practice at 87 Harley Street. Wendy also lives there with Nick and Pippa.

Alfie Collins is the apothecary at 87 Harley Street. His and Bea's romantic story is book 2, *The Scent of Intuition*. He studied in Vienna and completed an apprenticeship in ayurvedic medicine in Delhi, India before he returned to London and opened the practice with his friends. In his story, he administered a truth serum to Baron von List, which gives rise to some of the tension fueling the plot in the story you are about to read.

Dr. Andre Fernando is the orthopedist at 87 Harley Street, originally from Florence, Italy, and he is quite the heartbreaker. Although his past overlaps with that of his friends Alfie and Felix, his future has very different surprises in store. His story overlaps with the timeline of the book you are about to read and can be found in its entirety in book 3, *A Touch of Charm*.

Wendy Folsham is Nick's younger sister and the nurse who lives and works at 87 Harley Street. Alfie, Andre, and Felix treat Wendy as their little sister, too, watching over her and keeping her safe. In reality, it's Wendy's wisdom and good heart that help the young men. Her story follows this preface in *The Sound of Seduction*.

Dr. Felix Leafley is the dentist at 87 Harley Street, and a master of his craft. He suffers from a broken heart because he hasn't been able to be reunited with the love of his life. Read his story in book 5, *A Taste of Gold*.

Baron Wolfgang von List is a Prussian villain in this series and some of my other series, too. Suffice it to say his morals are questionable, his methods brutal, and his intentions violent. For more books with this villain and his story, please visit www.Sara Adrien.com—this is also where you can find out when he will be gloriously defeated by the heroes and heroines in my other books.

Several other medical professionals regularly visit 87 Harley Street and the nearby clinic. Find those stories as part of my contributions to the *Lyon's Den* series. For more information and a complete list of Sara Adrien's stories, please visit www.Sara Adrien.com.

Chapter One

August 1818, the Week Before Alfie and Bea's Wedding.

"IF YOU WANT to find the best nurse London has ever seen, you just have to call for Wendy at 87 Harley Street," her patients often said. But on this dreary morning at the practice, Nurse Wendy feared she didn't bring her usual vigor to the Monday routine. Amongst the cacophony of clinking vials, shuffling footsteps, and bustling conversations, Gwendolyn Folsham, affectionately called Wendy by everyone who mattered, usually thrived in this orchestra of care, but her mind was elsewhere today. Though technically a nurse, her role stretched far beyond the usual expectations of her station. She wasn't just supporting one doctor, but three, and the apothecary. Her hands had steadied patients during cataract surgeries just as deftly as they had fitted spectacles, delivered babies, helped set broken bones, or changed bandages.

She could do it all.

But not the one thing she longed for—to speak to the prince.

Nonsense, she thought to herself and yawned as she tied her white apron in the back. Princes were not for nurses, except in fairytales. Work called to her as it always did, but a whisper of restlessness stirred at the edges of her thoughts, only partially drowned out by the day's demands. With a stack of freshly laundered towels and bandages in hand, starched so stiff they practically stood on their own, she made her way to Dr. Andre

Fernando's treatment room, the orthopedist at the practice. Andre's skeletal chart loomed on the wall in all its bony glory and Latin terms, perched like a sentry over his latest invention.

"Oh, fresh bandages and towels, thank you, Wendy," Andre's eyes lit up as he spotted her. A smile broke across his features, and his voice was rich with warmth as if her arrival had brightened his entire day. "Thank you for always bringing me everything I need before I even know I do." He gestured to the empty cabinet where only one small towel remained.

He wasn't her brother—only Nick held that title—yet Andre, the orthopedist, Alfie, the apothecary, and Felix, the dentist, had all earned an honorary version of it. They had made it their business to shelter her as though she were their little sister. Sometimes too much so, like when they insisted she couldn't shop alone on Regent Street or when each of them came to wish her good night, taking turns as if she weren't perfectly capable of tucking herself in at two-and-twenty.

"You're welcome, Andre." Wendy's gaze landed on the small contraption atop the table. "Is it finished?" She leaned closer, curiosity flaring.

"Yes." He picked it up, his hands deftly adjusting the splint to show how it articulated at the hinges. "It's for a little boy with rachitis. He's coming today." *Rachitis*, he said, not the common *rickets* most would use. He addressed her as though she were a colleague, not merely a nurse, and the respect in his tone felt like a cherished compliment.

"The poor child—his legs barely hold his weight. He's never played outside like he should." Her throat tightened. Wendy thought about how many carefree days she'd had playing outside with Nick when they were children...before their parents died. Freedom had always been something she'd taken for granted— until now. At the thought of the young boy whose legs couldn't hold him, her shoulders slumped, and she stared at the floor, blinking rapidly as her chest tightened. "Andre, how will it work exactly?" she asked, her eyes fixed on the intricate device.

"The splints are designed to stabilize his legs while still allow-ing movement," Andre explained, gently turning the contraption to demonstrate. "The hinges here mimic natural joint articula-tion, so he'll be able to walk more steadily without locking his knees. It'll give him the chance to build up strength."

"So, he'll be able to walk?" she asked, a glimmer of hope in her voice.

"Yes," Andre replied with a slight smile. "With some practice, he might even play outside like other children."

Wendy gently traced the leather strap with her finger, admir-ing the careful craftsmanship. It was ingenious, truly. "Will you make more?"

"I must. There are so many children like him in London. Some call it *the English disease.*" His voice dropped with quiet frustration. "I remember in Florence when I played with my brother and sister. The children there ran free, and their legs never bowed. They basked in the sunshine, healthy, strong. It's not right that children who seem otherwise well suffer a life indoors."

"It isn't," Wendy agreed softly, touched by the tenderness in his gaze as he stared at the tiny splint. He carried a protectiveness born of grief because he missed his family, a side of Andre that always left her humbled. Perhaps that was why she was drawn so deeply to this practice, to this place.

And she'd never leave, she thought.

At 87 Harley Street, their clothes were plain, their pockets often empty, but their hands never stilled—operating where others didn't dare, treating those who had been said to be incurable, binding open wounds, planting seeds of hope for healing, offering light in the darkest corners.

But still, something shifted within her. Was this all she would leave behind one day? Splints, glasses, and tinctures?

"I might accompany you to Regent Street this week," Andre added nonchalantly, interrupting her thoughts.

"No need," she replied with a touch of levity. "Bea and Pippa are coming with me for the modiste to fit my gown."

For a moment, the wedding idea lingered warmly in her thoughts—until it soured. With Nick and Alfie's marriages to high-born ladies, things had already started to change. Besides, there'd be a ball after the wedding, an unusual celebration, and worse, there would be dancing. And she still didn't know how.

That unspoken chill of embarrassment pressed on her. When would she have had the time to learn dancing? It was a life for debutantes, aristocrats, and people like Pippa and Bea. Not a nurse. Yet, she couldn't deny the brighter side of the event— celebrating Alfie and Bea's wedding, the elegance, the promise of people whose lives seemed so impossibly larger than her own. It was a glimpse of a fairytale.

"Here comes the groom," Andre said with a smirk.

"Good morning, Wendy. Andre." Alfie's cheerful voice broke into her reverie as he entered carrying several porcelain pots on a metal tray. His arrival brought a faint bittersweetness as she eyed the salves inside. Some were for children whose skin chafed against their braces and splints.

"Stan needs our help with Baron von List," Alfie declared with a tone bearing bad news as he set the tray aside.

Andre's grip faltered, and the splint slipped from his fingers. Wendy caught it effortlessly, her reflexes honed by years of far messier mishaps. Andre's voice was sharp. "Not again."

"Yes, again. And I'm concerned. That truth serum we gave him… List is bound to retaliate." Wolfgang von List, with ties to the King of Bavaria—a confidant of Napoleon Bonaparte—was a man without scruples, preying on minorities, women, and those too burdened by honest labor to see the leech that thrived on their toils. It was generally known that List viewed Europe's fragile post-Napoleonic peace as a prize for his gain and that he was the kind of man whose presence could tip the scales of empires. And although Wendy had never confronted him personally, his name was not a name meant to rest idly in anyone's mind.

Her breath caught. Not from fear—but from calculation. It was only a matter of time before they were all pulled into the crosshairs of the discord between von List and the Hohenzollern-Sigmaringen royals.

One misstep, one whisper of impropriety, and List could twist it into a scandal—or worse—war. Not just for her—but for the clinic. For Nick. For Alfie, Andre, Felix. For Cloverdale House.

Wendy didn't have to strain to follow their words. She had heard the tale, the whispered accounts of the night at the card table when Prince Stan had outmaneuvered the notorious Baron von List using Alfie's alchemy. List had tipped his hand, revealing secrets he couldn't afford to lose. He wouldn't forget this humiliation and the information he'd involuntarily shared.

Just then, the murmur of voices down the hall sent shivers up Wendy's spine, and without turning, she knew. *Prince Stan was here.* Perhaps it was the creak of the floorboard or perhaps simply an instinct she couldn't seem to suppress. Her pulse betrayed her, quickening as though each beat announced his presence.

Prince Ferdinand Constantin Maximilian Hohenzollern-Sigmaringen—Stan, to those fortunate enough to stand beside him as equals or have earned his friendship—entered with a sweep of motion like a man who commanded not just attention but respect. His shoulders were pleasingly broad, his stride purposeful, and his hair defied the principles of civility as though no crown or comb could tame it, and Wendy found herself drawn in by the storm of contradiction that was Prince Stan. Power and poise wrapped in mischief and rebellion. If Prince Stan were a book, she'd not only read her copy but wear it down till the pages fell off the binding.

But this was no fictional fairytale prince. He had no spine of glue but a straight back and warm eyes. His front wasn't a mere gilded cover but a breathtaking display of masculine splendor. And his backside was not to be hidden behind dusty book covers but wrapped in the finest tailored wool coats that barely covered the perfect backside...oh, who was she jesting? He was perfection.

Too perfect. Too tempting. And far too dangerous.

She took a step back instinctively, willing herself to focus. She wasn't some giddy girl at a Mayfair ball. She was a nurse. One misstep—even a misread glance—could unravel everything.

She couldn't afford to long for him. Not when her name was tied to Harley Street, and one rumor could taint the very place she loved.

"Good morning, Miss Folsham." His voice reverberated through her bones as if she were a tuning fork that had only waited for him to set her in motion.

Still, Wendy straightened, willing herself to stay composed. She knew her thoughts were foolish; her dreams of him were nothing more than fantasies whispered to her pillow at night. Yet when his gaze wandered briefly to her, the intensity of being seen left her exhilarated and unnerved.

"Is List really that dangerous?" she asked before she could stop herself, her voice carefully even. But when Stan's eyes darkened, a single word slipped from his lips—a warning meant to echo.

"Very."

Her breath hitched. His voice was an undertow, pulling her further into the uncharted waters that were his blue eyes. A thought flickered, despite the majestic moment. Beneath her nurse's apron, beyond the tools of her daily life, she too could anchor something grander, like a quiet urge to break free from the boundaries she'd always known. Across the room, their eyes met—steady, searching—and the unspoken promise of change permeated the atmosphere surrounding them.

STAN WAS NO stranger to the sharp crack of a rifle. He'd been trained to handle some of the military's most powerful missiles and endure the brutal toll of battle. Pain was something he could suppress without flinching.

But nothing in his training could have steeled him against the jolt that surged through him the moment Nurse Wendy met his gaze with her beautiful eyes.

Next, a stronger blow followed; she blushed. Not subtly, but with a vivid fury that left no room for doubt, he was the reason.

It wasn't a mistake. This was deliberate, and it was aimed directly at him with the precision of a gunshot.

He shouldn't have looked. Shouldn't have noticed. But he did—and now he couldn't unsee her.

Not just her beauty, but her bravery. Her restraint. The quiet, stunning nobility in the way she held herself like a soldier under inspection.

And that was the problem. He wasn't safe for her. He didn't have a simple life. And getting close to her could mean dragging her into the line of fire.

For her sake, he had to turn away and pretend none of this stirred anything at all.

"Then how do we defend against him?" Nurse Wendy asked. A simple question that had such a complicated answer. It had taken him nearly two months in London to just charter its border—or better, List's wide reach of that forsaken and corrupt network of near-miss crimes he'd constructed.

There was no defense. Not for this. Not for her. Certainly not because he wouldn't try—he would have given half his fortune to conjure up some barrier between himself and the thrumming in his chest—but because he couldn't. Every hard-won ounce of discipline, every instinct honed for survival, seemed utterly useless the moment Nurse Wendy entered his proximity—and yet the closer she was to him, the more she could be in danger, like him.

"We stay away," Alfie said as if he tried to dismiss the idea of Wendy going anywhere near him because it was plain to see that List's assaults followed him like an unwanted shadow.

"But List won't stay away from *us*," Andre said.

"He won't stay away from *me*." Stan corrected them. "I'm his target."

"And now, we all may be," Andre added.

And that was one of the thousand reasons why he had to stay away from Nurse Wendy. He'd die a death worse than execution at List's hands if anything happened to his friends, the doctors at Harley Street, or Nurse Wendy.

She took his breath away in ways he couldn't fathom. And yet, it happened every time he saw her.

He'd seen her before, of course. Many times, in fact—often enough that her presence should no longer rattle him. As the oculist's sister, she'd been part of the clinic's daily rhythm. She was never insignificant. Her crisp white apron, her steady hands, her voice that calmly directed even aristocrats—she was not just a nurse. She was the linchpin of this place. It wasn't just admiration anymore. It was longing, and that made her dangerous. He had enemies. Loving her could destroy her.

Last month, when he'd begun staying at the Langley's townhouse upon his arrival in London, she had flitted in and out as part of the medical entourage for the pregnant Countess of Langley. The apothecary and the doctors came as needed, their presence a matter of courtesy or necessity. But Wendy…Wendy was never just a formality.

At first glance, she appeared to be the epitome of modest utility—a pretty girl in her crisp white apron, her hands methodical and steady. From the beginning, he noticed her attractiveness. He wasn't blind, nor was he immune to how her neat braid slipped loose by late afternoon, framing her face with a hint of chaos that contrasted with her precise movements. He contemplated how to tug at that neatly tied ribbon of her apron, envisioning various angles from which she would fall straight into his arms. The outcome existed only in his dreams at night, for he also imagined how he would unravel that ribbon and catch her—the best part. Still, he quickly dismissed the idea, much like one might disregard a glimmer on a distant horizon. It was there, yet inconsequential.

But then…

Then, he watched her work.

And that was when the glint became a beacon.

Wendy moved not with the clinical detachment he expected from someone assisting physicians but with a sort of quiet, unyielding purpose. She wasn't merely present; she was pivotal. Her deft hands anticipated what each doctor needed before they even asked. Her voice, calm but firm, without hesitation, directed aristocratic patients twice her age. It was in the way she leaned over a patient's bedside, her brow furrowed not in doubt but in determination, that he realized something startlingly simple yet irrevocably profound.

She healed.

People, objects, even his fractured patience as he waited hours in the Langley parlor for someone to tend to his hostess' nausea—everything Wendy touched seemed to mend under her care. And it had struck him harder than any bullet that she wielded her expertise without the faintest trace of vanity. Wendy simply…did. Wasn't that infinitely more compelling than any amount of artificial charm honed by the vain aristocratic ladies he'd been presented with for as long as he could remember? He may bear the title of prince, but that was only a courtesy of his bloodline; there was no kingdom nor principality he ruled over, despite the blue blood in his veins.

Now here she stood, blushing with a fury that seemed to set the room alight, and Stan felt something unravel within him. It wasn't her fault. He knew that. She was probably not even aware of what she'd done. But her cheeks, pink and burning, betrayed something that tightened his chest to the point of absurdity.

This wasn't admiration. Not anymore. Admiration didn't lance through a man's defenses and leave him raw every night— apparently now, also by day.

He should have looked away.

Should have folded this moment down like a military report—studied, filed, and dismissed.

For a moment, their eyes met again, and the air stretched thin between them. He was a soldier, a leader, a man trained to withstand harsher pressures than this.

But what training prepared a man to resist someone like her? Not when her mere presence could compromise his entire mission. And yet, here he stood, utterly unarmed in the face of a woman who didn't even realize she'd already conquered him.

Chapter Two

NO MATTER HOW many ways Stan dissected the threats posed by List, the danger remained the same. He had spent the better part of the morning discussing it with Andre and Alfie, but the weight of it still pressed heavily on his mind. Protecting his friends at Harley Street was non-negotiable, yet he couldn't face this alone—he needed their help. Even now, as he lingered in Andre's treatment room with the only two people he could truly trust—the unease refused to leave him.

"If they insist on coming to the wedding, we have to make sure they're safe," Stan said, glancing over his shoulder at the small group who had become—to his surprise—what he could for the first time in his life call friends. Truly. Until he'd met the doctors on Harley Street, he thought a prince couldn't have real friends—not ones he dared to trust fully, at least. Too often, people had vested interests in his fortune, his title, and even the alliances he was expected to forge. That's why he'd sent for his brother, Alex, when the trouble with List started to escalate.

He needed someone he could trust.

Trust, for Stan, had always been a guarded currency, spent sparingly. He had been careful even during his rare indulgences with women on the Continent. No names. No promises. No lingering attachments, not in the heart and not physically. There wouldn't even be a rumor to follow his trail.

It wasn't until Wendy appeared at the Langleys', that a woman took over his every thought.

And he'd never even touched her!

Except secretly, in the quiet of the night, Stan had entertained the treacherous scenes in his mind—where he untied those neat little ties of her bonnet, drew her into his arms, and kissed her until her blush deepened to a shade reserved only for him. Yet even his errant thoughts couldn't remain innocent. No, he'd seen what her blushes were truly capable of, and they tugged at him—closer, always closer.

Stop it!

The command to himself was rough and unheard.

Someone cleared his throat. "Nick?" Alfie called, his voice pulling Stan out of his thoughts. Stan stepped aside instinctively, unconsciously situating himself nearer to her. "Nick?" Alfie's voice echoed down the hall.

"I'm here," came the calm baritone as the tall, fair-haired oculist entered the room. Nick nodded toward Stan, treating him to a brief but exacting gaze. "Your Royal Highness, how do you do?"

Stan almost snorted. "Drop the formalities. Please," he added, a touch too dryly. "It's hardly amusing, given the circumstances." His gaze swept over the room. "We're all in grave danger."

"What happened this time?" Nick inquired, stepping to Wendy's side with the protective air of an elder brother—a gesture Stan recognized all too well, having a sister of his own. But Nick furrowed his brow and studied Wendy for a moment too long. "Are you all right?"

The question, direct and inquisitive, lit Wendy's cheeks anew. Her hands twisted together, and she cast her gaze downward. "I'm fine," she murmured, barely louder than a whisper.

"Wendy, you seem flushed," Andre chimed in, stepping forward. "Are you feverish?" He reached a hand toward her forehead.

Stan's jaw tightened. *She's not a child. Leave her be.*

"Here, allow me." Alfie intercepted, taking a gentle but confident hold of her wrist to feel her pulse. His expression barely shifted, though he hummed softly. "A bit quick," he noted.

"Perhaps you should rest instead of going shopping with the ladies," Nick suggested, crossing his arms in that insufferably practical manner of his.

Stan had to fight back a bitter laugh. If his own sister came into the room flushed and flustered in such a way, he might well have chalked it up to summer heat or exertion—anything to avoid entertaining the presence of a suitor. Of course, Nick likely didn't see *him* as anything resembling a suitor.

Would he even allow it, though? Would Nick approve, knowing Stan's rank, his known ties to danger, and his carefully veiled reputation as a man who left no traces? Stan knew Nick was no fool, unlikely to be dazzled by a title or royal lineage. He'd remarked—more times than Stan cared to recall—that being a prince was as much a burden as it was a danger and not something to envy. Stan had no illusions about earning Nick's blessing to court his sister. And who could blame him? To Nick, he likely seemed more a weapon to protect against, than a man worthy of his sister's heart—a testament to Nick's fierce love as a brother, even if it made Stan's path to Wendy all the more impossible.

Stan knew that their parents were no longer alive, leaving Nick as her only family. His wife, Lady Philippa Pemberton—Pippa for short—was the daughter of an Earl and an heiress with riches rivaling the Crown, though Stan was keenly aware of how carefully Wendy balanced her ties to nobility with her devotion to a simpler life among her patients, friends, and extended family. As for protection, the beautiful, capable nurse had the unofficial fortress of the fine doctors stationed at 87 Harley Street—some of the best—and they all seemed to guard her with the same vigilance one might a precious heirloom. And if Stan weren't an intruder in her innocent and shielded world, he'd simply be happy that she was cared for. The problem was, he wanted to be looking after her and taking care of her himself.

"Wendy, if you wish, I can brew some eucalyptus tea," Alfie said gently.

"And I'll fetch some ice to cool you down," Andre added, already half-turning toward the door.

"No!" Wendy's voice rose abruptly as she pulled her hands free from Alfie's grasp. Her blush deepened even more, and her eyes fluttered briefly toward Stan before shooting downward again. "I said I'm fine," she insisted, her voice firmer this time. Too firm, perhaps—but necessary. If she lost her composure now, if anyone guessed why... it wouldn't just be her pride on the line. It would be the practice. Nick's legacy. Everything that mattered in her life. *Not me.*

"Are you certain, little sis?" Nick pressed, clearly unconvinced.

"Nick!" she all but groaned, rolled her eyes, and shifted. Her shoes scraped the floor as she stepped away, gaze fixed downward, her cheeks still flushed. Each glance from Stan felt like exposure. She couldn't let anyone guess what stirred inside her. Not when a scandal could ruin everything. Still, her eyes didn't leave the hardwood floor as she straightened, a flush still staining her cheeks, like ripe peaches he wanted to reach for and taste.

Stop pining after her!

Stan rubbed his forehead, as if the tension between them could be wiped away. But it lingered—thick, and dangerous. Without saying a word, she turned and strode toward the doorway, her skirts swishing with a defiance that felt aimed at him.

Stan's eyes followed her, unable to look away. His chest tightened as he caught the smallest tremor in her hand when it brushed the doorframe for balance, her resolve strong but fragile in that fleeting moment.

Every part of him ached to follow—to close the space between them, pull her into his arms, and promise her the safety and comfort she deserved. He could almost sense the way she'd fit against him, could already hear the steadier rhythm her breathing would find there. But he stood frozen, his own reason bearing down on him.

It would only put her in harm's way. The harder he held on, the sharper he'd carve her path into the danger that loomed always just behind him.

She vanished down the corridor, taking the warmth of the room with her, leaving in its place the cold certainty he fought to live with every day—he had to let her go to keep her safe. But it hurt to watch her leave.

He inhaled deeply—steadying himself before his own composure shattered outright.

Nick tilted his head, watching Wendy's departure as he stood rooted in place. "Well," he said, plucking at his cuff. "She's somewhere between perfectly fine and completely overworked."

"She must be worried because of the danger," Andre said. "I warned you!"

"You can't warn us from the storm that's List because we can control him as little as the weather," Alfie said and tapped his foot on the floor as if List would come and strike any moment. "And he could strike us with the force of a lighting strike at any moment!"

"We know he will seek revenge for what we did. We should never have given him that truth serum and forced him to give up half his secrets. Who knows what the other half bears?" He pinched the bridge of his nose and exhaled slowly, his lips pressing into a thin line as though bracing himself to deliver grim news he wished he didn't have to share. "And she knows it, too. List preys on women." Nick swallowed visibly and glanced toward the door through which Wendy had just left. "And this leaves us all vulnerable. Pippa, Bea, and Wendy are—"

"Don't say it!" Alfie held his hand up. "I should have never listened to you and made the truth serum for him. It's because of me that we are in this situation."

"Not even a little bit, Alfie," Stan said. "I have it on good authority that he was already targeting Felix Leafley."

"What does he want from a dentist?" Andre said.

"It's not what but who." Stan lowered his voice. "Felix's suppliers are the Jewish jewelers. The Crown Jewelers. List is cutting their supplies off by stealing from my family and my people in Transylvania."

"I thought he was exploiting the gold mines in your region without—" but Andre couldn't finish. Nick slapped his forehead. "No! Please tell me that isn't true!"

"Oh, but it is." Stan cleared his throat. "List is stealing from Transylvania's gold mines and trying to blame it on the trade route of our Jewish friends! How am I supposed to protect the people of Transylvania, preserve the trade route, and stop List from exploiting innocent people as scapegoats? The Jews have done nothing wrong, and List has no right to embezzle the gold from *our* mines!"

"So if he succeeds, then Felix will be seen as little more than a thief for the Ton." Alfie lifted his chin as understanding dawned. "It would ruin us all."

"But that's a lie! Felix and the Crown Jewelers…I know them. They're the most upstanding, honest, generous men I've met!" Andre's voice rang with outrage.

Stan nodded once, grimly. "Which is exactly why they're useful to List. He doesn't care who he harms. He only wants to profit. And he needs a scapegoat for the collateral damage."

His throat tightened. That phrase—*scapegoat for the collateral damage*—lodged somewhere deeper now. It was too familiar. He thought of Wendy, of the fragile line between her quiet heroism and the noise List would make if he ever caught wind of her connection to him. She, too, could be used. Twisted.

And he was the one who brought that risk near her, he reminded himself.

"So, if he hurts any of us and we fight back, he'll make it seem like we attacked him? And that'll just draw even more attention to us?" Alfie asked.

"I don't understand what he would gain from hurting us or

the women we love." Nick blinked toward the door again.

He had the most to lose—his wife, his sister. But it wasn't just personal. If anything happened to Pippa, it would shatter Nick. If anything happened to Wendy…

Stan exhaled. Wendy was more than Nick's sister. She was the quiet strength behind everything Harley Street stood for. If List touched her, he wouldn't just be harming a woman Stan had come to care for. He'd be undermining the very heart of the practice. Discrediting her would discredit them all.

And Wendy would lose so much more than her reputation. Not just her safety. Her dignity. Her place. Her brother's legacy. The work they'd built with their bare hands.

The doctors at Harley Street weren't just a group of forward-thinking healers. They were a family. And List, if given the chance, would destroy them from the inside out. He had seen villages torn apart by threats like List—silent, creeping, cloaked in legitimacy until it was too late. But here, there might still be time to act. And it had to begin with protecting the women who carried their futures in hand and heart.

"They might be easier prey than we are." Andre shook his head.

"So, we protect Pippa, Bea, and Wendy," Nick said. "Right? We keep my wife, your bride, and my little sister safe."

Alfie nodded, and Andre joined in synchrony as if no further words were needed.

"It is my duty to protect them, too," Stan said. "I brought List closer than he might have come to you all…"

Nick and the others shook their heads, but Stan didn't hear them anymore. Wendy had her own royal guard, and for the first time in his life, Stan became the potential danger to the people he'd actually wanted to protect.

"About the corrupt Baron then…" Andre started anew.

"We knew he'd retaliate for the truth serum," Alfie added. "Where do we start building our defenses?"

But Stan said nothing. He couldn't. Silence was safer. His

mind was far too occupied with reliving the moment Wendy stumbled over her words and glanced at him—the way she'd looked at him. Because it hadn't been the gaze of someone embarrassed by polite company or overprotective brother figures. It had been something else entirely.

Something aimed at him.

And he only hoped he could be worthy of what she had to give without endangering her.

Chapter Three

S TAN NEEDED TO speak to Felix, too. He still carried his father's letter in his pocket.

My Dear Son,

The weight of our house and the fate of our people rest heavily on us, and now more than ever, you must act with vigilance and diplomacy. Protect those under our care, especially your brother as he journeys to Cornwall. For even the thinnest threads of our family's security are vital. Our enemy, List, is no better than his father, a man vile in his scapegoating of the Jews and cunning in evading accountability. His charm belies his true nature, and he grows more dangerous by the day. I trust your strength and decisiveness will meet the challenges ahead; this family and our people depend on it.

Your devoted Father,
Prince Ferdinand

But today, the hallway outside Felix's office at 87 Harley Street felt narrower than it should have, like a space that seemed to close in when tension filled it. Stan adjusted his stance, his boot squeaking on the worn oak floor. Felix stood stiffly in front of him, his face unusually tense, his jaw clenched as if holding back words. The sharp smell of mint poultices and something metallic drifted from the rooms beyond, but Felix didn't seem his usual composed self today. His hands, normally quick and steady, hung stiffly at his sides.

"I haven't seen you downstairs," Stan said when Felix gave him a smile that didn't reach his eyes. "Henry told me that you had to change his appointment because you didn't have enough material."

Felix flattened his lips. Of course, Stan didn't expect that any of the doctors at Harley Street would discuss private patient matters with him but since Stan lived with Henry, the Earl of Langley, he just happened to know.

"It's not because of me," Felix started, scanning the hallway before speaking again, quieter. "But about the Klonimuses."

The name landed like a blow. Stan's chest tightened as he straightened, his mind leaping to the six brothers. Kind men. Brilliant, even. Stan could still hear any of the six brothers Klonimus chattering while they bent over a delicate commission of the Grand Service for the Crown. They had served England with grace—and for that, they'd become targets.

"Are they safe?" Stan asked, his voice too sharp, betraying his nerves.

"For now," Felix replied with a grim edge. He folded his arms, his gaze fixed on Stan. "But it's List. He's not working alone. He's working with a man named Richard Nagy, calls himself a bailiff. The kind who'll do anything for coin and out of sheer hatred for us. And his men nearly killed Benjamin Klonimus."

Nearly. The word lodged in his throat like grit. Ben was a friend and one of the most honest and talented people Stan had ever known, just like Felix. And anyone who targeted his Jewish friends were enemies to Stan, too. His jaw clenched instinctively. He kept his eyes on Felix as if the calm demeanor might dull what was quickly blooming into anger. "What do you mean, 'nearly killed?' Is Ben all right?"

Felix shook his head, frustration flickering across his face. "He's well, which is more than we expected. They didn't find him, that's all. And List hasn't ceased trying. He's had others attacked already, and worse. Men like Nagy act with impunity under his name."

Stan felt the slow churn in his stomach coil and rise. Tactics. Orders. A pattern forming. He'd seen it before, knew it too well. "He's escalating," he said, though it felt more like confirming suspicions aloud.

Felix inclined his head, but the energy in his stance didn't shift. "And the brothers' gold," he continued. "It's nearly gone. They send me whatever meager amounts they can spare so I can treat patients, but… I don't know how much longer I can keep taking it."

There was more to this, Stan knew it. Felix wasn't a man to focus on his own troubles unless he believed something greater was at stake. Stan narrowed his eyes. "Gold for your patients. That's part of it, but it's more than that, isn't it?"

Felix inhaled through his nose and lowered his arms. "Yes," he said softly. "If word gets out that any of us can't treat our patients, it damages us all. The doctors, the rehabilitation center at Cloverdale House. Worse than that, though, this directly affects the brothers. They're the Crown Jewelers, Stan. If they can't supply Prinny with what he demands, the humiliation alone… You know how fragile England appears on the heels of Napoleon's defeat."

Stan's pulse quickened. This wasn't just about the Klonimuses or Felix's practice. This had layers, consequences stacked too high to ignore. And yet, the thought of six brothers being targeted for daring to exist was what burned brightest in his chest.

"It all leads back to List?" Stan asked tightly. "What's stopping him?"

"You? Or nothing yet," Felix admitted. His voice dropped further, and he closed the space between them. "He's been seen in the House of Lords, Stan. He's got men rallying to him. Some of them don't care what he stands for, as long as the money flows. Something is… deeply rotten."

Stan's thoughts swirled as Felix spoke. Enough. Stan had hoped he'd left the battlefield when he'd accepted his father's task to prevent the exploitation of Transylvania's gold mines from a position in England, or so he thought. But the knot sitting hard in his gut told him this was no different. Only here, it wasn't a field. It was the shadows in corridors, secret deals, attacks in the dark. Men like List didn't stop until someone forced them to.

He stared past Felix for a heartbeat, his earlier optimism now gone. If List succeeded, he could strip Transylvania of its gold and resources, turning it into a hollowed land mired in despair. The blame would fall squarely on Stan's family, left to govern an impoverished, depleted region. Their power would crumble, their coffers drained, and Stan and his siblings would face a future without wealth, influence, or hope.

"We don't have time to wait," Stan said quietly, more to himself than Felix. His voice carried steadily, though a part of him wanted to shout at the injustice of it all. "He has to be stopped before this web tightens."

Felix's gaze lingered on him. There were no promises exchanged, but there didn't need to be. Stan squared his shoulders. Whatever was coming, he wouldn't stand idle. There was too much at stake. And for the Klonimuses, for Felix, for Transylvania, he'd act before it was too late.

"Be careful," Felix said but Stan was already on his way out. He needed to think about his next move—if he could anticipate List's next attack, he could prevent it. Or perhaps, he could even stop List from getting away with wielding the forces of evil without scruples and punishment.

But the faint murmur of voices reached Stan as he paused in the hall on his way out. He recognized hers immediately—soft, warm, gently lilting like a summer breeze.

Wendy.

She was the ray of sun in the dark storm brewing in his chest. And like a ray of golden warmth, she had the unique ability to make him briefly forget the thunder brewing with the rays of her sweet and lovely voice alone.

Now, however, she wasn't speaking to him. But he couldn't ignore the pull that made his feet move toward the sound.

He stood outside Andre's treatment room, expecting to see the familiar tall figure of the physician bending over a patient. But Andre wasn't there. Instead, Wendy's voice carried through the cracked door, low and melodic. She was talking to someone—cheerful, tender, and unhurried.

"I don't want the other children to see me like this." A boy's voice now, timid and trembling slightly.

Stan frowned at the fragility in it, the kind of raw uncertainty only childhood could carry. That tone—he'd heard it before. In war camps, in exile camps. Dread of judgment.

"They won't know what to say," Wendy replied lightly, "because none of them have such interesting contraptions as you. It's a brilliant thing, see? With hinges, leather straps, and metal bars on the sides."

Her tone made Stan pause, his gaze resting on the narrow slice of the room visible through the gap in the door. He shouldn't be here. Shouldn't linger. Yet her words reeled him in—effortless reassurance and an ease that seemed to cradle the boy's insecurity in her capable hands.

"But my sister Charlotte said I look like I'm stuck in a birdcage," the child's voice trembled with another sniffle. It was muffled, as though he'd turned his face away.

Fabric rustled faintly. Stan leaned closer, his pulse ticking faster as though proximity would allow him into that space where Wendy's presence was the sun casting everything else in shadow. He dared a glance through the door.

She was crouched beside a boy, her skirts and white apron pooling in soft folds around her as she delicately dabbed a small handkerchief against his blotchy cheeks. The boy's shoulders curled inward, his thin legs bound in the contraptions he'd heard that Andre had crafted—splints of metal and leather to straighten bones and strengthen poorly healed fractures or to help children with rickets walk—Andre had mentioned it to Stan before. They did not resemble a birdcage though, Stan thought absently, more like the lanterns at Bran Castle perhaps. But that's what a genius's inventions often initially appeared like, didn't they? The world was rarely ready to accept medical breakthroughs in a timely fashion.

"It's not fair," the boy whimpered, his head bowed. "I can't walk unless I have the splints on."

Wendy sighed, a quiet and sorrowful sound that softened the air. Stan's gaze lingered on her profile as she bit her lip as if carefully choosing her words. A curl had slipped loose from the pins holding her hair up, brushing her cheek in a way that made Stan's chest tighten. "Look at me," she said finally, her voice threaded with calm authority and a trace of playfulness. "Thanks to this invention, you can walk. Your sister doesn't understand that this is temporary. Temporary means it won't last forever, do you know that?"

The boy sniffled audibly but shook his head, his small, freckled face peeking out from beneath the messy fringe of his red hair.

Wendy leaned in slightly, lowering her voice as though sharing a secret. "Do you know what I think? I think your contraption is cleverer than Charlotte realizes. She doesn't see what I see. It's like a magic trick." A pause, brief but deliberate, pulling the boy's attention away from his doubts. "You step inside it now, and one day, you'll step out stronger than you've ever been. You'll have straight legs, strong bones, and"—she smiled softly—"you'll be the last to laugh, like my father always said."

The boy peered at her, his tears momentarily forgotten. "You really think so? It's a magic trick?"

Wendy's smile deepened, filling the air with her quiet confidence. "I know so. When the human body heals, it's nothing short of a miracle! Magic, absolutely! And you can tell them you're the only one clever enough to wear it to help that magic along."

Stan's throat tightened as he watched the boy's shoulders

relax at her gentle reassurance. The smallest blossom of hope flickered in the child's tear-streaked face, and Wendy reached forward one last time, dabbing a stray tear away with her square of linen.

"Then Father must be right. He says that we're both miracles, Charlotte and I. All the time."

"And if your father says it," Wendy replied, "I'd wager it must be true."

Another pause, this one unbroken by the boy's voice or Wendy's. Only the sound of her skirts as she shifted slightly, a curl of hair bouncing free as she moved with some unintentional grace that Stan found impossible not to notice. She lifted her hand suddenly, as if remembering it was there, and tucked the rogue curl back into place behind her ear.

Then, she looked up.

Stan's breath caught and he froze. Her gaze met his—wide, unguarded—and for a breathless moment, the quiet room, the boy's splints, the entire world narrowed to just that look.

She saw him.

And worse—he sensed what it cost her to hold his gaze.

His chest tightened, not from nerves, but from knowing how fragile the moment was. This was the distance he was meant to keep.

Still, he stepped forward. His boots clicked softly against the polished floor, each stride a quiet betrayal of his caution. He met her eyes—steady, searching—even as every part of him warned that she could not remain untouched if he continued.

Her lips parted, just barely, as though she meant to ask something-or perhaps only caught her breath. Although her surprise lingered, what arrested him most was the way her expression softened, just faintly, not retreating but allowing him to be seen in turn.

And for Stan, that was it—the moment the lost pieces fell into place, like the shields of a Roman testudo snapping into perfect formation. His mind, trained in the art of strategy, recognized the pattern instantly, each piece locking together with purpose, and defense was futile. Whatever longing had clawed at him before felt sharper now, absolutely undeniable. There was no running from Wendy, no strategy that ended with escape. There was only her and him, rooted in the doorway, unable to prevent whatever came next.

This moment—Wendy in his arms, instinctively calm and focused even in the heat of intimacy—showed him something else too. She was not just the nurse who'd cared for him. She was someone who could stand steady at the helm of Cloverdale House, calm beneath pressure, bold without being reckless.

THE CORRIDOR FELL into a hush as Wendy gazed at Prince Stan standing in the doorway. For a moment, it was as if she'd forgotten to breathe—just her unsteady pulse filling the stillness. Then he shifted, bowing slightly, one hand pressed to his chest in that easy, regal way of his.

"My apologies, Miss Folsham," he said in his smooth and rich voice. "I didn't mean to interrupt."

Wendy's heart thrummed—too fast, too loud—and she pressed her palm to the edge of the treatment bed to steady herself. Could he hear what he did to her heart?

"Can I assist you in any way, Your Royal Highness?" she asked, a touch breathless but managing the question with a small, composed smile.

Her little patient, Eddie, stopped sniffling long enough to squeak, "Royal Highness?" His wide, skeptical eyes darted to the doorway, studying the prince.

Wendy flicked her gaze toward Prince Stan, a silent prompt he instantly understood. He tipped his head slightly and, with a slow smile, stepped inside.

"Yes, my name is Prince Ferdinand Constantin Maximilian

Hohenzollern-Sigmaringen," Stan announced with gravity, bowing low once more. He was too good to be real, and yet, there he was, true nobility impersonated.

The boy gasped, eyes lighting up like lanterns. "Oh boy! A real prince?" His excitement bubbled over, and before either of them could stop him, he attempted a leap from the high treatment bed.

"Eddie, wait," Wendy called, reaching for him—but the little boy's legs slipped.

Stan's movements were immediate and startling in their graceful precision. He lunged forward, pivoting with ease to intercept the boy as he toppled toward the floor. One arm swept beneath the boy's knees while the other supported his back, catching him mid-air before his splints or his pride could take any damage.

The room seemed to exhale as Stan crouched low, lowering Eddie gently to a standing position. His hands steadied the child's sides, just above his narrow hips, before he leaned back and knelt to meet him at eye level.

"See?" Stan smiled as if he didn't have a care in the world—only patience and encouragement in his voice. "You're standing!"

Eddie froze, blinking down at his legs as though the realization hadn't fully registered. The splints gleamed faintly in the soft light of the room, supporting him as his feet pressed firmly against the floor.

"I am," Eddie whispered with delight.

Wendy placed a steadying hand on the boy's back, her fingers lightly brushing over his thin shoulders. Tears pricked behind her eyes, but she pushed them down, focusing instead on the moment unfolding before her.

"The splints are holding me!" Eddie exclaimed, turning his head to peek at Wendy with wide, amazed eyes. "Look, Nurse Wendy! I haven't stood since Yuletide last winter!"

Her smile curved warmly as she glanced down at him. "You see? What did I tell you? Magic."

Stan surveyed her then, and his gaze was like the brush of sunlight against her skin. His smile deepened, sincere and dazzling. Wendy tried desperately so to keep her composure, but her heart was having none of it. It melted clean away as that breathtaking mixture of blue and green in his eyes pinned her in place.

"Magic indeed," Stan murmured, more to her than to the boy.

Eddie bounced on the balls of his feet, testing the strength of the splints.

"Well, Eddie," Stan nodded, "I'd say you're already getting stronger wearing those splints. Like a knight preparing for battle in a full suit of armor."

"Armor?" the boy asked eagerly, his face alight.

"Oh yes," Stan said, nodding as though the idea had struck him only then. His expression turned mock-serious, lips pursed as though he were carefully considering his next words. Wendy couldn't hold back a soft chuckle.

"I've seen many hopefuls come and go at Bran Castle," Stan continued gravely, "in the Carpathian Mountains. Not every warrior has what it takes to carry heavy armor and protect what's right."

Eddie's eyes went round as saucers, his breath hitching in awe. "I can carry armor. I can do it," he said firmly.

"I think you can, too," Stan said, straightening to his full height. He reached out a hand toward the boy. "You, Squire Eddie, strike me as the kind of knight who will finish training stronger than anyone expects."

Eddie shook Stan's hand solemnly, without hesitation. Wendy clutched her chest as if her heart could pop out with delight and break in two at the sight of Prince Stan towering like a sturdy oak above the boy, his smile both encouraging and kind.

And then Prince Stan looked at her again, his focus shifting entirely to her. Wendy's breath caught, the beginnings of a blush stealing over her cheeks at the depth of his gaze. He didn't need to say a word, not with that shimmer in his eyes—mischievous, yes, but also deeply understanding, as though he knew exactly what this moment meant for Eddie.

For her.

It wasn't the smile itself that undid her, but the way it reached his eyes, softening the edges, wrapping her in a glow that could banish the cold forever.

Wendy clasped her hands tightly to still their tremor, but her heart?

That was another thing entirely.

Eddie's parents arrived not long after, bustling into the treatment room with worried faces that quickly melted into gratitude at the sight of their boy standing tall. Stan remained gracious, offering a steady nod before excusing himself, mentioning something about needing to speak with Alfie in the apothecary. Wendy handed the child over with a few final words of instruction for the splints; her voice warm, but her thoughts distracted.

She smoothed a hand over her apron, the linen coarse beneath her fingertips. Stan's gaze wandered across the treatment room and lingered on Andre's diploma, sunlight glancing over its bold Latin text. *Universitas Vindobonensis, Scientiae Medicinae Doctor*, it read, University of Vienna, Doctor of Medical Science.

Stan's brow furrowed as he tilted his head to study the frame. "Andre's diploma," he noted. "He's fluent in German and Latin, I wager." He paused and cast a glance toward Wendy, his voice colored with a curious lilt. "Where did you hang your certifications as a nurse? I see each of the doctors has their own on the wall."

The question landed like a wet cloth splashing her face. Wendy hesitated, her heartbeat quickening. The mortar and stone walls, so much less forgiving than the village cottages she'd grown up in, offered her no escape from the question. She clasped her hands in front of her to keep them still, though her fingertips pressed into her palm, betraying her unease.

"I don't have one," she admitted, her voice soft but steady.

Even so, heat prickled up her neck, blooming across her cheeks. She risked a glance at him, already preparing herself for the flicker of disappointment. Or worse—pity. There it was again—the chasm between their worlds, deepened by paper and privilege.

"Oh," Stan said, the single syllable hanging awkwardly in the air between them. His gaze flicked away as if unsure where to land, and Wendy's stomach tightened.

She glanced back at him reluctantly, carrying the silence with her like a too-heavy burden. His brows drew together briefly, but then, just as quickly, his expression softened.

"My sister didn't attend university either," he said, leaning forward, his voice low in the quiet of the room. "Unlike my brothers and me. But truth be told, she's smarter without a degree than all of us together with our collection of papers covering walls." Wendy blinked, surprised enough to meet his gaze directly. His tone was warm, unassuming, and carried a thread of admiration she hadn't expected. "She's the one who sees what we miss entirely," Stan continued. His lips curved, just faintly, into a smile that felt meant for her alone. "I suppose you're like that, the axis that keeps things spinning. Without you, nothing works as smoothly here in the practice."

Wendy's throat tightened—not from shame, but from something rarer: recognition. Could he really see her? Not as a nurse, not as Nick's sister, but as someone worthy? She didn't speak, not at first, because she couldn't quite trust herself to. Her fingers, still knotted together, loosened slowly. Why did a compliment from the prince mean more to her than a degree on the wall would?

Stan shifted again, seemingly at ease with the confession he had shared. "I imagine it's the same here," he added simply, almost as though clarifying to himself. "You don't need a piece of paper when it's already clear how brilliant you are."

The words hung in the air, bright and solid, and for once, Wendy did not rush to chase them away. Instead, she nodded slightly, her lips curving in a brief but genuine smile. "Thank you," she murmured, the heat in her face softening into something less painful, something more like pride.

Stan returned that small smile, and for the first time in what felt like ages, the room wasn't weighted by pretenses or unspoken apologies but simply comfortable.

Stan left when Eddie did. Wendy felt the tug the moment the door closed behind the patient and his parents. The urge. She should clean up the treatment room. She knew that, but her feet itched to move before her mind could second-guess. She slipped into the hall, barely bothering to smooth her apron or adjust her bonnet.

There was no time; cleaning would wait. She hurried past the gilded mirror that hung just outside the waiting room, pausing only for a fraction of a second. Her reflection offered nothing particularly reassuring, but she decided it didn't matter. If her bonnet sat slightly askew, well, so be it. She wasn't sure what to expect from this impulse, only that she wanted—no, needed—to see him again.

The apothecary door stood partway ajar, and her heart gave a traitorous leap when she peered inside. There he was.

Stan stood at the counter, one hand resting lightly on its edge as he leaned in to speak with Alfie. His frame was purposeful even in repose, his voice low but carrying the faint cadence of dry humor.

"—List lurking with his plan for vengeance—nonsensical, naturally, but it seems alarmingly well-organized."

Alfie muttered something in response, but Wendy missed it entirely because Stan shifted then, just slightly. Her eyes drifted downward, unbidden. Oh dear.

His beige breeches, sharply tailored to perfection, framed his shapely behind, and Wendy's cheeks burned. This wasn't just shapely—it was everything in harmony. The cut of his breeches, along with the positioning of the seams in the most flattering places, complemented the serious lines of his tailcoat, yet couldn't hide the firm, lean strength she imagined underneath. A symphony of masculinity and strength, with the right measure of youth and a dash of refinement, made her forget how to speak.

But then Stan turned toward her, stealing her breath anew. His sideburns—trimmed to impeccable precision—framed a face poised with charm. And, oh, that slow smile. It wasn't loud or broad, more subtle than she'd expected, but it felt deliberate. Reserved for her.

"Wendy!" Alfie chirped, snapping her out of her spiraling thoughts. Stan turned fully toward her, his gaze steady, and she felt her throat tighten.

"Th-thank you," she croaked, then immediately flushed harder.

Alfie tilted his head. "For what?"

"She means me," Stan said with an arched brow.

Even that was perfection.

"Erm," Wendy blurted hastily. She cleared her throat, dipping into a slightly stiff curtsy as she addressed Stan. "Your Royal Highness, I mean—thank you for your help with my patient."

The curtsy was instinctive, yet it felt awkward when paired with her faintly trembling voice. Oh, if Pippa and Bea saw this, they'd probably send her to finishing school—she needed finishing, regardless of the full waiting room, waiting for her every morning.

"You helped her with a patient?" Alfie leaned back, his grin turning sly as his arms crossed over his chest. "Do tell, Stan."

"It was nothing, really," Stan said, brushing it off with a wave of his hand. "A boy who needed a little encouragement, that's all."

"That wasn't nothing," Wendy interjected quietly, drawing his gaze to hers once more. "It was awfully nice."

The corner of his mouth tilted up again—not quite a smirk, not quite a grin. Something softer. The warmth in it reached to his eyes, and she couldn't help the way her stomach fluttered like leaves caught in the wind.

Stan returned his focus to Alfie, but Wendy hardly noticed as the sensations washed over her. It wasn't just the princely ease with which he held himself, the quick wit, or the gentle manner with the boy. It was something more. Deeper.

She'd read too many bedtime stories to count as a child, tales of noble heroes who soared in to save the day. But Stan was different. He didn't sweep in with showy gestures or grandiose promises. He stood firm, steady, real. He made the fantastic seem tangible, as if the divide between dream and flesh could bridge two opposites with one glance.

And perhaps that was why she felt so rooted to the spot, heart thrumming and cheeks glowing. Not because he embodied the ideals of a prince from any story she'd known, but because he surpassed them. A man of action over pretense, conviction over performance.

Better than a fairytale.

Real.

That thought settled low within her, solid and undeniable, just as Stan caught her gaze once more. This time, she didn't look away.

— ❖ —

Chapter Four

AFTER HE'D SPOKEN with Alfie and Andre again, Stan turned to leave for the Langley's—but paused mid-step, one hand in his coat pocket. A voice cut through the corridor behind him.

He didn't need to turn. That clipped edge, sharpened by Prussian disdain, could only belong to Baron von List.

Sometimes speaking of the devil does indeed conjure him up.

Stan's pulse surged. Cold tension threaded through his shoulders, knotting at the base of his neck. He hadn't seen List since that cursed card game, but just the sound of him—here, this close—tightened every muscle into readiness.

So it begins. The one man who could unravel everything—Transylvania, Harley Street, the Klonimuses, Wendy.

He glanced left, toward the misty glass door of Alfie's apothecary. Inside, only shadows and streaks of light. But Stan didn't need to see. His instincts already screamed that whatever List was doing here, it wasn't by chance.

Stan stepped back, his heel brushing against the hallway runner and slowly leaned closer. A faint scuff of indistinct footsteps echoed from somewhere—farther down the hall or perhaps above.

The Baron's voice cut through again, low and deliberate. "So, you believe this to be only temporary?"

There was a pause—just long enough for Stan to crouch

slightly, feigning an adjustment to the buckle of his Hessian boots in case anyone found him—but he angled his head slightly toward the frame of the door.

"Entirely temporary," came the reply, Nick's familiar tone casual and breezy. "With due care and some chamomile compresses, I imagine it will improve soon."

The scrape of a wooden chair rang faintly through the threshold, followed by the tired groan of a floorboard. Stan held his position, an outer calm in sharp contrast to the twist in his gut. What fleeting ailment could List need curing here? What ailment at all, for that matter, when the man had the arrogant confidence of one impervious to such vulnerabilities? And what nerve did he have to seek advice from the doctors he was trying to ruin? He was the worst sort of hypocrite and no better than so many noblemen Stan knew all too well.

The door clicked softly, startling Stan upright. It opened with an insistent push, flooding the hallway with the menacing presence that List carried like a foreboding storm cloud. Stan barely had time to rise from his crouch and straighten his coat. Baron von List stepped out with the sharp discipline of a man accustomed to commanding attention, his frame creating a lean silhouette in the light.

Stan met his gaze—a steely, pale blue diluted further by disdain. The Baron's mouth curled faintly at the corner, his eyes drifting momentarily to Stan's hands near the Hessians, as though to silently comment on the awkwardness of his position.

"Prinz Hohenzollern-Sigmaringen, was für ein Zufall, nicht? What a coincidence, isn't it?" the Baron said, with a throat-clearing precision that seemed to rid the syllables of any warmth or sincerity.

Stan forced a flat expression, pulling his gloves from his pocket with deliberate slowness. "Baron," he said with a Germanic baritone in acknowledgment, giving no indication that he respected the man in the least but was a match to him regardless.

Von List lingered where he stood, motionless save for one

quick movement. Stan caught it—the subtle way the Baron's hand curled around something as he reached toward his coat and slipped something into a pocket. It was small and brown, catching the light briefly before vanishing from sight. A vial. Glass. The kind with droppers Alfie often used for exacting measures of tincture.

Stan's chest seized with suspicion; every nerve honed with sharp awareness. His face, however, betrayed nothing. He nodded once, tugged his gloves over his fingers, and pivoted to leave. But his steps—as even and precise as he made them—were slower than before. Each step made him painfully aware of the soft padding of boots behind him as List headed in the other direction.

Nick appeared at the doorframe, leaning casually against the wooden edge as von List left through the front door. Despite his rolled-up shirt sleeves, his easy manner contrasted with the keen sharpness of his worried tone.

"List's audacity to come to you for treatment is stunning," Stan said.

"Well," Nick said, his voice low but edged with significance, "that man's about as welcome as a fox in a henhouse. But if we turn him down, it might be worse." He crossed his arms, nodding toward the direction von List had gone. "No good's going to come of whatever he's plotting. You feel it too, don't you?"

Stan nodded, his gaze level and unreadable, but his brow slightly furrowed. "He wouldn't have come here without a reason. Whatever it is, it bears watching."

"It does." Nick exhaled heavily, some of his usual lightness returning as he straightened and took a step closer to Stan. He smiled, though it didn't quite reach his eyes. "He's the worst sort of patient, always threatening with his connections—as if he could pull a lever to ruin our practice at his whim."

"Yes, I know the kind. It doesn't behoove the nobility to threaten honest people who work for a living, hmm?" Stan frowned. He feared he'd be no better and deserve his title even less if he couldn't resolve the threats List meant for Transylvania, his home.

But then Nick's grin softened, and his voice lowered. "You can frown all you like, Stan, and even if you don't acknowledge it, I will. You might be a prince, but no one's more down-to-earth than you." He paused, shaking his head as if marveling at the thought. "It's not all men who'd get their hands dirty when they don't have to—you're a man of honor who happens to have a title."

Stan shifted uncomfortably, his mouth opening slightly as if to protest, but no words came. Instead, Nick clapped a firm hand on his shoulder and continued, completely undeterred. "And don't go forgetting this either—you've earned our loyalty not because of what you were born into, but because of the man you've chosen to be. If von List tries anything, you won't face him alone. You've got me, and more besides."

Chapter Five

Later that afternoon on Regent Street…

MADAME DUCHON'S FINE shop exuded elegance from every corner. The walls were painted a soft cream, punctuated by gilded mirrors that reflected light from the store windows as well as the lights inside. Bolts of luxurious fabric spilled from cabinets, their textures and hues tantalizing even to Wendy, who had never worn the finest styles she saw coming in and out of Harley Street. Ladies flitted across the room like butterflies, their voices blending with Madame Duchon's low, brisk French commands.

Wendy felt entirely out of place. She stood stiffly on a slightly raised platform in the back room, her plain shoes peeking out apologetically from beneath the hem of her gown. To her left, Pippa was reclining in a spindly chair, her perfectly coiffed blonde hair catching the light. Beside her sat Bea, a vision in her plum morning gown, adjusting the lace gloves on her delicate hands. They seemed effortlessly regal, every inch the noblewomen they were, and their ease only heightened Wendy's discomfort.

"Stand still, Miss Folsham." Madame Duchon fluttered toward her, scissors in hand, her sharp gaze as calculating as a surgeon's. "You mustn't twitch, or I'll ruin the hem."

Wendy obeyed, resisting the urge to fidget as one of the assistants adjusted the shoulder seam of the gown she now wore. She caught a glimpse of herself in the nearby mirror and blinked, hardly recognizing the young woman staring back. The dress—a deep hue of rose gold that shimmered with golden threads in the light—fitted her like a second skin. It draped fluidly over her frame, the skirts pooling into soft folds that swayed delicately when she dared to move. Wendy's curly blonde hair, hastily tied into a simple braid that morning, had somehow begun to suit the richness of the gown, the lighter strands picking up the warm tones in the fabric.

She liked what she saw even though it felt strange and out of place. Who didn't want to be like a princess if given the chance?

But giving in to the idea—even imagining it—was going to be trouble. And Wendy knew it.

"Turn, won't you?" Bea's voice broke through her daze as soon as the modiste refrained from fussing and stood back.

Obediently, Wendy pivoted, her cheeks burning. She felt as if every eye in the shop was on her, dissecting the way the gown hugged her waist and flared at her hips.

Bea's sharp inhale was the first sound to break the silence. "You're... radiant," she said, her warm eyes widening. "Doesn't she look radiant, Pippa?"

"She does," Pippa answered easily, leaning forward with a smile that could charm the entire room if she wanted while she pushed her spectacles up her nose with a discerning gaze—as if she knew the fine fabric of the dress. Her tone carried the smooth confidence of someone born to be admired. "Rose blush and gold suits you perfectly. And the shimmering shot silk—it catches the light just so. Doesn't it, Bea?"

"Changeant, we call it," Madam Duchon mumbled. "Two colored threads are woven in different directions, blushing pink and gold, to catch all the light in a dazzling ballroom."

Bea nodded eagerly. "Oh, it does. It's positively dazzling. Wendy, you'll outshine half the girls at the ball."

Wendy's fingers curled into the folds of her skirts. "I hardly think that's likely with you as the bride," she murmured. The words came out quieter than she'd intended, but they were sincere. She wasn't dazzling. Not like Bea, with her lush strawberry-blonde hair that gleamed with coppery hues and the poised confidence of a woman well-versed in Society; nor like Pippa,—but rather, the commanding presence they both carried at a ball. Her own hair, a tumble of wild golden curls that caught the light unevenly, seemed a rebellious imposter beside Bea's sleek shine—a reckless scribble on the page where Bea was the artist's deliberate stroke. Wendy thought her existence had always been practical, not ornamental—surgeons didn't care how prettily a bandage was tied; they cared that it held. "I'm not certain this suits me. It's too much."

"Nonsense," Pippa said, dismissing her in the same tone she used when scolding Nick for eating too many biscuits. "You'll walk into that ballroom, and no one will suspect you haven't always dressed like this."

"They will when I trip over my own skirts." Wendy frowned. "It is so silky, I am afraid to tear it."

"Then we will be there to lend a hand. I assure you, I'm the reigning queen of mishaps at balls, and I won't let you earn the title on my watch," Pippa said with a wink.

She was so kind, Pippa, her new sister-in-law. Wendy wished she didn't like Pippa so much, but she did, even though Pippa competed with Wendy for Nick's protection—or was it his attention rather?

"If only you could see yourself," Bea added gently, sensing her unease. "You look..." She paused, searching for the right words. "Like a dream. Truly."

Wendy glanced down, unable to meet their warm gazes. "Well, it's not every day I look like this. Or wear anything like this," she admitted. "I don't suppose I'll fool anyone for long."

"Don't be silly," Pippa chimed in briskly. "You'll be perfect. I'll make sure of it. You've already survived our wedding. This will be easy."

But Wendy couldn't shake the tension coiling beneath her ribcage. Nick's wedding had been different. She had been the groom's sister, unobtrusively tucked into conversations or helping direct wandering children after the celebratory breakfast. No one had minded that she hadn't danced; in fact, hardly anyone had noticed. But now, she'd be stepping into a ballroom filled with England's elite, where partners would stretch out their hands and expect her to know steps she'd never been taught.

And then there'd be *him* to witness her embarrassment.

Her breath hitched slightly at the thought. A prince. He'd be there. The prince.

The man who managed to stride through rooms as if he belonged everywhere, and yet had those damnably mischievous eyes that hinted otherwise.

Wendy forced herself to take a calming breath. She'd kept to fairytales for precisely this reason—they were harmless stories, but when their elements crept into reality, the line between wonder and apprehension easily blurred.

"Fairytales aren't for women like me," she muttered under her breath—*not ones who stitch wounds and disappear.*

"What was that?" Pippa asked, raising a brow.

"Nothing," Wendy lied nervously. "Just reminding myself not to step on anyone's toes if I'm forced to dance."

"The dances will begin by rank," Pippa shrugged as if it were nothing but common knowledge.

"Since Violet is pregnant, I don't suppose the Earl and Countess of Langley will follow the bride and groom, will they?" Bea asked.

"Not if Prince Stan will be there," Pippa said. "He outranks them all, even though he's not English."

"Oh, the villagers will speak of the balls at Silvercrest Manor for months!" Bea said excitedly.

"We're certainly bringing some of London's finest to our grandparent's old country estate," Pippa added with an arched brow.

"It's been made for elegance, and we've let it slumber far too long." Bea blinked in Wendy's direction.

Pippa laughed, but it was Bea who stood and placed a hand on Wendy's arm. "You'll be splendid, Wendy. Even if you *do* step on someone's toes—they'll still thank you for it."

The sincerity in Bea's smile was disarming, no wonder Alfie was so smitten with her. And for a moment, Wendy felt a flicker of comfort break through the nerves twisting inside her.

"Turn again, Miss Folsham!" Madame Duchon's voice commanded from the far side of the room. "I must see the back."

Wendy sighed and obeyed, the muslin skirts brushing softly against her legs. The lightness of the gown felt foreign compared to the ones Wendy usually wore to work. But it's sheen and the brightness seemed oddly grounding, like armor for the evening to come. She squared her shoulders, glancing nervously at her reflection one more time. This was a gown to catch the eye, not allowing her to blend into the background.

The empire waistline, adorned with a creamy-rose satin ribbon, drew the eye upward, while the low square neckline—modestly daring—framed the décolletage without overstepping propriety. Fine embroidery, like frost on a winter pane, traced the hem and bodice, catching the light in hushed, glittering whispers. The sleeves, mere wisps ending just below the shoulders, lent cherubic purity to the audacious elegance that made Wendy weigh the words she'd use to describe her reflection. It was elegant. Refined. Splendid.

Except somewhere in the depths of her mind, "splendid" sounded awfully close to "terrifying."

MEANWHILE, IN ANOTHER part of London, Stan adjusted his gloves and watched from the shadowed alcove as the Langleys, servants bustling around them, issued crisp instructions for the upcoming trip. By now, every corner of the grand townhouse was filled with the sounds of trunks being hefted, feet hurriedly scuffling across polished wooden floors, and the occasional sharp call from the steward ensuring not a single satchel would be left behind.

And Stan didn't want to cast a shadow over the excitement before the journey to Alfie's and Bea's wedding in Kent, even though his mother's letter was pressing down on him.

My Dearest Son,

The burden of the world seems to press upon us, and my heart cannot rest knowing the peril in which all my children now stand. Thea, cast adrift and a fugitive in all but name, bears a danger I scarcely dare to imagine. Alex is soon to follow, burdened with the grave task of securing a match to cement our family's fragile standing. And you, my steadfast son, must shoulder this storm with courage beyond your years.

How cruel it is that I must send my children into such a maelstrom when I would sooner send an army if only it were within my power. The thought of my family scattered in distant lands, exposed to treachery and peril, breaks what little strength I have left. Were there but a stronghold for us in England, a sanctuary to shield and aid you all, I might find some ease.

The whispers have grown louder—Baron von List is not merely threatening your allies but boasting that he will begin by 'erasing the women who stand beside the men.' The gossips say he believes that by removing the caretakers and healers, the warriors will crumble next. It is not just vengeance—it is strategy, cruel and precise. Please, my son, do not ignore this. Do not make Thea the first to pay because she's the closest to you.

Yet we must persist. You must persist. Protect Thea, guide Alex when he arrives, and hold fast to the resolve I know resides within you. The fate of our house and our people is in your hands now, and though it grieves me, I know there is no one stronger to bear it.

Yours always and unrelentingly,
Your Mother

Stan patted his pocket where he'd put the letter after he read it. It meant too much to set aside and held too much power lest it fall into the wrong hands. Except Stan didn't want to worry his friends, the Langleys, either and yet, he feared that List would strike and endanger the people who meant so much to him.

Violet, the Countess of Langley, radiant despite her condition, stood near the base of the sweeping staircase, her ruffled lavender day dress brushing the crimson carpet. Pregnancy softened her otherwise poised figure, though she carried herself with the same self-assured grace of a young countess who had commandeered ideals of propriety long before she gained the title. Not that Stan cared for such formalities. What truly concerned him was the rather inconvenient and dangerous truth of Violet's determination to travel. He already had to keep watch for Lady Pippa, Lady Bea, and Nurse Wendy. The expectant countess was another woman who would surely be at the top of List's candidates for prey.

"Are you certain this is wise?" Stan asked, stepping forward into the flurry of activity. His tone was deliberate, masking the discomfort edging at his words. He glanced between the Countess and the Earl, searching for some sense of practicality to anchor the reckless idea she was presenting. "Forgive me for speaking plainly, but you're carrying a child. The trip to the countryside, no matter how short, can hardly be without risk."

Violet turned toward him, an exasperated smile brightening her fair features. "Stan, I appreciate your concern, truly. But we're practically traveling with a caravan of our own private doctors from Harley Street." Her blue-gray eyes held an unshakable resolve. "Plus, I won't miss Bea's wedding. We were at finishing school together. Bea and I have been through too much over the years for me to stay behind now. Confinement can wait."

"You're hardly confined, but—"

"I'm barely five months. And this dress hides more than there is to hide." She interrupted with a soft laugh, her fingers brushing over her barely noticeable bump.

"I understand, but—"

"The carriage ride is less than three hours, Stan," she interjected again, though not unkindly. There was a musical quality to her voice, one that could drown out even his stiffest objections. "And it's in daylight. Hardly an ordeal."

His hand instinctively went to the back of his neck, fingers rubbing at the tension mounting there. "Less than three hours becomes far too long if it turns dangerous."

At this, the Earl of Langley, tall but lean in figure, stepped up beside Violet, having given a few more orders to pack the carriage. If Stan had hoped for an ally in the Earl, that hope dwindled when the man rested a hand comfortably at his wife's elbow, his expression unreadable but unmistakably firm.

"I can't very well allow her to go alone," Langley said, casting Stan a sidelong glance. "Would you?"

"Of course not," Stan replied sharply. "But that's not the point." He motioned broadly toward the open windows. "There's a reason I've been keeping an eye on everyone."

"Paranoia?" Violet asked cheekily.

"Preparation." Stan crossed his arms.

"For what, exactly?" Violet asked, her voice softer now but tinged with curiosity.

Stan tilted his head toward her, studying her for a long beat before answering. "For Baron von List."

Her hand faltered on the embroidered cuff of her sleeve, and her brow knit faintly. "How do you know we're his next targets?" she asked, a hint of incredulity creeping into her tone. "He hates so many people, the Crown Jewelers, Baron Stone, Dr. Leafley, he could pick on anyone."

"Which is why he must be stopped." The Earl nodded at Stan.

"Considering that the Ton won't want to miss Lady Bea's wedding, I think it would be unwise for him to strike at the wedding. He has enough to do in London with his own wife."

Violet waved in the direction of the carriage, and the footmen carried her trunks to the front door. "There will be so many doctors at this wedding, it is as if I was going to a clinic. Right? No party without medical supervision."

Both Stan and the Earl stared at her, their expressions making it perfectly clear that the answer should have been obvious.

Stan folded his arms and glanced at the parlor door down the corridor. "It was Alfie who made the truth serum. And all of us—every last one—were right in that parlor over there when we poisoned the man against his will."

Violet paled slightly, though her chin lifted in defense. "That was done with good intentions. We…the circumstances demanded it."

"Intentions only matter to those concerned with morality. Those on the right side of it, to be exact." Stan's voice darkened, his thoughts pulling him back to von List's calculating gaze, his predatory stance even as the serum forced truths from his lips. "He isn't on any side. He's on his own. He's gotten away with exploiting the Transylvanian gold mines for too long. Alfie's serum—and our interference—humiliated him. It stripped him of power and control. If you think he isn't plotting his revenge at this very moment, you're being naïve."

The Earl's hand tightened slightly at Violet's elbow, but she didn't falter, her jaw set in stubborn defiance.

"And yet, wolf or no wolf lurking beyond that door, I can't abandon Bea. Not now—not for anything," Violet declared, leaving no room for protest.

Stan exhaled through his nose, biting back the retort hovering on his tongue. Society events were far too important to London's Ton—Violet and Bea being right in the midst of it all. And logic wasn't going to win here; it never did when it came to friendships and the bonds women seemed to hold so fiercely. He tried again, his voice lower, quieter. "Bea wouldn't forgive herself if anything happened to you—or the baby—because of this trip."

"It's an argument I can't win," the Earl said with a faint shrug, tilting his gaze toward Stan. "Believe me, I've tried."

Stan gave the man a flat look. He didn't appreciate Langley's surrender, but he wasn't entirely surprised by it either. For all his supposed influence, his wife already had him wrapped around her smallest finger—a talent Stan was beginning to see Violet employed quite well.

"Three hours in broad daylight is manageable," Langley continued lightly as if dismissing Stan's concern entirely.

Manageable? Stan wouldn't go so far with the looming shadow of von List darkening every move they made. "I'm taking my carriage with Andre and following close by."

Still, before he could utter another remark, Violet pivoted on her heel, glancing back at one of the hurried footmen. "Were the trunks loaded properly?" she asked, her voice floating so composedly above the whirlwind around her.

Stan watched her go, shaking his head to himself even as his thoughts churned. She didn't pay heed to the gravity of it—the fact that von List wasn't finished with them yet. He was certain of that much. The Baron had let some of his motives slip the day they poured that truth serum into his drink, lost his dignity, and there was no telling how far he'd go to reclaim it.

This wasn't over. Not by a long shot.

The impending ball felt like a narrow valley with sheer cliffs on every side, and List was the predator perched above, waiting for the moment Stan's guard faltered to rain arrows down. Stan knew List preyed on the undefended, those too weak or unsuspecting to strike back. He had seen the malice etched in the man's actions, from the threats that drove their Jewish friends to trembling silence to the venomous grin that promised vengeance against Violet, Pippa, and Bea. Their involvement in poisoning him—instigated by Stan himself—made them perfect targets.

He needed a battalion—but all he had were friends too loyal to stay safe.

And the women List would target first.

And Wendy—who'd already become too much to lose.

❖

Chapter Six

A N HOUR BEFORE they were supposed to leave for Silvercrest Manor for Alfie and Bea's wedding, Wendy stood in the center of her chambers in the new townhouse. Her fingers fumbled with the last few buttons of the gown. She had to try it on again before she could muster the courage to face people in it. And by people, she meant *him*, of course. Not that she'd ever admit that.

The rose-gold silk dress had arrived earlier that morning, carried in by the milliner's assistant with so much care that she half expected it to waltz into the room on its own. Now, it hung awkwardly from her shoulders, elegant in its design yet stubborn where it refused her reach. Twisting to catch sight of her back in the small, spotted looking glass only made the situation worse. She jerked forward, grabbing the back of the chair nearby to steady herself. Her grip wasn't enough. The chair tipped, her stockinged foot caught on the hem of the gown, and with a gasp, she landed in an undignified heap on the rug.

For half a heartbeat, she just lay there, the tight bodice of the gown pressing against her ribs, her pride bruised worse than any bone might have been. The scent of dusty lavender sachets from the corner chest mixed with the sharp tang of floor polish, grounding her in the absurdity of the moment. She wanted to laugh, but the sting of humiliation crept up faster, pooling hot behind her eyes. Wendy bit her lip instead and pushed herself upright, brushing silk out of the way to inspect her ankle. Fine. At least she'd kept that intact.

The voices came faintly at first, muffled by the closed door but unmistakable in their urgency. Her heart lodged in her throat as footsteps thundered up the stairs.

"Wendy? Are you all right?" Pippa's voice shot through the crack under the door, followed immediately by Nick's deeper tone.

Before Wendy could respond, the knob turned. She scrambled to her feet, the half-fastened gown slipping down one shoulder as the door burst open. Pippa and Nick stood framed in the doorway, their expressions painted with concern that quickly turned quizzical. She barely had the chance to tug the gown into place when another figure loomed behind them.

"Oh no," she whispered, more to herself than anyone else. Andre's unmistakable baritone was followed by a clipped phrase she didn't catch, and then—there he was. Prince Stan stepped into view, taller than she remembered and uncomfortably breathtaking in his easy elegance. Why had he already come to pick Andre up and begin their journey to the country?

The room felt suddenly stifling, the scent of lavender overwhelming with the warmth of too many bodies in such a small space. Wendy's face burned hotter than the midday sun. She folded her arms over the drooping neckline and dipped her eyes, erring on the side of fervent pleas that the floor might swallow her whole.

Wendy didn't even reach the bed on her own terms. Andre's insistent hand on her shoulder pushed her down until she sat perched on the edge, her skirts puffing awkwardly around her. Before she could regain any semblance of control, Pippa's sharp gasp struck her like a slap.

"Oh no, is the gown torn?" Pippa's horror was palpable, her hands flapping as if she could somehow smooth the fabric from across the room.

"I think the gown has survived," Andre said, kneeling as if addressing some battlefield wound. "Her ankle is my concern. Did you see how she winced?"

"My ankle is fine!" Wendy blurted, her voice high-pitched and slightly wild, but it was already too late.

With infuriating efficiency, Andre flipped the hem of her dress up to her shin, exposing her bare ankle to the room. She hadn't put the stockings on to try her dress on in the privacy of her own chambers.

Yes, a judgment error.

The cool air prickled along her skin, but the mortification burned hotter than anything she'd faced in years. Wendy's hands shot to the fabric, trying to pull it back down. "Andre! Propriety?"

"She's not fainting if she can still complain," Nick quipped, lightly slapping Andre on the shoulder. "That's a good sign."

"I am sitting right here!" Wendy hissed, darting a glance at the prince. Oh, he was looking—no, more *staring*—which was somehow worse. His gaze wasn't leering or even overtly inappropriate, but it was attentive, deliberate, and utterly unrelenting. The intensity of it nearly sent her sliding off the bed, petticoats and all.

"Shh," Andre said as if soothing a skittish horse. "If you keep wriggling, I won't be able to check for a decreased range of motion."

Pippa groaned, throwing her hands up. "And now she's squirming! Wendy, if the bodice twists, I don't think the modiste will forgive you."

Andre ignored her protests entirely, one hand circling Wendy's ankle with the effortless authority of someone who clearly thought decorum was optional. He prodded, tilted, and—oh heavens—pressed the tips of his fingers along the tendon in a way that made Wendy jump out of sheer indignation.

"That's tender!" she snapped, the pitch of her voice climbing dangerously higher.

Andre seemed unbothered. "I didn't say it wouldn't be. No

break, though. You're lucky."

"Lucky," she repeated, the word strangled as her skirt slipped higher under Andre's inspection. Only her petticoat shielded her from complete indecency, and even that felt woefully thin.

Nick crouched beside Andre, squinting at her ankle as if it might reveal some hidden truth. "Seems fine to me. No bruising yet, but you should keep off it." His tone was firm, laced with concern he barely tried to hide.

"I told you, I'm fine," Wendy snapped, yanking her foot back. The motion sent her skirt sliding dangerously high, and Nick's face darkened as he muttered, "For crying out loud, Wendy," yanking the fabric back down.

She flushed, opening her mouth for what promised to be a sharp retort, but yelped as Andre caught her heel mid-air, steadying it deftly. "Careful," Andre said lightly, his grip secure but gentle as he glanced at Nick for approval.

Nick exhaled, a grudging nod acknowledging Andre's effort. "Right. No sudden movements if you don't want to make it worse—or take him down with you." He gave Andre a pat on the shoulder, the gesture oddly fraternal, though his jaw remained tight.

From the corner of his eye, Nick seemed to have caught Stan watching. The sheer casualness of the man's gaze knotted something protective in Nick's chest and Wendy could tell. She knew what her brother was thinking even when he didn't say It aloud. When Nick shifted closer, subtly angling his body as a shield between Stan and Wendy, his hand hovered near her hem again, as if silently vowing there weren't enough pairs of eyes in the world to justify leaving her vulnerable.

"You'll twist it further," Andre chastised, gripping her ankle firmly and pinning her in place. "For your own sake, Wendy, stop thrashing about like a trout out of water."

"I'm not thrashing," Wendy snapped, her cheeks burning anew. "And I'm perfectly fine! I don't need your help." Her voice wavered, and she swallowed hard, trying to steady it. But there it was—that awful lump rising in her throat as if her own body delighted in betraying her.

She sucked in a breath, determined to speak more forcefully, but the words tumbled out in a rush instead. "If I do twist my ankle, Andre, it won't be because of this—it'll be because I can't dance at Alfie and Bea's ball!"

"Why not?" Nick asked, his tone light, as if this entire spectacle wasn't already unbearable enough.

"Can I dance? Have I *ever* learned how to dance any of the refined dances of nobility?" It had been one thing to skip and twirl to the merry strains of a fiddle at a rustic country gathering, but the ball would be another matter entirely. Wendy flung her arms up in exasperation, the motion unrestrained and impulsive. Dancing at a ball… and Prince Stan would be there to see her… It wasn't until the cool draft swept across her shoulders that she realized the full catastrophe of her outburst.

The gown—unfastened and hopelessly delicate—slid down her torso, pooling unceremoniously at her waist and leaving her clad in nothing but her chemise from the ribs up. A collective intake of breath filled the room, though Wendy's own lungs appeared to stop functioning entirely.

For a horrible, frozen moment, she could do nothing but stare at the stunned faces around her. Andre blinked at her, his focus mercifully shifting to the ceiling as his jaw tightened. Nick, on the other hand, had the decency to whirl around so quickly he narrowly missed colliding with Pippa, who promptly shrieked, "The gown!"

The prince's stare landed on her like a misplaced anvil, his brows rising high. For one excruciating moment, his mouth hung ajar, a perfect picture of unpolished shock that turned her stomach into a knot. She might as well have been a clumsy fawn, limbs askew, caught mid-somersault. The realization struck her like a slap from a wet glove—this wasn't a prince; this was just a man. A very *aware* man. And she? She was now the embodiment of calamity, a spectacle he could neither unsee nor, apparently, look away.

Wendy's senses returned in a rush, and she scrambled to snatch the dress back up, hauling the silk over her shoulders with shaking hands. Her fingers fumbled desperately to cover herself as she pressed the bodice tightly against her chest.

The silence that followed was deafening. Nick blinked at her, Andre hesitated mid-grip, and Pippa clamped a hand over her mouth, her eyes suspiciously bright as if stifling laughter.

And then there was Prince Stan. Wendy dared a fleeting glance in his direction only to find his expression utterly indecipherable; his brows arched the faintest bit.

The comparison stunned her into a momentary silence, during which Pippa flounced closer, muttering about crushed silk and scandalized men. But for all the chaos erupting around her, Wendy could think only of him—Prince Stan, still leaning against the doorframe like he had all the time in the world to watch her humiliation unfold.

He hadn't said a word, hadn't moved an inch, but the intensity of his gaze sent ribbons of heat lacing up her neck. If only she could formulate some clever comment or demonstrate even a shred of poise. But no, there she was, hoisted up like a specimen while two men debated the state of her ankle and a third silently judged her from his elevated perch.

"Perhaps," Wendy said finally, her voice trembling as she snatched her dress down from Andre's grasp, "we can leave my ankle's future to its own devices. It seems fully capable of surviving without an audience. So, please stop looking!" she pleaded, her voice strangled with equal parts fury and mortification.

"No one's looking," Andre said curtly, though the faint strain in his voice betrayed him.

"I'm not even in the room anymore," Nick declared from somewhere behind the doorframe, though she could still hear the laughter he failed to suppress.

And Prince Stan was gone.

Pippa, meanwhile, rushed forward, fingers flying as she attempted to re-secure the gown. "Oh, Wendy, *honestly*! Why didn't you call me or a maid to help you tie the gown? A situation like this—this is the sort of clumsy thing that would happen to me, not you!"

"I suppose this is why Bea said women need attendants." Wendy bit her cheek.

"Yes. We shall fix it, of course, though whether your dignity survives is another matter entirely!"

"Thank you, Pippa," Wendy muttered through gritted teeth, flattening her lips into a tight line as waves of embarrassment crashed through her. Her cheeks radiated heat, her hands clutching the slippery fabric as if her life depended on it.

But at least her new sister-in-law was by her side, and she didn't have to endure it alone.

And then there was the prince. Slowly, against all reason, she allowed her gaze to flicker toward the door through which he'd just left.

Wendy revisited the moments in her mind. Prince Stan hadn't moved, nor had he looked away. His expression betrayed no shock or discomfort, only sharp, unwavering attention that made her knees soft like pudding. There was the faintest lift at the corners of his mouth—enough to suggest either mild amusement or perhaps subtle admiration—though Wendy could hardly fathom which.

"Do you think she's all right?" Wendy heard the prince's voice in the hallway.

"She's usually not this clumsy," Nick said, Wendy hearing it all.

Pippa, however, seemed to tactfully pretend not to hear.

"...glad she's unhurt," the prince's voice now fading as he was probably downstairs already.

And just like that, the last string of Wendy's dignity snapped. If there were a less graceful end to a morning, she could not imagine it. But the faintest glimmer of humor in his voice left her wondering if maybe—just maybe—she hadn't entirely lost his favor. For now, though, she only wanted her floor to swallow her whole.

FOR STAN, THE tranquility of Nick and Pippa's new townhome on a quiet Marylebone street starkly contrasted with the storm inside him. Breakfast had been served in the drawing room, as the breakfast room had yet to be furnished. However, since he was a prince, Pippa insisted he be served elegantly in the drawing room. She was just as kind as Nick and everyone else from Harley Street—all potentially in danger from List because of him.

It's all my fault.

The soft clink of porcelain and the faint shuffle of servants in the corridor punctuated the otherwise still space, a calm utterly at odds with his thoughts.

Stan should have taken a walk like Andre, who had strolled the short distance from 87 Harley Street to the townhouse on what seemed like a windy day, leaving Andre more disheveled than usual as he deposited his trunk at the door for the servants to load into the waiting carriage. Meanwhile, Stan had arrived in his own carriage at Pippa's insistence, drawn into her whirlwind of preparations to accommodate her seemingly infinite collection of trunks and valises. Between Andre and him, their meager travel necessities scarcely filled a fraction of the allotted space. He hadn't minded the task at the time; in truth, he hadn't given it a thought. But now, seated amidst the unnerving quiet, it struck him that perhaps agreeing to help had been nothing more than a prelude to some grand cosmic joke, one designed to leave his mind in greater disarray.

Wendy's mishap upstairs, just as Stan arrived, left him completely unraveled.

Nick and Pippa had excused themselves minutes earlier, providing Stan with a brief reprieve from Pippa's enterprising tone of giving instructions to the servants. This left him alone at the table with Andre, who appeared to be in no hurry to speak, allowing Stan's thoughts to wander unchecked. Wendy seemed to remain hidden upstairs, but Stan couldn't help glancing at the door every minute or so.

He stirred the cup of tea in front of him absently. Wendy hadn't been down for breakfast. Her absence thudded in his chest with a fury he couldn't explain—not aloud, at least—and between each sip, he found himself wondering when she might emerge from her chambers.

He'd stared.

The memory unraveled him further, a sharp pang of guilt twisting in his chest. Like a besotted idiot, he had been rooted to the spot, his breath a traitor caught between gasps and stillness when she'd fallen. He should have moved—should have shielded her. But he hadn't.

Worse, he was the humiliation incarnate.

Instead of helping her up, he had been useless, struck dumb, his body locked in a wretched stupor while time seemed to freeze around the soft, silken tangle of her. The sunlight had caught the sheen of her chemise, its pale ivory clinging to her form like morning dew to petals. She had been...enchanting. Utterly undone, yet so whole in her unassuming grace, like a flower toppled in the breeze but not yet plucked.

It had been ungentlemanly, shameful, a betrayal of every lesson ingrained into him since boyhood. A prince does not ogle. A man does not freeze in helpless lust while the object of his folly fumbles in embarrassment. And yet, for all his remorse, he couldn't unsee her—not the way her skin had glowed in the filtered sunlight, nor the delicate twist of her ankle as she'd shifted to sit. She hadn't looked at him in that moment, but if she had... he wasn't sure he'd have been strong enough to meet her eyes without giving his feelings away.

He released a tight breath, one hand dragging over his jaw as if to wipe the heat of the memory away. Had she noticed his impropriety? Did she remember the humiliating pause, the beat where he had hesitated instead of helping? His chest tightened painfully at the thought. If she avoided him now, he couldn't blame her.

Andre ate with the unbothered ease of a man ignorant of Stan's torment, slicing into his scrambled eggs with deliberate precision before sweeping them onto his toast. The soft crunch carried through the quiet room. His own plate sat before him, untouched save for the glisten of butter pooling on a single slice of toast. The bread's golden edges mocked him with their mundanity. Instead of eating, Stan's stomach churned; his appetite, like his etiquette, had entirely abandoned him.

Wendy seemed to have that effect on him.

Her innocence, her quiet strength, her beauty left him pulsating with need. His greatest disgrace wasn't in staring too long; it was in knowing that, given the chance, he'd likely do it again.

He clenched his jaw, his pulse drumming in his ears. It was bad enough that he often imagined her with her tidy coiffure undone, her lips parted in breathless surrender, her form pressed against his, bare and unguarded. Those thoughts were unbidden, uncontrollable—and every time, he forced himself to shove them aside with no success. But now, the reality of her beauty, even if only accidentally exposed, rendered his fantasies wholly insufficient, cruel by comparison.

"I'm ready," she said suddenly, stepping into the doorway. "When are we leaving for Kent?"

Wendy's presence seemed to ripple through the room, a quiet force that never left—even when she wasn't there. Every thrum of his pulse echoed the same maddening refrain. He was falling. Or perhaps he already had.

She finally arrived, framed in the gleaming arch. For a moment, she lingered, smoothing her hands nervously over the pale muslin of her gown—a gesture so uncharacteristically hesitant that it froze the air between them. Stan straightened, his chest tightening as he took her in. The gown, simple and elegant, caught the light just right, accentuating something she herself didn't seem to grasp. She looked radiant, effortlessly so.

Andre, of course, filled the silence first, leaping to his feet with a dramatic sweep of his waistcoat. "Wendy," he exclaimed, a teasing grin lighting his face, "if I didn't know better, I'd say you raided the wardrobe of a queen for Silvercrest's grand halls!"

Stan knew the coach was ready, and the others would follow soon. They were all bound for Alfie and Bea's wedding in Kent. But in this moment, no one seemed in a rush to move. Even as they all prepared to leave, something about Wendy held Stan captivated—tied to her.

Stan glanced at Wendy, his brow furrowing as her lips pressed together, her eyes cast downward. The faintest flush crept across her neck. She didn't meet Andre's gaze, nor, Stan noted, anyone else's.

"You truly look…" Andre continued, his voice softening. "Beautiful. Like a lady in every sense of the word." For once, the usual edge of jest was gone from his tone, and Stan felt a pang of unease, though he couldn't say why.

"Do stop, Andre," Wendy murmured, her sharp wit softened into something reluctant, shy even. "I'm neither a duchess nor a lady. This is merely my new carriage dress and a new spencer. Bea insisted I not disgrace her wedding in road dust." She waved a hand, dismissive. "Nothing special."

Stan shifted his stance, clenching his hands behind his back. Nothing special? She couldn't have been more wrong. She looked… well, he wasn't sure he had the words. Sophisticated. Lovely. And entirely unaware of it. There was a tight pull in his chest at the thought.

"You're wrong about that," Andre said, his grin fading into something kinder, gentler. He reached for her hand, lifting it to his lips with a lightness foreign to his usual antics. "You'll turn heads at the ball," he murmured. A beat passed before he added, softer still, "All grown up."

If Wendy was still flustered, she hid it behind a faint smile, though Stan caught the way her fingers trembled just slightly as Andre released her hand. The sight stirred something within him—a need, perhaps, to shield her from the attention she wasn't sure how to bear. He cleared his throat, stepping forward at last as Andre glanced his way, amusement flickering in his expression.

"That's true," Stan said, his voice steady, though his eyes lingered on Wendy. "He's right."

Wendy blinked at him, an unspoken question in her gaze, but she said nothing, only twisting the edge of her glove between her fingers. Stan held her gaze for an instant longer before glancing back at Andre. The room had grown quieter, but not any more comfortable. Stan clasped his hands behind his back again, willing the tension from his posture. The wedding ball would be long enough without Andre putting ideas in anyone's head to woo Wendy before he had the chance.

But Stan didn't share any of the brotherly affection for Nurse Wendy that Andre did.

Oh no!

She was a woman all grown up, that was for sure. Fresh and ripe.

Must. Not. Pick. This. Flower.

From his seat at the table, Prince Stan lowered the edge of his paper, though he didn't speak. His dark eyes lingered on her a second longer than polite, sparking a rush of awareness that flickered in her eyes. She parted her lips as if to say something—anything—but Stan, as though sensing her thoughts, promptly raised the paper again, dismissing her words before they could find air because they weren't alone. Oh, how he longed to be alone with her!

"Wendy," Andre said silently. "About earlier—"

"My ankle is fine," she said. "Thank you."

"Not that." Andre rubbed his neck like a green boy.

Stan narrowed his eyes.

"I didn't know you couldn't dance properly." Andre winced when he said it.

Wendy stiffened and seemed to avoid looking in Stan's direction. Yet he saw her over the newspaper's edge. "I… I meant to learn," she stammered, tucking a stray strand of hair behind her ear, "but there never seemed to be time."

"I can teach you." Andre kicked an imaginary pebble on the Persian rug. "I've had formal lessons with my own sister."

"In Florence?" she asked, eyes wide.

"Yes. There will be a cotillion for certain." Andre said as he bent down. *No!* He bowed deeply. "May I, Miss Folsham?"

Wendy chuckled and let Andre lead her to the center of the drawing room, her hands resting lightly against Andre's as he explained the steps of the cotillion. Her pale cream frock, simple yet fetching, fluttered as she curtsied, earning a crisp nod of approval from Andre.

Stan hated every moment of watching her take a dance lesson from Andre—it should have been him.

Yet, seated at the table, Stan held the newspaper aloft, though the print was nothing more than a jumble of meaningless black on white. His jaw clenched as he tried to concentrate on the words, but every laugh Wendy released cut through him like the sharpest of swords. He dared another glance above the paper. Andre had positioned himself next to her now, one hand at her waist, the other guiding her arm in an invisible arc. Wendy stumbled over a step, giggling as Andre steadied her, and the sound—her sound—ignited a chain of envy so fierce that Stan bit the inside of his cheek in frustration.

He was the royal in the room and yet, found himself relegated to the sidelines, watching helplessly as another man gleaned her smiles. Crushing the pages of the newspaper a bit too tightly, he cleared his throat, though none looked his way.

"Perfect, just like that," Andre murmured, stepping nimbly back before bowing in exaggerated courtly form.

Wendy's laughter was musical, her curtsy playful as she replied, "If only it were that easy. You make it seem effortless."

"I assure you, it wasn't always the case," Andre countered,

bringing her back into position for another pass. "I had plenty of lessons myself—often with my sister, who was forever telling me I lacked elegance."

"Did you?" Wendy teased, tilting her head as if mocking disbelief.

"To hear her tell it, I was hopeless," he replied with a grin. "Hopeless until she conceded I'd surpassed even her expectations. She always claimed I danced with her only because no other lady would suffer my missteps."

Wendy chuckled. "You don't seem so hopeless now. I think you're quite good."

Stan lowered the newspaper with a deliberate thud. "Quite good," he repeated, his tone laced with a shadow of something unreadable. "Except you seem to have overlooked the most important steps."

Andre paused, eyebrows raised, his expression uncharacteristically blank. "Have I?"

Stan stood, peeking out from behind the newspaper with slow precision, his gaze pointedly catching Wendy's just long enough to make her look away.

"The steps are different for any dance in three-four time," Stan said.

"In a waltz," Andre said flatly, the declaration hanging like a scandal in the air. "Surely you don't mean to credit me with skipping over what is hardly a proper dance by certain accounts."

Stan shrugged. "Call it what you will," he replied evenly, his voice betraying nothing. "It's the one worth remembering." And with that, he held the paper up, leaving Wendy's gaze lingering on him, sending a shiver down his back.

"Your Royal Highness… is your paper upside down?" Wendy asked.

Stan froze mid-turn of the page, his princely façade crumbling just enough for that betraying heat to rise to his collar. With agonizing precision, he set the paper down, his composure recovered in an instant.

"It's an editorial trick to test the most astute of readers," he quipped. He glanced at Wendy fleetingly, but his gaze lingered in the air between them, heavy with something unsaid.

"Why not show how it's done then?" Andre said, stepping away with a bow to Wendy. "I'll let you cut in."

Stan tilted his head; his heart apparently had forgotten to beat. "I could, though perhaps advice from Andre would suffice." He paused, and when he turned his focus fully to Wendy, the change was palpable—soft, searching, almost tender. "Unless you'd prefer otherwise?"

Chapter Seven

W ENDY NEVER WANTED her first dance with the prince to be in her drawing room, but considering that it was happening at all made her quiver with joy that she thought she'd snap in two like a twig. When Prince Stan stepped forward, tall and confident, his shadow stretched long and commanding across the wooden floor. Wendy soon forgot to breathe again. He bowed slightly when he stood just behind Andre, an elegant gesture that sent a tingle skittering down her spine.

"And this is how a gentleman cuts in," Andre said as he bowed to the prince as he stepped back from Wendy.

"Would you do me the honor of permitting that I lead you in your first waltz?" the prince murmured, his voice low and impossibly gentle. Before she could collect herself enough to refuse—not that she truly wished to—he extended his hand. With trembling fingers, she placed hers in his, the warmth of his grasp searing. He drew her closer, the faint scent of cedarwood and clean linen enveloping her as if the very air he breathed carried its own comfort.

"I don't know what to do," she whispered, glancing over her shoulder.

"He will show you. Let me check when the carriage is ready and if Nick needs any help." With those words, Andre left the room.

Alone.

With the prince.

Her giddy heart thundered in her chest, her breath catching as his gaze met hers. Her knees wavered, a trembling betrayal beneath his closeness.

"Relax your shoulders," Prince Stan said softly, his other hand settling lightly at her waist, firm but respectful. His touch was unshakably steady.

She forced herself to look up, meeting his dark-blue eyes that seemed to hold the secrets of the world—and her heart—in their depths.

"This is all about trust," he continued, leading her in a slow, careful step. His voice rumbled through her chest before his words reached her ears. "Just follow me. One step, and then another."

"W-Where am I stepping to?" she asked.

The prince looked down, and Wendy followed his gaze. There was a small distance between their bodies.

Yet any distance felt like too much.

"Imagine a square on the floor. We must only step inside its four corners."

She looked down, but her mind stayed blank.

"Begin with the left foot. Step forward with the left foot on count one, step to the side with the right foot on count two, and close the left foot to the right foot on count three."

One, two... *thud!*

She had bumped right into him.

He only rumbled a laugh, gentle, not mocking. She was so close she could sense the vibration. Wendy looked down again, but no coherent thoughts came to her mind.

"Left foot. Step forward, step to the side..." Yes, she could do that.

Thud! Again.

She was so close that his wonderful laugh vibrated through her bones. Then she stepped back. "You need to mirror my steps,

Miss Folsham." He extended his arms and invited hers in. "Steady your frame with your arms. You already have impeccable posture." *Impeccable. She was impeccable?*

"Step forward with the left foot on count one, step to the side with the right foot on count two." He started to move. "See? It's easy, one, two, three."

Easy? No.

"One, two, three," she mumbled.

The prince is dancing with me. What are you doing? This isn't safety. This is surrender. But her traitorous body kept time to him like it had waited years to belong.

Their movements were tentative at first, her nerves making her misstep more than once. Yet each time her foot faltered, his presence was there to steady her, to guide her with infinite patience. Gradually, an unspoken rhythm passed between them, and she began to trust the silent language of their joined hands. How he wielded his strength—to support her, not control her— softened her knees.

They turned in a slow, graceful circle, the faint strains of imagined music filling the room. His closeness felt intoxicating, yet achingly safe. For an instant, the chaos of her world outside this room ceased to exist. There was only the warmth of his hand, the quiet assurance in his step, the soothing scent curled around her like a favorite novel—warm, unforgettable.

When he smiled, it stole the air from her lungs, leaving her helpless in the gravity of his presence. "You're a natural," he whispered, his voice a velvet caress that wrapped around her like the lingering warmth of a summer sunset.

A nervous laugh bubbled from her lips before she could stop it. "I hardly think so," she murmured, her words trembling under the moment, her heart pounding louder than the music that surrounded them.

"You're better than you think," he said, his voice low and intimate, each word a confession only for her. His eyes locked onto hers, a smoldering promise hidden in their depths. The world around them faded, the waltz forgotten as the space between them disappeared entirely. It wasn't the dance that kept her steady—it was him. His unyielding strength, the way his hands guided her with effortless confidence, and the unspoken desire that lingered like a spark waiting to ignite.

Her breath hitched as his hand slid ever so slightly over her back, pulling her closer. If she moved just a fraction closer, his lips would be... *Dare she think it?*

"Am I interrupting something?" Nick's voice cut through the moment like a sharp wind, shattering the fragile tension. They broke apart as though caught in the act, the spell broken.

Nick stood in the doorway, arms crossed, an eyebrow raised, and his smirk equal parts amusement and suspicion. "Didn't mean to interrupt your... dance lesson," he added, though the warning undertone in his voice said otherwise.

She stepped back, breathless and flustered, avoiding both of their eyes. "Of course not, Nick," she said quickly, her cheeks burning.

Prince Stan, however, didn't even flinch. His gaze lingered on her for an agonizing heartbeat longer before he straightened, his expression unreadable. "We'll have to finish this at the ball," he said softly, meant only for her ears, before turning and walking away, leaving her heart racing for entirely different reasons.

Chapter Eight

Silvercrest Manor in Kent. One day later, at Alfie and Bea's ball in honor of their wedding…

THE BALLROOM WAS a marvel of light and sound. Coffered ceilings adorned with chandeliers dripped with crystal, casting a kaleidoscope of brilliance over the parquet floor as the string quartet began its lively waltz. Every detail, from the sweeping drapery to the polished silver trays in the hands of the quick-footed footmen, was exquisite. It was a scene straight out of a fairytale, one Wendy felt she had absolutely no business being in.

She stood at the edge of the crowd, a fixed smile plastered on her face that she hoped appeared pleasant rather than pained. Her rose quartz gown shimmered under the gold-tinged light, the golden threads in the fabric catching every angle just as the modiste had predicted, making her stand out more boldly than she expected—or desired. The truth was, she felt like a pink cake—overly sweet, overly seen, and waiting to be devoured by aristocratic stares.

Her gloved fingers toyed nervously with the fabric of her skirt as Alfie, dashing in his evening wear, led a radiant Bea onto the dance floor. Alfie's hand rested confidently at his bride's waist, and Bea, in her summer-sky blue silk gown, was the picture of grace as they began their first dance. Around the room, delighted whispers and approving smiles followed their steps. A circle of guests formed to admire the pair, champagne glasses clinking softly as onlookers leaned in for a better view.

Wendy shifted uncomfortably. The music swelled, spiraling higher, and her stomach twisted matching its rhythm. This was the moment she usually avoided. She would normally excuse herself discreetly, dodging the peacock parade of silk and shot silk before anyone could notice her absence.

But tonight, escape wasn't so simple.

Pippa, hosting the happy couple for the evening, soon followed Bea onto the dance floor, her champagne-colored gown glittering with every step. She moved with her usual elegance, arm-in-arm with Nick, whose sharp black coat and tailored trousers made him look like he'd wandered off the pages of a painting. Wendy had often relied on Nick for an exit strategy at these grand events, but there he was, spinning across the parquet with his new wife—a vision so polished, they seemed to belong to another realm entirely. Although Wendy's own gown shimmered in the candlelight, every facet catching the grandeur around her, the brilliance only made her feel more exposed. If she could vanish into the gilded walls, she would. But when her heel caught on the hem of her gown, she swayed—too visible, too exposed. She stayed rooted, not by choice, but by the sheer impossibility of escape.

The crowd around her had tightened, the guests whispering and shifting closer to see the spectacle of Bea and Alfie opening the ball. She couldn't move. Glancing around helplessly, Wendy clasped and unclasped her hands as she tried to find a place to disappear quietly. Nick's gaze found hers from across the room. He tilted his chin faintly, giving her a slight nod.

At first, Wendy thought it was one of Nick's reassuring smiles, checking on his little sister.

But then Alfie did the same from the ballroom, which was a little odd, wasn't it? Why would he, the groom, look to her during his first dance with his bride?

Then Bea—smiling mid-spin—caught her eye and tilted her

head in the same direction.

What did they mean? Why were they nodding at her?

The dances will begin by rank.

Wasn't that what Pippa had said at the shop?

Wendy looked for the Earl and Countess of Langley but couldn't see them.

A low wave of whispers resonated through the crowd of guests, but Wendy couldn't make out what they were saying as the music soared around her.

She blinked, and then her heart lurched.

The crowd began to part. Like ripples spreading outward in restless water, the space between the guests widened suddenly, leaving a clear path through the throng. A gasp caught in her throat as she recognized the man moving toward her.

It was him.

Her knees locked in place as Prince Stan stepped forward, the curling tails of his black evening coat swaying behind him. His cravat, pressed and folded with military precision, was as crisp and white as the snow-capped peaks in Alpine paintings. His dark hair, smooth and neatly combed back, gleamed under the brilliance of the chandeliers. Yet it was his eyes—those impossible, intense eyes—that struck her hardest. They locked onto hers as though no one else existed in the entire ballroom.

Wendy's pulse jolted painfully. It couldn't be. Surely, she was mistaken.

But then he came straight toward her, no hesitation in his stride, his tall frame commanding the sea of silk and diamonds that rippled away to make room for him.

Her heart stumbled over itself as the crowd around her began to murmur, and then he stood still.

Right in front of her.

Wendy's lips parted in a rush of breath she'd forgotten she'd been holding. She stared at him as the gasps and faint whispers quieted around them. The air between them felt charged as if something unseen—something pressed by the curiosity in the room—demanded recognition.

And then he moved.

Prince Stan, the man who had eclipsed the splendor of even this ballroom, bowed. Deep and deliberate, the motion was perfectly executed, yet it sent a stark shock up Wendy's spine.

Every thought swirled in her head. How could this be happening to her? Would someone pinch her and let her scurry around the practice with a pile of clean towels any moment? Or, surely, someone would tap her shoulder any time now and inform her that this was a misstep, a wrong turn in the orchestra of events, and they were expecting someone else entirely.

But his eyes stayed on hers as he straightened, the look in them unyielding, focused.

Gentle, she'd say, with a tinge of vulnerability that woke her from her stupor.

"Miss Gwendolyn Folsham," he began in a deep, even tone that made her break out in goosebumps.

Her heart, already thundering, skipped so violently she feared it might leap entirely out of her chest. One word—the simplest greetings—and her carefully constructed walls began to tip.

Reality twisted uncomfortably close to the whimsical fairytales she had once adored. It couldn't be that simple.

And yet, here he was.

Just a minute earlier...

STAN STOOD TALL, his eyes scanning the room with practiced precision. A ballroom like this—bright with countless lights casting their brilliance on gilded trim and gleaming parquet floors—should have been a sanctuary of celebration, not a stage for tension. And yet, here he was, every nerve honed and attuned to threats as though he were on a battlefield instead of a polished dance floor.

The crowd was alive with chatter and laughter, the swirl of ladies' gowns creating a palette of color as if a painter had swirled his brush too vigorously. Stan's gaze swept past diplomats engaged in polite conversation, their laughter too hollow to be genuine. He noted the presence of Langley and Violet, who stood near the far wall, their attention caught by a French emissary's animated gesticulations. Violet looked serene in her ivory gown, though Stan knew Langley's hand resting at her elbow wasn't for effect. She leaned on her husband just enough to betray her delicate condition, though only someone looking closely—as Stan always did—would notice.

His gaze shifted, and there they were—Baron von List, leaning back with unsettling ease, and his wife, a portrait of poise on his arm. She tilted her head towards her husband as he murmured something in her ear, her expression unreadable. Her eyes, dark as ink but cold as ice, cut sharply across the room, a predator's gaze wrapped in civility. Stan tensed. Criminals always adopted masks in polite society, but with the Lists, it wasn't a question of deception. It was an inevitability. They weren't watching the ball. They were watching *him*.

The music swelled, and the crowd shifted around the dance floor's edge, creating a wide circle as Alfie led Bea out for the first waltz. The newlyweds stepped into the light, their hands joined, Bea radiant in her gown and Alfie's confidence a match for his bride's loveliness. Stan's lips twitched faintly with approval. If anyone deserved a reprieve from danger, it was the pair of them.

I'll stand guard for you.

He scanned the room again, intent on keeping the Lists and other suspicious figures in sight. But the forming sea of murmuring guests created a wall of colored silk and black tailcoats, limiting his vision. Awful crowds. Height helped, but nothing fixed limited sightlines when bodies jostled, and heat gathered like fog rising on a battlefield. His instincts were screaming. Something didn't seem right. He couldn't place it, but his stomach knotted tighter with every measure of the waltz.

"Stan." Andre's voice at his side caught his attention. Stan turned, noting his friend's calm but intent expression.

"You see them?" Stan asked, nodding slightly toward the Lists.

"I do," Andre confirmed briefly. His words were measured, and his tone was low to avoid attention. "But we need to focus elsewhere tonight."

Stan raised a brow. "You don't say."

"This isn't up for debate. You're the next highest-ranking guest in attendance," Andre added with a subtle tilt toward the dance floor. His meaning was as clear as daylight.

Stan frowned. "You're telling me to waltz while the Lists watch us like prowling wolves?"

"I'm telling you to do what's expected," Andre replied before shifting his gaze. "And to keep her safe in your arms. I would, but you outrank me by far."

Stan's eyes followed Andre's line of sight until they found her—Wendy. She hovered near the far edge of the floor, her posture impossibly still. Her rose-colored gown shimmered faintly as the light teased the golden threads woven through the fabric, but her expression was what caught him. Fear. Not alarm or panic like that borne of battle, but the kind that softened into dread, the unmistakable look of someone seeking an escape they couldn't find. Had List delivered a threat?

Oh, if he as much as breathed in Wendy's direction, Stan would … oh, he would do his worst with bare hands.

Andre clasped Stan's shoulder briefly, his message delivered. "Your duty lies there," he said softly before stepping away.

Stan exhaled slowly, his thoughts a storm of responsibility and instinct. Traditionally, etiquette dictated that he'd dance with the highest-ranking aristocratic lady in the room, but there was no contest in his mind. None outranked Wendy—not in his eyes. The Lists would not take her. Not if he could shield Wendy with his body.

Oh, the thought alone made him hard, his body over hers...

but this wasn't the moment.

Nor was it allowed. His world was dangerous, and he couldn't ever approach her as he'd wished.

Except that Andre had given him one chance: a dance with the woman of his heart.

The music played on, blending seamlessly with soft laughter and murmured conversation as he approached her. Step by deliberate step, he charted a course across the polished parquet, weaving past the observing crowd. He moved purposefully but not too quickly, giving her enough time to notice him. Enough to steel his thrumming heart—the rest of him was harder than diamonds when he saw her.

Her head lifted when he was nearly there, her wide eyes locking onto his. Something about that look—the uncertainty mixed with undeniable recognition—felt like a stitch pulling tight in his chest. Her reaction wasn't that of a court debutante eager for glory. She wasn't one of them. And yet, she stood there like a vision, unassuming but breathtaking, wearing the trappings of elegance as though they were borrowed rather than her due. She was so very much herself, unmolded by this glimmering crowd.

At last, he reached her, his chest tightening further when she dipped her gaze, a blush warming her cheeks. Her hands curled tightly into the folds of her gown, and for a moment, he thought she might take a half-step backward. But she stayed.

"Miss Gwendolyn Folsham," he began, his voice balancing formal and intent, "would you do me the honor of this dance?"

She blinked up at him, her pink lips parting slightly in surprise. Her hesitation was brief but palpable. Then, as if buoyed by some strength he hadn't expected, her gloved hand unfurled and reached tentatively for his; he took it gently in his own, his fingers steadying hers as much as leading.

The room around them shifted faintly, and guests turned to notice the prince leading someone onto the floor who surprised them. Yet, Stan ignored them all. For now, the Lists, their dangers, and the room's edges blurred and faded entirely as he led

Wendy to the center of the parquet.

WENDY'S HAND IN his felt warm and steady, as if it belonged there. It was absurd. She had no place stepping into the light, not alongside him. But Stan's unwavering grasp made escape virtually impossible, and so she followed him, her pulse racing as if trying to outmatch the soaring melody of the string quartet.

She had grown up in rooms that smelled faintly of clove oil and belladonna, where her father's unwavering focus was on his patients' wellness and her family rarely entertained grandeur. She was educated, certainly, and her work as a nurse at the practice made her useful in ways that mattered. But none of that belonged here, amidst crystalline chandeliers and gilded splendor. The sister of a doctor, the daughter of a dead one—what claim did she have to this polished world where a prince as dazzling as Stan commanded attention with little effort? Her gaze darted to the faces in the crowd, noting the murmurs and stolen glances from familiar patients. They knew who she was. Just a nurse. That truth pressed down harder than the glittering silk of her gown. And not even Wendy dared mustering an explanation of why the prince had chosen her.

The shimmering skirts of her gown flowed over the petticoat that brushed against her ankles with every step. Around them, the ballroom hushed slightly, the collective hum of curiosity buzzing in the air. Wendy scarcely registered the stares, the barely concealed whispers, as Stan guided her to the center of the parquet. She could only focus on the firm, confident hand at her back, anchoring her as the crowd softened into blurred shapes and colors at the edge of her vision.

Ahead, Nick spun Pippa elegantly across the floor, his expression a mixture of pride and joy as his wife laughed softly at something he murmured. Wendy caught his eye briefly, and the look he gave her interrupted her mid-breath—the brotherly kind of glance that spoke without words. Approval, encouragement, and something infuriatingly protective. He didn't seem surprised to see her escorted by a prince. Wendy envied that certainty in him, as if he believed she had any right to be there.

She dragged her gaze back to Stan and stumbled slightly as he turned to face her at the center of the dance floor. Now that they were still, she felt every stare upon her. Her throat tightened. She wasn't built for waltzing under gilded chandeliers or dazzling members of the Ton. Her place was quieter, simpler, away from the polished scrutiny of ballrooms. But she was here.

Stan's deep voice reached her over the low hum of the string quartet as he stepped closer. "Is something the matter?"

His question was soft, yet it grounded her. His dark eyes held hers, steady and intent, pulling her from the haze of growing panic. She nodded faintly, but her lips parted, and the confession escaped before she could stop it.

"I shouldn't say," she mumbled, feigning a smile for the on-lookers.

"If you don't tell me, I can't help you," the prince said.

It was absurd but also terribly sweet.

Under normal circumstances, it was her offering help and service. How often she'd said this exact phrase to patients, she couldn't even count. And it was true; he couldn't offer a cure unless she told him her symptoms. And the only cure for standing still on the parquet at a ball with what felt like a thousand eyes on her would be the one thing she didn't know how to do.

"I still can't really dance." Her voice was a whisper, barely audible amid the sweet swell of violins, but Stan heard it, his brow lifting in faint surprise before his expression softened. He didn't scoff. He didn't falter. Instead, he stepped back slightly, his movements deliberately measured as if addressing a far greater concern than an untrained waltz partner.

"You can," he said simply, his tone kind but firm, leaving no room for doubt.

"I… no," Wendy stammered, shaking her head. "I truly can't."

His hand tightened gently at her back, his other resting lightly on her gloved fingers. "Just follow me like you did in London. That's all you have to do."

His calm was maddening, yet it worked through her jittered nerves. Follow him. Surely, it couldn't be that simple.

STAN REALIZED THAT being with Wendy was as simple as breathing.

Essential.

Instinctual.

And now that he felt her in his arms—her warmth molding to him softly, her lace-gloved hand resting so delicately in his own— he didn't know how he'd survived for a whole day without her presence. He inhaled deeply, his chest expanding as her subtle scent wrapped around him. Roses and apricots mingled with the clean, straightforward simplicity of soap. It was intoxicating in its purity. Briefly, he closed his eyes, committing every detail to memory as though he needed this moment to sustain him.

Something profound had happened, and it had taken him completely off guard. Stan, raised to master strategy and diplomacy, found himself disarmed—not by war or intrigue—but by the quiet courage of a nurse who didn't belong in this world, yet had shaken his to its core. He hadn't seen this coming—not when his eyes were fixed on Baron von List, nor when his thoughts were tangled in Transylvania's impending doom at List's hand.

But all that fell away. Now, holding Wendy and swaying to the waltz's tender rhythm, Stan knew he was experiencing something immeasurable. Not glory from his rank nor from the accolades he had received in battles or ballrooms. No, this was an entirely different honor—Wendy Folsham had given him the privilege of her first dance at a ball.

"Put your hand like this," he instructed gently, guiding her trembling fingers to settle against his shoulder.

Her touch was feather-light at first, as though she feared overstepping, but she followed him, trust evident in her wide-eyed gaze. And—he sighed—her innocence gutted him. Not innocence born of naivety but of unspoiled simplicity. That rare kind, tinged with strength. She was a woman who knew who she was and carried herself gravely, though she wasn't hardened by life.

And yet, she was inexperienced in all the things he'd gladly teach her—if only she'd be safe by his side.

Stan would guide her wherever she allowed him. Tonight held danger, duty, and the responsibility pressing on his shoulders. But for this moment, he only wanted to hold her, to cherish this fleeting dance with her—the woman who stirred something raw and primal in his chest.

He pulled her a little closer, cherishing her warmth seeping through the layers of fabric between them. "Count with me," he said, voice low. "One, two, three."

Her lips parted, her pretty head tilting back as she looked up at him. A nervous laugh bubbled from her throat and spilled out between them, and he couldn't stop his grin from spreading. Of all the things to paralyze him—her laughter. Light and musical, it softened the air and eclipsed every harsh murmur of his mind.

"Did you make that rhyme for me on purpose?" she asked, her voice teasing, her white smile radiant.

"Perhaps," Stan replied, a low chuckle rumbling through him. He tightened his arm slightly at her back, drawing her closer to his control.

"Why am I not surprised, Your Royal Highness," she quipped, but there was no malice in her tone, only warmth.

"Feel my steps," he instructed, keeping his voice firm but soft enough to coax her. "And trust me. You're safe in my arms."

She dropped her gaze briefly, hesitating. He felt her knee brushing his leg, her wide eyes met his again, and his breath hitched. She nodded, her fingers curling lightly against his shoulder, holding a bit firmer.

"One," he began, stepping smoothly into the waltz. She moved with him, awkward for a heartbeat, until he guided her hips with the subtle shift of his frame. "Two," he continued, tone low and steady, counting softly against the hum of the orchestra. She stuttered only momentarily until her body began to follow his instinctively. "Three," he said, adding the faintest pressure to her waist to guide the next turn, his hand at her back firm but gentle, tethering her to him. Her body adjusted, falling into a rhythm—not with the music, but with him. His steps, his lead.

There was a shift in her frame now—the moment when her movements softened and became intuitive. She didn't move like someone being led awkwardly across foreign terrain. No, Wendy glided now, her body learning the language of his guidance with astonishing grace.

Wendy's shoulders dropped as she exhaled deeply, visibly relaxing even as her nervous laugh returned. "You make it seem so easy," she said, her lips curving into a shy smile.

"It is," he replied against her ear. "When you trust the partner who's leading you."

Her lashes fluttered briefly as she swallowed, and he couldn't resist tightening his grip just the slightest, propriety and boundaries be damned.

"See?" he murmured, his breath brushing her temple as they turned smoothly. "You're practically a natural."

"Don't jinx it," she teased, though her voice carried a tremor that didn't match her playful words.

Stan angled his head slightly to see her face better. Her cheeks were flushed, the delicate pink matching the gleaming fabric of her gown. Yet her expression truly struck him—not shyness, or embarrassment, but something else entirely.

She wasn't surrendering—she was choosing. *Him. Here. Now.*

In front of the assembled Ton.

And List.

They turned once more, their joined movements seamless, and for those few moments, nothing else existed. Not the gilded chandeliers blazing overhead nor the crowd's murmurs of surprise and curiosity. Not even von List, with his sharp, calculating stares from the rim of the ballroom.

It was just him and Wendy.

One, two, three.

Trust in me.

Chapter Nine

STAN HAD SEEN beauty before—countless painted, powdered, and polished women dressed impeccably, each parading their graces as if vying for a crown. Yet none of them had prepared him for this. Wendy. The woman in his arms with her dazzling smile and rosy cheeks. She was… breathtaking.

She wasn't like the rest of them, the ladies who prattled about ribbons and coiffures while they polished their nails to perfection, or those who danced mindlessly, unaware of the wars that raged outside their gilded walls. Wendy was different, unspoiled by the frivolity of such trappings. Her hands had saved lives, steady and sure as she tended to the broken and ill on Harley Street. She didn't polish herself for praise—she trained her hands for healing. And to Stan, that made her more graceful than any duchess in diamonds. And she was utterly, devastatingly beautiful.

Stan's chest tightened as he stared down at her, the dimples at the apex of her softly curved shoulders peeking out just enough to disarm him entirely. Her cheeks, already flushed from dancing, held a bloom that no amount of rouge could replicate, while her lashes framed wide, earnest eyes that made fools out of men like him. He lost his grip—on himself, on the dance, on whatever soldierly instincts usually kept him protected.

His mind faltered.

Sweet and oblivious, Wendy moved instinctively, stepping

forward when he should have led her to step back. He blinked, momentarily stunned as she unknowingly took the lead. Her glove brushed his hand lightly, her movements uncertain but determined—it made something almost painful curl inside his chest.

He tightened his hold deliberately, grounding her as much as himself. "I'm leading," he murmured, his voice deeper than he intended.

Her eyes darted up to him, a flicker of confusion softening at the edges. But before she could speak or laugh nervously, he guided her back into the rhythm of the waltz. One firm step forward, coaxing her into step with him. The violins sang their soft strain, the room around them swaying, but Stan was singularly focused on the woman in his arms.

Her breath hitched as he turned them in a wide circle, her skirts brushing against his calf. Her hand at his shoulder tightened reflexively as he easily pulled her into his orbit, silently urging her to trust his lead. She was pliant now, yielding to him entirely, and Stan felt a quiet triumph at the way her body moved to follow his.

She exhaled softly, and he was sure he felt it—like the faintest whisper against his jaw.

He shouldn't feel this way. She wasn't meant for him; this grounded woman with real hands and real skills that mattered in ways Stan never could. He wasn't made for women like her. Uprooting her, transplanting her into the fine halls of his world, filled with egos and politics, would destroy her. She'd wilt. He couldn't do that—he wouldn't pluck her from the soil that nurtured her vibrance—the practice that gave her purpose.

But at this moment, with her heart drumming so close to his, Stan couldn't stop himself.

His fingers tightened at her back, pulling her impossibly closer as the waltz quickened. Her breath tangled with his own, her head tilting slightly toward him, and for one maddening moment, he thought of leaning down, whispering something reckless against her ear.

The music slowed, the last gentle notes stretching across the room. And then it stilled entirely, leaving the crowd to break into soft murmurs of approval. The spell shattered too, though Stan's reluctance to release her grew.

He pulled back just an inch, his gloved fingers loosening their hold on her waist.

"Thank you for the immense honor of this dance, Miss Folsham," he said, though the words felt too small for what had just transpired between them.

Wendy's lips trembled faintly before she offered a sheepish smile. "It's I who should thank you," she replied softly.

But Stan didn't want to just thank her. He longed to hold her tighter, pull her away from the gawking members of the Ton, and kiss her until she forgot they existed altogether. Instead, he gave her his arm, his grip steady and certain as he led her toward her brother.

Nick turned toward them before they fully reached him, his expression unreadable for a moment before a faint smirk betrayed his thoughts. He looked at Wendy first, his usual protective pride gleaming in his eyes, before directing a pointed, knowing look at Stan. Was it that obvious something had happened between them?

"She's in one piece, then," Nick quipped, offering Wendy his hand.

More than I can say for myself, Stan thought when cold air took the place where Wendy's hand had just lingered. *If a dance with her had this effect, what would a kiss do to him?*

Stan forced himself not to clutch at the void her absence left on his arm. Instead, he bowed slightly.

"Your sister is a remarkable dancer," he said to Nick, though his words were meant entirely for her.

Wendy blushed immediately, and her hand fluttered at her side. "You flatter me, Your Royal Highness."

"Not nearly as much as you deserve," he replied, his tone

lower than he intended.

Then he caught it—a cold stare piercing through the gathered guests. Stan turned his head slightly, focusing on the back corner of the ballroom. There stood von List, his expression unreadable but his intent unmistakable. He was watching.

Stan's pleasure drained like spilled wine. The moment—sweet and fleeting—was over. He straightened, gloves crisp again.

Duty called.

Chapter Ten

Baron von List was not on the guest list. Yet there he stood—shoulders back, smirk in place—as if the crest above the ballroom door belonged to him. Stan knew immediately: bribery or deceit had bought the Baron's entry.

The violins soared, oblivious to the rot threaded through the gold-tipped splendor. Shoes swept across parquet, the dancers moving in practiced grace, but Stan felt no solace in the music. Not with Wendy's laughter still echoing in his mind—soft, unguarded, dangerous.

He scanned the crowd again, searching for her, but instead met the unmistakable stare of List—sharp, amused, and aimed directly at him. A cold spike of warning shot down Stan's spine. That look—sharp, predatory—sent a chill rippling down Stan's spine.

The Earl of Langley's voice, clipped and rife with tension, broke the glamour of the moment. "Stan, List hasn't taken his eyes off us. What do you think he's planning tonight?"

Stan followed Langley's warning glance, the Baron's cold smirk chiseling into his attention. List stood close enough to snuff the joy from the celebration like a billowing curtain dousing a bonfire. Discretion urged Stan to turn away, but fury niggled at his composure. "Andre and I are leaving," he muttered to Langley, the words weighed against his unease. No sooner had he spoken than Andre approached his shoulder. Stan felt thankful for his friend's calming presence—a mind so utterly practical that not even vipers like List could unsettle it for long.

"Why are you on the sidelines?" Alfie, the groom, laughed as he joined them. His conspiratorial tone roughly masked an attempt to bring levity amid tension. He bowed briefly to Stan but looked more earnestly at the other man.

"Just keeping the prince here company until we leave," Andre replied smoothly, his grin polite but distant, as if his mind were already a thousand miles from the ballroom's golden glow. He had perfected the art of being present without sinking too deeply into any interaction, a skill Stan increasingly envied. "It's a beautiful celebration," Andre added as Bea approached, her cheeks tinted with the blush of the newly wedded. Stan greeted her too, momentarily masking his internal storm with as much grace as he could muster. Still, his gaze flicked back to List, whose lurking presence loomed large in his periphery.

"He's looking at us," Stan said.

"As long as he's just looking," Alfie chimed in quickly, though palpable disdain curdled his words.

"He's probably plotting his ne—" Andre began, but Bea's laugh interrupted, slicing the moment cleanly, a gentle curtain between tension and celebration. She slipped her arm affectionately into Alfie's, and the two radiated a complete happiness that felt invulnerable. Or maybe that was just the illusion love demanded.

Stan exchanged a glance with Andre, signaling they should leave the ball while discretion still allowed it. Perhaps, if Stan left, the Lists would also go, and the women would be safe at the ball. Together, Stan and Andre began weaving through the crowd toward the exit. The conversation shifted sharply as they moved, Andre muttering cold remarks about the Baron's aura of malice. Though the dialogue hooked into his ears, Stan wasn't truly listening. The closer they approached the carriages, the more one thought drowned out all others—the sweet nurse in the rose gown with golden threads.

By the time their boots struck the gravel outside, Stan's thoughts had fully escaped his control. Wendy. Just a short while ago, her dress had shimmered in the ballroom's light, her delicate smile igniting a dangerous yearning in him. She was a bloom he couldn't touch. A woman who deserved a man with promises for the future, and not only his shadowed past. Wendy had a brother, Nick, who had proven that a man could seek both love and honor in the same dance with his aristocratic wife, Lady Pippa. But Stan? He felt burdened by his title, his obligations, and the dark pull of conflict. Love, if he even dared call it that, was his greatest risk. Anyone he dared love was a vulnerability. Wendy's life couldn't afford his dangers seeping in—yet that didn't stop the pang of regret tightening in his chest as he stepped into the carriage.

Andre's hand gripped his shoulder firmly, grounding him. "Stan," he said in a low murmur, his tone both an anchor and a caution. "The Baron's presence is no coincidence. But he wasn't invited."

Stan's jaw tightened, but his gaze rested on the dark road ahead, and not back toward the man they were fleeing—or the woman he was leaving behind.

WENDY STOOD AT the edge of the ballroom, her gloved hands curled tightly around the golden fan that dangled from her wrist. The violins played another lively waltz, the music swirling with the laughter of elegant dancers twirling across the polished floor as though it demarcated another world entirely. A world she wasn't part of—not truly, not when it came to her because she was only a nurse to the Ton, a guest of the Ton; not part of the peerage who could expect a second dance—or a third—from a prince.

Her gaze flitted to Nick and Pippa, who stood nearby, perfectly poised as they exchanged pleasantries with other guests. Pippa's easy grace made her seem as if she'd belonged to this glittering crowd forever. And Nick—well, when had her brother become so comfortable here? To see him at ease in a world of dukes and viscounts beyond his treatment room simultaneously warmed Wendy's heart and twisted something deep within her.

A flicker of movement caught her attention, pulling her thoughts elsewhere. Wendy glanced across the room, her breath catching. By the far wall, Andre and Alfie were speaking with the prince, their tones low but strained, their expressions taut. Alfie's jaw worked as if biting back some retort, and Andre's gaze was sharp enough to cut glass. Wendy frowned, a faint unease crawling up her spine. It wasn't like Andre to wear his emotions so plainly—especially not in a public hall like this.

He must have been worried.

The unease grew colder when she noticed Baron von List at the edge of the shadows. He stood as if carved from stone, his dark, assessing eyes fixed on Andre and Alfie with unnerving intensity. Or was it the prince he'd made his target? Wendy couldn't pinpoint what it was about List that radiated malice—the rigid stillness, the faint smirk, or the fact that it felt like he seemed to take in far more than one ought in such a setting. Whatever it was, it brought with it a chill that settled deep in her chest.

She couldn't look at this man anymore.

Her gaze swept the room, searching almost unconsciously for the prince's dark hair and commanding silhouette that had been so distinctive on the dance floor, but now... where was he?

Her pulse quickened, the fan dangling from her wrist swaying slightly as her fingers flexed. Andre was missing too, she realized.

Wendy rushed to Pippa who'd just refilled her glass with punch.

"Have you seen them?" The question slipped out before she could stop herself, the words as quiet as the flutter of her fan. Pippa blinked at her, tilting her head curiously.

"The prince and Andre," Wendy clarified, her voice catching

slightly. "I don't…" She trailed off, aware of how silly she sounded. Why would their whereabouts matter to her? Yet the question burned anyway, the silence between their last dance and now seeming far too vast.

Pippa's lightly lilting voice broke the spell. "The prince? Oh, Bea and Alfie went to say good-bye. He left just moments ago," she said, answering a question Wendy hadn't even realized she'd asked aloud. "Andre went with him, back to London."

The words landed harder than Wendy had expected, pulling her thoughts sharply away from Baron von List. "He… left?" Wendy echoed, voice taut with effort. Her fan snapped open with too much force, trembling fingers betraying more than she wished. "Andre and Prince Stan left together?"

"Yes, dear," Pippa managed with a gentle squeeze of Wendy's wrist before she nodded in Bea's direction and made her way through the crowd near the perimeter of the dance floor.

Right, it was a ball.

One of those events Bea and Pippa knew to maneuver, but not Wendy.

She swallowed hard.

Prince Stan had gone. Without a word.

It shouldn't matter, she scolded herself fiercely. She swallowed, each breath heavier than the last. Prince Stan had gone. No farewell. No explanation. She wasn't foolish—only a nurse. Whatever warmth he'd shown had melted away with the night. Yet the understanding did little to soften the ache unfurling in her chest.

Her eyes slid unbidden to the ballroom's center, where they'd danced just an hour earlier. The memory was still warm, vivid, his steady hand guiding hers through turns and steps, the way the music had seemed to bend for them alone. And now, like a candle snuffed out, that warmth was gone, replaced by the icy realization of her reality. Duty, danger, and the shadow of aristocratic divides pulled him away. It wasn't her world, and it never would be.

From the corner of her eye, Nick's voice tugged her back into the moment. "Pippa was just saying that Cloverdale House should be ready soon," he said. His words were calm, but there was a tautness to his posture, his attention undoubtedly still lingering on whatever had passed between him and Alfie a moment ago. "The architect gave her the good news that he's obtained all the necessary permits for the construction."

"Cloverdale House," Wendy repeated, more to steady herself than to truly answer. Her brother nodded, his face softening as Pippa chimed in about the grand effort to turn the elegant estate into a place of healing. Wendy tried to focus, but her own thoughts still churned. She nodded along, catching only fragments of Pippa's enthusiasm, but her focus kept deteriorating.

Caught between worlds. That's what she was. Not quite belonging, not quite excluded, always poised at the threshold of something that promised both joy and sorrow. Society's rules, Nick's warnings, her own insecurities—they all formed a net that held her tightly.

And yet... and yet she couldn't erase the warmth of Stan's hand, the way he'd pulled her closer on the dance floor. How could something so fleeting unmoor her so fully? Even now, she could picture him—not the prince, not the nobleman—but the man who had looked down at her as if she were the only person in that glittering crowd.

But that moment, however sweet, changed nothing. Out there—beyond the music, beyond the chandeliers—duty awaited. Danger loomed. And men like Prince Stan didn't belong with women like her.

Not for the first time that night, Wendy forced herself to breathe deeply and plant a faint smile on her face. She was here for Nick, for Pippa, Alfie and Bea, Felix, and Andre—her family. For her meaningful work. If dreams of princes lingered dangerously near her thoughts, they were only that—dreams. Nothing more.

Still, she couldn't quite resist one last glance across the room, past Nick and Alfie, to where Baron von List still lingered. His expression seemed changed. Pleased. Smug. Triumphant. As if her pain were part of his design. He'd been over on the side of the dance floor for a while. And then, his gaze flicked to hers, a chill that froze her from the inside out. And then the violin's crescendo pierced the crowd, but the sound only seemed to heighten Wendy's disquiet—her hands grew cold and unsteady as the icy stung of Baron von List's stare pressed down on her, chilling her spine, and leaving her frozen in place, unsure where to turn or how to escape his unsettling gaze.

No wonder Prince Stan wanted to get away.

$$\sim \cdot \sim$$

Chapter Eleven

ANDRE SEEMED READY to return to London, but Stan wasn't so sure this had been the wisest move. They'd been in the carriage for more than half an hour, but Stan had not wanted to leave the ball. Least of all, without exchanging another word with Nurse Wendy. Her delicate hands in his, the sensation of leading her in rhythm with the waltz lingering in his thoughts, a tether he hadn't wished to sever so abruptly.

Just then, the sound of distant hooves broke through the peaceful hum of night. At first, it was almost ghostly, faint and rhythmic, but then it grew—a heavy, menacing cacophony crashing through the silence. It didn't sound like another carriage with travelers. Stan tensed, his ears straining as the dirt road beneath them seemed to vibrate in warning. The air thickened, the scent of damp leaves and earth suddenly laced with the sharp tang of something colder.

Danger.

His pulse quickened, pounding like war drums in his chest.

He turned to the carriage window, catching Andre's uneasy glance.

"Lock the door," Stan said, the words clipped, his voice low. He snapped the latch into place himself and moved back, one hand already brushing his boot where the concealed knife waited. Somewhere in the shadows, something was coming for them.

No, not something—someone. And Stan had the terrible suspicion they had been waiting.

The cries came next. Sharp, jagged screams sliced through the muffled drumbeat of hooves. A chill clawed at the base of his spine, coiling there like a snake poised to strike. Hell was bleeding into the night, its entry marked by shouts in a language that made his blood burn. Prussian. He clenched his fists, his nails cutting into his palms. This was no coincidence. No accident.

The carriage jolted. Stan caught himself against the door as the horses reared up, their terrified whinnies shredding the quiet. His body moved almost independently, a soldier's reaction carved deep into instinct. He stepped between Andre and the door, his stance rooted, braced, as though no force of nature could move him.

"Do you have a pistol?" he barked. The words were sharp, deliberate.

Andre shook his head, his expression one of raw fear. Stan kept his gaze forward, his jaw locked. He expected nothing less. Andre was a healer, not a fighter. The burden would fall to Stan. It always did.

The handle rattled violently, the sound of metal grating against itself sending adrenaline surging through him. Stan's body tightened; every muscle taut as a bowstring drawn too far.

"Stay back," he growled; words meant as a command, not a request. His heart hammered against his ribcage, its rhythm reckless and wild, but his breathing remained calm. Focused. The soldier within him awakened.

The door flew open, crashing against the frame with shattering force. Before they could drag him out, Stan surged forward, meeting the first attacker with his fist. His punches were swift and calculated—a fury honed by necessity. If he survived again, he could protect himself.

The man staggered, his mouth twisting open in a snarl, but Stan's next blow silenced him. The crunch of bone cracked against the night air, sharp and satisfying, but Stan had no time to relish it. Another shadow loomed.

Stan ducked just as something heavy sliced through the air where his head had been. The club swung wide, the whoosh of near impact brushing his ear. He pivoted low, his hand flashing to his boot—and there, the cold bite of steel greeted his fingers. He slashed upward sharply, catching his second assailant along the arm. Blood sprayed across his sleeve, dark and viscous, and the man howled as he stumbled back.

The stench of cheap liquor clung to the air, thick and suffocating, as if his attackers had bathed in it before descending on him and Andre in this forsaken wood. Stan's lungs burned with each shallow breath, and his eyes darted toward the fast-moving chaos, seeking his next move. But then, beyond the furious swings and grunts of the brawl, he caught the flicker of a silhouette—a woman's shape illuminated briefly in the moonlight.

He blinked, unsure if his weary mind was playing tricks on him. Another blow came swinging toward him, and he barely twisted in time to avoid it as the attacker's knuckles slammed against his ribcage. The pain spread, dull and hot, but he gritted his teeth, shoving the man back. Another scent—the iron tang of blood—curdled the air. Somewhere amidst the shouts and scuffling boots, a gasp rang out, light but piercing enough to slice through the fog of battle.

Stan's head whipped around despite the risk it posed. An attacker ripped the sack off a figure hunched to the ground. The fabric fell away, and moonlight caught the cascade of her hair, loose and soft, glowing like liquid silver. His blood ran cold, freezing him in place for the heartbeat it took to whisper, "Thea?"

My sister.

Before the name even fully left his lips, a heavy fist slammed into his jaw, snapping his head to the side. Pain erupted, white-hot and blinding, and he stumbled back into the fray of bodies. His heart hammering against his ribs as his vision cleared just enough to see her—the woman who was with a child. He blinked but couldn't understand. His lungs seized. He'd left to keep

Wendy safe and there was… No, not Thea.

Her face came into sharp focus despite the chaos. Tears tracked glittering paths down her cheeks, her wide eyes locking onto his. The raw fear in them tore at him more deeply than anything his adversaries had inflicted. For a fragile moment, the battle seemed to slow, the sounds dulling as he stood transfixed by the face he'd never wanted to see here, in a place like this. Why was she here?

Another attacker lunged, and Stan moved without thinking. His hand clasped his sister's trembling arm, half-hauling her to her feet as he propelled her roughly toward Andre. "Protect her!" His voice was rough, almost a roar, as he spun to intercept the next blow aimed at her.

Her tear-filled eyes lingered—fear and apology locked in them. But there was no time. He swung his blade upward, catching an assailant's shoulder with just enough force to drive him back, and wrenched his focus away from her. His arms felt heavier now, his stamina fraying under desperation, but there could be no hesitation.

"Inside!" His shout merged with the hollow clang of steel meeting steel as another attacker closed in. His sister was disappearing behind Andre's frame, but the lingering chill of her presence stayed with him, sharper than any blade that had struck him.

They were shadows in his periphery, barely there—but their fear hit him like a sword to the chest. Failure was not an option. Failure meant blood and death.

Stan lunged. A third man barreled toward him, his dagger gleaming like a second moon. Their blades met in midair, the metallic clash screaming against Stan's eardrums, vibrating up his arm. He shoved forward, snarling as their bodies collided. The earth beneath them seemed to tilt. Stan's back hit the dirt hard, the impact jarring through his frame, but he twisted, rolling free before the man could pin him down. He came up swinging, slashing. A vicious slice opened his attacker's thigh, a cry tearing from the man's throat like an animal wounded. One down.

Still, they came. Shadows emerged from the edges of the lantern light, more hits, more weapons. Stan's skin glistened with sweat, every muscle burning, but he held his ground. Pain flashed from a strike he couldn't dodge in time—a fist catching his ribs like a hammer to glass. He fought regardless, his blade an extension of himself, cutting and stabbing with ruthless precision.

A girl's whimper cut through the chaos, sharper than any blade. Stan twisted his head toward the sound; her small, tear-stained face shone like a beacon in the dark. The child was clinging to Andre's leg like he was the last solid thing in the universe. *Why was a child with Thea?* Her cries gutted him, but his distraction cost him—a stray boot collided with his side and sent him sprawling.

"I said go inside!" Stan shouted.

Stan hit the dirt again. His vision blurred momentarily, stars bursting against the black cloak of the night, but his grip on the blade remained steady. A roar erupted from his mouth as he surged upward, plunging the knife into the thigh of the man above him. The attacker spasmed, his breath hitching in a crude, guttural sound before crumpling beside him.

The remaining few attackers faltered then, hesitation curdling their momentum. Shadows receded; the clang of weapons replaced by retreating hoofbeats. His enemies melted into the forest, leaving only their failure behind.

Stan staggered toward the carriage, his lungs heaving, his fists burning, and his blade still clutched tightly.

Thea.

His sister's face came into focus, pale and trembling beneath the lantern's glow.

"Eşti rănit?" Are you hurt? His voice was low, frayed, the Romanian rolling from him almost without thought—

She shook her head but collapsed into his arms, her body wracked with fear.

Why was she here? How? And who was the little girl?

He held her firmly, his frenzied heartbeat just beginning to return to pace. Andre still stood nearby, quiet but unshaken, the girl tucked protectively in his grip. He nodded once—a silent assurance they were safe for now, though Stan doubted that. These were the precursors of war, small battles with surprise hostages. Whatever this night had wrought, Stan knew one thing—it wasn't over. List's threat coated this night like a shadow too thick to shake. This had been a warning or else they would have killed him.

But why?

What gruesome plans did List spare him for?

$$\sim\!\!\bullet\!\!\sim$$

Chapter Twelve

I T WAS TIME to return to London and Wendy couldn't wait to see Prince Stan again. The carriages lined the drive at Silvercrest Manor, their polished finishes glinting in the soft, wintry sunlight. Footmen bustled, lifting trunks and hatboxes with swift efficiency, while the distant nicker of horses punctuated the crisp morning air. Wendy stood near the edge of the gravel path, her shawl pulled tightly around her shoulders to guard against the chill. Her traveling bag rested at her feet, but her eyes were drawn to the manor house.

The magnificent estate loomed against the pale sky with its ivy-laden towers and soaring windows. It seemed absurd that only one day ago, its halls had been filled with music and laughter, the revelry of the ball now faded like a distant dream. Wendy's gaze lingered on the stately façade, an ache tightening in her chest that she didn't quite understand.

"You'll come back, won't you?" Pippa's voice broke through the din, soft and warm. Wendy startled slightly and turned to find her sister-in-law standing beside her, elegantly wrapped in a velvet cape trimmed with brocade. There was something maternal in Pippa's smile, as if she could sense the turmoil Wendy wasn't ready to voice. "Silvercrest is your home now, too, Wendy. You're part of the family."

The words struck her harder than she expected. "Thank you,"

Wendy managed quietly, though her voice trembled. Family. Pippa's tone should have comforted her. Instead, doubt coiled tight. She glanced away, back toward the manor, where the gilded edges of the windows caught the weak glitter of sunlight.

"Oh yes," Pippa added, more brightly now. "Perhaps you'll even have your wedding here someday!" She teased as she adjusted the clasp of her cloak. "Wouldn't that be something?"

Before Wendy could respond, a soft laugh echoed behind them. Bea stepped forward, her bonnet tilted slightly as the breeze toyed with her loose curls.

"It suits you," Bea said, smiling kindly, her gloved hands clasped neatly in front of her. "Silvercrest has a way of beckoning like home."

For a moment, Wendy could only manage a nod. Bea's words were sincere, her smile unguarded, but guilt gnawed at Wendy just the same. She should have felt welcome among these women who spoke to her with such ease, such affection. But it only made her more acutely aware of how misplaced she felt, stranded somewhere between two worlds.

The others bustled around them, Nick overseeing the loading of the carriages while Alfie spoke quietly with Felix just ahead. They were all kind to her, truly, but Wendy couldn't shake the impression of being a permanent bystander. She wasn't a doctor like Nick, whose hands helped build their practice from the ground up. And unlike Bea or Pippa, she wasn't born into this gilded world of titles and ballrooms. She was simply… Wendy. A nurse. An observer. She knew how to bind wounds and comfort patients, not how to weave effortlessly through this glittering tapestry.

"I mean it, Wendy," Pippa said gently, drawing her from her thoughts. "You're always welcome here. Don't forget that."

The sincerity in her voice caught Wendy off guard, and for a moment, she could only stare at Pippa. She opened her mouth to respond, but instead of words, her mind reeled with memories of the past night. Prince Stan's hand guiding her through the waltz.

His steady voice murmuring the steps. The way he'd looked at her afterward, his expression unreadable but piercing and lingering long after the music ended.

"Thank you," she murmured finally, her voice barely above a whisper.

Pippa reached out, brushing a strand of hair off Wendy's shoulder in a gesture so familiar it made the ache in her chest deepen. "Now, let's return to London. We have work to do." She turned gracefully, heading toward the carriage, leaving Wendy standing just beyond the gravel path with Bea still lingering close by.

"Wendy." Bea's quiet voice pulled her attention, her gaze warm, but searching. "You *do* belong, you know."

The kindness in Bea's words tightened Wendy's throat. She forced a small smile and nodded, though she couldn't bring herself to answer. How could she explain the storm that churned within her? The noise of the Ton, the judging gazes at the ball, and even worse, the voice in her own head whispering that she'd never truly fit in the prince's world.

Wendy turned back once more as the first carriage creaked forward. The estate seemed impossibly large now, as though it were swallowing her in its shadow. She tried to shake the thoughts that pressed at the corners of her mind, but they always returned to one thing. Or rather, one person.

Stan. What could she offer him, truly? She had to stop pining after him, no matter how fiercely her heart protested otherwise.

Chapter Thirteen

AT CLOVERDALE HOUSE in London, Stan clenched his jaw against the faint sting of antiseptic, the sharp smell mingling with the sterile chill of the bed chamber that had been converted to a treatment room as Andre methodically unraveled the bandage from his aching shoulder.

The late afternoon light caught the edges of Andre's instruments, all neatly arranged on the table nearby. Andre fussed over them, his sharp gaze darting between Stan and the tools he'd brought.

On the desk sat the letter from home, its broken seal a silent rebuke. It had arrived days earlier at Langley Hall and was forwarded to Cloverdale—another problem added to the pile. But Stan's pain was not just his shoulder. His failure to stop List gnawed at him harder than the wound. List was still out there, bleeding Transylvania dry. Yet, here he was, bleeding instead of fighting, no closer to capturing the man responsible.

Andre cleared his throat, dragging Stan from his turmoil. "You look terrible, and you've been avoiding me since you received your post. You must rest or it'll all hurt worse than it already does." His tone was brisk, but Stan caught the thread of worry beneath it.

Stan managed a dry smile, though it didn't reach his eyes. "It already does." He glanced back at the letter, his mother's words pounding at the edges of his mind.

He will begin by erasing the women who stand beside the men.

But Thea wasn't the only woman close to him anymore. List's target.

Wendy.

Stan clutched his heart instinctively, as if he'd already been shot.

If Mother knew the full truth—Thea's close calls, his festering wound—would she rage? Collapse? Demand the impossible? List's men were stripping the mines bare, their greed draining not only the earth's riches but the lifeblood of the people his family had sworn to protect. How could they protect anyone when they couldn't even shield their own?

But she was right in that he needed a stronghold in England, an embassy perhaps.

Stan shifted to give Andre better access, wincing as Andre poured a strong-scented liquid over the wound. Andre's sharp eyes surely didn't miss the flinch, but Stan tried to ignore the burn. Only four days since the ball, and it had all unraveled— Wendy's laughter echoing faintly behind the chaos. He should have said something. Done something. Sent flowers? No—that would have been unwelcome. Nick would never forgive him for drawing Wendy into his chaos, not when his shadow carried the threat of a criminal who could so easily make her collateral damage in List's schemes. A war was coming. Nick would never allow Wendy to be caught in its crossfire. Stan had to catch List, stop him, but how? He had no idea. Perhaps it already was too late.

Before the thought could fully form, a sharp tug on his shoulder forced a wince from him.

"Have the guards arrived yet?" Stan asked.

"Yes, Nick and Andre showed them everything. I hope they'll be trustworthy," Andre said, laying his hand carefully on Stan's shoulder but Stan nearly jumped from the pain of even the lightest touch.

"Is it really necessary to change the bandage again?" Stan snapped, his irritation spilling over.

Andre didn't glance up, his focus locked on the dressing as he peeled it away. "Unless you're keen to have the infection take its course and spare you all future worries—yes. I don't re-dress wounds for sport," Andre drawled, though his tone stayed even. "This is not a trifle injury."

Stan scowled, biting back a retort, but the hiss he couldn't suppress as the dressing pulled from raw skin said enough.

"Thought so," Andre muttered. "It tore open again when they attacked you the second time." He gestured lightly at the wound on Stan's side, an injury he'd gotten when List's men took Thea after the wedding ball. The latest skirmish when Thea had been taken to the woods had aggravated it, leaving it raw and angry. But Andre had saved her then and was now setting his healing hands on Stan. Andre's movements, as always, were precise. If it hadn't been for him, that second attack on Thea could have turned out far worse than leaving her with the shock of it altogether. Moreover, since there had been a second attack, Stan feared for a third.

"I'm aware," Stan said tersely. His voice dripped with bitterness, his frustration flaring. "It's difficult to forget being tossed aside like a ragdoll while two men tried to drag my sister away."

"I prevented that—"

"And I'll be forever grateful. But they will be back."

Andre paused briefly, then turned to dab a cloth soaked in medicinal oil along the inflamed edges of the wound. Stan tensed his jaws against the sting.

"It's worse than I feared," Andre said, a note of concern sliding beneath his usual calm. "Stan, have you noticed you're burning up?"

"No," Stan lied, though every breath he drew seemed to feed the heat suffusing his body. He could feel it crawling beneath his skin like fire licking at dry kindling.

"Mm-hm." Andre's brow lifted, unconvinced. His hand

pressed against Stan's forehead, an action efficient but bordering with exasperation. "You have a fever," Andre confirmed, his tone leaving no room for argument. Not that Stan didn't try.

"And what of it?" Stan shot back.

Andre surveyed him as if he were a particularly stubborn case study. "What of it? You're flush with fever, your shoulder's inflamed, and you're sitting here asking 'what of it.'" He stepped a pace back, his hands falling to his hips in disbelief. "People with infections of this magnitude don't typically sit upright, Stan. Most *certainly* not while barking orders."

"I don't have the luxury of being laid low," Stan bit out, leaning forward despite the ache in his muscles. "Not while von List's men are still after Thea. Fool me once, shame on you. Fool me twice…" He trailed off, shaking his head. The words curdled in his throat, pressing hard against his chest. He would not remain idle, awaiting yet another misfortune to befall them, for twice was already more than enough.

Andre's expression softened—slightly. "You said yourself they shoved you aside. What happened wasn't a failure," he said evenly.

"It wasn't me who saved her, Andre. But thanks to you she's safe." Stan's voice dropped, the words tangling with his guilt and frustration. "Do you understand what that's like? Two men came into that house and made me powerless. They laid their hands on her, my sister." His fists curled on instinct as though the memory alone required a physical response. "And it's all because I took on List."

For a moment, silence stretched between them, broken only by the rustle of bandages in Andre's capable hands.

"With your fever and that shoulder, I'd hardly call standing upright a failure," Andre finally said dryly, though the edge of his voice softened in reproach. "Most men would be halfway to a grave by now. The fact you were upright at all is nothing short of a miracle."

"I don't dream of miracles; I need solutions," Stan muttered, the fire of his anger dimming slightly, smothered out by exhaustion. His shoulders sagged momentarily, though the fight in him persisted.

Andre tied off the fresh bandage carefully. "A good start might be resting for more than an hour between brooding sessions," he offered lightly, though his gaze grounded Stan. "And letting the wound air might do better than wrapping it again."

Stan gestured dismissively, the idea of surrendering to rest agitating him further. "I can't."

"You *won't*," Andre corrected without missing a beat.

Stan ignored the comment, his thoughts drifting to familiar territory—the face he hadn't been able to get out of his mind. Wendy's smile flickered in his memory, her tone soft but steady. For days now, she'd lingered at the edge of his every thought like sunlight through a haze.

"If anything had happened to Thea that day..." Stan began, then cut himself off, his mind catching the parallels before he could stop them. Could he bear to involve Wendy further when his own life was this volatile? Nick certainly wouldn't approve, and Stan could hardly fault him for that. He'd nearly unraveled entirely when List's men took Thea. To bring Wendy any closer felt like folly.

And yet...

"I need a private nurse if you want me to stay locked up till the fever breaks," Stan said abruptly, breaking the tension with the force of the confession. He hadn't intended it to come out quite like that, but Andre stilled, his attention now wholly on him.

"A nurse," Andre repeated, measuring his words. "And by that, you mean?"

"Miss Folsham. Nurse Wendy," Stan said evenly, though the heat climbing his neck betrayed him. "At Cloverdale House. If I'm to recover, it must be someone I can trust—and someone with skill that you approve of. It's safe here with the new guards in place."

Andre's mouth curved faintly, a subtle shift that could have passed as indifference, yet Stan felt the air tighten between them. Their eyes locked, and the room stretched quiet except for the muffled ticking of the mantel clock. Nothing was said, but the silence resonated louder than words.

Stan stiffened, his shoulder aching, but the discomfort barely registered. His thoughts pulled sharply to Wendy—her steady voice, the way she met his gaze without flinching, her gentleness wrapped in an iron will. Andre had always spoken highly of her, but now Stan understood the depth of that admiration. It was more than appreciation. It was protectiveness—sharp and uncompromising, woven into every careful motion of Andre's hands as he adjusted Stan's bandages and tied off a sling to support his arm.

"You want Wendy as your private nurse?" Andre seemed to test the words with the protectiveness of a big brother. Stan understood why. Of course, he did.

His jaw tightened, but his expression smoothed into neutrality, save for the slight lift of one dark brow. He didn't need to say anything. Andre's own stance answered questions unvoiced. His shoulders were squared, feet planted firmly as if bracing against something unseen. The message was clear—and Stan didn't miss any part of it.

Andre's closeness to Wendy wasn't born simply out of respect. It ran deeper, a connection strong enough to make any man cautious. Stan didn't falter under Andre's gaze, though a flicker of heat crept across his skin from restraint. He turned his attention inward, deliberately keeping his emotions penned tightly where they couldn't betray him. He liked Wendy, perhaps too much, and Andre would know it, even without Stan admitting it.

The pulse of tension hummed between them, filling the chasm of unspoken truths. But just as Stan began to settle into this unyielding exchange, another connection struck him—a thought so sudden it hit like a blow. Thea.

"You saved my sister." Stan narrowed his eyes slightly, observing Andre with renewed scrutiny. There it was again—that faint flicker, that hiccup of hesitation in the otherwise calm fortitude Andre carried. It was gone as quickly as it came, but not before Stan noted it. His brow arched a little higher, his expression cool, as if asking, *Shall we talk about you and Thea, then?*

Andre remained silent, his steady hands folding the used towel over and over until it was a lumpy ball, though his jaw flexed. A crack in his control. That was all it took for Stan's suspicions to slip into sharper focus. Of course, Andre would never overstep, yet the thread of something lingered—proof etched in the slight shift of his mouth, the tension in his grip. Stan tapped his fingers idly against his thigh, feigning nonchalance to mask the new string of questions unraveling in his head.

"When people need my help, I try to be there." Andre reached for another cloth, his movements more clipped than usual. He settled the bandage in place with a final tug, firmer than before.

"Is that so?" Or, *is that all?*

"You're fortunate this hasn't worsened," Andre said, his voice steady but just a shade colder than usual. "It should hold for now, but only if you rest. No excursions. No lifting swords. No making life harder than it already is."

Stan tilted his head, offering a slight nod as though acknowledging the words, but his mind lingered on the changes he'd seen in Andre. The moments were fleeting but all too telling, and not just about Wendy. He straightened, his posture sharper despite the dull ache settling deeper in his body.

It was laughable—the notion of him being scrutinized over feelings for another man's sister. Yet, here he was mirroring Andre's own exacting nature, shielding Thea as fiercely as Andre guarded Wendy.

Andre finally stood back, brushing his hands together as though shaking off the tension along with the task. "You should be sleeping right now," he added, his voice far less pointed, though his stare hadn't lost its sharpness.

"I'll think about it," Stan replied, his tone carefully neutral. He rolled his shoulder, testing the bandage's hold, but his thoughts collided inwardly. The bond between Andre and Wendy might have been clear, but something stirred deeper—and just as quietly—involving Thea. The irony wasn't lost on him.

With a slight shake of his head, Stan exhaled through his nose. "Thank you," he added, softer this time, though as he turned, a flicker of dissatisfaction curled in his chest. He wasn't only thanking Andre for the care. That unacknowledged respect simmered beneath. Perhaps that's why nothing more needed to be said. Neither man wanted to dissect uncharted territory, not when it entailed too much.

Even so, Stan wasn't blind to the deeper intentions wrapped tightly with their mutual silences. These threads—woven and unspoken as they were—wouldn't unwind easily.

"I wonder whether it's the safety that draws you," Andre remarked airily, turning away to tidy his supplies.

Ignoring him, Stan stood on slightly unsteady legs. "I'll arrange for more outside guards as well. Baron von List won't just—"

"Rest," Andre interrupted firmly, his voice sharp enough to cut. "It's admirable to protect others, Stan. But remember, you can't protect anyone if you can't stand. You may think yourself invincible, but even princes can crumble."

Stan wanted to argue, but his fever clouded even his stubbornness. He nodded curtly, but inside, resolve churned with emotion he wouldn't admit outright. Wendy. He would see her again, heedless of his better judgment or the warnings coiled in the back of his mind. Admitting it was dangerous. But not seeing her? That was unthinkable.

Chapter Fourteen

AT THE SAME time, Wendy was on the way back to London with Nick and Pippa. The carriage wheels clattered over the cobblestones, the steady rhythm weaving through the faint hum of conversation inside. Wendy sat opposite her brother and sister-in-law, her gaze flitting between them as they spoke. Pippa leaned slightly forward, her hands clasped tightly together, as though her excitement couldn't be contained any longer.

"The workers should have started this morning," Pippa said, her voice bright and lilting. "The architects promised to oversee every phase, but I told them I'd be there as often as possible. I need to keep an eye on the progress myself. It's not just about construction—it's about creating something with purpose."

Nick's mouth curved into a fond smile as he adjusted the cuff of his jacket. "And you don't trust their competence unless you witness it firsthand?"

"Not that," Pippa insisted with a good-natured laugh. "But yes. I want to see the rehabilitation center take shape. To know it's becoming real—what we've worked toward, what we've dreamed of. Can you imagine it? A space like Cloverdale House, transformed to help so many?"

Wendy studied her sister-in-law, noticing the light blush on Pippa's cheeks, the fervor in her expression. Even as Wendy's thoughts lingered elsewhere, Pippa's enthusiasm softened the tightness in her chest. It was clear Pippa's heart was firmly invested. The idea of the home, once lavishly idle, now repurposed for something meaningful—it was admirable.

Nick reached across the space and covered Pippa's hand with his. "It's beyond generous. Opening Cloverdale to high-ranking officials for treatments when it could be rented or sold for some grand profit... Not every woman would choose so selflessly."

Pippa wrinkled her nose as though dismissing the thought entirely. "What use is fortune if it can't help those in need? And think of the officers who served to protect us—of the families breathing easier knowing their husbands, sons, and brothers will be treated with dignity, surrounded by beauty. Most soldiers never return. But those who do? We will never turn them away. Healing isn't a small thing. I'd like to put my inheritance to good use. Plus, we owe them since they defended us and the hegemony of powers in Europe." Pippa waved as if it were nothing, giving up one of London's largest estates for the purpose of a sophisticated hospital, even if this was not what they'd call it.

Nick's nod carried quiet pride.

Wendy smoothed the folds of her plain dress, her gloves lying unused in her lap. For a moment, Wendy felt a tug of wistfulness—and then quickly tucked it away.

The ball four days ago felt like a dream now, a fleeting moment of effervescence, and one she could no longer afford to entertain. The cobblestones gave way to a smoother path, and Wendy stole a glance through the carriage window as Cloverdale House came into view.

Though she had visited before, seeing it now stirred something new within her. The façade, bathed in the pale morning light, stood tall against the bustle of the surrounding streets. The muted grandeur of the home felt inspiring, not ornamental, as though steeped in the promise of what Pippa envisioned, and Wendy would be part of, in converting the estate into a true rehabilitation center. Wendy tapped the crunched-up gloves she held lightly against the seat, waiting for the carriage to roll to a stop.

"I only hope it will be safe with the new guards," Nick added after a beat, his voice slipping into a lower, protective tone. "Not everyone agrees with the changes to Cloverdale. Some see its use as a rehabilitation center as an affront to its history."

"Isn't it the opposite if it becomes a place where those who defended what's good and right come to heal?" Wendy asked.

Pippa's lips curved slightly in response, but she swept a stray lock of hair behind her ear, a flicker of determination flashing in her hazel eyes. "Then they can argue with results. Time will prove us right." Turning to Wendy, she softened her tone. "And you'll tell me the truth, won't you, Wendy? If you see something that doesn't work?"

Wendy blinked, brought back fully into the moment. "Of course," she said, nodding. A smile tugged at her lips despite herself. "Though you hardly need my advice. You seem to have thought of everything."

Pippa beamed, her delight unmistakable. "Hardly everything. But between Nick's counsel and your steadiness, I know it will succeed. Andre is there already and Nurse Shira and Dr. Phil Rosen, too. With all your doctor friends from Harley Street, this will be the grandest establishment in London."

The carriage slowed, the jarring halt of the wheels signaling their arrival. Outside, she could see the entrance staff assembled, and the faint din of workers echoed from somewhere beyond. Wendy's heart nudged forward in her chest, quick and unsure, as she shifted in her seat. It might've been Pippa's vision—or something she hadn't let herself name—but the house bristled with newness.

"Welcome back to reality," Wendy murmured to herself under her breath as the footman reached for the carriage door, though her voice held no bitterness. Nick must have heard because he chuckled as he stepped out and extended a hand to her and Pippa to exit the cabin.

She would step forward, as always, steady and prepared. Whether for dreams to take root—or for them to be left behind entirely. The air in London was unlike that at Pippa's country estate, laden with the faint tang of damp stone and chimney smoke.

Back to work, Wendy! Time to exchange that shiny ballgown for a proper white apron and to help people.

Her heels clicked softly on the stone as she walked the few steps up to the door. The glow from within signaled that someone was inside, which didn't strike her as unusual since Andre was supposed to tend to any emergencies until she and the others returned. When she entered, the warmth inside greeted her, along with the faint scent of cloves and witch hazel lingering from treatments conducted earlier in the day.

The butler arrived and Pippa instantly gave a slur of orders. Nick seemed instantly distracted with some mail the butler handed on a silver platter and Wendy snuck into the corridor where the new treatment rooms were being set up.

"Andre?" she called softly, shutting the door behind her when she found the second on the right which was supposed to be his. The house stood quiet, but faint voices carried from the corridor leading to Andre's treatment room—a low, familiar cadence coupled with someone else's more clipped tones.

Curiosity drew her forward, and just as she reached the hall-way, a figure emerged from the shadows of the dim light. Wendy froze mid-step, her breath catching audibly in her throat.

"Stan?" she said, her voice almost a whisper. "I mean, Your Royal Highness." She curtsied deeply.

The man before her looked both strikingly familiar and pain-fully altered. His usually proud posture was diminished; his left arm rested in a sling, cradled close to his chest. The pristine tailoring of his coat was out of place against the pallor of his face and the faint sheen of sweat glistening under the light. His hair, often perfectly arranged, fell slightly out of place, and dark circles sat beneath his eyes.

Stan turned his head sharply at the sound of her voice, but the movement drew a visible wince from him. He quickly masked it with a strained smile. "Nurse Wendy," he said, his voice hoarser than she remembered.

"What happened to you?" she burst out, stepping closer. The soft light drew sharp lines on his face, and her eyes darted unbidden to the sling, to the tired slump of his shoulders. "Your arm—did you break it?"

He gave a small, dismissive gesture with his good hand, though the motion looked more like surrender than reassurance. "It's nothing," he said. "A mere… complication. I didn't know I would find you here. Did you just return to London?"

"Yes." But all that mattered was her prince.

He's not your prince.

"Complication?" she repeated, her brows knitting. "You look dreadful."

His lips twitched, as though her bluntness amused him despite himself. But before he could answer, she noticed something else—a faint, unnatural flush to his cheeks that stood out against his otherwise pallid complexion. And then there was the faint jitter in his hand as it dropped to his side. *Tremor.*

Her heart tightened with worry. She narrowed her eyes as she went over the symptoms in her mind. He looked strained but bowed and she dutifully extended her hand. When he reached for it, his palm felt cool and moist.

Clammy skin and sweat. Fever. *Calor.*

He'd winced when he moved the arm in the sling. Pain. *Dolor.*

"How were you injured?" she pressed, stepping even closer as she studied him.

Stan exhaled, glancing towards the hallway like he was willing someone—Andre, perhaps—to interrupt and save him from the inquisition. When it became clear no one would, he relented. "It was the night we left for London," he began, his voice deliberately measured. His eyes met hers, steady but shadowed with unease. "List's men—or likely them. They had a Prussian accent—"

"List?" she interrupted, frowning. "List's men attacked you?"

"Not me," he said tightly, a muscle in his jaw flexing. "My sister. They took her."

A princess? The thought barely had time to settle before another wave of confusion followed it. "She was abducted? But how—why?"

Stan's shoulders stiffened—a reflex of frustration, perhaps, or defensiveness. It was hard to tell. But when he spoke again, his tone carried an edge of weariness. "Their agenda is unclear, though I have no doubt it involved ransom. The timing was deliberate. They knew exactly when to intercept us." He shifted on his feet, his free hand balling into a tense fist. "They cornered us on the road. I took care of one of them, but... there were three."

"How—what about this?" she asked, gesturing toward his injured arm.

"Oh, this?" Stan gave a faint, rueful smile, though it fell short of any genuine amusement. "Just a slice in my shoulder. It's already healing."

Slice? Princess abducted?

Keep your distance, Wendy. You manage the injury but not the royal mess of his life.

Her eyes narrowed, suspicion flaring. Not about the little nagging voice of reason but because of her concern for her prince.

Still not your prince, Wendy.

"Wait, what healing? Stan, you winced just now. You're in pain!"

"It's nothing," he insisted, though the strain in his voice betrayed him when he wiped beads of sweat from his forehead. If anything, his attempt to move his arm in demonstration only deepened the grimace etched on his face. He quickly abandoned the effort, his pride clearly battling his pain.

She touched his forehead, her concern overriding all propriety. "You look fevered—have you rested at all? Has Andre given you anything for the injury?"

He hesitated, and that singular pause spoke volumes. Wendy could see the tension in his stance—the stubborn determination not to show weakness clashing with the very real signs of exhaustion etched into him.

"Andre's in there with my sister."

"Is she injured, too?" Wendy asked, ready to go to Andre and assist him.

"No, she's perfectly fine now, but if they don't come out of there, he might be—"

"Oh!" Wendy's hands flew to her mouth. *Andre and a princess?*

"Oh indeed." He arched a brow and there was a glint of boyish mischief that sent Wendy's heart into a wild flutter. But then it melted away as if the fever burned his spirits.

Without fully realizing it, she reached out, her fingers brushing lightly against the fabric of his sleeve just above the sling. The warmth radiating from him confirmed what she already suspected. Her throat tightened as worry tunneled through her.

"Your Royal Highness," she began softly, her voice steadier now despite the storm of emotions fighting for space in her chest. "You need to rest. Whatever this is—whatever you've endured—you can't simply push through it."

He looked at her for a long moment, his dark gaze lingering on hers in a manner that made her heart stumble. There was gratitude there, though unspoken, hidden beneath layers of pride and fatigue. Finally, he dipped his head, just a fraction. But even as he conceded, she noticed the faint hint of defiance still glittering in his eyes.

"Perhaps you're right," he said quietly. "But first... I need to speak with your brother about the guards."

Wendy pressed her lips together, resisting the urge to argue further. Instead, she gave a short nod, watching him closely as he straightened, visibly steeling himself against his weakness.

But as she followed him down the corridor, her mind churned with questions and a growing unease. The Stan she knew was always composed, unshakable. But tonight, she had glimpsed something else entirely—a man who was, perhaps for the first time, pushed to the brink. And she couldn't shake the awareness that he hadn't told her the whole truth. But what could the prince, who clearly suffered from an infection, hide from her, a mere nurse?

Chapter Fifteen

The next day, back at 87 Harley Street…

THE LIGHT FILTERED softly through the windows of 87 Harley Street, painting pale streaks on the polished floorboards. The treatment room was quiet, save for the faint clink of metal as Wendy arranged instruments on a tray near the carved wooden counter. Thin scissors. The smallest forceps. A triangular scalpel. Her hands moved methodically, performing the familiar task with care, though not without effort; her fingers trembled just slightly as she positioned the final tool. Wendy paused, drew in a steadying breath, and forced herself to focus. She had promised to split her time between the two places, but this morning, Harley Street needed her. By midmorning, patients would arrive, and Nick would need everything prepared. This, at least, she could manage without fault.

"Thank you, Wendy," Nick said. He stood at the back of the room, poring over a sheet of paper littered with calculations. Angles, lenses, equations. Usual work for the week's cases, though his tone was preoccupied. "Have you seen the vial of belladonna that was on the small desk?"

Wendy furrowed her brows, glancing up briefly. How unusual for Nick to ask about the little bottle with the dropper, the one he used to dilate patients' pupils for their eye exams. "No," she replied, though her curiosity over the missing vial quickly gave way to the need to finish her preparations.

The instruments rested in neat rows on the tray, gleaming in the light. Her trembling hands stilled as she stood back, willing herself to push the gnawing anxiety aside. There was work to do, and that was where her focus needed to be.

"Do we have enough clove oil for tomorrow?" Nick looked over his shoulder at the half-empty bottle on the metal tray on the side table.

"I put a spare bottle in the cabinet," Wendy said just as Pippa swung into the room with an exuberant energy Wendy both admired and envied.

"Did he say anything?" Pippa suddenly asked, breaking the clinical focus with the kind of indulgent and amused curiosity that was typical of her. Wendy glanced toward her sister-in-law, who stood at the mirror, removing her gloves and unbuttoning her pelisse, her ochre gown catching the morning light. Pippa's expression was expectant, the beginnings of a smirk playing on her lips.

Wendy turned back to the tray, her throat tight. "Who?"

"Who indeed," Pippa teased. "The prince, of course! What did he say while the two of you floated across the dance floor, wrapped in whatever enchantment he cast over the room?"

Nick stilled but remained silent.

"I don't believe we floated," Wendy snapped, her tone harsher than intended. "It was just a dance."

"Oh, Wendy, don't insult my intelligence," Pippa said, her voice lilting with humor. She stepped closer, scrutinizing her reflection as she patted her curls into place. "Even with my diminished eyesight, it was plain. There was such tension between you. Everyone felt it. The way he looked at you—it was as though the rest of us simply vanished from the room. He didn't say anything to you at Cloverdale House yesterday?"

Wendy's chest tightened, the boundaries she had so carefully maintained threatening to crumble. Her older brother stared at her with a completely new expression she couldn't decipher. Not precisely bewilderment or shock, but something in the general range of fear mixed with anger.

Oh dear.

So, Wendy decided to focus on her chest, willing her lungs to fill evenly with air, steadily. "You're imagining it."

"I'm not, and neither were the other guests. By the look of half those matrons with unwed daughters this season, you may already have enemies." Pippa clasped her hands together with glee. "You looked so beautiful in his arms."

Nick recoiled, his eyes widening as though he'd just been told the moon had fallen from the sky. He sputtered, clenching his cravat as if it had turned into a noose, and then broke into a cough.

Pippa, suppressing both a grin and a sigh, hurried to his side, her hands gentle as she patted his back. "Do breathe, Nick," she teased. "It's hardly a death sentence to be the belle of the ball in the arms of a prince."

He rubbed at his temples as if reason itself were slipping through his fingers, his voice low and half-muffled. "Perhaps this is my punishment for letting her waltz with a prince," he murmured, his mouth pulling into a rueful grimace before sighing.

"Pippa," Wendy warned, an edge creeping into her tone.

"All right, I'll stop," Pippa replied, though her grin remained as she kissed Nick on the cheek. "At least for now. Don't think you've escaped me entirely, Wendy."

"Shall I walk you home?" His gaze lingered on Pippa with indulgent affection. "I'm afraid I have a long day tomorrow and need about another two hours to prepare and come back." He looked at Wendy, who gave a faint nod. "The emergency from this morning will return tomorrow for a change of bandages, Wendy." As if no further explanation were needed for Pippa, he added, "Have you seen the belladonna vial? The one with the dropper to dilate the pupils?" Nick searched the room, his gaze narrowing as he pursed his lips and eyed the spot on the exam table where he usually kept the brown bottle.

Whatever he didn't finish, Wendy gladly prepared. She'd be there for as many patients as possible. She clung to her need for distraction more than usual.

"Very well," Pippa replied with mock submission. Her hand brushed his as she prepared to leave, but she turned back once at the door, her gaze briefly meeting Wendy's. "I shall pay Violet a visit after I meet with the architects for the rehabilitation center. I will ensure that dinner will still be hot no matter how late you both come home."

Wendy didn't respond, locking her attention instead on the tray before her, but Pippa's words echoed with unnerving weight.

When the door shut behind her, the room seemed emptier, though the sunlight and faint scent of Pippa's perfume still lingered. Wendy adjusted a scalpel slightly as Nick came to stand beside her. His hand landed firmly on the back of the chair; she didn't have to look to know his gaze had turned to her now.

"This is the first time we've been alone in a while." he said with brotherly bluntness. "You're moving like someone half-asleep."

Wendy forced herself to smile. "I'm fine. I've assisted with surgeries on less rest than this."

"That's not what I meant." His tone softened slightly, and when she glanced at him, the sharp, evaluating stare of a surgeon was gone. Replacing it was something harder to face—concern.

Her hands slipped. The tray tilted; metal clinked loudly against metal. Wendy caught it before an instrument could fall but the tension snared her breath tight in her chest. "It's nothing," she said quickly, lifting the tray and crossing to the counter, desperate for distance. "I'll—I'll boil these again."

"Wendy." Nick's voice was calm but steady. Unwavering. She glanced back reluctantly. He had moved to sit against the surgeons' desk, arms crossed as he studied her.

"What?" she said—a little too defensively.

"I should've asked sooner," he said, his gaze unwavering. "Do you have any affection for him?"

Her pulse thudded. The instruments lay heavy in her hands, too sharp, too cold. "I… I'm not sure what you're after."

"You know exactly what I'm asking," he replied gently. "Do you like him? Prince Stan, I mean."

Her throat tightened around the words she didn't want to speak, words that crowded her mind with emotions she couldn't untangle. *Like* wasn't the word. Not for the way her chest had warmed under his gaze or the fragility in her limbs when his hand brushed hers during the waltz. Admiration, longing—just the memory made her want to step closer to some invisible warmth that lingered. But then came the other side—the chill tether of reason.

She cleared her throat to break the tense silence. "It doesn't matter, does it? He's… a prince. I'm no one."

Nick's brow furrowed, his expression a study of disquiet. "Don't say that."

Wendy shrugged and dropped her head, suppressing a pout.

"Never say you're less than what you are." There was no heat in his voice, only a raw insistence that made her pulse falter.

She turned away, her gaze dropping to the polished wooden counter in front of her. "Nick, I'm a nurse," she said softly, the words deliberate, as though each one carved the truth she'd resigned herself to. "I organize linens, clean instruments for surgery, and help you all. That's all."

"You're more than that," he replied, his tone sharpening with certainty. "None of us could run this practice without you, don't you know that?" She shook her head, swallowing to try to rid her throat of the lump forming. "Wendy, as much as it pains me to warn you that Stan is entangled in some very dangerous business, it is not because of your differences in stations that I think you should stay away from him."

Her hands trembled as she gripped the rim of the counter, his words too much and too little all at once. She wanted— desperately—to believe him, but doubt clung to her like a shadow. "I know my place," she whispered, barely loud enough for the words to escape. "It's here. With the doctors on Harley Street, not a prince."

Nick groaned, dragging a hand down his face as though his thoughts had settled there, and muttered, "It's a cruel twist of fate, watching your sister cease to be a child right before your eyes." He sighed. "And yet I often wish Mother and Father could see you. They'd be so proud. At least as much as I am."

Wendy willed herself not to cry and shifted her stance. "Well, I'll stay as long as I'm needed here—but once things settle, I'll return to Cloverdale House to help oversee treatments." Wendy tried to smile, but her lips wobbled, and she felt tears pooling.

Nick inhaled sharply and stepped closer, his presence firm but his voice quieter and calmer now. "Will you?"

"Of course. I'll always be there for you just as you're always there for me."

Nick slumped his shoulders. "But I haven't been there enough since Pippa and I…I mean…"

"Oh, please! I know you fell in love, Nick. I'm glad you did." Wendy wiped the tears from her face with one of the towels she'd just prepared for surgery, making a mental note that she'd have to boil and press at least three more for tomorrow morning. "Pippa is wonderful, and she's the sister I never had. Don't worry about me, I'm not a little girl anymore."

"Tell me this, Wendy—what would you have said to me if I had thought myself unworthy of Pippa? If I had convinced myself that her title or my lack of it defined us? Would you have told me I was right to believe that?"

She swallowed hard, biting her lip as emotion welled in her chest. She didn't answer, couldn't answer, and shook her head.

Of course not. And yet…

He pressed on. "Don't limit yourself," but even though his voice was steady as a soft tide, it betrayed more than he seemingly intended. "Don't look at him and see only what you aren't, Wendy. That's no way to measure anything." He pulled each word from somewhere deep.

"You don't think I should let him… allow him to… um…" It was too difficult to tell her older brother, who had stepped into the role of both parents at such a young age and had always been present. For him to get married meant that Wendy would move into a house with him and Pippa. But if Wendy ever thought about marriage, she would have to leave her brother. The idea of not living together for Wendy and Nick was absurd. Other siblings certainly had no issue with it, but Wendy and Nick—Nick and Wendy—brother and sister; they were always together, committed to being there for each other since their parents died.

Thus, she couldn't go and explore what these feelings were for Prince Stan. She wasn't able to untie the chains of her life if those very chains kept her safe and tied closely to her beloved brother who had been the only man in her life.

Until now.

Her throat burned with unspoken words, but her fingers moved of their own accord, crumbling the tear-stained towel, and brushing lightly over the cold steel of the instruments she worked with daily. They felt familiar—solid, grounding—but couldn't quiet the wild, uncertain hope that had begun to stir deep within her.

The dance. The prince's eyes on hers. The way he had spoken, as if the rest of the world had faded. It wasn't supposed to matter, and yet it did. Too much.

Nick's hand, firm but gentle, rested on her shoulder. It was the only reminder she had of where she stood at that moment, in that room. "Wendy," he said, and his voice was kinder now, almost solemn. "You've always been everything you needed to be. Don't forget that. Don't be afraid to ask for more." Tears stung the edges of her vision, though she blinked them back. Slowly, she managed a nod. "But can you do me a favor, little sister?"

"Anything."

"Don't let the prince's sparkling smile and manners trick you into his world. He is in much danger, and I fear it has just begun. I just signed off on a contract for outside guards at Cloverdale House."

"What if it's too late?" Because she prioritized the prince's safety over her own, it was too late for her to turn a blind eye, wasn't it?

"Wendy?" With a long, theatrically drawn-out sigh, Nick raked his fingers through his hair and muttered, "You were supposed to stay eight years old forever. How am I supposed to survive this torment? What if something were to happen to you?"

"I won't allow it." It wasn't an agreement not to let the longing for the prince take root, but an acknowledgment that she'd chosen her brother if ever faced with a decision between one or the other, a promise she wasn't entirely sure she could keep, not yet. But when Nick gave her shoulder a small, reassuring squeeze, she leaned into his touch, letting the faint warmth of his support steady her.

"So, you'll be careful?" he pressed on.

She wasn't ready to say yes—to choosing her own path, to leaving Harley Street, to following her heart—not yet. But for now, she could hold onto the words her brother had spoken and the love that had shaped them.

And for the moment, it was enough. It had to be.

Chapter Sixteen

Later that night at Cloverdale House…

THE WAR RAGED within him, burning hotter than the chaos waiting just beyond the carriage door. And the heat was relentless, an iron weight pressing down on Stan's chest and muddling his thoughts. Around him, the chamber rocked like a horse galloping toward battle, dim shapes of furniture appearing and vanishing with each slow blink of his eyes. Sweat slicked his skin, soaking the linen beneath him, and his left shoulder burned, a hot and furious ache radiating through his entire arm. If he moved, even the slightest shift, the pain blazed brighter, sharp enough to twist his breath into shallow gasps.

Something white flickered at the edge of his vision—a sleeve, perhaps, or a gown. He couldn't lift his head to confirm, the effort too great and the fever too cruel. A voice, calm but firm, sounded nearby.

"Keep the wound clean." That was Andre, the unmistakable lilt of his Italian accent cutting through the heavy fog of Stan's mind. "He won't admit it, but the pain is worse than he lets on. The fever must break soon or else—"

Then a woman gasped.

The response came, quieter, but with an urgency that cut through the haze like a blade. "And the princess? Is she—"

Stan's breath caught. Wendy. The soft twang of her vowels and her tone's precise warmth—his Wendy. Andre had allowed her to be his private nurse then?

He tried to turn his head to see her, to make certain it wasn't a fever dream conjured by weeks of longing and misery. Instead, his vision splintered into watery lights, and the swish of her movement blurred into the shadows.

"She's safe," Andre replied, though Stan barely caught the word before the thrum of blood in his ears swallowed it.

Wendy. She was here. Despite her work at Harley Street and the risks involved, she'd come.

He wanted to reach out as he had earlier at the practice, to tell her something, anything, but his limbs wouldn't obey him. Heat roared through his body, and the world tilted sideways. A sharp pang flared in his chest, and then there was nothing but darkness.

When the light returned, it wasn't the dim glow of his bedroom but the pale, soft radiance of summer in Transylvania. Stan's childhood home unfolded before him; each detail impossibly vivid despite the swirls of mist clouding his thoughts. The pine-clad hills stretched endlessly toward the horizon, rugged and proud, and in the valley below lay the estates he'd sworn to protect since he was a boy. His home, Bran Castle, loomed with its great stone walls stark against the lush greenery surrounding it.

But the edges of the image wavered, and he couldn't taste the crisp mountain air or feel the sun warming his face. Instead, a cold dread curled in his stomach. He couldn't move forward—his feet seemed rooted to the earth—but through the fog, he saw the doors to the castle thrown open. Inside lay responsibilities he had neglected during his time away. His people needed him.

Thea, his sister, was in danger. The affairs of state escalated and could force his father to declare war. His family, his everything, needed him.

Someone called his name—it sounded like a whisper carried on a distant breeze.

"Stan," the voice said again, sharper now, pulling him back, yanking him away from home to a body stretched on a bed too soft and too foreign, with linens damp from sweat and the ravages of fever burning him alive.

He fluttered awake, if opening fevered eyes could be called waking. The light hurt, low though it was. He tried again to find her—a glimpse, a hand, anything. Instead, he felt the crushing helplessness. The fever pressed him down, pinned him, stripped him of himself. But she was here, wasn't she? Wendy was here, her voice curling around him like a lifeline he couldn't yet reach.

The agony in his shoulder pulsed again, tethering him to the now. The ache of infection threaded with her name, glowing faint and enduring in his mind. And though everything else swam in confusion, one thought burned bright through the fever's relentless haze—she had come for him.

The shivering started in waves, only half-registered at first, until cold wracked his body with such force it seemed to shake his very bones. Stan groaned, the sound low and ragged, as if torn from his throat. He rolled his head weakly to the side, his lips parting to draw in air that felt both too shallow and too sharp. He struggled to hold onto something, onto anything, but he was slipping again—slipping into the shadowy folds of his fevered mind.

This time, the ballroom unfolded before him with cruel familiarity, like a premonition about List. It shimmered, impossibly bright, chandeliers dripping with endless crystal light that spun and danced in time with the violins. Wendy was there, a vision draped in white instead of the shimmering pink dress etched so vividly in his memory. The apron clung to her figure, stark, plain, practical. And he wanted to tug at the bow and take off her apron, bring the pink gown back and make her his princess. Why was she wearing this plain apron here, in this place of finery and grace?

Didn't she know she needed a gown to fit into his life? Oh how he wanted that more than his next breath.

He reached for her hand, his fingertips brushing against hers, warm and steady. The violins changed—the tune he so vividly remembered giving way to a lilting waltz as he led her to the floor. With him, she could dance. He'd taught her. He'd given her her first dance and wanted to give her so many more. But for that, he had to live.

He smiled faintly, lips moving numbly as he heard himself whisper, "One, two, three. Follow me." Their feet glided in perfect synchronicity, the world narrowing to the space they occupied together. Her green eyes lifted to meet his, yet something lingered there, something unreadable. When the violins stopped, her gaze slipped into shadow, her figure retreating. She was leaving. *Again.*

Stan's fingers tightened in the dream as he tried to hold onto her, a low plea slipping past his lips, soft, desperate. "No, my sweet Wendy, stay with me..." But her form dissolved, as if caught in the frantic swell of the fever burning through his body. "Wendy, please!"

His eyelids fluttered, heavy as iron weights. He tried to lift them, but the effort was Herculean.

One, two, three. Follow me.

Heat poured through his muscles, every joint, every tendon, as if someone had flayed him leaving him raw and exposed. His breaths scratched against his throat, coming too fast, too shallow. Something cold pressed against him, shocking his senses and pulling him closer to wakefulness. The touch hit his shins first, the chill spreading through his limbs. Then it moved to his forehead, a cloth soaked with winter and mercy.

He stirred. His lips moved, dry and cracked, forming shapes that never quite became words. Another chill surged, resetting the rhythm of his heart, anchoring him back into his body. Somewhere beyond the fevered hum in his ears, he heard her voice. Soft and insistent, a lifeline pulling him out of deep waters.

"One, two, three, Stan. Breathe with me." Her tone was steady, commanding, yet threaded with a tenderness he thought lost to him. "One, two, three, stay with me." His lashes parted, slowly, painfully. The dim light above shimmered more shadow than gold, but there she was. Wendy. Her face was flushed, framed by flying strands of loose hair. Her lips moved with precise care as she repeated the words, a mantra that bound him to the present. "Please, stay with me!"

For one crushing moment, his heart seemed to freeze—trapped, his chest swelling with a sensation foreign yet weighty. He knew this feeling, at least its echo. It was in the surrender. He had felt it before, on battlefields and in drills, the moment when you had no choice but to yield to the inevitable. Now, he knew, this was no battlefield. This was something sweeter, dangerously so.

And if he let the fever take him, he'd lose her.

His voice rasped, barely there, breaking against the air. "Wendy…" It wasn't much, but it was everything. Whatever battle he fought before, he could not fight this. Not her. Not now. Not when all he wished to do was stay in the orbit of her presence, the only thing tethering him to life. She had conquered him, and he submitted without struggle, his heartbeat catching in its new rhythm—*one, two, three. Stay with me.*

THE HOURS DRAGGED on and the oppressive heat radiating from Stan's body twisted Wendy's insides. She sat at his bedside, wringing out another strip of linen into a bowl of tepid water. Her hands, though steady, bore the stiffness of endless repetition. Compresses off, saturate, wring, compresses on. It was an endless, numbing rhythm, yet she never faltered. His fever was too high, his pulse too erratic for even a moment's hesitation.

A knock on the door gave her pause.

"May I come in?" a gentle voice asked.

Wendy couldn't say anything. The woman was breathtakingly beautiful in an unassuming way, and yet she had a poise that demanded attention. "Are you Nurse Wendy? Is my brother waking up yet?"

Oh, her brother!

"Your Royal Highness," Wendy set the cloth aside, dried her hands as she rose and curtsied at the same time, thinking how clumsy her manners were compared to the princess.

But when she saw how gently the princess laid her hand on Stan's forehead, the raw concern of a sister for her brother—it warmed Wendy's heart. If it were Nick's life in danger, she would also want to be with him and do anything in her power to help bring him back. That was when the princess sat at the foot of Stan's bed.

"When I was little, Stan was always the first to save me." The princess wrung her hands. "I once brought home what I though was a puppy. But Stan saw it was a wolf cub and returned it to the forest. And when I climbed a tall oak, he was the one to help me down the tree. And now... I ran away, and he was hurt because of me." She heaved and wiped a tear from her cheek. "What can I do?" she asked.

"Nothing," Wendy said, picking up the cloth again and continuing the cold compresses.

"But Andre... ahem... Dr. Fernando said the next hours will tell whether he shall live." Concern was etched on the princess's face, even though she spoke with the grace of a woman who had much training in dealing with bad news. It was a rare and taxing skill Wendy knew all too well dealing with noble patients.

"I'm keeping him as cool as possible. May I propose that you rest in case he needs you in the morning?" Wendy said more as sister-to-sister than nurse-to-princess. "He spoke your name, he worries about you. Don't give him a reason that could weaken his condition."

The princess nodded and rose, the reluctance weighing her graceful movements down. "Will you call me if I can help, please?"

"Certainly," Wendy said with a curtsy.

"Thank you, Nurse Wendy. Your work tonight is deeply appreciated. I shall forever be in your debt." And with these words, the princess left.

Yet, Wendy couldn't fathom being anywhere else. And there was nothing to repay her with, no debt, only Stan.

Oh, please be strong. Please live.

His face, normally so composed—even imperious—lay stripped of all dignity by the fever. He didn't look like the intimidating royal anymore. Gone was the precise movement of his training as a soldier. All that was left just seemed like a very young man, devoid of the boyish mischief and struggling with the inflammation in his body. His eyes were shut, lids fluttering as if a struggle waged underneath. He parted his lips in uneven rasps of harsh breath.

Once again, Wendy pressed the damp fabric to his brow, gentle but firm, and trailed another along the burning planes of his cheeks and neck. He didn't stir. He hadn't stirred for hours now. Not even when she'd carefully peeled back the corner of his soaked shirt earlier to inspect the infected wound that had brought him to this wretched state. She'd had to bite the inside of her cheek to keep herself steady, for the ragged edges of the gash told the story of his pain more vividly than she could bear.

Not your prince, Wendy.

The thought struck her again as her hand smoothed the compress over his forehead, her cuff dragging slightly against the coarse stubble on his jaw. Not your prince. Nursing was her duty, her calling—that was all. And yet, the steady intensity of her care betrayed her heart, a heart she repeatedly chastised for yearning where it shouldn't.

A noise at the door startled her. She turned, her hand stilling mid-motion, as Andre entered, his expression grim. A leather bag hung from his arm, and behind him trailed a servant balancing a bucket filled with ice—the kind procured at an exorbitant expense, especially this time of year. Wendy didn't dare speak, but the quick glance she cast at the doctor's furrowed brow told her what she already feared.

This wasn't working.

"We'll need more water. Tell them to bring it cold." Andre gave his orders swiftly, his voice clipped in a tone that allowed no arguments. He shot a look at the already cooling compresses, though the reprimand in his gaze wasn't for her. "The ice will help a little, but it's not enough."

The servant hurried out, and Andre moved quickly to the bed. He leaned close to inspect Stan, pressing deft fingers to the artery in his neck. Wendy saw the faint shake in his hand as he withdrew it but said nothing. He turned to her. "Has he woken at all?"

Wendy shook her head. She'd worked with Andre at the practice for years now, but this was new. The rehabilitation center at Cloverdale House was for intense care and she'd see her first patient before going back home to Harley Street.

I can't believe my first patient here at Cloverdale House is my prince.

"Take the coverings off. He mustn't trap the heat," Andre said and pulled the covers off the prince. Without hesitation, Wendy folded back the heavy blanket, her fingers nimble as she peeled the damp sheet that clung stubbornly to Stan's chest. The saturated fabric dropped to the floor with a faint thud, but neither she nor Andre paid it any mind. The doctor reached for his scissors and pressed them into Wendy's hand.

"You'll do it faster," he said curtly. "Don't lose time with the buttons."

Wendy worked with a precision born of knowledge rather than instinct, the fabric of Stan's shirt parting cleanly under the blades. She peeled it away, leaving only his breeches in place, which were already rolled up over his knees—both for propriety and necessity. His broad chest, glistening with sweat, rose and fell shallowly under the reddish flush that marked the fever's relentless grip. The stitched wound, angry and seeping, stood out against the heat-mottled skin, and Wendy noted it silently, her mind already planning its next steps.

Andre's instructions were sharp. Together, they maneuvered Stan's still form, lifting him just enough to place his feet into the ice-water bath. He was alarmingly limp in their grasp, heavier than Wendy would have imagined in his unconscious state. Somehow, she managed to keep her grip steady, her movements firm yet careful. Andre, for all his briskness, softened slightly as the task came to completion, his trained efficiency revealing the smallest glint of hope.

"Perhaps this might bring relief," he said.

But his unspoken fears pressed down on her as they adjusted the basin beneath the bed. It wasn't just fever that hung in the air but something heavier, darker. Wendy had seen the coma claim others, and too often, it refused to give them back.

Andre poured the remaining ice alongside the water and leaned back as if to appraise the battlefield. "If it lasts," he muttered, half to himself, "it could shut everything down. Heart. Lungs. Brain." His jaw tightened. "And I'll not have the prince die here. Not with his sister sleeping in the room above us."

Stan wasn't just a prince, Wendy thought, irrational anger spiking beneath her worry. He was a man—her prince, her treacherous heart whispered—but his life hung by a thread so fine, a spider might have as well spun it. She adjusted another fresh compress to his forehead, her fingers brushing against his hairline. He didn't move, didn't give any sign of life beyond the fragile rhythm of his chest.

"Am I missing anything?" Wendy asked, her voice low but steady as her fingers worked another damp cloth over the prince's fevered brow. Despite the calm she projected, a knot twisted in her stomach. There was no room for error, not tonight. Hadn't he suffered enough already?

Andre adjusted the basin of melted ice water by the bedside before straightening. His steady eyes turned to her, interpreting the strain in her question.

"No," he said firmly, though there was a gentleness beneath

the word. "You're doing everything I would do."

She hesitated, her hand stilling for a brief moment. "Were you there?" she asked finally, biting her bottom lip. "When he was injured?"

Andre exhaled a long breath, wiping his hands on a linen towel. "Yes. It was madness," he began, his voice quieter as he recalled the events. "The attackers came out of nowhere. He fought them alone, drove them back until they ran. Brave as hell." Andre's lips twitched with something close to respect. "One of them got lucky, sliced his shoulder with a filthy blade in the struggle. He never faltered. Just—" He paused, his jaw tightening briefly. "His sister and her ward were in danger. He shoved them into my arms and ordered me to take them to safety." A ghost of tension flickered across his face. "It happened fast. Too fast. And through it all, he stayed on his feet. Didn't so much as wince on the carriage journey back to London."

Wendy's fingers pressed a cloth against Stan's temple, her hands steady despite her pounding heart. Andre's recounting painted an agonizing picture. She could almost see Stan—defiant, untiring even as blood soaked through his shirt, even as the hours passed before Andre could finally clean the wound and stitch him up. Her chest tightened.

"But now..." Andre's voice snapped her attention back, and she realized with a start that he'd been studying her—noticing the way her hand had pressed too long in one spot. "This battle," he said softly, gesturing to Stan's pale, sweat-slicked form, "is one he fights alone. No weapons in his hand this time."

Wendy nodded, unable to speak. Her throat felt thick. Admiration flared in her chest, unbidden and overwhelming. His bravery, his strength—none of it surprised her. He walked through fire for others when most would turn away—it was why he'd come to London to face Baron von List. She knew enough to understand the urgency. Yet the thought of him here, defenseless against the sickness tearing through him, made her eyes burn. She blinked rapidly, brushing another fresh compress over his brow.

No tears. Not now, not tonight, not when her hands were his only armor.

Andre must have seen her falter because his voice broke through her thoughts. "We keep him cold. Keep the fever from baking him alive," he said, and then, softer, "You're doing well. I'll come back to look after him or should I take over for a while now?"

"No." *He's my prince.*

Andre nodded as he left but she didn't need the reassurance, though there was some strange comfort in it. She'd learned to steel herself against the worst in her years of her training, practiced keeping a trembling hand steady while her brother operated on patients far worse off than this. But here, with Stan burning under her care, every touch, every decision struck deeper than she'd admit.

Swallowing hard, Wendy wrung out another compress and placed it methodically over his brow. She gently smoothed it as her lips tightened into a firm line. No, not her prince. But tonight, she would be his guardian for every drop of sweat she wiped, for every furious whisper of fever she soothed, for every icy measure purposed to cool him. Whether he lived or died, she would not falter. Not once. And if her hands trembled when they finally stilled, that was no one's concern but her own.

Then something happened.

The sudden rigidity in his body froze Wendy in place. His muscles tensed as if an invisible force had seized him, his head jerking sideways on the damp pillow. Her hand hovered over his chest before trembling fingers sought his brow. It was still burning. Still perilously hot. Yet this movement—this spark of life—was unexpected.

If he was dreaming, she thought wildly, wasn't that proof it wasn't a coma after all? Or was he waking up?

Her throat tightened. "Stan?" she whispered, her voice trembling as she gently replaced the compress on his temple with a fresh one. The cool fabric brushed his flushed skin, and she thought she saw his head shift slightly toward it. He moved again, faint but deliberate, his lips parting with a dry, chapped smack. "Stan, it's Wendy," she tried again, leaning closer. "Can you hear me?"

For a long moment, there was nothing but the sound of her own shallow breaths and the faint trickling of the water as she wrung the compress. Then his lips moved again—a low murmur at first, unintelligible and drowned in fever. She bent lower, her ear just above his mouth, the scent of sweat and heat filling the space between them.

"...One... two... three..." The words came in fits, broken by uneven breaths. "...Follow... me."

Wendy froze, her heart catching mid-beat. She clutched the compress, pressing it too tightly to his skin as gooseflesh raced up her arms. Her stomach churned at the words' familiarity and the unmistakable strain in his tone.

"That..." she breathed, blinking rapidly. "That's what you said. At the ball." Her voice caught at the memory, vivid despite the weeks that had passed. The way he had spun her with such purposeful grace, the warmth of his arms around her, the way he had whispered that very line. But this time it wasn't a flirtation. This time it sounded like a plea. Was he calling for help?

His eyelids fluttered briefly, a glimmer of his lashes catching the candlelight before they fell still. "Stan," Wendy urged, her free hand brushing a damp curl from his forehead. A lump rose in her throat. Sometimes, patients needed to be called back, needed a tether to hold on to as they climbed out of the haze.

"Stan, please," she pleaded, her voice soft but firmer now. "Don't leave me. Fight. You are stronger than this."

But there was no reply, no movement, nor the faintest flicker of recognition. He had slipped back into the depths, his breathing shallow, as if retreating further from her reach. Tears pricked her eyes, but she clawed them back before they could fall. This wasn't her pain to carry—it was his fight, his battle, and all she could do was keep his body cool and his time short for as long as fate allowed.

Still, as she wrung the compress one more time, her trembling lips bent close to his ear, her voice raw and small. "Don't leave me, Stan," she whispered again, though she wasn't sure whether the words were meant for him or herself.

Chapter Seventeen

"One, two, three," Wendy whispered, her voice fraying at the edges. "Don't leave me."

Her voice broke as she pressed the fresh compress against Stan's brow, her other hand trembling around his wrist, with the faintest pulse kick against her fingertips. She leaned closer, her breath warm and feather-light near his ear.

"One, two, three," her voice cracked now, and the tears rolled down her cheeks. "You're so close."

The words slipped out again, soft and desperate, her lips barely moving. They weren't just for him anymore. They were for herself, a thread to hold as everything else threatened to unravel. "Fight this. Don't leave me," she repeated, her whisper growing louder, firmer, like a plea to the universe itself.

Before she could breathe another word, his entire body jolted faintly beneath her touch. Wendy gasped, pulling back just slightly, her eyes darting to his face. His chest rose with a sharp inhale. The tiniest flicker passed through his features—his brow twitching, his lips parting, his lashes trembling as if dragging himself out of the abyss.

And then—his eyes opened.

Wide and unfocused at first, they roved the room as though seeking something. Then they found her, and everything stilled.

Wendy's breath caught in her throat. Her hand froze mid-motion, her damp cloth dragging to a stop against his temple. His hazel gaze was murky, shadowed with fever's grip, but he was there. He was looking at her.

"One, two three. Don't leave me," Wendy murmured again, the words spilling out too easily now, her mind trying to catch up to what she was seeing.

"Never," came his cracking voice—hoarse, barely audible, but unmistakably his.

The sound of it hit her like a blow, striking something unbearably tender inside her chest. All the tears that had been threatening for hours finally welled in her eyes, slipping down her cheeks. She had thought she might never hear that voice again, never see that gaze sharpen with recognition, and yet here he was. Broken, weak, but here—alive.

"Stan…" she whispered, her voice thick with relief. She pressed the back of her hand to his cheek, noting the persistent heat but relishing the way his skin shifted under her touch, no longer deathly slack. "You're—You're awake."

His lips turned in the faintest flicker of a smile, weary but full of something warm, something steady. "You called me back," he rasped, his eyes still locked on hers.

Wendy's chest tightened, her pulse thundering in her ears. "I couldn't—I wouldn't…" Her words tangled, her gaze falling to her lap for a brief moment before she met his eyes again. "You're too stubborn to leave anyway," she added, trying for levity, though the shaky laugh that escaped her betrayed how close she was to falling apart.

His hand shifted weakly on the bed, fingers twitching as though trying to reach for hers. She noticed, and without hesitation, she clasped his hand between both of hers, and kissed his thumb, her grip firm despite the warmth that lingered on his fevered skin.

"Stay with me," she said softly, her throat tightening, the words laced with everything she couldn't say aloud in that moment.

His grip, faint as it was, tightened around hers. "Always."

The single word, resonant and solemn, sparked something fierce in Wendy, something she couldn't describe and didn't dare try to name. The storm of anguish and fear that had gripped her all night began to subside, leaving a fragile but undeniable hope in its wake. For the first time since it all began, she allowed herself to believe. He might just make it.

And if he did… what then? How could she possibly go back to pretending none of this mattered—pretending he didn't matter?

The door creaked open, and Wendy turned her head, startled by the quiet intrusion. Andre entered, his expression carrying its usual calm authority, though his eyes softened at the sight of Stan's now-open ones. Relief flickered across his face.

"Oh good," Andre approached and set a fresh basin of water on the bedside table. "You just can't stay out of trouble, can you?" His tone was light, but his hands moved efficiently as they examined Stan's pulse and leaned closer to check his breathing.

Stan gave a faint chuckle—or was it a groan?—and closed his eyes briefly, as if Andre's words didn't require a response. Wendy, perched on the edge of her chair, felt torn between lingering, and leaving. Her relief at seeing Stan awake weighed heavily on her chest, but a strange exhaustion began to creep into her limbs. She wasn't sure how long she'd been sitting there, but now that Andre was present, she felt her knees weakening. Or was it the effect of the moment between her and Stan rather than fatigue?

"Wendy," Andre said gently, without looking up from his work. The use of her first name caught her attention more than his tone. "Let me take over a little. It's four in the morning, take a turn to rest."

Her hands twisted in her lap, reluctant to obey. "But—"

Andre glanced up then, cutting off her protest with a pointed look. Yet his voice remained kind, steady. "You'll do him no good if you collapse. Leave him with me now." He paused, cocking his head. "You look like you've been through a battle of your own."

She opened her mouth to argue but saw the truth in his

words. Her hands had lost their earlier steadiness, and her nerves were frayed to the point of snapping. She nodded slowly, rising to her feet.

Her gaze lingered on Stan's face as if to reassure herself that he truly was awake—he truly was here. His heavy eyes fluttered open for the briefest moment, landing on hers, and his lips curved into that faint, tired smile. It was a promise disguised as gratitude, a reassurance that she could step away. Andre distracted him, murmuring something technical as his experienced hands moved efficiently over the bandage at his shoulder.

With nothing left to do, Wendy slipped out of the room. The corridor was dim, lit only by sparse sconces, and the quiet felt oppressive after the hours of tension. She pressed her palms together, suddenly aware of how much they trembled now that the fear of losing Stan was no longer pulling her strings.

But what was she doing?

Her legs threatened to buckle as she took slow, cautious steps away from the door. She should be relieved—Stan was awake. But what lingered now wasn't entirely relief, or maybe it was, only tinged with something deeper. Something that made her heartache oddly sweet.

Something had changed when his eyes met hers. She was sure of it. They had shared… something. A moment beyond words, one that sent ripples through her, deep even now. Even in silence, it was an acknowledgment, like a confession—one neither of them had spoken aloud. Yet she knew, with a certainty that made her cheeks warm, that it was there all the same.

Wendy paused by the staircase, gripping the banister to steady herself. Could it be possible? Had Stan felt the same pull, the same raw connection that she had? Unspoken though it was, it left her shaken. She bit her lip, struggling to chase away the nervous trail her thoughts were beginning to take.

She had crossed a line tonight. And maybe, just maybe, she didn't want to cross back. Not now. Not when her heart beat in time with his. Not when she'd witnessed what nearly losing him felt like.

For now, she allowed herself a shred of hope, like a spark held carefully in her hands. Perhaps, just perhaps, she wasn't alone in how she felt. But that thought would wait until morning.

With a quiet breath, she began her slow descent, her body craving the rest her heart would not yet grant her.

◆

Chapter Eighteen

MORNING LIGHT SLIPPED through the parted curtains, warming the deep amber hues of the polished wood. Yet Stan still winced, his shoulder throbbing as his gaze lingered on the bowl of fresh water glinting on the side table. Andre had already made his final checks, his calm yet satisfied expression declaring to anyone who might care that the fever had, at last, broken and Stan was on the way to betterment.

Then why didn't that heaviness in his chest lift?

Stan adjusted himself carefully against the pillows, his body still sore and his shoulder throbbing faintly under its fresh bandage. He was raw—both physically and in some unspoken way he couldn't quite explain—but alive. That counted for something.

The creak of the door drew his attention, and when he lifted his gaze, Wendy was there. She hesitated as if she weren't certain she should enter, her fingers wound tightly around the edge of the doorframe.

He took her in, the dark shadows under her eyes painting a picture of how her night had been—worn down, worried beyond reason, but undeniably lovely. She seemed to glow even through her exhaustion, and the sight stirred something deep in his chest that had little to do with his injuries.

"It's only seven in the morning," he said rough from disuse

but warm with curiosity. He tried for a half smile; it hurt a little less than he expected.

She nodded, stepping further into the room, and her soft-soled shoes barely made a sound as she crossed the space. "I was—" Her words faltered, and she exhaled quietly before starting again. "I was waiting for Andre's report... Needless to say, we're relieved."

"Relieved," he murmured, letting the word stretch lazily from his tongue. His gaze searched hers. "Is that all?"

Her faint laugh fluttered in the room, and she lowered her eyes. She blushed so easily.

"What happened last night?" he asked after another moment, his tone turning serious. "Andre didn't say much, and I remember nothing... yet, I think I owe you my life."

Her eyes darted to his, startled at his abrupt sincerity. "You shouldn't speak like this, Your Royal Highness," she fumbled for words before gathering her thoughts. "You were feverish. We didn't think you'd wake. But I..." Her cheeks pinked again, and she tightened her hands in front of her. "I did what I could."

What. She. Could.

Stan's throat tightened, and he lowered his gaze briefly to take in her small, weary frame. "Then it seems I owe you more than I can say," he murmured, tipping his head slightly.

She waved his gratitude off, looking embarrassed. "I only followed orders. You would have done the same for anyone in need of care."

"Perhaps," he replied, his voice dropping slyly to a murmur, "but I doubt I would have looked so radiant doing it."

She froze, unsure how to respond, but his grin deepened. It was fun, seeing her flustered like that—a delightful distraction from the ache in his shoulder.

"Can I get you anything, Your Royal Highness?" she asked suddenly, as if working around his teasing to find solid ground again.

"Just Stan, please. I owe you everything and hate the distance of formalities between us." He pushed himself carefully upward, propping himself higher on the pillows. The movement was slow but deliberate. "I only need to sit up," he said, gesturing vaguely toward her as pain flickered through his arm.

"Yes, of course—here," she replied, rushing forward to help. Her hands came gently under his arm, and she stepped closer, leaning in to steady him. He stopped mid-motion. It was only then that he noticed.

No shirt.

His stomach tightened faintly in shock—or was it something else entirely? He glanced down at his bare chest, his bandaged shoulder, and felt the faintest flush rise beneath the scruff on his jaw. Then his eyes darted up to catch hers, just as quick.

"And where, pray tell, might my clothes have gone?" His smile curved lazily now, a fox's grin despite the moment's heaviness.

Her reaction was immediate and delicious. Her eyes widened just a fraction, cheeks blooming with crimson as she stepped back reflexively, her hand suddenly hesitant where it had supported him. "I—I had to cut it. It was—it was in the way, and we had to act quickly," she stammered, clearly mortified.

"Did you now?" His mouth lifted further, and there was no denying the amusement gleaming in his eyes.

She turned her head abruptly, her gaze fixed on the low stool in the corner—on what remained of his shirt, tucked unceremoniously over the back of it.

"I'm sorry." Her words sounded unconvincing.

Stan laughed softly, which hurt his chest more than he'd admit, but oh, it was worth it. "A tragedy," his voice low and teasing. "But if it had the privilege of being in your capable hands, I'll forgive its demise." His grin flickered wider.

You can tear my clothes off any time you like.

Wendy frowned at him, her lips pressed tight, but the redness in her cheeks betrayed her. She busied herself smoothing the blanket at his waist.

"What can I do for you?" she asked suddenly, almost like a challenge, her words crisp but also concerned.

He quirked an eyebrow at that, admiring the determination radiating off her. "I don't think you can help," he said honestly.

But she stiffened at his reply, her gaze snapping to him with a spark of defiance. "I'm your nurse. If there's something you need, tell me."

"That's so?" His grin widened as he shifted slightly, testing the warmth in his limbs before gesturing vaguely upward. "What I need, my dear nurse, is a bath. Could you ring for my valet?"

Wendy blinked at him, repeating his words without saying them out loud, and then squared her shoulders as if preparing for an argument. He made a faint move to rise, but the second his weight shifted, dizziness gripped him. He fell back onto the pillows with a sharp inhale, grimacing.

"I gave him time off. You need a nurse." Wendy reacted quickly, leaning into him again, her hands coming to his shoulder and back to steady him before he fell outright. "Perhaps it's too soon for a bath," she said breathlessly, adjusting her grip to be sure he was secure. "After a fever, the body may not adjust to temperatures readily. And water might cool you down too quickly."

He doubted that even an ice bath would cool him in her presence, and then it became worse.

She met his gaze—level, steady. "But a sponge bath? Partial, perhaps?"

Stan froze, startled by the very idea of it—this beautiful woman who had most likely saved his life offering to stay by his side, a nurse in name but so much more to him in every other way. Her suggestion hung in the air, equal parts logical and utterly enticing.

"Let me make sure I understand this correctly: You gave my valet time off so you can give me a sponge bath?"

She furrowed her brow and was so sweet that he wanted to reach out and pull her close.

"No, Your Royal Highness." She turned beet red.

So terribly sweet.

"As I said, please call me Stan. I owe you my life. Forget the formalities." He swallowed hard, wondering if it was the fever that still had a hold of him or just her presence that made his pulse leap. "So, a sponge bath? Madness," he murmured, more to himself than her biting away a grin. When she tilted her head in confusion, he added with a soft smirk, "It's madness to think I'd want to subject such fine company to that."

She rolled her eyes faintly, fighting a wry smile. "I nearly did it already," she replied, nodding toward the cool basin beside the bed. "All those hours with the cold compresses…"

Her words trailed off, and an odd silence lingered between them. Unspoken tension bubbled just beneath the surface, and in her dark, tired eyes, he thought he saw it—that flicker of acknowledgment from the night before.

His flirtation softened for just a moment as he reached with his free hand to lightly graze her wrist. Her gaze snapped back to his, startled at the contact.

"Even though the fever broke, your road to full recovery is long," she said.

"I'm beginning to think," he murmured softly, his voice low and intimate in the quiet space between them, "I might just keep you as my private nurse for a very long time."

Her blush deepened, the pink spreading to her throat. But just like at the ball, she stayed where she was, her breath catching faintly over his.

And just like at the ball, something unspoken flared between them—tenderness wound so tightly around attraction that it ached.

She should have looked away. She should have moved. But instead, Wendy remained frozen in place, her fingers still brushing his wrist.

It was enough for now. Just enough to know she didn't run. Not from him.

THE ROOM WAS quiet except for the faint water splashing as Wendy wrung a soft cloth over the basin. The morning sunlight streamed in through the lace curtains, painting the chamber in hues of gold but nothing compared to the royal figure making her fingers twitch. She could hear her own heartbeat—a persistent thrum she willed to calm. In the center of the room, Stan sat on a chair with a towel on his lap, bare-chested, watching her with an intensity that made her breath hitch.

"I can't imagine how you convinced me to agree to this," he murmured, his deep voice laced with equal parts amusement and… something else she couldn't quite name.

She glanced at him and frowned faintly, trying to focus on the task at hand. "It isn't as though you're in any condition to argue with a nurse," she replied lightly, though her cheeks burned as she stepped closer with the damp cloth.

Her gaze flickered, despite herself, to the broad expanse of his chest. Her hand paused mid-air as she took in the way the hard planes of muscle shifted with the rise and fall of his breathing. His skin was slightly bronzed, faint scars marking his body like a story waiting to be read.

"Something on your mind, Nurse Wendy?" Stan's lips quirked into a lopsided grin, and she froze, realizing she'd lingered too long.

"No," she replied quickly, blinking away her wandering thoughts as she pressed the cloth gently to his shoulder. "You're just…" she hesitated, her voice faltering. "You're surprising, that's all."

"Surprising?" he echoed, his amusement growing. Beneath the damp cloth, his muscles flexed faintly, involuntarily, as though testing her resolve.

Her hand moved with careful precision, tracing the curve of his shoulder and down the well-defined planes of his arm. "You don't look like a prince," she admitted finally, her words almost shy.

Stan chuckled low in his throat. "I'll take that as a compliment being that I'm half-naked," he said. His gaze drifted to her face, and though her expression was composed—focused—the faint blush coloring her cheeks betrayed her. "Years in the military will do that to a man."

Wendy glanced up at him, curiosity lighting her features despite herself. "What did you do in the military?"

He nodded, his posture easing slightly into the pillows as if the memory carried him somewhere far off. "I served under the Austrian Emperor," he explained. "My training began when I was barely more than a boy. Day after day of drills, sparring, learning to endure." His voice softened, though a hint of pride lingered. "You'd be amazed how quickly a soldier learns his limits when frost covers your boots, but quitting isn't an option."

Her hand slowed, and her expression softened. She hadn't considered this side of him—the discipline, the effort shaping the man before her. "It must be difficult," she said quietly. "Living that life."

Stan's eyes met hers, and for a moment, the teasing glint faded, replaced by something contemplative. "It's a life," he said after a moment. "But I wouldn't trade the lessons it taught me."

She nodded, the intimacy of his admission lingering in the air between them. Her hands worked across his chest now, her fingers brushing against the ridges of his muscles as she cleaned away the last traces of the previous night's fever.

"What about you?" he asked suddenly, his voice drawing her gaze back to his face. "How did you become a nurse?"

Wendy blinked, momentarily caught off guard by the directness of his question. She hesitated, lowering the cloth to dip it in the basin again. "It wasn't something I planned," she admitted eventually, wringing out the excess water. "After Nick and I lost our parents, he took it upon himself to look after me. He studied medicine in Vienna. It meant long hours and then, during his apprenticeships, never being in one place for too long. I suppose I tagged along at first just because I didn't know what else to do."

Stan tilted his head, his expression thoughtful as he listened. "But you stayed," he said.

"Of course," she confirmed, moving to the other side of him, her hands working methodically though her voice grew softer. "When Andre, Alfie, and Felix joined us and they founded the practice, I... well, I just started helping wherever I could. They taught me everything—the basics, at least. Enough to be useful. I owe them more than I can say. They made me who I am."

Stan frowned faintly, turning his gaze toward her even as her hands fluttered near his side. "You're wrong about that," he said unexpectedly firmly.

She paused, puzzled, her brow furrowing slightly. "What do you mean?"

"They need you," he said, and the way he spoke the words made her cheeks warm again. "You're the one holding them together. The practice would be in chaos without you. Don't think I haven't noticed." His lips curled faintly into a smile. "How you hand them their patient cards each morning. I've seen how you keep track of every name, every appointment. Those men wouldn't last a week without you keeping them—how do I put this politely?—in check."

Wendy gaped at him, a mix of surprise and indignation brimming under the surface. "That's—" she stopped, searching for the right words to refute him, but they didn't come.

"You're too modest, just like at the ball," Stan added, lowering his voice as if it were a secret meant only for her.

Her hand tightened around the cloth, the moment settling heavily in her chest. For a man who was supposed to be recovering, Stan had a remarkable way of disarming her—of peeling back the layers she wore as armor, leaving her exposed without her even realizing it.

"You've been looking after me all night," he murmured, his gaze holding hers. "Who looks after you, Wendy?"

The question hung in the air, spoken so softly she might have imagined it. But the warmth in her cheeks and the fluttering sensation in her stomach told her she hadn't.

Her throat bobbed as she attempted to speak, but no words came. Instead, she settled for dipping the cloth back into the basin, her fingers trembling faintly as she wrung it out.

"My brother..." she began, but her voice faltered. She had been worrying for a while about what would happen if Nick and Pippa had a baby. "But recently... Erm... I shouldn't say."

"Why not?" he asked, leaning back slightly, though his eyes never left hers.

"Because it makes me forget I'm supposed to be your nurse," she replied quietly, her voice barely above a whisper. She wasn't sure whether she intended for him to hear it, but the way his faint smirk softened told her he had.

He exhaled deeply, his skin warm beneath her touch as her hands moved again, this time slower, each motion stretching the space between them. Neither of them spoke. The tension did plenty of talking.

And somehow, amidst the quiet breaths and tender gestures, she knew that whatever it was had changed something between them. Would it last after he healed and left that bed behind?

She wasn't sure she dared to find out.

Chapter Nineteen

S TAN STOOD BY the window, feeling almost—almost—himself again. Two more days had passed since that wretched night had left him battered, bones weary, and spirit shaken. The haze from the ordeal had begun to clear. it was her—that quiet certainty—he remembered everything about her.

Wendy.

Clear as crystal. The brisk, cool press of her fingers against his fevered skin. The focus in her eyes that stayed just as steady while he thrashed helplessly, as it did when she paused to dab sweat from his brow. He closed his eyes, and there she was, hovering in his mind as vividly as if she were still standing at his bedside.

Those wispy blonde curls framing her face, combined with the intelligent and discerning look in her eyes, made his insides melt—but not from a fever this time.

A sharp knock at the door snapped him from his reverie.

"Come in," Stan called, voice still hoarse but stronger than it had been in days.

The door opened with a creak, and Andre strode in first, his bottle-green coat flaring sharply around his knees. Wendy followed closely behind, holding a metal tray with bandages, a jar of ointment, and scissors.

Andre spoke first, his tone clipped and professional.

"Stan," he greeted without flourish, eyeing him like one sizes up a patient who is entirely too stubborn for their own good. Andre gestured lightly toward Wendy. "You're up again?"

"I can't lie in bed all day, Andre. Nothing will be resolved that way," Stan quipped.

"Well, I'm here to assess whether you've undone all the mending from the past two days."

"Hmm," came Wendy's soft, thoughtful hum. She stepped closer than Andre, near enough for Stan to catch the faint hint of her lavender soap underlined with something warmer—clove or anise perhaps? Certainly, one of the scents from the practice at 87 Harley Street. Her head tilted slightly, assessing him like an artist gauging the flaws in a newly stretched canvas.

Her gaze settled on him—deliberate, steady, and so thoroughly scrutinizing that for a moment, the room stilled. He felt flayed open, laid bare beneath her eyes—not from pain, but from how intimately she seemed to see him. His neck prickled beneath her critical eye, the sensation spreading across his skin like the warm fizz of *ţuică*, the Romanian plum brandy, rolling down one's throat. Something flickered in her features, unreadable as always, but Andre's voice sliced cleanly through the room before he could find his footing with words.

"It's von List that worries me." Andre glanced pointedly back at Wendy for some unspoken exchange before he turned sharply to Stan. "He's not someone to be left unattended. His men could have—"

"I know. They had Thea twice." Stan's resolved hardened to confront List. Whatever came next was harder for Stan to hold on to. Andre's matter-of-fact tone shifted each word into static, each syllable tumbling into the buzz of thought suddenly coursing through him. Von List. He had enough information about him now thanks to the truth serum Alfie had made. With the right angle, there should be a way to send List back to where he came from.

He felt the prick of anxiety drill low in his stomach, but Wendy's stare lingered even as Andre finished speaking. Without waiting for a response, Andre pressed a hand briefly to Stan's shoulder, a physician's touch of finality.

"I'll look in again later," Andre said over his shoulder from the doorway, already departing briskly. "Don't be this difficult a patient when she changes your bandages."

The latch clicked softly behind him, leaving Stan alone with her.

Silence stretched before Stan finally wore it down. His voice met the air without apology. "I must go after him. Von List."

It sounded solid when he spoke the villain's name aloud. Certain.

"Not today." Wendy's voice danced past him, light yet firm.

"Today, tomorrow—it doesn't make a difference." His jaw tightened slightly as his words pressed against her reason. "It's Wednesday. He lingers at White's after lunch. Civil as places go—I'll find him there."

Wendy exhaled faintly, a flash of disbelief flickering across her features. A pause, a shift, before she folded her arms across her middle with a small shake of her head.

"You think they'll take you seriously like that?" Her eyes swept him again—leveled at him, unwavering, edged by challenge.

"This?" He gestured toward his day-old linens and the unruly fall of his hair. He scoffed faintly. "My valet—"

"Will do a perfunctory job," she cut in, lips curving into something faintly mischievous. "He wouldn't dare show actual initiative."

"And why is that?" Stan asked.

"Because he's intimidated by your title."

"And you're not?" He raised a brow, nearly giddy for her sly retort. Truth be told, he loved the fact that she didn't mind formalities. And when she did, she erred. Perfect. These days, honesty was rare to come by, especially as a royal fourth son.

"This—" she drew an imaginary circle around his head, "needs work."

His brow lifted faintly, his own challenge lighting his tone. "So, you think you can do better?"

Wendy stood perfectly still for a moment, her gaze holding his like a hand brushing the surface of a flame. That spark between them caught again—quiet, electric, impossible to ignore. Then, as though the idea required no particular weight of thought, she turned just enough to glance over her shoulder.

Her words came lightly, lazily hedged in amusement, yet they landed with startling precision.

"Absolutely. As soon as I change your bandage."

WENDY BENT TO place the bowl of water on the table near his chair, her movements deliberate yet unhurried. The light in the room was muted, softened by the overcast sky outside Stan's chamber. Her gaze flicked to him—dark brown waves unruly as they fell across his forehead and curled at his crown and nape. Longer than a prince's hair ought to be, certainly, but there was something else beneath the untamed locks, something far more captivating.

He was still recovering, yes, but even that couldn't disguise the pull she felt. His presence had an undeniable gravity that drew her in.

She had seen him at his most vulnerable. Sweat-soaked and feverish, an injured warrior's body—a man—battling his demons. And now, to see him upright, even flirtatious, an undercurrent of strength animated every movement he made. That strength drew her in until even breathing felt magnetic and it was so hard to fight the attraction.

"Don't tell me nurses are in the habit of cutting hair," he said, the lilt in his tone as teasing as the amused arch of his brow.

Wendy allowed him only the shadow of a smile. "I can't speak for most nurses, but I've had very comprehensive training.

A brother who's an eye surgeon ensured I could learn everything he could teach me."

Stan crossed his arms, leaning back slightly, an inquisitive tilt softening his usual royal demeanor. "You cut Nick's hair, then? Your mysterious skill has nothing to do with being a nurse."

Oh, he was sharp. The way his lips slightly curved pulled the words from him like silk from a spool, making mischief simmer beneath the room's quiet lull. Wendy pressed her lips together and looked away before her smile betrayed her amusement.

"You know," he continued, with a faintly conspiratorial edge, "I have a sister too. You can't fool me."

She breathed softly, steadying. Fooling him wasn't what she wanted. Touching him, though... well, that was a different matter entirely. Her fingers tingled at the thought.

"Please pull your shirt down. I'll change your bandage," she said evenly, concealing those betraying impulses.

His hesitation was brief, just a fraction of a second before his hands reached up to untie the collar and, with a practiced tug, pulled free the fastening at his shirt. He crossed his arms and pulled the hem of his shirt first and then over his head to reveal... well... his entire torso in all its muscular glory.

Wendy did not mean to look. Truly, she did not. But her gaze couldn't seem to obey her better judgment, drawn, as if by its own will, to the sight before her.

His shirt, discarded in a casual heap, left every inch of him on display.

The planes of his torso were defined, each muscle standing out as if carved, the faintest shadow tracing beneath each line. His shoulders were broad, strong, and purposeful, tapering down to a chest that suggested strength held firmly in control. Beneath his skin, the sinew shifted with every small movement he made—a turn of his head, the subtle stretch of his arm—each motion revealing the seamless coordination of form and function. The perfection was almost unsettling. He resembled the ideal proportions Wendy had once seen sketched in a reproduction of a

Leonardo da Vinci sketch belonging to her brother, though Prince Stan felt more vivid, more alive than any preserved parchment could capture.

Her breath shallowed, though she quickly pressed her lips together—anything to stop herself from making a sound.

The wound.

Tend to the bandage.

With the small scissors from her tray, she cut the muslin and peeled it off carefully.

Wendy frowned slightly as she leaned in, examining the healing gash. The deep cut was closed now, the angry flush faded, and the swelling in the area greatly reduced.

"You're healing well," she said as she discarded the old bandage with the faint yellow crusted edges. It assured her that nature was taking her due course, and her prince was recovering.

Not. Your. Prince.

Her hands worked carefully, deft fingers unwinding the older muslin before reaching for fresh strips. She didn't rush. The muslin lay smooth between her fingers as she carefully folded it, her touch deliberate as she spread the chamomile and calendula salve over the wound. Why, she hadn't even the grace to glance away! The warmth of his skin met the cool balm—almost intimately, almost tenderly. And just like the balm melted, so did the distance between them.

There was power there—real, tangible power—as if his body had been forged for more than courtly pursuits. Wendy wondered whether that explained the ease in his movements or the slightest air of command that came with him, even half-clad in the morning.

Somewhere—between her work and the tranquility of the room—came a sound she wasn't prepared for. Low and rich, the quiet groan he emitted reverberated down his back, through his ribs, vibrating beneath her steady hand. A manly sound, it burrowed deep, too personal for reason. Wendy's breath hitched imperceptibly as warmth spread low in her own chest. The sound of seduction, surely, though it might have been unintentional.

"Your recovery is remarkable," she managed finally, desperate for any words to anchor her composure. Carefully, she pressed the edges of the fresh muslin to his skin, securing it with nimble precision before her hand, traitorous, lingered. She suspected she could map every muscle beneath her palm if given the opportunity. His build was something more reminiscent of a soldier than sheer royalty. The inherent strength in his frame, tempered with a heart she suspected was capable of rare tenderness, made the injury seem cruel. It was some cosmic injustice that she couldn't name.

She allowed herself one more indulgent moment, tracing along his back—just a whisper of touch, the curve of her thumb following where muscle met bone.

Stan's voice interrupted the hazy thought forming in her head. "I shouldn't have been injured in the first place. It cost me too much time."

"It nearly cost you all your time. You could have died."

"I know. List is dangerous." His tone dipped lower, carrying the weight she imagined he saved for the gravest of matters. "He already proved what he was capable of when he captured my sister," he went on, words tight now, his hands curling into fists at his sides. "Still, I should've seen it coming."

"Surely," she began tentatively, "you could appeal to the English royal family. Or... perhaps your own family? Isn't that what they're for in matters as critical as this?"

Stan turned toward her, a flicker of something unreadable crossing his expression before his lips curved into a faint wry smile. His dark eyes, keen and steady, rested on her, though there was no mirth in his tone. "You think too highly of royal families, Wendy. My title is courtesy, not authority."

She frowned, her confusion deepening. "But you are of nobility, are you not? Surely your bloodline must still carry some influence?"

He gave a slight shake of his head, his voice quiet but firm.

"Not the kind you're imagining. I am not of a reigning monarchy, nor do I hold a throne to summon aid from lofty courts. My title is ancestral, a relic of the past. Decorative at best." A pause lingered as he studied her, his gaze softening. "It's me, Wendy. I'm what Transylvania has in England, for better or worse."

Still, she pressed on. "There must be someone else. Surely, you cannot bear this alone."

His smile turned faintly indulgent, though his eyes held steady. "It's not a choice, Wendy. It's my responsibility, my fight to take up. I've called on my brother for what help he can give, but this rests with me. That's why I'm here."

Wendy swallowed hard, her heart tightening. She wanted to argue, to insist it wasn't fair, but the quiet determination in his tone silenced her. All she could do was hold his gaze and pray he understood the unspoken words in her heart. "I see," she said at last, though the words felt feeble in the face of his resolve. What she saw, most of all, was that he stood alone, and something about that filled her with an ache she couldn't name.

"Until I stop List, the responsibility lies with me—I'm the only one here."

There it was, a sharp pang inside her chest, accompanied by a dreadful thought. When the time came, he would leave. For how could his integrity of such admirable magnitude remain bound in any one place when his country demanded him back?

Her hesitation filled the gap between her confession of worry and her desire to console. Her hand moved again, trailing over the landscape of his back—a brave trespass, guided by the quiet confession trailing her thoughts. Here he was, too resolute for his own good.

Stan shifted abruptly, interrupting her near-reverie. His pivoting brought his eyes square to hers, and Wendy's hand froze mid-motion at the nape of his neck.

Caught.

She drew in a sharp breath and, as though to cover the unspoken folly of the moment, her fingers lightly scraped at the longer strands of brown curling at the back of his neck.

"Are you finished?" His words were laced with curiosity, hovering at the edge of amusement.

Wendy's lips parted faintly before recovering. "You tell me," she replied, feigning all the calm her pounding heart refused her.

Then he picked up the small scissors she'd set aside after cutting off his bandage. He handed them to her, holding the blades in his hand and offering her the finger loops. Stan had her gaze a moment longer before nodding, settling back in the chair as though offering her free rein.

And yet, the depth of his stare lingered, heavy with unspoken intent, leaving Wendy to wonder if she had just been handed freedom—or something far more perilous.

Chapter Twenty

THE TOWEL SETTLED over Stan's shoulders, soft but at first cool and rough against his skin. Wendy's hands brushed the edges, ensuring it was snug before stepping away. There was an unhurried elegance that made his pulse thrum with sharp awareness. He exhaled slowly, watching her scan the room, her gaze darting to the table, where she finally found a comb. She picked it up with a faint smile that hinted at amusement, as if her search carried secrets he wasn't privy to.

"Is this silver?" she asked.

"Yes, I've had it all my life."

Then, Wendy returned to him. Slowly, tenderly, she lifted the comb and began. The first touch of its teeth against his scalp sent a shiver down his spine. Her hands followed, slipping through his hair with gentle insistence, her fingertips grazing his skin now and then. It wasn't just the motion—though that alone was enough to seize his attention—but the way she loitered, as if every stroke held a purpose beyond mere practicality.

Then she went to the wash-table in the corner, wet her hands, and returned to him. She drove her fingers through his hair.

Her fingers slid deeper, weaving through the unruly waves, tugging softly at the ends of his hair when they caught. Each pull was tantalizing, a temptation dragging him deeper into thoughts he had no business entertaining. Time seemed to stretch absurdly long beneath her touch, yet every second she spent combing felt stolen, and wrong to want, and impossible not to.

"You have beautiful hair," Wendy said at last, her voice low, intimate, the words rolling easily, as though speaking them aloud was indulgence enough. "Thick and dark...it's the kind of hair most people envy."

Heat flared across Stan's chest and climbed his neck, invisible flames she couldn't possibly see—or could she? He didn't dare look at her, not when every nerve, every corner of restraint in him, was locked on guarding that thrum of tension building steadily within. Instead, he remained silent. Gathering what control he could, Stan leaned over, snagged another towel off the side table, and settled it across his lap casually—or as casually as one could when his body felt charged, every pore aching with awareness.

Stan rested his hands on the towel to keep it stretched in place.

Wendy resumed her work. Scissors whispered through the air, sliding steadily as she trimmed the sides, focusing with a precision that exposed him to every careful motion. The back of his neck tingled when the scissors moved lower, and then her hand—her fingers—brushed lightly against the nape. The faint sensation set him on edge. By now, her proximity alone was wreaking havoc, the whispers of her touch a distraction that left him half-mad with the effort to remain still.

When she finally dusted him off, picking up another towel and brushing the soft fabric over his neck and shoulders, Stan almost cursed aloud. Her touch, featherlight, laced with care, was far too gentle. Even her scent—clean and floral—drew him further from reason.

She reached diagonally past him, stretching just slightly to retrieve something on the far side of the table. Then it happened—her footing faltered. He saw it in the sway of her frame, the stagger of movement as she overreached, and his instincts kicked in without thought.

"Wendy," he called, sharp and gravelly, catching her as she toppled.

The world tilted briefly—the soft curve of her body collided against his, her fall folding neatly into his lap. His hands steadied her, one resting against the smooth line of her back, the other splayed instinctively across her waist. Her breath rushed out, warm across his neck, and the intimacy of the moment struck like lightning. Neither spoke. Her face hovered close to his, startled eyes wide and soft lips parted slightly, as if she was too stunned to force words.

Stan swallowed thickly, every muscle winding tighter, harder. The shape of her shoulder beneath his hand, her narrow waist, the rise of her chest as she inhaled—everything sharpened to her presence. And in her gaze, he saw it too—that spark of realization, the same one he felt driving through his pulse like a drumbeat. Her mouth twitched at the edge of a smile, but it was fleeting, her composure seemingly struggling to cement itself.

She stared at him for a moment longer, her expression un-readable but heavy—too heavy—with layers neither dared to voice aloud. Then, as though sensing the precipice waiting in both their silences, Wendy shifted. A faint tremor in her smile appeared as she scrambled to straighten herself, to stand and reclaim composure from where it had been left discarded between them.

But it never came back.

Stan's hand cupped the curve of Wendy's cheek, his thumb tracing a deliberate line across her skin. Her warmth seeped into him, grounding him even as his pulse quickened. The softness of her skin was mesmerizing, the smooth heat under his touch tying him to the moment.

So precious.

So perfect.

Even with his hand on her, he still thought she was too good—out of reach.

Every shallow breath she took brought her closer to him, her trust palpable in the way she tilted her head into his palm. She might as well have handed him the reins to her heartbeat.

But she remained still, watching him intently. Then she tilted her head slightly to the side and put it trustingly in his hand. He swallowed hard, his own heartbeat thundering in his chest as her gaze caught and held his. Her eyes didn't waver; they didn't invite, they dared him—dared him to break the carefully maintained distance he'd sworn to keep. She was temptation woven in silk, and he was too far gone to resist.

It was a gesture that spoke louder than a thousand words. She trusted him.

But she shouldn't. It was unwise.

His thumb lingered on the corner of her mouth, brushing just enough to relish in the softness of her lower lip. Her lips parted on a silent gasp, both innocent and knowing, sending a jolt of heat straight through him.

"I'm no fairytale prince, Wendy."

"I know. You're better. You're real." And with this, her gaze fell to his mouth.

"Wendy…" he rasped. And then words failed him. What more was there besides Wendy? She was all he had on his mind, his priority—even more important than his life. "I'd do anything to make you happy."

She closed her eyes and slightly parted her lips. Her breath trembled, her chest rising and falling as if it took all her strength to stay as still as she was. The space between them dissolved, every inch closer like an unraveling thread. Their foreheads almost touched, and his breath mingled with hers, the intimacy of it raw and intoxicating. She tipped her chin up, her lashes fluttering just before her eyes closed. He couldn't look away; she was beautiful in her quiet vulnerability, in her unguarded certainty.

"Please tell me to stop," he whispered, his lips hovering just a breath away from hers. His voice was thick, pleading, even as every fiber in his body screamed to close the distance. But Wendy didn't speak. She simply opened her eyes again—not wide, but enough to offer him a quiet, resolute answer before her lids drifted shut once more.

So, he kissed her. Slowly, reverently. Her mouth was soft, yielding, and the slightest pressure from her lips sent tremors coursing through him. Time stretched, fragile, and crystalline as her fingertips brushed his jaw, hesitant and featherlight. He deepened the kiss, coaxing rather than demanding, his palm still cradling her cheek as if afraid she'd slip away.

It was undoubtedly her first kiss and yet she knew what she wanted. And he was at her service. He'd take it as slowly as she wanted, or as fast as she wished, so long as he could be with her.

When her lips moved with his, her timid confidence blossoming, it undid him completely. There was no one else in the world, no sound but the faint rustle of her skirts and their shared breaths. Each touch of her lips was a discovery, each sigh a promise. And for the first time in his life, Stan forgot every rule, every doubt—because there was only her.

WENDY'S BREATH HITCHED as Stan's lips brushed hers, soft and unhurried. Her pulse fluttered wildly, her heart thundering in her chest like an untamed thing. This was her first kiss—her first real kiss. This was something altogether different from a respectful kiss on her knuckles, something so overwhelming it left her trembling. Her fingers, hesitant at first, touched his sleeve, the fine fabric beneath her hand a reminder of who he was—what he was. A prince. And yet, here he was, kissing her, holding her as though *she* were the precious one.

The world around them blurred, fading into a quiet haze where nothing mattered but the taste of his lips, the strong yet gentle way his fingers cradled her face. She had always wondered what a kiss would be like, but nothing had prepared her for this. It was a cascade of sensations—his warmth, the faint scrape of stubble against her skin, the steady exhale of his breath mingling with hers. It should have been too much. It should have left her overwhelmed. Instead, it anchored her, made her cling to this moment as if it were the only thing tethering her to life.

Her free hand curled against the front of his chest. She couldn't stop herself; it was instinctive, this need to be closer, as if the space between them was unbearable. And instead of pushing her away as she thought he ought, he put one hand over hers, pressing her hand firmly down to his heart. His lips moved against hers—patient, deliberate—and her nervousness began to melt. She didn't know what she was doing, but he made it easy, guiding her with steady tenderness. He tasted faintly of tea, richer than anything she'd imagined. Her cheeks burned, though she couldn't say if it was from the kiss itself, or the realization of what they were doing.

A prince. *Her prince.* Not in the storybook sense, not a knight in shining armor come to rescue her, but Stan—solid, real, and undeniably human. The man who had stolen glances at her over dinners, who had made her laugh when propriety dictated silence. The man who now kissed her as though they weren't bound by titles or expectations, as though the world outside this moment didn't exist. It was intoxicating—headier than the strongest spirit—and she wasn't sure she'd ever felt so alive.

When he pulled back just slightly, her chest tightened, and she found herself leaning forward, unwilling to break the connection between them. Her eyes fluttered open, meeting his, and she drew in a shaky breath. His expression was unreadable, though his gaze held her captive, searching her face as though committing every part of it to memory. Her lips tingled, and she absently raised her fingers to touch them, the sensation as foreign as it was thrilling. She couldn't bring herself to say anything, her thoughts too scattered, still caught in the echo of his kiss.

He didn't speak either—not immediately. Instead, his fingers skimmed down from her face, lingering for a moment at her jaw before falling to her arm until he let go, as if he, too, was reluctant to sever their connection. She hated how empty she felt without his touch, how her body ached for the warmth of his hand once more. But his lips parted, and a hint of a smile ghosted over them, tinged with uncertainty.

"Wendy," he murmured, her name like a vow on his tongue. His voice was low, rough with emotion, and it sent a shiver skimming down her spine. "Are you all right? I fear I might have been…" He trailed off, his hesitation surprising her. It almost made her smile—that this man, this prince who commanded rooms with his presence, could be so unsure about something as simple as a kiss.

"Yes." Her voice wavered, quieter than she intended, breathless and unsteady. But when she saw the relief that flickered across his face, when she noticed the way his shoulders relaxed slightly, she cleared her throat and tried again. "I mean… I—yes, I'm all right. More than all right."

It wasn't enough, not even close, to encompass what she was feeling. But how did one put into words the way her heart lurched? Like it was breaking free of its constraints, the way her very soul seemed to shift and settle when he held her gaze like this? Words failed, so she didn't even try. Instead, she allowed herself the indulgence of simply looking at him—the prince who had just dismantled every carefully constructed thought she'd had about what a kiss would be.

His thumb brushed over the back of her hand—she hadn't even realized she was still holding onto his sleeve. Her grip loosened, but as soon as she slackened her fingers, his hand caught hers, lacing their fingers together. Her racing heart stumbled, then sped up again, the simple touch more intimate than the kiss had been. If she hadn't known before that her world had changed in those few minutes, she knew it now.

"I—" She started to speak, unsure of what she meant to say but desperate to fill the silence creeping between them. Yet, as soon as the sound left her lips, he squeezed her hand, shaking his head slightly.

"Don't." His voice was soft but firm, and as her mouth snapped shut, she realized he understood her—understood the whirlwind of emotions she couldn't untangle. The lines around his eyes softened, his smile returning, this time with genuine warmth, and she felt the knot in her chest loosen.

It struck her, as they remained there, that her life would never be the same. Stan wasn't just a prince; he was *her* prince now, whether she liked it or not. Since that fateful night when she nearly lost him, as they counted together and he returned to her through sheer willpower and inner strength, even as his body was losing the battle against the fever, he was hers. This was how he became hers, whether they'd talked about it or not. Some truths can be felt long before they're voiced. When the prince's life nearly ended, they had begun something new together instead. And though she couldn't say where this tentative beginning might lead, she knew one thing for certain.

"Please say something." His voice was a plea of uncertainty that surprised her.

She hesitated, biting her lip. "I didn't expect that."

"That?" he echoed, his thumb brushing lightly over her knuckles as if he'd only ever be allowed to kiss her there again. His touch was gentle, yet it sent shivers rippling through her.

"The kiss," she admitted, her head dipping. "I mean, I thought about it—wondered what it would be like—but I didn't think it *would* happen."

Stan's free hand slid to her face again, his fingers warm against her skin as he guided her gaze back to him. "I didn't plan it either," he confessed. "But the thought of not kissing you, not knowing what it felt like to hold you this close… I couldn't stand it anymore."

"I've dreamed about you."

"Only at night or also in daydreams?" he asked, a teasing glint in his eye.

"Both," she replied, her cheeks warming as she dared to meet his gaze. "Somehow, you always find your way into my thoughts."

I wish I could find a way into your heart, too.

Her breath hitched, her chest tightening but not entirely unpleasant. "You're a prince," she whispered. "You have duties, expectations. And I'm—"

"You," he interrupted firmly before she could finish. "You're Wendy. And all I want, all that matters. More than I ever dared hope for, but everything I ever dreamed of."

She stared at him, her thoughts tumbling over one another. His words were so earnest, so unshakably genuine, yet the enormity of what he represented weighed heavily on her. "Stan… what if this isn't enough? What if I'm not enough?"

His hand lingered against her cheek, tender and steady, as though grounding her fears. "Wendy," he murmured, his voice low and reverent, "you're already more than I could have dreamed. You're everything. But if you'll allow me, I want to show you. To woo you. To earn the right to kiss you, to fight for you, to make you believe what I already know."

Her breath hitched, her heart at war with her doubts. "And if I can't believe it?"

He stepped back then, inclining his head in an unmistakable gesture of deference. "Then I'll wait," he said softly, his voice unwavering. "For as long as it takes, Wendy. Just grant me the chance to try."

The prince bowed to the nurse with a tilt of his head, but she could tell that he put her above him and all the hierarchy of social standing.

But he never took his hand off her cheek.

Her throat tightened, the vulnerability in his words catching her off guard. She nodded slowly, her lips curving into a small, hesitant smile. "Yes," she murmured, her voice barely audible.

"Yes?" he echoed, his mouth lifting as though the simple agreement meant more to him than he could say. For a moment, neither of them spoke, the air between them thick with unspoken emotion.

Finally, Wendy's grip on his hand tightened just slightly. "Stan?"

"Yes?"

Her cheeks flushed, but she met his gaze head-on. "Will you kiss me again?"

Stan barely waited for Wendy's words to settle, the sound still hovering in the air before he closed the distance between them.

Yes.

So simple.

And yet, it meant everything.

His lips met hers with the same measured gentleness as before, but this time, there was no holding back the urgency simmering beneath his restraint. It wasn't rushed—it never would be with her—but it pulled him entirely into the moment. The kiss felt impossibly intimate, as though they'd done this a hundred times and yet were discovering it anew.

Her hands came up, hesitant at first, then firm as they anchored themselves to his shoulders. That single motion made him forget to breathe. She wasn't retreating; she wasn't uncertain. She was holding onto him, pulling him closer, and that knowledge sent a jolt of something deep and searing through his chest. His hands cradled her face, fingers brushing softly against her skin, and a part of him swore her pulse fluttered under his touch, quickened and alive. It felt like the most important thing he'd ever done, being here and kissing her like this.

Everything else—the duty and the expectations waiting for him beyond this moment—fell away. His world, once dominated by rules and roles, now narrowed entirely to her. She reset his perception because, from now on, there would be Wendy before anything and anyone else. The warmth of her lips, the faint tremble in her grip, and the subtle scent of something soft and flower-soapy that clung to her—all of it held him in place, as though he had found the one thing he hadn't known he needed even more than air.

When he finally eased back, Stan's forehead came down to meet hers, unwilling to part completely. Their breaths tangled in the fragile quiet between them, and he couldn't stop himself from searching her face, needing some signal that she felt it, too—that this wasn't just him being swept away, that she was right there with him. Her flushed cheeks and the way her chest rose and fell unevenly grounded him, a subtle, unspoken answer to his silent question.

"Wendy," he said softly, his voice rough from the emotion tightening his throat. He knew no other words would suffice but the simple truth. "I'm yours. No matter what happens, no matter what comes—it's you. Only you."

But the danger that Baron von List would come, that was for sure. And it was an uncalculated but enormous risk. He'd attempted to murder Benjamin Klonimus, stolen from the trade route, infiltrated the House of Lords, kidnapped Thea, and sent his lackeys to try again. There was no doubt that even when List didn't personally attack, he was sending the attackers.

He could see her breath hitch, hear the faint gasp as her fingers curled tighter against the towel draped over him. Stan braced himself for hesitation, for the shadow of doubt he'd grown so accustomed to seeing in her eyes when the reality of who he was loomed between them. He was the person between the doom List could cause and the safe and happy life he wished to give Wendy. But she didn't pull away. Instead, her lips tilted into the smallest smile, and one of her hands lifted to touch his face in return, a touch of a caress that sent heat coursing through his veins.

"I'm not going anywhere," she said, her voice quiet but firm, her gaze settling on his. Her words struck him like a sharp pang in his chest—breathtaking and raw. She paused, and he held his breath, not daring to interrupt her. "Not now, not ever."

His heart stumbled at her meaning. He wanted to respond, but the seriousness in her gaze stilled him, urging him to listen.

"I don't know what the future looks like," she continued, her laughter soft but tinged with a vulnerability that made his chest ache. "But I don't want to—can't—waste another moment running from this. And yet, wherever this—" she laid a hand on his arm, "leads me, I will never leave my brother."

Never leave her brother… Stan nodded and inhaled deeply. Understood. She must have given this some thought. Well, so had he.

Her courage astounded him, but more than that, it unraveled something inside him. He lifted his hand to cover hers as it rested against his cheek. "You don't know what it means," he began, his voice thick, "to hear those words."

"I think I do," she replied, her tone trembling but certain enough to root him to the spot. Her cheeks flushed deeper, and when she hesitated, looking away, Stan didn't push her. Every passing moment felt like an unraveling for them both—the layers of doubt, fear, and hesitation falling away to reveal something starkly real. Finally, she braved his gaze again and whispered, "You make me believe I can be more for the first time and yet, I remain anchored to London and my brother."

Stan swallowed hard, gratitude laced with determination surging within him. Words seemed a poor substitute for what she'd gifted him just now—her trust, her willingness to meet him halfway—but he couldn't leave her words hanging unanswered. He leaned in again, brushing her lips with his, slow and deliberate. This wasn't a kiss meant to claim or persuade. It was a promise—a tangible expression of the vow he'd made the moment she walked into his world.

But his world was laced with intrigue, danger, and the ever-simmering fuse to wage war. Wherever he went, he was a representative of the conflict of the European hegemonies—or lack thereof. Trouble didn't follow him by chance. It followed him by definition.

He shouldn't drag her into this.

"Wendy," he murmured, his voice low but weighted, "My name alone draws danger the way a storm draws lightning. Wherever I go, it follows. You'd be safer without me." Stan swallowed the rest of his words. What an idiot he was, longing for her and then, when she finally kissed him, warning her that he'd be nothing but trouble.

Yet, he cared for her safety and wellbeing more than himself. Although he couldn't quite understand it, he knew it to be true.

But then she leaned into him, her response unguarded now, and it was freeing in a way he hadn't expected. He felt her melt into the kiss, and beneath the press of their mouths, under the shared breath and warmth, Stan could sense the faintest shift in the way she held onto him. It wasn't nervousness, nor was it uncertainty.

It was trust.

And it made him hold her closer, cherish her all the more.

When she finally pulled back, her face was so close to his that her exhale brushed his lips. "You're wrong," she said simply. "You don't attract danger. You attract honor. Loyalty. The sort of people who would lay down their lives to keep you safe, not because they have to, but because they want to."

Her words cut deep, in a way no blade could. He laughed softly, incredulously, though the sound carried no humor. "Loyalty doesn't stop wars, Wendy. It doesn't dismantle schemes or keep someone out of their sights. I can't promise… I can't promise I'll never ask you to leave with me someday. I don't know how this life will shape us or what it might demand of me." He hesitated, the sincerity of his own confession dulling the air between them. Her eyes searched his, unwavering. "But if that day comes," he continued, more urgently now, "I will promise this: I'll always bring you back. Back to your brother. Back to safety. That, I swear to you on my own honor and the life you gave me back."

She smiled so softly, so achingly tender, that it nearly undid him. "Stan," she whispered, brushing her fingertips lightly over his cheek, "the danger that follows you doesn't scare me. The idea of not being here with you—that's what I can't face."

It wasn't trust anymore. It was something stronger. Something unshakable. For the first time in years, Stan felt the faintest flicker of hope catch fire in the corners of his heart. Without a word, he cupped her face in his hands, leaning down to steal another kiss, one populated with every unspoken promise he couldn't yet put to words. For now, this moment was enough. For now, he'd surrender to her faith in him, and he'd carry it with him like armor.

I'll keep you safe.

Somehow… unsure how and yet sure of it, nonetheless.

When he finally pulled back again, she lifted her eyes to him, her lips parted as though she hadn't yet caught her breath. But there was no question in her gaze this time, no hesitation. "We'll figure it out," she murmured, a steady confidence in her voice that made his chest swell with something dangerously close to hope. "Together."

Stan's hand dropped to hers, his fingers lacing through hers with an ease that felt as natural as breathing. Her words, simple yet all-encompassing, felt like a tether and a lifeline all at once. "Together," he repeated, a smile of quiet joy settling on his face, but he knew it was wishful thinking. An impossibility he'd trained not to underestimate as a soldier.

Never think you are prepared for the enemy.

He couldn't claim to know what challenges lay ahead. The world outside these walls, the burden of titles, responsibilities, and expectations—they wouldn't disappear overnight. But as he looked into her unflinching gaze, Stan made a silent vow to himself.

Whatever came, whatever battles awaited, he would fight for her. For them. Because Wendy wasn't just a fleeting moment of happiness for him. She was happiness, his present, and—a hope he dared not voice yet—perhaps even his future. All he could do now was hold onto her fiercely and cherish her, with everything he had.

Chapter Twenty-One

THE EVENING SHADOWS stretched long across the walls of Cloverdale House as Wendy left Andre's treatment room, having prepared everything for the next day. Her steps unhurried though a quiet unrest prickled beneath her calm. The silence of the house, save for the creak of floorboards and the distant rustle of trees beyond the windows, felt profound. Andre had departed earlier that day, leaving a curious quiet in his wake.

Wendy wandered toward the former breakfast room, now a space transformed into an office for Pippa. She had peeked in before when the light still streamed golden through the windows, but now the scene was marked by the glow of a single oil lamp, its flicker casting long shadows over the disarrayed plans that cluttered the table.

Pippa leaned over a wide roll of paper, her fingers skimming its surface with a sense of purpose that made Wendy's throat tighten. She didn't look up immediately. Her spectacles sat askew, and her hair, usually tucked neatly into a knot, had loosened into stray wisps that framed her face. A pot of tea sat abandoned, the tea's surface dark with flecks from where it had gone undisturbed for hours.

Her slippers barely whispered over the floorboards as she stepped inside. "Are you converting all the rooms to chambers for patients?" she asked, her voice steady though a thread of steel ran beneath the words. Where would Stan go once he was well? And where would that leave her?

Her ties to Nick, the practice, and her work at Cloverdale House tugged at her.

Pippa startled, straightening too quickly as a flush of color rose to her cheeks. "Oh, Wendy!" She fumbled with a teacup and saucer, placing them rather indelicately on along the border of the blueprint. Her smile was bright, too bright, as though she'd been caught rifling through someone's private letters.

Wendy's gaze swept the table. The rolls of paper unfurled here and there revealed tantalizing glimpses of plans. Details leaped out—angled corners, marked measurements, an elegant curve that suggested something too grand to be mere practicality. Yet nothing immediately declared itself as a patient's chamber.

"Why shouldn't I know what you're planning?" she asked, clasping her hands in front of her skirts, holding them there to disguise the tiny, restless motion of her fingers. The question hung in the air, soft but insistent.

Pippa didn't answer at once. Instead, she fiddled with her lace cuffs, her eyes darting briefly to the papers before landing on her sister-in-law with a practiced look of nonchalance. "Of course you'll know. Just not yet," she said with an airy laugh that tugged Wendy's defenses taut.

The lamp flickered again, catching the gleam of the tea's surface as Pippa adjusted the saucer. Wendy took in the scene— the slightly crumpled edge of a blueprint now bearing the faintest ring of condensation, the guarded brightness in Pippa's tone, the deliberate ease of her movements. Something important was hidden here, something meant to be meaningful—but who was it intended for? Wendy had always found secrecy unsettling.

Wendy's breath caught, not from surprise but the old ache of standing just outside the frame of grand plans—useful, necessary, but never central.

"How much longer do you think you need to remain here?" Wendy asked gently as she approached.

Pippa glanced up, blinking as though surfacing from deep concentration. She adjusted her spectacles and straightened in her seat. "Nick said he'd see to a matter at the practice and return to collect us," she replied, her tone breezy but the furrow of her brow giving away her wearied focus.

Wendy moved closer, noting the neat—or perhaps nearly chaotic—array of parchment rolls, sketches, and neatly scribbled calculations. Pippa pushed at a particularly rebellious scroll to keep it from curling.

"What are these?" Wendy asked, nodding toward the plans.

"The architect's designs," Pippa sighed, her tone betraying a mixture of frustration and fondness. With a shuffle of papers, she pulled a new sheet forward. "And this," she added, nudging it toward Wendy, "is the report on today's excavation."

Wendy took the proffered paper but found her attention drawn to Pippa's growing frustration. "Is something amiss?"

"Not precisely," Pippa said with a sigh, frowning at the sketch before pushing it aside. She studied Wendy with a most serious expression, as though about to announce a grave situation. "It's… well, it's hedgehogs."

"Hedgehogs?" Wendy echoed, her brow lifting in amused surprise.

Pippa nodded solemnly, adjusting her spectacles as though preparing to deliver an important lecture. "Yes. A whole family, right in the middle of where we planned to connect the orangery to the carriage house. Two adults and—" she paused for theatrical effect—"five tiny babies."

"Five?" Wendy asked, clasping her hands together, her tone caught between curiosity and delight.

"Yes," Pippa confirmed, her tone grave, as if the tiny creatures had personally thwarted her grand architectural vision. "Happily nesting in the very path we intended to clear. They've undone all forward progress, those prickly little sweethearts."

Wendy angled her head, smiling fondly at Pippa's dramatics. "Do tell, what shall be done about such formidable opponents?"

Pippa huffed softly, gathering her composure. "The adults are clever and hardy—no doubt they'll find a new home soon enough. But the little ones…" She trailed off, the line of concern creeping back to her brow. "They are so small, Wendy. Little bundles of quills and fur who've no concept of avoiding harm. And the nights, though not frigid, are hardly kind to such defenseless newborns."

Wendy bit back a laugh, though her smile couldn't be helped. "And so, five tiny hedgehogs have outmaneuvered the architect and delayed the grand designs of Cloverdale House?"

"They may soon be under your purview," but Pippa paused and seemed to bite her tongue. *Whatever did she mean?*

With a resigned shrug, Pippa tossed her pencil lightly onto the table. "They cannot possibly understand the inconvenience, poor dears. I suppose we'll delay the work. For their sake, of course."

"For their sake, of course," Wendy repeated, attempting a tone as serious as Pippa's, though her lips twitched with amusement. "And what shall become of them now, these interlopers?"

Pippa hesitated, fidgeting with the corner of a parchment roll. "I-I may have requested that the workers guard their nest." She glanced up with a shy smile, her cheeks tinged pink. "Just until they're big enough to manage on their own."

Wendy pressed a hand to her mouth to stifle her laugh before leaning forward warmly. "Pippa, do you mean to say that the progress of construction halts entirely at the mercy of five hoglets?"

"Well," Pippa said with a trace of defiance, though her smile clung to the corners of her mouth. "They've lived here as long as we have, I dare say. Perhaps longer. It's only right to consider such longstanding tenants before proceeding with any eviction."

Wendy couldn't stop the giggle that spilled at that. "You've a softer heart than you care to admit, Pippa. And a most noble ambition—even the hedgehogs of Cloverdale are shielded under your stewardship."

"They hardly asked to be born in the middle of my plans," Pippa replied, crossing her arms with mock indignation. Her eyes, however, sparkled with humor.

"Indeed," Wendy said, nodding thoughtfully. "I should think history will remember this moment—how Cloverdale House came to a halt for the smallest and prickliest of residents."

Pippa laughed at last, shaking her head and straightening the plans before her. "It isn't ideal," she admitted ruefully. "But neither is the work of disturbing what's already well-settled. And besides..." she smiled, a little sheepishly now, "they *are* rather delightful."

"I'd love to see them," Wendy said warmly, wondering not for the first time how Pippa balanced her exquisite plans with such endearing sentiment. Certainly, Cloverdale House was all the better for it.

"I can take you outside right now if you'd like," Pippa said, pushing her chair back and standing with a small stretch. "There should be a worker keeping watch over the nest, lest a predator decide to have a late supper."

"Or early breakfast?" Wendy's eyes lit with interest as she set the excavation report down.

"Yes, of course. They are nocturnal." Pippa furrowed her brows and hooked her hand into Wendy's arms.

"You are quite serious about this, aren't you, Pippa?"

"Entirely," Pippa replied, adjusting her spectacles with mock gravitas before gesturing toward the doorway. "Come, Wendy. Let me show you."

Chuckling, Wendy stepped past her, and the pair made their way through the quiet halls of Cloverdale House. The oil lamps along the walls lent a warm glow to their path, while their footsteps echoed softly against the wooden floors.

When they stepped outside, the cool night air greeted them with a gentle hush, carrying the faint scent of earth and greenery. The crescent moon hung low, casting a silvery light on the neatly tended grounds. Fireflies blinked lazily in the distance, dots of luminescence dancing just above the hedges.

"Do you think they have any idea how much trouble and expenses they've caused you?" Wendy teased, clasping her hands behind her back as they strolled toward the orangery.

"Not one whit," Pippa replied, a faint smile tugging at her lips. "Though I daresay I would expect no less from nocturnal creatures. They are far too busy scampering about and causing mischief under the moon's watchful eye to concern themselves with anything so tiresome as construction plans."

"Scampering and causing mischief?" Wendy repeated, unable to suppress a grin. "You make them sound like tiny rogues of the garden."

"Oh, they are," Pippa said with mock indignation, lifting her chin. "But animals are rather fascinating, wouldn't you agree? The world changes so at night—it belongs to different creatures entirely."

Wendy glanced up at the moonlit sky. "Moths instead of butterflies, owls instead of sparrows…" Her voice softened, and her smile grew wistful. "And foxes, of course. I always imagine foxes darting through the shadows, quick as ghosts because they are crepuscular and usually seen at dusk or dawn."

"You're not far off," Pippa said, her tone thoughtful as she brushed a stray lock of hair from her cheek. "The foxes here are a regular sight, though they never linger. I'd wager they've caught wind of the hedgehogs, which is precisely why the workers have posted a guard."

"Ever vigilant," Wendy said warmly. "Though I hope the foxes find their supper elsewhere. The hedgehogs are, after all, under your protection."

"That they are," Pippa said, nodding. "And if you look close-ly, you might just find a badger nosing about as well. They're less stealthy than foxes, but far too clever to discount."

"But where's the guard?" Wendy asked, her voice hushed as she glanced about. The owl's hoot from the trees above hung in the stillness, blending with the faint clatter of distant footsteps on the street. The house behind them stood quiet, the windows dark, and the surrounding garden seemed to hold its breath.

Then, a twig snapped. The sound, sharp and sudden, made Wendy jolt, her heart leaping into her throat.

Pippa, however, crouched down without hesitation. "They shouldn't have left the nest yet," she murmured, her hands gently parting the low bushes. "The babies are likely close by, but I won't disturb the nest. Mama hedgehogs are easily scared. And the little hedgehogs are hardly adventurous at this age."

Wendy tried to steady herself, following Pippa's movements and waited to see whether a hedgehog would snuffle out of the nest. But before either of them could look further, a sudden click sounded—a door opening behind them.

"What are you doing out here?" The deep timbre of a man's voice broke the quiet with startling force, resonating like a clap of thunder.

Wendy straightened immediately, turning to Pippa, who rose in a swift, jerking motion. All the color drained from her face as her spine stiffened. Wendy caught the fleeting look of shock on Pippa's features. Then fear. Without a word, Pippa dropped into a hurried curtsy, eyes lowering to the ground as though she scarcely dared to breathe.

Wendy turned, her chest tight, to meet the source of the voice. There stood Stan. His figure emerged from the dark with startling clarity, the simple white of his shirt and the pale beige of his breeches catching the faint moonlight. Though stripped of its usual finery, the plainness of his attire did nothing to soften his commanding presence.

His expression was unreadable, his frame upright with an almost studied ease, but his gaze—his gaze made Wendy's breath catch. It wasn't fury in his eyes. It wasn't even frustration. It was something raw, something unmistakable, yet buried like a hidden current beneath the cool surface of his demeanor.

Fear.

"I asked what you were doing out here," Stan repeated firmly, though his voice had softened as he stepped toward them, glancing sharply around the garden as he spoke. He came to stand beside Wendy, a looming presence of authority and tension.

Wendy felt the chill in the air anew. "We—Pippa wanted to check on her hedgehogs," she began, though her words faltered at the sight of him up close. His face was clear, expression tight yet veiled, but those eyes... They mirrored a memory, a flicker of terror she'd seen before. That night.

"Baby hedgehogs," Pippa interjected, her voice rushing into the silence. Nervous but eager to explain, she stepped forward, clasping her hands together. "There is a nest, you see, right under the hedge. I was only ensuring they were safe. We meant no harm—"

"And the hedge will still be standing come morning," Stan interrupted. He swept a hand toward the door in a brisk, no-nonsense motion. "Both of you—inside. Now."

"But—"

"Inside," he repeated, his voice carrying just enough steel to leave no room for further debate.

Wendy moved first, though the heaviness in her chest made her limbs slow. Pippa hovered uncertainly, shooting longing glances back at the bushes before Stan gestured again, stronger this time. They stepped through the open doorway, the warm light of the interior breaking the spell of the shadowed garden.

"The baby hedgehogs—" Pippa started again as Stan closed the door behind them, the latch clicking firmly into place.

Wendy barely registered Pippa's words. Her attention was entirely on Stan now, the line of his jaw tight, his hands braced against the doorframe, his posture still drawn taut like a bowstring. He looked in control, yes. But she could see the cracks—cracks no one else might notice.

The same cracks she'd seen before, that night when the world had seemed to tip sideways, and the threat of danger had settled squarely on his shoulders. The same fear that had burned in his eyes then burned now, though tempered by his quiet resolve.

Pippa, bright and entirely oblivious, continued as though nothing were amiss. "I don't see why we couldn't simply check for a moment longer. Hedgehogs are quite nocturnal, you know. Anything could happen while we—"

"Enough," Stan said firmly, though not unkindly. He turned to face her, his expression clearing into something gentler, though still touched with urgency.

"I didn't mean to cause alarm." she murmured.

"You didn't," he said, softer now, though his gaze lingered only briefly on her before flickering back to Wendy. "This is your house, Lady Folsham." But Wendy saw everything—his control, his struggle to mask what he truly felt. While Pippa babbled apologies she hardly needed to give, slipping toward the stairs, Wendy stood rooted. She couldn't look away from Stan.

Stan shut the door after he looked behind himself one last time, as if he wanted to make sure nobody had followed them. "And I mean no disrespect, but until Nick is back, shouldn't I keep his family safe?"

Pippa arched her brows and cast Wendy a look.

"Thank you, Your Royal Highness. But it was merely some nightly invaders of the four-legged sort that we were after," Pippa said.

"It's not about who you're after but who may be after you. Or me. They attacked my sister twice already. And since he knows I am here, I pose a risk to you."

He turned to her fully, his composure reasserted, yet the echoes of his fear still lingered behind his eyes.

For a moment, neither spoke.

He turned toward her, his protective instincts etched in every line of his body. And Wendy, caught in the pull between duty and longing, could no longer pretend not to feel it.

"You were afraid," she found herself saying softly, the words tumbling out before she could stop them.

Stan's lips parted—not in denial, but as though caught unprepared for her insight. Finally, he exhaled. "It's late, Nurse Wendy.

Go and see to your rest."

"I shall gather the plans before Nick comes back to fetch us." Pippa turned and left.

But far too much had passed unspoken to leave it there. Wendy hesitated, her heart warring with her sense. "No one meant harm. Truly."

"It isn't harm that you mean, that concerns me," he said, quieter still, his expression unreadable once more. "Where is your brother?"

It wasn't a command. It wasn't a dismissal, either. It was something heavier. Something that made her hesitate only long enough for the growing pull of everything yet to be understood.

"Wendy?" Stan's voice was a low murmur, scarcely more than her name carried on a breath.

She blinked up at him, her pulse quickening as the space between them seemed to collapse. The air was thick now, charged with something unspoken yet unmistakable. Her hands trembled at her sides until, as if drawn by some unseen force, she reached out and brushed her fingertips against his.

He didn't withdraw. Instead, his hand turned instinctively, his palm cradling hers with a tenderness that sent heat rushing to her cheeks. She felt the roughness of his skin, a silent testament to strength and grit, yet the way his fingers curled gently over hers spoke of care, of warmth.

The movement was slow, deliberate. Her breath caught as their fingers intertwined, slotting together as though they had done so countless times before—as though hours ago, in another fleeting moment, their hands hadn't already whispered secrets of this connection.

His gaze held hers, unwavering, and in it she saw everything that words could not express. The moonlight filtering through the windows softened the angles of his face, casting shadows that only made his bright eyes seem more piercing.

Her heart swelled as his thumb brushed lightly across the back of her hand, a simple touch that made sparks dance beneath her skin. Neither of them moved closer, yet the unspoken pull between them was undeniable; every inch of space seemed to hum with the possibility of being closed.

"Stan…" she whispered, the name trailing off her lips like a prayer, her voice trembling with equal parts wonder and hesitation.

"I saw you through the window in the dark and was alarmed. If something happened to you… you and Thea—" He took a deep breath. "I need to know that you are safe."

He leaned in slightly, his presence so near now that the faint warmth of his breath brushed against her skin. The world around them seemed to fade, and Wendy felt as though she stood on the precipice of something boundless and irrevocably beautiful.

Then—"Wendy?" The spell shattered as Nick's voice called from the hall, clear and entirely banal against the fragile magic of their moment.

Wendy started, her hand slipping from Stan's as though retreating from something forbidden. Her eyes darted toward the doorway where Nick's shadow lengthened, heralding the intrusion of duty.

She turned back to Stan, and her heart clenched at the sight of him. He had stepped back, his posture composed and his expression carefully neutral once more. Yet there was a flicker of something in his eyes—reluctance, perhaps, or the faintest echo of what had just passed between them.

Her breath hitched as she reluctantly relinquished his hand, fingers uncurling one by one. "Over here!" she called, forcing brightness into her voice, though she felt the wistfulness tugging at her chest.

Nick appeared in the doorway, his easy smile in full force. "Oh, there you are," he said, glancing between them pleasantly. "Good evening, Stan."

"Good evening," Stan replied, his voice as steady as ever, though Wendy thought she caught the faintest edge of restraint in his tone.

"Would you like to join us?" Nick asked, stepping further into the room. "Violet mentioned that we ought to reconvene for dinner, and it seems Pippa has agreed at the mention of a hot roast."

Stan gave a brief nod, his hands falling to his sides.

"Wait!" Wendy said.

⇒⇒⇒✕⇐⇐⇐

STAN'S LIPS PRESSED into a thin line as Wendy spoke. "I ate when the patients did," she said, her tone light and convincing enough to fool anyone who wasn't paying close attention. But Stan wasn't so easily deceived.

He'd seen the staff arranging the dinner table hours ago when he'd descended the stairs, taking care to remain unnoticed. He knew the schedule well enough by now. Wendy, for all her selflessness and dedication, rarely remembered to tend to herself, especially on busy days like this. It had been that very thought that had spurred him to step outside in search of solace, only to stumble upon Wendy and Pippa in the garden.

Now, as he stood across from her in the soft glow of the drawing room, he narrowed his gaze, his thoughts swirling as he considered her. She had a way of deflecting concern so deftly, turning attention elsewhere with a bright smile and a charming remark. But the faint shadows under her eyes and the slight tension in her posture betrayed her.

She needed someone to look after her.

Wendy must have felt the magnitude of his scrutiny because she looked at him then—a searching look that made his chest tighten. She was expecting something from him. What, exactly, he could not say, but the vulnerability in her gaze stirred something deep within him, a longing to protect her from every discomfort the world might throw her way.

"It's truly some ices I'd much prefer," Wendy continued,

tilting her head with a small, wistful smile that nearly made him forget his thoughts altogether.

"From Gunter's?" he asked, raising a brow.

Her face lit up, and her eyes opened just a touch too wide. "Oh, the one, you know! Mandarin and rosewater," she said, her voice a bit too eager. "Unless it's closed this late."

Stan's lips quirked in the faintest of smiles. She was playing at innocence, though it was clear she was fishing for something—and perhaps not only the ices she claimed to crave.

Before he could respond, Pippa's voice drifted from the hall. "Nick, are you coming?"

Nick, who had been standing nearby, shifted awkwardly, his retreat more of a stumble than a step. "Should I come and pick you up later, then?" He asked, his glance darted between Wendy and Stan, as if he'd stumbled into a scene he shouldn't have witnessed.

Stan saw his opportunity and seized it with the calm confidence that came naturally to him. "No," he spoke measured but firmly. "Allow me to thank her with some ices and then bring her home to your townhouse in my carriage."

Wendy turned her head toward him quickly, her brows cinching together in surprise.

"That's hardly proper," Nick protested, his expression tightening. "You two shouldn't be seen alone together."

"I'm still a patient at Cloverdale until I've been officially dismissed," Stan replied smoothly, his voice steady with reason. "This isn't socializing. This is ensuring I remain safely under my nurse's care."

Wendy arched a brow at her brother and added, "Precisely. I'm his nurse, Nick. My priority is his wellbeing, nothing more."

Nick hesitated, his frown softening at their reasoning but not entirely vanishing. Wendy drew her eyes wide and gave him a look that almost dared him to argue further.

"If you're certain, Stan," Nick said reluctantly, his voice nearly mumbling.

"I am," Stan replied simply, his tone leaving no room for

debate. His gaze flicked back to Wendy, catching a hint of softness in her eyes before she quickly turned away.

Stan shifted his focus entirely back to Wendy now, watching as her expression softened, her lips curving into the faintest shadow of a smile. She dipped her head once, a quiet acceptance that made his pulse quicken.

He could not say whether his offer stemmed from pure chivalry, concern that she hadn't eaten properly, or some deeper, unspoken desire to extend their time together. Perhaps it was all these things; perhaps he did not care to question it too deeply. What he knew was this—he wasn't ready to see her go just yet. Choices for which there were no words often felt the truest.

"I shall have the carriage prepared at once," he said, the slight incline of his head wholly formal. But when Wendy lifted her gaze again to meet his, something far less composed stirred between them.

Nick excused himself kindly, heading toward Pippa and the others. As the hall quieted once more, Stan extended his arm toward Wendy—a simple gesture, yet one brimming with unspoken meaning.

"Shall we?" he asked, his tone steady yet touched with warmth.

Her fingertips drifted against his sleeve, feather-light. A pulse leapt in his wrist before he could still it. The space between them contracted, charged and breathless, as if the air itself dared not interrupt. Her eyes sparkled with a playful light that caught him unguarded, sending an unexpected ripple of giddiness through him, as if the room itself had grown warmer. She looked up, her gaze glinting with restrained mischief—or was it hope? "I suppose it would be improper to deny His Highness's gracious offer," she teased softly, though her quiet laugh masked something more tentative lurking beneath her words.

He smiled at that—not widely, not openly, but enough to sense the corners of his guard shift. Cracks of something new and unfamiliar edged into the quiet between them as they turned toward the door together.

Chapter Twenty-Two

THE CARRIAGE LURCHED down the cobbled streets, the rhythmic clatter of hooves underscoring the quiet tension inside. Stan adjusted the collar of his greatcoat, the chill of the night of the night lingering even within the enclosed space. Across from him sat Wendy, wrapped in her pelisse, her cheeks flushed from the cold—or perhaps something else entirely.

Hopefully me.

She fidgeted in her lap before clasping her hands together, her excitement visible in every small action she made. The way her foot tapped lightly against the carriage floor, the unconscious tilt of her head as she glanced at him with wide, sparkling blue eyes—it all struck him like a bolt to the chest. He wanted to pull her into his arms, to feel her warmth against him, but the weight of knowing he was skirting propriety held him back.

"I can't believe my brother truly allowed this," she said, her voice low yet teeming with energy. A mischievous grin tugged at her lips as she sat straighter, her posture alive with confidence, as if the sheer improper nature of it had added to her daring. Her shoulders rose in an eager shrug that made his heart clench. That small, innocent motion undid him completely. She trusted him implicitly, unreservedly, and this trust filled him with guilt that gnawed at the edges of his control.

Stan forced himself to look at the passing scenery, willing his thoughts to steady. Yet even as he did, her presence consumed him, bright and undeniable. He didn't understand it fully, but he felt it deep and resolute. There was no one else, and there never would be. Just Wendy. Only Wendy.

He leaned back against the seat, his muscles relaxing outwardly but his thoughts anything but. Nick's blind trust in him wasn't something to trifle with. This wasn't about duty or obligation to a fellow man—it was a brother-to-brother and friend-to-friend sort of trust, thus something far simpler and far more meaningful than what he'd initially envisioned, time alone with Wendy. Yet, he didn't even mind the implication of escorting her through the cool evening alone. It just wasn't as simple as that with a woman like her. Although she didn't have a title, she had class, honor, and a loyal brother. Plus, others who were like brothers to her: Alfie, Andre, and Felix. They'd kill Stan with something untraceable and quick—he mused—considering their collective knowledge of the workings of the human body— or probably stop it from working. Not that they'd ever harm a man, but if anyone were alone with his sister, he and his brothers would be no less vicious than … But there was one problem: He wanted to be here more than anywhere else in the world. With her. Not as a patient grateful for her attention, but as a man cherishing the company of a woman. Wendy.

He sat forward slightly, considering her, and then said, quieter than before, "Perhaps your brother wanted to give you a moment's happiness… as much as he wished to give me the same."

Wendy's hands stilled mid-fidget. She met his gaze, her brows pulling together before lifting her chin with quiet defiance.

"I'm fully aware of what's proper," she said, her tone measured but firm. "But propriety doesn't dictate my choices. I didn't need my brother's permission, and I certainly don't need a chaperone to sit in a carriage with you."

Stan leaned back slightly, feigning contemplation. "If propriety doesn't concern you, then I have no objections. But perhaps I should send for my sister to ensure appearances?" His voice was even, but the corner of his mouth quirked upward, teasing.

Wendy's arms crossed, her expression unflinching. "If you think I need appearances preserved, you misunderstand me entirely."

For a moment, silence stretched between them, thick with tension. Then Stan's composed demeanor wavered as a low chuckle escaped him, growing into a warm, genuine laugh that filled the carriage.

Wendy dipped her chin, her expression somewhere between bewildered and bemused. "Care to share the jest?"

He leaned forward, his dark eyes softened with humor. "Only that I never doubted you. I simply wanted to give you an escape route, should you want one. Chaperones, I think we can agree, are unwanted here."

Stan watched as her lips curved, the faintest smile disturbing her otherwise guarded composure. She unfolded her arms but leaned back still, as though to keep her distance. "Then we can agree on that, at least," she said, her voice light yet laced with something unspoken. The charged silence that followed pricked at him, filled as it was with truths too delicate to voice aloud. He knew, clumsy though the exchange had been, that their hearts had chosen. For him, it felt as right as air drawn into his lungs, wholly unbidden.

"But," she added softly, her gaze falling, "I must discharge you. You're healed enough to leave Cloverdale House."

His brow rose slightly. "And so, I'm to pay my dues and be on my way?"

Her tone faltered. "No. I don't want you to leave. Only... I am no longer needed as your nurse." She paused, her voice barely a breath, the sadness woven through it unmistakable. "I've already told my brother you're quite recovered. Pippa will see to the... financial arrangements."

"So, this is to be a purely transactional affair?" he asked, his words quieter this time.

Her gaze lifted, and though her expression remained steady, there was a flicker of resolve beneath her words. "It is necessary. For you to see me as I am—not merely a nurse, but a woman. I don't want to be just an affair." She hesitated before continuing, drawing strength from somewhere deep within. "And Nick and I have redirected all our wages to Cloverdale House. Alfie has invested his earnings to restock the apothecary for the rehabilitation center. We cannot afford stagnation, no matter the cost."

"And how could I cause stagnation at Cloverdale House?" Stan pressed on.

"If you catch List, will you go back to Transylvania and forget me?" The words struck true, clean and sharp, and Stan found his throat too tight for speech. Her fire—her fearlessness—both humbled and unsettled him. He clasped his hands, resisting the urge to reach out, because if he touched her now, he might never stop.

I'd never forget you. I never want to leave you. But what if I don't catch List?

He didn't know where to even begin to answer. But his instinct guided him, and he leaned closer. "I think of you," he began, his voice warm and teasing, "as a heroine of medicine. One of the most talented and caring women I've ever known."

Her brows rose, a smile pulling at her mouth like a secret too pleased to keep. "And what makes you so certain of that?"

Oh, she's playing coy. This will be fun!

His grin widened, bright and utterly disarming, as though meant only for her. "Several reasons," he said, his voice dipping low enough to spark warmth in her chest.

"Such as?"

"You saved my life," he said lightly, though his gaze said it meant everything. "You mend children with rickets. You've the sweetest lilt in your laugh..." He paused, watching her cheeks flush, then added with deliberate precision, "And you've never kissed anyone before me, have you?"

"And just what do you mean by that? Was I... was I so bad?"

she asked. Her voice tumbled out, rushed and pink-cheeked. Stan's grin spread farther, lighting his face in a manner that made her breath catch. Stan leaned in just enough to catch her gaze fully, forcing her to meet him—no shields, no retreat. "Worse than 'bad'? W-was it because I've never kissed before?"

She leaned forward, her lashes lowering. Stan felt the intensity of her gaze as her tongue darted out, wetting her lips. The world outside dulled to silence. It was only them now, in the hush between heartbeats.

※》》》✕《《《

WENDY'S HEART RACED, every beat loud and insistent as Stan's voice dropped, each word curling between them like rising steam from a kettle—tangible, dangerous, impossible to ignore. "I kissed you, Wendy. And you *allowed* me. But that's different," he murmured, his eyes tracing hers with unsettling precision. "You haven't yet kissed me back. Not properly. Do you wish it?"

Her pride straightened her spine even as her pulse stumbled. "How exactly does one 'return' a kiss?" She blinked, then tilted her chin with a hint of defiance. "I'm not giving it back!"

Stan's brows shot up. Yet, Wendy's expressions changed and slow grin replaced surprise, teasing glinting behind dark lashes.

"You're asking me that?" His voice carried just the faintest incredulity, and his smile deepened, warm and maddening.

"Yes," she said, her words clipped despite the soft flush warming her cheeks. "Show me!" The moment stretched unbearably taut.

"Now?" he asked, his grin widening. His teeth flashed, perfectly white, his charm spilling over with effortless ease. It was unbearably distracting, the effect he had on her—not that she dared admit it.

"Yes." Her voice came small, trembling but resolute.

His smile lingered for a beat longer before quieting, softening.

He tilted his head, studying her intently, and in that pause, the air itself seemed to hold its breath. "Hands-on learner, are you?" His voice dipped just enough to unsettle her composure.

Her lips parted as a steadying breath escaped her. "Always," she whispered.

Wendy leaned in slightly, her heart threatening to betray her resolve every step of the way. But this was her moment. If she had uncovered anything from the fairy tales of her childhood, it was that heroines did not shrink from their trials. They were bold, even when the ground beneath them trembled. And weren't the best stories forged in courage?

The corner of her mouth hesitated before curving softly. "Tell me," she said, her voice quiet but unwavering, "what to do. Step by step."

Stan's smile remained firmly in place even after he looked at his hands for a moment as if stifling a laugh, and he licked his lips, though the sharpness in his dark eyes made her painfully aware of how close he was now. The space between them no longer felt like a barrier but a thread, a mere breath away from binding them together. Enveloped by his warmth, she could almost count the seconds between his subtly uneven gasps of anticipation.

"Are you trying to memorize the steps?" he teased, his voice a low murmur that sent a shiver racing down her spine.

"Of course," she replied, her hands clenching and unclenching in her lap to steady herself. "It's a simple operation, isn't it?"

Stan tilted his head, amusement softening the sharp cut of his features. "No."

Her lips parted, surprise flickering across her face. "But anyone can do it." She fought to keep her voice confident, but there was no masking the nervous energy bubbling beneath her words.

"Not well, no," he said, his gaze unwavering, as though he were daring her to challenge him.

That slight smirk tugged at his mouth again, and Wendy stiffened. "How do you know?" she asked, her chin lifting stubbornly. "Do you have so much experience?"

His brows rose slightly before his expression sharpened into something more deliberate. "Yes."

Her stomach twisted, heat rushing to her cheeks as she leaned back abruptly, crossing her arms over her chest like a shield. "I don't like that."

The smirk just came, and he seemed genuinely happy. Flattered. "Are you jealous?" he asked, his tone light but far too knowing for her comfort.

She hesitated, considering his question. *Was she?* Every inch of her pride tried to push the thought away, but honesty wasn't something she could easily deny—and not with him watching her like that. Finally, she gave a small nod. "Yes."

Then she gasped and covered her mouth with her right hand. "Oh dear! It's terrible! I'm… I'm a bad person!"

"You could never be," Stan said teasingly.

"B-but jealously is not nice. Soon, I'll turn green with envy and—"

The sharpness in his gaze softened, replaced with something that made her pulse quicken. "You don't need to be," he murmured, leaning slightly closer. "I have an inkling you could kiss me breathless, so thoroughly I'd forget everyone before you."

Wendy's breath caught, her heart pounding harder with each beat. She tried to speak, to counter him with something witty or clever, but his words rendered her silent. Her arms dropped as her fingers gripped the folds of her gown in her lap.

"How?" she finally managed, her voice quiet and uneven.

"With affection." His voice dipped into something rich and warm. "I've certainly never felt about anyone the way I do about you."

A pang of sadness wrung her heart, her thoughts quieting into an ache she dared not fully examine.

"Me neither," she admitted, the honesty in her voice surprising even herself.

Stan's smile softened, as though her words meant more than a mere agreement. "Then may I kiss you again? Please?"

She blinked, her resolve returning as if sparked by his quiet invitation. Slowly, she gave a small but determined nod. When he leaned in, she followed, closing the space with a surge of courage.

Her breath mingled with his, her pulse racing as she prepared for this moment—not as a timid heroine from a storybook but as herself, Wendy, who was ready to learn something new and face it head-on.

STAN LEANED CLOSER, his breath mingling with Wendy's, a shared warmth in the chilly confines of the carriage. His eyes traced the curve of her lips, soft and slightly parted, as if inviting him forward. He fought the pull of instinct, held himself in check— not out of propriety, but something far more thrilling.

"Wendy," he murmured, his voice low and steady, though his pulse raced faster than any words could admit. "If you'll trust me… part your lips. Gently. Just a touch."

She did—tentatively, hesitantly, her gaze flicking between his mouth and his eyes, searching. The uncertainty in her expression was as endearing as it was intoxicating.

He swallowed hard. "Now, if you wish, close your eyes, and follow my movements. Copy me." His thumb brushed her cheek—a light, fleeting touch, enough to calm her while his restraint frayed. "Grant me access, Wendy. Only if you wish it."

Her lashes lowered, and for a moment, he wasn't sure she understood. But then her lips softened beneath his, telling him everything. Her tentative trust opened the door just wide enough to unravel him. He pressed forward, capturing her mouth and coaxing her into an entirely new experience.

This was not a tumble as earlier at Cloverdale House.

This was deliberate.

Intentional.

Thrilling.

Heat spiraled between them, slow at first, a warm tendril winding through the cold air of the night. Her lips yielded to him tentatively, her inexperience painfully sweet and wholly undoing. He deepened the kiss, and for a moment, the air around them vanished.

Stan tried to focus, to continue his whispered instructions, but the taste of her—like something forbidden and stolen—drew the thoughts right out of his head. She was delicious, soft, and utterly consuming.

Her hands, he noticed, hovered awkwardly between them, fingers curling and uncurling like she wasn't sure what to do. He grinned faintly against her lips and pulled back just enough to speak, his voice rough. "Your hands," he whispered, taking them gently and guiding them upward. He placed them against his chest, a solid barrier of warmth beneath her touch. "You can touch me anywhere you want."

Her fingers trembled briefly before sinking into the fabric of his coat, her gaze darting back to his. "Me too," she whispered, her voice husky, desire threaded through her words.

Her hands drifted upward, threading into his hair, her touch bolder now. She raked through the strands, and the sensation pulled a shiver from him that he couldn't suppress. His mouth moved against hers again, possessive now, and when her tongue darted out to brush his lower lip, he groaned low in his chest.

Stan opened his mouth, and she flicked her tongue hesitantly into the warmth of his. He didn't guide her this time, couldn't have spoken if he'd tried. Instead, he cupped the back of her head and tilted her just enough to take her deeper. When she mimicked his movements, shyly at first but with growing enthusiasm, it felt as though his heart cracked to lock her in.

A deep, guttural growl escaped him, raw and unbidden. Wendy broke the kiss only to catch her breath, her chest heaving against his own. Her wide eyes sparkled with mischief and discovery as she whispered, "I know this sound now."

Stan blinked at her, still half-reeling, his breath ragged. "What is it?"

Her lips curved into a small, devilish grin. "The sound of seduction."

He stared at her for what felt like an eternity, the words a spark in the tinder of his desire. With no further warning, his hands slid lower, tracing down her back, over the curve of her hips. She gasped softly as his grip tightened, and in one fluid motion, he grabbed hold of her bottom and lifted her.

Wendy moved without hesitation, her skirts brushing his legs as she straddled him. For someone so new to this, she was a quick learner. *Talented. Hands-on indeed.*

And Stan knew, without a shadow of doubt, that he could never keep his hands off her.

Chapter Twenty-Three

MINUTES LATER, THE steady rhythm of hooves ceased, and the carriage came to a halt before Gunter's Tea Shop at 7-8 Berkeley Square. The amber glow of the shop's windows bathed the quiet street with warmth, a contrast to the chilly evening air. Stan stepped down first, his shoes landing firmly on the cobblestones, before turning to assist Wendy. She placed her gloved hand in his, her grip delicate but certain, and descended with a just-kissed flush that drew his gaze for a moment longer than necessary.

Wendy's earlier delight lingered on her features, her cheeks faintly pink from the cold—or perhaps from their shared breathless moments in the carriage. Her smile was so unreserved, so vivid, it tightened something in Stan's chest, though he didn't dwell on it. He offered his arm, and she took it lightly, her fingers brushing his sleeve as though this was where they were meant to be.

Stan pushed open the door, the bell above chiming softly. A gust of sweetness enveloped them—a blend of citrus and faint floral notes mixed with the spicy undertone of cinnamon wafting from behind the counter. Wendy blinked, slightly off balance as her gaze swept across the shop. Rows of neat jars and tins lined the pastel-painted walls, their contents etched in neat lettering. Beneath glass-domed trays on the polished counter sat the famous ices in appetizing hues—pale creams, soft yellows, delicate pinks—half-melted under the warmth of the lamps that lit the space.

Stan took in the tiled floor patterned with faint geometries, the meticulous order of the display, and the weary clerk wiping his hands on a linen towel behind the counter.

"Sorry, we've just closed," the clerk said, his tone matter-of-fact but not entirely unkind. "Was just about to lock up for the night."

Stan stepped forward without hesitation, Wendy keeping pace at his side. He stopped when they looked at the counter, his hand steady on the frame of the door, holding it open as though to leave no room for negotiation.

"Can we purchase the mandarin ice with rose and take some with us, then?" Stan asked.

The clerk hesitated, glancing toward the glass-domed trays across from him. His eyes lingered on the emptying remnants within. He sighed softly, finally bending to retrieve a small tin. "We have a little left," he admitted, his tone reluctant but yielding.

"I'll pay double," Stan said plainly. There was no bravado in his voice, only the quiet conviction of a man accustomed to getting what he wanted.

Before the clerk could respond, another voice broke through, jagged and unfamiliar.

"No, I'll take the last of it."

Stan's spine stiffened at the grating accent threaded through the words. It was peculiar and harsh, each sound fractured and scraped against the warm cocoon of the shop. He recognized it immediately, but he refused to react too soon. Instead, he turned slowly, his composure unshaken but his senses on full alert.

The long-fingered hand pushed the door open, slipping past Stan's grip and catching his attention first. It was wrong—bluish, cold, too still. Stan's eyes moved upward, taking in the figure now standing a step too close.

Baron von List.

The coat fit him well, it's dark tailoring cut to his tall, broad frame, but there was no mistaking how alien his presence felt within these walls of civility and comfort. His face was almost sickly pale but sharply angled, his cheekbones high and hard against skin that seemed to glisten under the lamplight. Deep-set eyes locked onto Stan's, with more disgust than respect, though his faintly blue-tinged lips twisted upward in what might have been amusement or danger.

Wendy shifted next to Stan, her fingers tightening reflexively on his arm. He felt her tension and adjusted his stance to shield her from List without thinking.

"You'll find another flavor," Stan said evenly, his voice cutting through the space between them. He held List's gaze, unflinching. This wasn't just about ice—it was about drawing a line, here and now. When my love wants mandarin rose, she gets mandarin rose ice. He didn't dare look at Wendy, not now—not when the weight of what she meant to him had just been exposed in the worst way possible. List's lips curled faintly, though there was nothing pleasant in his expression. His cool blue eyes swept over Stan once, lingering only briefly on Wendy, and that was enough to set Stan on edge.

"I doubt the others will suffice," List replied smoothly, his accent slicing through each syllable. "Mandarin happens to be the Baroness' favorite. She's expecting, you know." List arched both brows as if he'd accomplished something fantastic, but Stan knew that his wife was no better than List, and they'd hatch nothing better than the devil's brood.

Stan did not move. The icy calculation in List's tone was not unfamiliar, but it set Stan's resolve deeper. His hand fell casually to his side, steady as he positioned himself more fully in front of Wendy. The clerk remained frozen at the counter, the tin in his hand seemingly heavier with every passing second.

"I'm afraid the ice has already been claimed," Stan said, his voice cool but bordering on sharp. Each word carried a warning he dared List to test.

"Has it?" List countered, his tone laced with mock astonishment. He gestured subtly toward Wendy. "And the girl as well?"

Stan's spine went rigid. Every instinct screamed to strike—but not here, not with Wendy watching, not with witnesses. "If you would like a reminder of proper decorum, I would be glad to educate you," he spoke in a low, deliberate, and menacing voice. "Starting with how to address me—as Your Royal Highness."

The faintest flicker of something passed through List's gaze before it was buried under cold indifference. He moved his weight slightly, his coat shifting as though to reassert his presence.

The room went silent. The clerk's nervous shuffling echoed in the stillness that followed, even the distant sounds of the street outside drowned out by the thick tension in the air.

Finally, List's lips curved again, his gaze settling coldly on Stan. "We'll meet again," he said, his accent curling over the words like a veiled threat. "Hopefully at your funeral, if not sooner." With calculated ease, he turned and retreated toward the street, the bell above the door offering a hollow jingle as it closed firmly behind him.

Stan stood motionless, the air heavier in the baron's absence. The scent he left behind clung to the shop like smoke, a sickly mix of decay masked by something sweet. His chest tightened, tension uncoiling in his shoulders but refusing to dissipate completely. The urge to act—to strike out at such a festering evil—still burned in his veins. Wendy's hand rested lightly on his arm, a tether, soft but secure, that held him steady in the storm of his thoughts.

Her voice cut through the dense silence, quiet but laced with disbelief. "Do you think he's ever truly killed anyone?"

Stan's jaw tightened as he glanced down at her, the grave question mirrored in her wide eyes.

Slowly, he nodded. "I know he has." His voice dropped, each word a damning weight. "More times than I care to count. And he's brought his depravity to London with him."

Wendy's gasp was barely audible, but her fingers curled against his sleeve, clutching tightly as though trying to anchor herself from the horror of it. "And no one stops him?" she whispered, her voice trembling with both anger and unease.

"He's like smoke," Stan murmured bitterly. "You see him, you smell him, but try to grasp him, and there's nothing there. He's always gone before the noose can tighten. He slips through every law, every border. And now he knows who you are to me." He forced himself to unclench his fists, though the tension remained locked within him. "He bribes, he threatens, he bends men to his will. No matter what he's done, there's always a greater devil willing to protect him if it favors their cause."

Wendy's brows furrowed, her lips pressing into a thin line as her gaze shifted toward the door, as though she could still see the shadow of him slipping into the night. "How can someone so vile go unpunished?"

Stan's chest rose with a deep breath, but still, the weight didn't lift. "Because men like him wield power the honorable cannot fathom." His words were quiet but hard, steeled with the bitterness of truth.

The baron's shadow weighed heavily on them both, a stain on the quiet of the night.

He turned toward the counter again, his tone steady once more. "Now, shall we finish arranging the ice and leave?"

WENDY HUGGED THE cool paper-wrapped tin close to her chest as Stan assisted her into the carriage. The sweet scent of mandarin and rose mingled with the cool night air, and she allowed herself a moment to savor it. Once she was settled, Stan followed, pulling the door shut behind him.

The carriage rattled to life, its wooden wheels clattering softly against the cobblestones as they headed toward Hyde Park. Wendy glanced at Stan from the corner of her eye, noticing the tension in his posture despite his efforts to hide it. His jaw was tight, his gaze distant, and his usually calm demeanor seemed eroded by something far heavier.

She reached out, her gloved fingers lightly brushing his. "Everything felt almost... normal until he appeared," she ventured softly.

Stan looked at her then, his expression softening marginally. He sighed as though the weight of the evening rested firmly on his shoulders. "It is my job to be certain that nothing touches you, nothing as dangerous as him."

"Baron von List," she said, testing his name as if it might make sense of the cold shiver he caused.

Stan gave a curt nod. "List is not a man to trifle with, Wendy. He's a coward and doesn't get his hands dirty but his intentions are rotten." His gaze darted briefly to the window before returning to her. "I should have seen this coming."

"Why was he so important that you came to London?" she asked gently.

Stan hesitated before answering, his voice low with restrained anger. "Because he's already stolen too much from my family, and we are responsible for so many people at home. It's personal now, too. Twice, he's captured my sister, Thea. She... she lives, but the fears from those encounters—visible and otherwise—remain. And he continues to steal from the gold mines in Transylvania; he's unstoppable, no matter how hard I try." His hands curled into fists before relaxing as if realizing they betrayed too much. "And if List even so much as tried to lay a hand on you..." He stopped, exhaling sharply.

Wendy's heart ached at the sheer vulnerability she saw in him. "He won't," she told him with quiet assurance. And for the first time, she didn't want to shield herself from that ache. She wanted to carry it with him.

His eyes fixed on hers, then, a devastating mix of frustration and regret flashed in them. "Now that he's seen us—me protecting you, you holding onto my arm—he'll know exactly where to aim the next time he wants to hurt me." His expression searched hers, jaw tense. "I brought him into your world. I never meant to, but I did."

Wendy tightened her grip on the tin in her lap, her chin lifting slightly.

I'm the risk he can't afford.

And yet, leaving him now would be the greater danger—to both of them.

With this realization, she knew her time with Stan would be short-lived.

"I won't make it so easy for him," Wendy said.

Stan flinched at her determination. She was resolute, radiant in her courage. And it terrified him—because it made him want to believe they could truly have something more. He reached for her hand and looked at her as if he'd done something terribly wrong. "I should take you to Nick," his voice clipped. "He's dining at the Langley's. You'll be safer there than with me because List knows my whereabouts now."

"No." She leaned toward him, her voice clear and resolute. "I'll pay the Countess a visit tomorrow, but for tonight, I stay right here. With you."

He shook his head, visibly torn. "We may not be safe."

"I don't care," she said, her voice softening. "How much longer will you even be in London, Stan? I don't want to waste a single moment with you—not talking about him, not letting him take even more from us. not letting him scare us into silence. We still get to choose how this story unfolds." She met his eyes, daring him to argue. "You told me once I was the brave one. Let me be that now." Wendy sighed. "His people attacked you that night, didn't they? It was his command. You almost died because of *him!*" Her voice broke and wobbled slightly, she couldn't hide it.

And her words hung in the air between them, heavy but

earnest. Stan's shoulders relaxed, just slightly, and he nodded once.

The carriage slowed as they approached the Gardens near Cloverdale House with their wide expanse of shadowed rows and placid waters. When they stepped down, the world felt quieter here. Although the chill of the night wrapped around them, the sky above was clear, and the soft shimmer of moonlight reflected off the dark glass of the Serpentine. It gleamed as if scattered with liquid stars, its small ripples catching the gentle breeze.

Stan retrieved a horse blanket from under the seat of the carriage and led Wendy toward the water's edge to a bench. They spread out a thick blanket on the damp grass, and the distant lantern glow from the park's entrances was the only other illumination. When they settled, Wendy unwrapped the tin and scooped the now-softening ice into two delicate silver spoons. The fragrant sweetness of mandarin and rose filled her senses when the first bite melted in her mouth.

Stan sat beside her, close enough that their knees brushed. He didn't need to speak for her to know his thoughts still lingered on List, on the way he hadn't been able to protect Thea, and his fear that history might repeat itself.

Wendy reached for his hand, her fingers wrapping around his larger ones. The warmth of his touch comforted her more than she expected. "You'll find a way to keep us safe," she said quietly. Her certainty seemed unshakable.

His gaze searched hers. "You have too much faith in me."

"Because you've earned it," Wendy replied simply. "Not through titles, Stan. Through every step you take toward protecting what's right."

Something in him softened then, a subtle shift that made the tension around his eyes ease. He leaned forward, one arm bracing against the blanket as he brought his free hand to her cheek. His thumb moved gently over her skin, warming her against the night's chill.

Their foreheads nearly touched, their breaths mingling in the stillness. The quiet park and shimmering water stretched before him, a patchwork of moonlit paths and shadows cast by the tall hedgerows. Stan took a steadying breath, his gaze fixed on her. Wendy blinked at him, her eyes catching silver from the starlit sky. She turned to him then, her pale pelisse shimmering faintly as it moved with the soft breeze, her eyes bright and searching. Something in their stillness captured his very soul.

He closed the distance toward her, his boots crunching softly against the gravel. The faint scent of mandarins and rose lingered in the air, mingling with the cool earthiness of the night. She did not retreat, did not so much as tremble, though he suspected her heart must race like his. The night felt poised on the brink of something unnamed, their breaths mingling with a tension that begged to be broken.

Finally, Stan closed the distance. He lifted a hand and rested it lightly beneath her chin, tilting her face toward him. By the flickering light of the nearby lantern from the carriage, her features seemed impossibly lovely, a portrait of serenity hiding the storm he could sense beneath. Slowly, as if testing the bounds of reality itself, he lowered his lips to hers.

The kiss was gentle at first, a quiet promise in the stillness of the garden. But the second touch, more certain, unraveled all the restraint he had known. The world shrank to this—her warmth, the soft tremor of her breath against his mouth, the brush of silk against his fingertips as his hand slid to the delicate shape of her neck. The distant night sounds of owls and rustling leaves dissolved entirely, leaving only the steady beat of his heart and the intoxicating closeness of her.

When they drew back, the night air kissed their faces, cool and startling in its sharpness. Wendy's eyes held his, her lips curving into a smile so tender it caused a pang deep in his chest. The fountain behind her shimmered, its gentle cascade reflecting the scattered moonlight like fractured diamonds.

"There is nowhere else I would rather be," she said softly, her voice as delicate as a ribbon catching the air.

Stan's lips tugged into a smile, slow and unguarded, a response he had not given anyone in what felt like a lifetime. "Nor I," he replied, his voice rich but laced with quiet sincerity.

Then she closed her eyes.

He reached for her hand, drawing her knuckles to his lips for a lingering kiss before tucking it into the crook of his arm. Together, without urgency, they got up and began to wander down the moonlit path, the neatly trimmed hedges framing their private escape. The night, so still, seemed to hold its breath for them, as though even the stars had gathered to watch.

Chapter Twenty-Four

Harley Street just after ten o'clock at night...

KISSING IN THE carriage turned out to be the best sort of fun and yet it never seemed to be enough, Stan thought. In front of her home, only a short distance from the practice, he helped Wendy down from the carriage, his hand steady beneath hers as they stepped onto the quiet street just down the street from the practice where she now lived with Nick and Pippa. Wendy's lips curved in that soft, determined smile of hers.

"The house seems dark; they are not home yet. Could we stop by the apothecary?" she asked, almost innocently. "I need to find something before I go home."

Stan glanced toward the dark windows of 87 Harley Street, his jaw tightening briefly before he nodded. "Of course."

Thus, they walked in silence, closely together, for about two minutes until they reached the front door of the practice. Inside, the house was eerily quiet, and Stan couldn't shake the prickle of unease along his spine. The dim entryway bore no signs of life; the Langley's were hosting dinner for Nick and Pippa, Alfie and Bea were on honeymoon, and Felix and Andre were scattered between Cloverdale House and their friends at 91 Harley Street probably. Wendy's voice pulled him from his thoughts.

"We're all alone here?" he asked casually, opening the door to 87 Harley Street.

"I think so."

Stan froze as Wendy turned on two gas lights, his breath hitching involuntarily. The sudden brightness flared against a memory—the night he bled out on this very floor. Pain and duty, always intertwined. He said nothing, clenching his fists briefly at his sides to steady himself the shadows in his mind receding only as Wendy's voice reached him again.

Wendy turned right and made her way to the apothecary, pushing the glass-paneled door open without hesitation. Stan followed, his broad figure brushing the frame of the door as he entered and leaned against the counter.

"What are you looking for?" He didn't need to hide his curiosity.

"That—I'm not exactly sure." Wendy began opening the small drawers along the wall, the light glinting off her golden hair as she focused intently on her task.

Stan crossed his arms, one brow lifting slightly. "Is it all right for you to take whatever you need?"

"Oh, yes." She threw him a quick smile over her shoulder. "I just need to mark it in the ledger for Alfie to restock and set the pricing later."

Stan relaxed a bit but kept his eyes on her. "Are you looking for a salve for me, then?"

She paused but didn't meet his gaze, her tone unusually hesitant. "Not exactly."

"And yet, you don't seem to know what it is," he pressed, half-amused, half-bemused.

"I know it's here somewhere," she replied, leaning down to rummage through another set of drawers. "I'll recognize it when I find it."

"Describe it. Perhaps I can help."

Wendy straightened just enough to glance at him briefly before continuing her search. "It has to do with frogs."

Stan arched a brow, a smirk tugging at his lips. "Frogs?"

"Yes, something related to external fertilization." The words left her mouth with such matter-of-fact certainty that Stan's train of thought promptly derailed. He scratched his neck, trying to process her logic.

"What exactly does external fertilization in frogs have to do with me?"

Wendy didn't look up, still engrossed in her search. "There's something here that stops fertilization. Surely, it's in one of these drawers."

Stan frowned, pushing off the counter as he stepped closer, towering over her petite frame as she bent beneath the counter. "Wendy, I am trying, but I don't follow." *He did, of course.* But he needed to make sure she meant what had been on his mind for a while.

"It's all biology," she said simply, as if that explained everything.

"And which part of biology," he replied, his voice dipping, "are we addressing?"

She straightened, still concentrating on the rows of tiny drawers. "I've seen babies born, helped the process even. Stan, I assisted with all kinds of pregnant patients. But I'm not ready for all that myself."

"Birthing a baby?" he asked, as an unfamiliar heat rose in his chest and neck. A few kisses and ices and yes, he knew he was in love, deeply and irrevocably, but how did her mind trail to babies already?

"Not yet. Which is why I need this," she said firmly.

Stan faltered. "Why are you suddenly worried about a baby?" *Perhaps he was the frog prince since his voice resembled a croak now.*

Wendy groaned quietly, tapping one of the drawers closed with more force than necessary before she finally turned to him. "Because... In the carriage." Her cheeks turned the faintest shade of pink.

"The carriage," Stan repeated, his voice thick with skepticism.

"Yes, the carriage. But there's more to come, isn't there?" she leveled him with a look, still not elaborating as her focus darted back to the apothecary shelves.

He folded his arms, studying her closely. "Are you—are you looking for a letter?"

"Yes, it must be an envelope or some folded paper," she said triumphantly. "I expect it's in French. You speak French, don't you?"

Stan sputtered. "A French letter?"

"Yes," Wendy said brightly, as if the revelation solved everything. "Alfie has some here, I know it."

Stan drew a sharp breath, his lips twitching as he wrestled against laughter. "Wendy, you have no idea what a French letter is, do you?"

"Well, obviously you do," she countered. "Have you seen them? Can you translate for me what it says, what to do? Where would he keep them?"

He almost choked unsure whether to laugh or cry. "Wendy…" He pinched the bridge of his nose, his voice shaking with barely restrained laughter. "French letters are not for reading. And they are certainly not about external fertilization of frogs."

"But they don't let fertilization happen in humans. So, it becomes like with fr—" Her expression faltered, her brow creasing as she considered his words. "Then what—erm. How do humans avoid… prevent…" She wrinkled her nose and narrowed her eyes in thought.

Stan exhaled slowly, his voice softening as he stepped closer, cupping her face with an almost reverent tenderness. "Wendy, please listen to me. There's no need to rush toward any of this— babies, letters, or anything beyond what's here and now. And I would never—" his thumb brushed against her cheekbone with quiet promise, "—I will never take what you're not ready to give. No matter what I want."

Before she could reply, a sound broke the stillness—a faint click of the front door.

Wendy's eyes widened, and in an instant, she turned off the gas light, whispering urgently, "Felix and Andre?"

Stan barely had time to react before Wendy grabbed his hand, pulling him through the hall as voices echoed from the entryway. Before he knew it, they were rushing up the darkened staircase, her quick, determined steps leading them to a bedchamber. She pulled the door closed behind them, her breathing soft but quick in the sudden quiet.

Stan stared at her in the faint moonlight streaming through the curtains, torn between shock, amusement, and an undeniable affection for the breathtakingly beautiful, innocent, and brilliant woman standing so resolutely before him—*in her old bed chamber.*

WENDY TURNED THE doorknob with deliberate slowness, her heart pounding in harmony with the muffled voices drifting up from the lower floor. The faintest click of the door closing behind her was soundless to anyone but herself—and to Stan standing so close she could sense the warmth of his presence.

"This is my old bedchamber," she whispered, her voice barely carrying as she tilted her head toward him.

"I know."

Her brows lifted, curiosity chasing back the thrum of her heartbeat. "You do?"

Stan stepped closer, the distance between them narrowing until his body seemed to fill all the air around her. His lips curved faintly, but not with his usual teasing smirk. This was something else—soft, unguarded.

"I've been in love with you far longer than I've admitted, Wendy," he murmured, his voice a low caress that seemed to settle onto her very skin, "but I waited—because wanting you is dangerous. And still I can't stop. I love you, Wendy Folsham. So much!" His breath brushed the shape of her ear, sending a shiver all the way down her spine.

Before she could gather a response, his hands settled at her waist, firm and steady, grounding her and igniting something restless all at once.

"But it's only recently," he continued, dipping his head closer so that her breath caught entirely, "that I gave up trying to resist you. I'd rather try to keep you safe than risk a safe distance from you that might imperil us both."

Her chest seemed to tighten, not in fear, but in anticipation so sharp it almost ached. She barely had time to register the swoop of movement as his hands guided her gently but firmly, turning her to face him fully.

The closeness was intoxicating. Wendy felt her heart stumble, forgetting for a moment the delicate rhythm it was supposed to maintain. Her fingers brushed instinctively against his chest, and the strength beneath her palms was quietly reassuring.

"Do you want me to leave?" he asked softly, his voice a mix of vulnerability and something darker she couldn't quite name.

She shook her head, unable to speak past the lump in her throat.

"Should I take you home?" he asked again, his tone carrying the same low intensity, though his lips pulled into a faint smile.

Again, she shook her head, her voice still refusing to cooperate. Her gaze, however, wandered to his lips, drawn there as if by an invisible force.

He licked his lips.

The motion was nothing if not simple, yet the effect on her was anything but that. Warmth unfurled low in her stomach, curling inward and spreading in waves that made her knees wobble.

A smile teased the corners of his mouth as though he were fully aware of the effect he had on her. He raised a hand, his palm resting against the back of her head, his fingers tangling lightly in her hair before guiding her toward him.

Wendy felt herself dissolve as his mouth met hers.

The kiss was patient yet consuming, like the slow pour of liquid honey. Every brush of his lips against hers unraveled her composure, pulling her deeper into the moment. Her hands gripped the lapels of his coat without thought, anchoring herself as her world narrowed to the soft sound of their breaths mingling and the steady press of his touch.

The floor creaked faintly somewhere down the hall.

Wendy froze, her lips hovering just a whisper away from his as voices filtered faintly through the doorway. Felix and Andre were still talking, their conversation indistinct but close enough to send a jolt through her.

Stan's arm tightened around her waist instinctively, his body tense but unmoving. They stayed locked in place, barely breathing as Andre's louder-than-usual laugh echoed through the quiet house.

Wendy pressed her forehead lightly against Stan's chest, stifling the nervous, fluttery laugh threatening to spill out. His hand traveled to her lower back, a silent reassurance that they remained unseen, unnoticed—safe, for now. But the thrum of their shared moment, the charged current between them, didn't subside.

"They won't come in," she whispered against his chest, the words more for herself than him. "I don't think they know that I am here."

Stan lifted a brow as he met her gaze, heat and mischief flickering in the depths of his dark eyes. Before he could say anything to tease or distract her, she reached up, grabbing the front of his coat and pulling him down closer.

Her lips sought his quickly, desperate to reclaim the kiss they'd so rudely abandoned. He responded instantly. There was nothing tentative now. His fingers slid into her hair as their movements became bolder, though still silent.

Footsteps stirred again beyond the door—retreating, then pausing. Wendy's breath hitched as she caught Stan's gaze mid-kiss. It burned with a challenge, one she couldn't resist any more than she could resist him. When the voices finally faded and a door clicked shut upstairs, Wendy dared to draw back just enough to whisper in his ear.

"Felix and Andre are in their rooms now. Nobody else is on this floor. They can't hear us."

Her cheeks flushed even as she said it, the intimacy of their stolen moment swelling in her chest. This wasn't how it was supposed to be—but it was real. And it was hers. The moonlight sifted in through the thin curtains, but her resolve didn't wane.

Stan didn't reply right away. His gaze held hers, intense and unyielding, before he gave a slow, satisfied smile. The quiet depth of his expression sent a warmth running through her.

Wendy bit her lip and took a careful step backward. She tugged him with her, her lips never quite leaving his as each step lengthened the stretch between them.

He followed her lead anyway, his movements steady even as the tension thickened—that fragile, forbidden sweetness of their secrecy wrapping around them like morning fog.

Her legs hit the edge of the bed, she kissed him again, her hands lingering just a moment longer against his chest before sliding down.

"I won't do anything even close to the things that require a French letter. But if you allow me, Wendy, I'd like to show you something I don't think you know about the human body."

Wendy arched a brow. "Truly?" She whispered.

"You know medicine, functions of physiology. But allow me," he whispered, brushing her hair back, "to show you what it means to be desired—with reverence."

She bit her lip when he said it. And for the first time in her life, Wendy couldn't care less about what came next—only that it was him.

—◆—

Chapter Twenty-Five

WENDY'S CHAMBER WAS quiet save for their faint mingling of breaths and the soft rustle of moonlit shadows chasing each other along the walls. Her old bed, small and intimate, bore the gentle echo of memories now being transformed into something entirely new. Stan stood beside the bed, his gaze riveted on her as if she were a star fallen to earth, lighting the dim space with her very presence.

A nervous laugh caught in Wendy's throat, but his eyes, dark and unwavering, stole the sound before it could escape. He guided her gently backward, his hand warm and firm on her waist as he eased her onto the covers. The care with which he cradled her head as her body met the mattress made her breath hitch—something about Stan's touch was tender enough to make her ache in ways she could hardly put into words.

He hovered above her, a heartbeat of hesitation between them before he dipped his head and brushed his lips softly against her own. One kiss, then another, then another. Each one deeper, slower, unraveling her as if the air had been drawn from the room.

His hand skimmed up her cheek, tangling briefly in her hair before trailing down her throat, his lips following the path of his fingertips. When he reached the base of her neck, his kisses slowed, lingered, and the seductive heat of his breath blossomed over her skin. Stan shifted slightly, his solid chest pressing against hers as he murmured something low, something she couldn't quite make out past the roaring in her ears.

With exquisite care, his hands found the buttons of her pelisse. His fingers worked skillfully, though he took his time, each undone button exposing more of her skin to the cool air and his searching mouth. His lips moved lower, kissing where her dress still covered her, his restraint evident but no less maddening.

"Stan…" she whispered, though whether it was plea or prayer, she couldn't say.

His movements stilled briefly at the sound of his name, his eyes flicking up to hers. She met his gaze, her heart hammering as an unspoken understanding passed between them. Slowly, achingly slowly, he resumed his ministrations, peeling back the fabric as though unwrapping a treasure he'd been waiting his entire life to hold.

When his hands reached the delicate lace of her shift, just above the mounds of her breasts, he paused. His eyes, burning with unspoken devotion, locked with hers once more. Everything about him—his breath, his body—seemed to still as if waiting for permission he dared not ask.

Wendy's own breath hitched as she lifted a hand, trembling slightly, to the back of his head. Her fingers threaded through the dark strands of his hair, and with a delicate but deliberate motion, she urged him downward.

The heat of his mouth bloomed through the fabric as he kissed her above her dress, reverently savoring the moment as his hands found the laces of her gown. The ribbon yielded easily, the practical simplicity of her dress offering no resistance to Stan's careful undoing. The sensation of his fingers brushing against her bare skin as he unfastened the bodice was electric, sending tremors through her body that made her toes curl.

And that gave her a pang of courage.

She became brazen even—not because she'd forgotten the risks, but because for once, she chose herself.

Not to do the unspeakable but to take as much from him as he was willing to give.

When the last lace was undone, he paused, taking a deep, measured breath as the garment fell open, revealing her stays and corset under her sheer chemise.

"You're so beautiful," he whispered, his voice rough with something deeper than desire. His hands slid gently down her sides, and he leaned forward, pressing a kiss to her collarbone, then lower, and lower still.

Wendy's breath caught as his hungry black eyes roamed over her, devouring her every curve like she was the only thing that could sate him. The heat of his gaze burned through her, leaving her trembling, her pulse pounding in time with his touch.

The first brush of his lips against her now-bare skin was fire. Stan kissed her breasts with a tenderness that unraveled her entirely, his warm mouth exploring her curves as though committing them to memory. When his lips closed over her nipple, Wendy arched into him, the sensation pulling a soft gasp from her lips she hadn't meant to utter.

The sound seemed to unravel him. Stan groaned low in his throat, the reverberation of it against her skin heightening the exquisite sensitivity of her body. His hands, strong and deliberate, cradled her hips as he continued his careful attentions, his mouth worshiping her chest with no doubt about the depth of his devotion to her.

She knew this couldn't last. But she brushed any thoughts aside.

This was her moment to revel in her prince.

For now. Just tonight.

Because if she thought of what might come after—of what she might lose—she'd never let herself feel this.

Wendy's hands found his shoulders, gripping tightly as he drove her further into the intoxicating haze of his touch. For once, her mind was utterly blank, her world narrowing to the press of his lips, the sweep of his breath, and the steady, grounding presence of him above her. It was too much and not enough, all at once.

Stan never rushed; each kiss, each touch carrying an almost excruciating patience that made her feel treasured, adored—a sensation so profound, it brought tears to her eyes as she lifted her head to meet his gaze once more. His breeches remained on, but the hard press of his arousal against her hip made her acutely aware of just how much this restraint cost him.

Stan's lips curved faintly as though he could hear her silent realization, and he kissed her once more, his tongue tracing slow, languid patterns against her skin before he drew back just enough to speak.

"You're everything, Wendy," he breathed, his voice husky and unsteady. "You'll always be if you allow it."

Her answer came not in words but in the way she reached for him, pulling him down to kiss him fiercely, her own walls crumbling completely in light of everything she couldn't yet say.

And in the stillness of her old room, as the moonlight bathed them both, the rest of the world melted away.

⟫⟫⟫⟨⟨⟨⟨

STAN COULDN'T BELIEVE how perfect she was. It was almost impossible to separate the image of the fiery, brilliant nurse he knew with the impossibly soft, glowing woman lying beneath him now. If she hadn't saved his life, he would have never had a chance to experience *her*. List had brought him pain, but he had also led him here. To her.

She was his calling. And she was his weakness.

He'd imagined this—oh, how he'd imagined it—on those endless hours spent watching her work in quiet fascination. He'd dreamed of tugging at the white apron ties she wore so effortlessly, of pulling her flush against him and finally knowing the way her body fit to his. But even in his wildest imaginings, what lay beneath those simple dresses was a level of beauty he could never have anticipated. And now that he had her, he feared the cost. How long could he stay in London, keep her safe from the demands pressing in on all sides?

She was exquisite, soft, and radiant in the dim light filtering through the curtains. Each newly exposed inch of her skin stole the air from his lungs, her trust in him written in every curve, every fluttering breath. And as much as he longed to claim her fully, greedily, this wasn't about him. Not now. This was about her—her pleasure, her discovery, her peak.

Her first time to trust him with this.

And if he knew one thing as a prince, it was not to disappoint people who put their faith in him.

Breaking their kiss, Stan stood smoothly, his knees brushing the side of the bed as he began to shrug off his coat. The material slipped from his shoulders and landed in a heap at his feet. His fingers found the buttons of his shirt next, undoing them deftly despite the tremor in his hands. He tugged the shirt free and tossed it aside, exhaling deeply as the cool air met his skin.

His boots followed, kicked off with a haste that delayed none of his purpose. But as much as he longed to shed everything, he stopped purposefully at his breeches. They stayed on—for safety, for respect, for control. He didn't trust himself to take them off, not with her looking at him like that, her lips swollen from his kisses and her chest rising and falling with soft, shallow breaths.

She was everything he'd tried not to want—soft, good, and impossibly brave. And he worshipped her not just for her body, but for trusting him with it.

Wendy was everything he'd tried not to want—soft, good, impossibly brave. And the deeper he fell, the harder it would be to let go.

Despite the restraint he showed elsewhere, what flooded through him as he returned to the bed, lowering himself beside her, was anything but restrained.

"Wendy," he murmured, the hoarseness in his voice making her eyes flutter open to meet his gaze. Her name was reverence, worship, a whispered prayer against the backdrop of the vulnerability between them.

She didn't speak, but she didn't need to. The way her lips softened, the way her hand timidly reached for him, fingers brushing his jaw before slipping to his shoulder—it was answer enough.

His hands found her waist, sliding down and around with deliberate slowness, memorizing the curves he'd only dreamed of touching before. He leaned forward, pressing a kiss to her collarbone and lingering there.

The rustle of the sheets created a quiet song beneath them as they tried to remain as silent as possible—a reminder that they weren't entirely alone in the house. Even as her hands found their way to his hair, gripping softly, and her body instinctively arched toward him, that knowledge lingered in the back of his mind. He didn't resist it. Instead, the fear of being overheard, the necessity of holding back—the secrecy—only made it all the more intoxicating.

When his lips trailed lower, skimming the delicate column of her throat with featherlight kisses, her fingers tightened instinctively in his hair. Stan couldn't suppress the smile tugging at his lips against her skin. She was holding back, too—doing her best to stay quiet even as her body betrayed her.

He kissed a trail downward, following the soft curve of her chest now barely covered by her loosened bodice. When his lips found the barest edge of fabric, his restraint grew taut. Instead of urging the material away immediately, he kissed the line where her skin met cloth, teasing her with the knowledge of what was to come.

She whimpered softly, the sound escaping in a breathless gust, and his body tightened in response. Every nerve in him was screaming for more, begging to shed that last scrap of modesty that stood between them. But instead of yielding to that primal urge, he drew on every ounce of self-control he possessed.

"Patience," he whispered, though whether he said it for her

or for himself, he couldn't say.

The word hung between them, electric and unspoken, and she sat up a little so that he could slowly peeled the remaining fabric away.

When her skin was bare beneath him, he paused, eyes roaming over her with an unhidden awe. His breath caught. He hadn't prepared for this—not truly. She was so beautiful it ached. But as his eyes met hers, something shifted.

She looked at him, and suddenly it wasn't about him anymore.

WENDY COULDN'T THINK. Every touch was a distraction, every kiss an invitation to abandon the logic she clung to. She shifted slightly under his gaze, but when her eyes met his, there was no mistaking her trust, her longing for him.

Her thoughts spun: the deeper she fell for him, the harder it would be to choose. And yet, what choice did she have? Nick. Cloverdale. The practice. Her life in London wasn't negotiable. But her heart—her heart didn't know that.

"Perfect," he breathed. The word broke from him like a revelation, his fingertips trailing reverently down her sides as though relearning what he had yet to touch.

His lips resumed their path, dipping to the sensitive swell of her belly, where soft sighs escaped her lips in time with his kisses. She twirled her fingers through his hair, as if she wanted to guide him on his path down. Lower—slower still—his lips dipped, each touch deliberate and gentle, igniting her skin in a way—he thought—she hadn't known before.

Stan steadied himself, his hands firm at Wendy's hips as she moved beneath him, her body completely abandoning the restraint she seemed to fight to hold onto. The way her fingers clung to his shoulders, pressing almost desperately into the hard muscle there, sent a torrent of sensation coursing through him. There was something primal, raw, and fierce in the way she held onto him—like he was her anchor.

But all Wendy could think was: how long did they have? Would he be sent away? Would duty call him back to fight List, to protect his country, to fulfill some prince's obligation she'd never be able to follow?

Her reactions were mesmerizing, drawing him into a trance he couldn't escape and wouldn't want to, even if he could. Her body trembled and writhed in his hands, the smooth curve of her back arching toward him like a supplicant drawn to something divine. The sound of her breath, shallow and uneven, filled the quiet room, each little gasp and whimper like a spark igniting the wildfire that burned within him. Every shift, every quiver, was a revelation—a language without words in which he was becoming fluent, one whispered sigh at a time.

"I didn't know…" she whispered.

"That it feels like this?"

"That my body could do this." She closed her eyes and let him continue.

He felt the heat of her body beneath his palms, the delicate tremble of her thighs against his shoulders. The tension in her muscles thrummed against his fingertips as if she teetered on the very edge of something impossible. But what undid him most was the audible evidence of her restraint—the small, ragged breaths that didn't quite become moans, each one bitten back in an effort to remain silent. They couldn't be caught; he knew it as well as she did. But the secrecy of it all, the fragility of this stolen moment, only heightened the intensity.

He paused, his breath warm against her, and the sound of her gasp—soft but nearly broken—washed over him. He couldn't drag his eyes away from her, couldn't stop himself from memorizing the way her hips lifted instinctively toward him, chasing whatever he gave her without hesitation. She was fire incarnate beneath his hands, molten and honest, her body moving with a rhythm that sang only of need. The sight of her—bare and unguarded there in the moonlight—was more than he could have prepared for.

When he lowered his mouth again, the silken warmth of her folds spoiled him, ruined him entirely. He moved deliberately, each touch of his tongue as calculated as it was reverent, knowing exactly how to draw those trembling, feather-like gasps from her lips. Her taste, the softness of her skin pressing against his mouth—it was everything he hadn't allowed himself to imagine. He closed his eyes for a moment, letting himself be consumed, seized by the enormity of their intimacy, by the quiet sounds she made, so much louder in their stolen silence.

Her thighs pressed closer around him in helpless reaction, her body shifting as though it had a mind of its own, surrendering to the inevitable. He felt her fingers in his hair, the way they dug in, as though desperate to keep him there. He tilted his head slightly, the faint graze of his stubble brushing against her vulnerable skin, and the way her body trembled in response sent a jolt of something unbearably sweet and wild straight through him.

That soft, breathless whisper of his name—"Stan..."—rose from her lips, and it was all he could do not to lose himself entirely. He didn't need her to say anything more than that, didn't need any other affirmation but those two syllables trembling in the air between them. It carried everything—her trust, her longing, her belief that he was exactly who she needed at that moment.

For a moment, he lifted his eyes. Tasting her, he licked his lips, and she lifted her head.

This was a meeting of minds, hearts, and soul. Her eyes were black, her mouth parted, and her chest rising and falling with needy gasps.

He answered not with words but with action as he dipped back down. His hands steadied her hips, anchoring her as her body threatened to arch beyond his grasp. His movements remained steady, slow, maddeningly precise, drawing from her the kind of whimpers and half-sounds that would be loud enough to awaken the entire house if she didn't fight to contain them. But oh, how glorious her restraint made it—the way she burned under his deliberate touch yet refused to break. He marveled at her, utterly entranced by her strength, her vulnerability, her beauty.

What if this moment—this breathtaking, trembling now—was all they would ever have? What if he left? What if this, right here, was her only memory of him?

"Tell me what you like," he spoke against her folds.

"I don't know," she cried, ashamed of her inexperience but too overcome to hide it. Every brush of his fingers unraveled what little composure she had left, and still she feared what surrender might cost her. What if this moment—this breathtaking, trembling now—was all they would ever have? What if, in a few day, Stan was gone and everything between them was reduced to a memory too dangerous to revisit? Her body cried yes even as her heart begged her not to fall further.

"This?" Stan teased her pearl with his index finger.

"Deeper." Her voice came forced.

And so, he inserted one finger.

"More!" she cried.

He inserted another. She arched into his hand, and he nearly lost himself when he felt her warm and wet tightness twitching against his hand with need. "Stan!" Her breaths quickened, shallow and sharp, her chest rising and falling in uneven bursts that made an unshakable satisfaction settle deep within him.

"Here, my love," he said, his voice raw with reverence, inserting a third finger and settling his thumb over her pearl. He came back to face her, and she grabbed his head, pressing her mouth against his. Their kiss was deep and open, swallowing her cries in the darkness of the night. The fire building within her was unmistakable, vibrating against him like the hum of something alive and untamed. He felt her inching toward release, the tension in her body coiling impossibly tight. Yet still, he refused to rush;

he refused to do anything but savor her every subtle shift and shake.

She moved involuntarily, her head tossing to the side, her hands tangling in the sheets beneath her, searching for something, anything, to hold onto. To him, she was devastating—utterly, heartbreakingly beautiful. The soft, restrained cries she fought to contain filled the room like the most beautiful symphony. He had memorized so many details about her before this, but he committed this, this sacred moment, to memory with the reverence only a man who knew he'd been forever changed could feel.

Their world narrowed to this single, shattering connection. Every glance, every touch, every whispered breath spoke volumes, weaving an unspoken trust and devotion that eclipsed the need for words. Wendy's eyes caught his, luminous with vulnerability and wonder, and in that exchange, Stan felt the earth shift. She was a constellation of light and fire in his arms, and he, a man who had never quite believed in redemption, found himself humbled, worshipful, and utterly hers.

Her trembling hand rose, brushing against his cheek as if memorizing the lines of his face in the twilight. "Stan," she mouthed, her voice breaking as if it carried her. It wasn't a cry of surrender—it was a claim. He was hers now, whether she dared believe it or not.

He caught her fingers, pressed his lips to her palm, and closed his eyes as if to preserve the memory forever. This wasn't merely the height of pleasure; it was something infinite, unyielding, a release tempered by awe. Their barriers, fears, and pasts seemed to dissolve in that tender collision of hearts and spirits. Whatever they had been before mattered little; together, they were something new, something extraordinary, something unbreakable.

It left him raw. The need to remain quiet, the tense secrecy of it all, made this moment burn brighter, sharper, and more unforgettable. His name on her lips, the tremble in her hands, the way she trusted and gave herself to him—it was everything. This was theirs alone, a fragile and precious thing born of whispered secrets and moonlit surrender. And as he moved in deliberate, steady reverence, Stan knew he would carry this moment, this connection, with him for the rest of his life.

$$\textit{Chapter Twenty-Six}$$

BIRDS CHIRPED AND there was noise coming from the street. Wendy blinked against the pale gray morning light filtering through the worn lace curtains. Her mind was sluggish, heavy with the lingering fog of sleep. She squinted toward the window and noticed condensation on the glass, a faint trail where cold air kissed its surface. A shiver ran down her spine, and she instinctively tugged at the covers, comforted by their weight as she buried herself within them.

Then, she froze.

There was a sound—voices, faint but distinct, traveling up from downstairs. Her heart stuttered. Something about it rang familiar. She scanned the room quickly, each object settling into place as recognition dawned with startling speed. The dresser. The quilt. The faint scratch above the doorframe.

This wasn't just any room. This was her *old* room.

Her eyes widened, the realization sending her bolt upright. The covers slipped slightly, exposing her bare shoulders to the cool air, and her startled gaze landed on the form beside her.

Stan.

He was sprawled on his side, unmoving save for the steady rise and fall of his chest. His face was perfectly calm, a boyish serenity softening the strong line of his jaw. There was an innocence in his expression, so at odds with the wickedly consuming man he'd been the night before.

Oh. The memory slammed into her, vivid and clear, making her skin flush hot despite the chill in the room.

"When did I fall asleep?" she whispered to no one in particular, tugging the end of the blanket higher. Her movements must have stirred him. He groaned softly, his voice rough with sleep as he shifted and rolled closer.

"Stan!" she hissed, attempting to tug the blanket away from him without dislodging it further from herself.

He mumbled incoherently and reached for her, his arm looping around her waist with a lazy confidence. Then he pulled her in, his warmth enveloping her like a furnace. That's when Wendy noticed—became painfully aware, actually—that she was completely, utterly, and irrevocably naked.

Her entire body tensed.

And she realized a soreness in her middle. That was new.

Meanwhile, Stan remained blissfully oblivious, tucked under her blanket, her only shield of modesty. He, on the other hand, was fully clothed—or nearly so. He lay on top of the quilt, his broad chest brushing hers, radiating warmth like a furnace.

"Stan, wake up!" she demanded, keeping her voice low but sharp as her embarrassment spiked.

He groaned again. "Hmm?" Barely coherent, his grip tightened, and his face burrowed against her as though he had every right to remain in a world where nothing else mattered but holding her.

"Wake. Up," she tried again, her voice a hurried mix of urgency and exasperation.

"If you insist," he muttered, sleepily grinning against her skin before slowly pulling himself upright. The blanket twisted with his movements, threatening to betray her further. Her mortification deepened when his shirt budged, revealing a glimpse of his deeply tanned chest—a chest that would put any carved marble sculpture to shame.

She shook her head firmly. Not now. This was no time to

admire him!

Wendy nearly giggled at the stray thought, but another sound caught her attention. She froze again, then scrambled out of bed, clutching the blanket, and dragging it around her like a makeshift cloak. Her bare feet hit the wooden floor, chilly against her skin, and she padded quickly to the window.

Peering out, she saw movement below.

Oh no!

Nick and Alfie were directing a carriage, their arms waving wildly as they attempted to guide the driver closer to the house. Just behind them, she noticed Andre hoisting a trunk over one shoulder with casual ease. The realization struck her just as a startled gasp caught in her throat.

"Stan! They're moving supplies to Cloverdale!" she exclaimed, whipping her head toward him.

His response was sluggish at best. He sat up slowly, rubbing the sleep from his eyes, and muttered groggily, "Good morning, my beautiful love." His voice—low and unrefined—sent an involuntary shiver through her. She might have melted at the sound of it—if her heart weren't already tangled in dread. Because now that the night was over, reality was here, and it had sharp teeth. What if this moment unraveled everything she'd fought to build? What if one whispered truth, overheard or guessed, cost them both everything?

"Stan!" she barked, refusing to be distracted by his tousled hair and endearing sleepiness, or the thrill of hearing him call her "my love."

He stretched lazily, cocking one eyebrow as if amused by her frantic state. "Wendy, what time is it?"

"Look!" She waved frantically toward the window, willing him to catch up with the gravity of the situation. Stan's shirt and much of her clothes lay on a pile on the floor.

At last, Stan dragged himself to his feet. Standing there in nothing but his crumpled breeches, he looked far too smug for her liking. He wandered closer, raking a hand through his already messy hair, and leaned casually against the window frame, completely unconcerned by the commotion below.

"They're moving medical supplies," Wendy hissed, stalking back toward him. The blanket trailed behind her like the world's most awkward train. "To Cloverdale. They're all here! Awake!"

Stan only grinned wider and crossed his arms, his casual composure as frustrating as it was unshakably charming.

It was going to be a very long morning.

STAN'S HEAD SHOT up, his heart slamming into his ribs at the distant sound of voices wafting up from downstairs. For a moment, his mind blanked before realization struck him like a cold slap. Nick was here. Oh no, Nick.

No, no, no!

He ran a hand through his already messy hair and scrambled for his shirt, the wooden floorboards cold beneath his bare feet as he began pacing. "I can't get out unseen," he hissed, glancing back toward Wendy, who was clutching a blanket so tightly to her chest that she looked ready to fuse with it.

"Yes!" she replied, not helpfully, her eyes wide and filled with an emotion he was pretty sure mirrored his own. Panic. Great, all-consuming panic.

They froze for a moment, listening. The muffled murmur of voices faded slightly, replaced by the heavy creak of wagon wheels and the clatter of boots. From the sound of it, one carriage had been loaded and left.

"Perhaps they're waiting for the next one," Wendy whispered, hovering by the window now, her toe sneaking out from under the blanket to lightly tap the floor. Her voice wavered, betraying an optimism even she didn't believe. "They're probably inside now."

He wasn't willing to bet on "probably." Stan peered past her, glancing out the window and noting the distance to the ground below. Not insurmountable. His gaze moved to the horizon, where his rented carriage was parked beyond the turn of the street, looking abandoned.

"I'm going out the window," he declared, moving with purpose toward it. *He'll kill me just as I would a man who touched my sister.*

Stan suppressed an inward smirk. *But that touching, oh that was so good.*

"Stan!" Wendy's voice pitched higher, equal parts disbelief and exasperation.

"Look," he said, swinging the window open and sticking his head out into the bracing morning air. The crisp breeze bit into him, but he waved it off. "My carriage is just around the corner. My driver must have fallen asleep. I'll get his attention."

She folded her arms, the blanket slipping precariously low on one shoulder, though she seemed not to notice. "Do you have much practice sneaking out of women's rooms in the morning?"

He glanced over his shoulder with a cocked brow. "No, but I have climbed down from Bran Castle, which is perched on a mountain. This?" He gestured at the modest drop to the ground below, "is child's play."

Wendy opened her mouth—probably to argue—but he didn't give her the chance. He swung his legs through the window frame. The slight groan of the wooden sill beneath him was the only hesitation he allowed himself. "One story up," he muttered under his breath. "I can drop onto the horse. Probably."

"Probably?!" Wendy's disbelief followed him as he carefully maneuvered to the ledge, his fingers gripping the edge tightly.

But just as he adjusted his stance, a new voice reached his ears—soft but insistent. "I'm going with you."

He craned his neck, blinking up at her in utter confusion. "What? Why?"

Her cheeks flushed, though she kept her chin high. "Because if I'm found here, it won't matter what excuse I give. Do you think anyone will believe I came to your room to discuss the weather? Or that I simply got lost on my way to the library?" She sighed. "And I don't want Nick to find out like this. I want to tell him about us properly."

Stan opened his mouth, then closed it again. She had a point. "All right, fine," he muttered quickly, now more concerned with the quickly collapsing timeline than with logic itself. "Wait until I bring the horse closer. I'll catch you."

Before she could counter with another protest, he dropped down, landing with a dull thud that shot up his knees but didn't quite dampen his pride. He stood, brushing his hands off against his breeches as he scanned the area.

And then he froze.

Around the corner, stepping out into full, damning view, were four men. Felix. Alfie. André. And Nick.

Each of them stared directly at him, their expressions ranging from wide-eyed shock to pointed disapproval. Nick, in particular, looked less surprised and more sharply annoyed in a protective, big-brother sort of way.

Stan swallowed hard.

There it was—the look. That look. The one that said: You've taken what you shouldn't have. And now you'll answer for it. Not with swords, but with silence. With exile. With the cold severing of trust from a man who had always kept Wendy safe—Nick— and might now decide Stan couldn't.

He cursed under his breath. He'd been caught.

For a moment that stretched a little too long, no one moved. Even the morning seemed to pause, holding its breath for what would come next.

"Good morning," Stan said, his voice forced into a feigned and utterly unconvincing calm. He gave the smallest, most awkward of nods, which went unreturned.

Nick's eyes narrowed. Alfie smirked. André crossed his arms and cleared his throat. Felix adjusted his gloves, looking like he was ready to start sharpening knives.

And then—another sound. The faint scuffle of feet above. Wendy.

Stan's head jerked upward just in time to see her climbing out the window, the blanket still tangled around her. He stepped forward instinctively. "Careful!"

Her hair tumbled into her face, the blanket slipping lower than was proper. Her face went white, then red, then white again as she looked down.

"Oh no!" Wendy said faintly from above.

Silence. Four very male, very judgmental stares.

Nick's gaze moved from Stan to Wendy dangling from the open window above them. Then back again. Slowly. "You have thirty seconds to explain," he said, his voice quiet. Which was worse than shouting. So much worse.

Wendy's voice cracked as she tried to summon words. "It's not—it's not what it looks like."

Stan, standing half in front of her now, glanced sideways at her, then back at Nick. "No," he said quietly. "It's exactly what it looks like."

Nothing could possibly go right with this.

Absolutely nothing.

Chapter Twenty-Seven

THE EARLY LIGHT revealed too much—his unbuttoned coat, his disheveled cravat, and likely the flush of a man who had just climbed down from a lady's window. He straightened his spine, meeting Wendy's brother and his band of allies directly. There wasn't much left of his dignity, but he'd spend every last scrap fighting for hers.

"I know what this looks like," he began, his voice even, though his chest tightened with every second Nick's cold, unyielding gaze stayed locked on him.

Nick tilted his head, his expression as clear as a loud sermon in a silent chapel. He wasn't looking at Stan as royalty, a prince, or even as an equal. He looked at Stan like a common thief—one who had dared to enter his house to steal a treasure: his sister Wendy.

It was true, wasn't it?

Stan dragged his gaze away from Nick's hard stare to Alfie. He was supposed to be still basking in that warm newlywed glow of love that softened other edges. But no. Alfie's mouth was a grim line, his eyes sharp and contemplative. It was a gaze Stan recognized all too well—the same look Alfie had the night he measured out drops of truth serum with chilling precision to extract information from Baron von List. Alfie had weighed that decision then, and Stan could sense he was weighing something now. Only this time, Stan realized, Alfie appeared to see *him* as the threat.

Stan swallowed and looked next to Felix. Quiet, steady dentist Felix. Reliable, even soothing, until you put tools in his hands. The thought made Stan's palms sweat. Felix looked as calm as always, though his lips pressed together tightly, his gloved fingers curling lightly at his sides. Stan didn't need to guess what he was thinking—Felix's gaze was sharp as a scalpel and full of warning. A man who carved teeth and hammered gold into them for a living clearly didn't mind a bit of blood if necessary.

"I have a sister, too," Stan said into the charged silence, his voice steady despite the tension curdling in his gut. "I know what you must be thinking."

Andre, standing at Felix's side, tilted his head and arched a single dark brow, as though to say, *Do you now?* Stan's jaw tightened, but before he could try again, Nick cut in, his voice like a blade.

"Wendy didn't come home last night." He wasn't speaking to Stan. He didn't even look at him. Instead, he spoke to Alfie, Felix, and Andre as though laying out evidence in a courtroom. But each word hit Stan hard enough to stagger him. "I thought she was looking after patients at Cloverdale House."

All four men turned their heads in unison, gazes snapping to Wendy's window above. Stan's pulse thundered in his ears. He followed their stares, though every fiber of his body told him not to.

Then he saw it.

A slender leg—perfect, undeniably feminine—emerged from behind the curtain, clad in nothing more than the sheer sheen of stockings. Her foot slid, audacious and teasing, against the brick wall as though searching for a steady foothold. His breath halted somewhere between his chest and throat, the sound catching faintly.

All at once, the air seemed to buzz with disbelief. Nick's sharp intake of breath punctuated the moment like a musket shot; his boots scraped against the gravel, grounding him as though preparing for battle. Stan fought the urge to step back, the sound alone thick with the promise of judgment. But then Nick froze, motionless as a statue carved from righteous fury, and his eyes—all their eyes—stayed glued upward.

Stan knew better than to follow their gaze this time, though curiosity pulled at him like a fisherman's net. He already half guessed what they were seeing. He just didn't want to confirm it.

"Oh, bloody—" Alfie's mutter cut the tension, sharp but low, his expression a half-step between alarm and exasperation.

Felix tilted his head, one gloved hand hovering near his face as though to shield his eyes—or perhaps his dignity—as the movement above caught the light. "Is she…?" he murmured, but his voice trailed off as Andre, too, leaned forward for a better view.

For a moment, the only sound was the faint scuff of silk on brick as Wendy—*Wendy!*—hooked her foot against the wall, the dainty toe of her stocking catching, slipping, catching again, refusing to stay still.

Nick's hand shot out, jabbing toward the window, his face twisting as words finally boiled to the surface. "What in the devil's name is she doing?!" It wasn't so much a question as an accusation hurled at the group around him, as though he had somehow convinced his sister to clamber out of a second-story window.

"She's climbing, I think," Andre supplied dryly, his voice lined with equal parts amusement and disbelief. He crossed his arms and watched, almost intrigued, as Wendy's other leg appeared, pressing against the brick in an awkward attempt at maneuvering. She wiggled farther out—too far, in Nick's mind, judging by the controlled snarl that escaped him.

"Gwendolyn Folsham—if you step *one inch* more—!" Nick's voice rang out, brittle with a fury so tightly restrained it nearly shook. Whatever was left of his composure threatened to snap as he turned, throwing Stan a look so venomous, it burned. "*This* is your fault."

Stan opened his mouth, floundered, and closed it again. He tried not to wince as Wendy, above them all, raised an arm—was she waving?!—as though utterly impervious to the storm brewing below her.

"I'm going to fetch her," Felix called as he darted into the house, remarkably calm, though his brow furrowed as if silently judging just how far Wendy would fall if her grip slipped.

"Or perhaps a straitjacket before Nick throttles someone?" Andre said, walking closer to the wall, as if he were estimating where she might fall—if not from the second floor, then surely from grace.

There was no question in their minds, she'd fall. And if—no, when—she got hurt, it would all be Stan's fault.

"I'll throttle you if you don't stop enjoying this," Nick snapped, turning back to the scene above, his arms flailing in something caught between despair and rage. "Wendy! Get back inside this instant!"

Her answer came in the form of another wiggle, more determined this time, that sent her skirts shifting precariously against her legs. The slight flash of skin underneath shot through the group like a lit fuse, and Nick visibly reddened—though it was hard to tell if it stemmed more from anger or embarrassment. "I *swear*—" Nick's mutter dissolved into incoherent sputtering before his voice rose again. "Tell her to stop!" he barked at no one in particular.

"She's your sister," Alfie quipped, his tone far too relaxed for the moment as he leaned just slightly away from the inevitable eruption. "I think that's your job."

Nick whirled around, pointing an accusing finger at Stan, his face thunderous. "*You!* What did you do to her?!" His voice practically cracked under the pressure of sheer, unbridled protective instinct. "If she falls, I'll—"

But no one finished the sentence. Because at that very moment, Wendy paused her descent just long enough to glance downward at all of them—a shy little tilt of her head, her hair spilling over one shoulder like innocent curls on a child, though there was nothing innocent about the way she dangled there, smug as a cat who'd caused a vase to fall.

Stan should have protested. He should have spoken, thrown himself on what little mercy existed, or even tried to offer an explanation. Yet, all he managed to do was stare, his chest tight with some unnamable blend of concern and outright admiration. Because when Wendy grinned—a flash of delight that dared everyone below to *stop her*—he knew that no one, not even Nick, had a chance of reining her in.

WENDY GRIPPED THE windowsill, her fingers curling tight against the cold wood. It *felt* higher from here, far higher than it had seemed when she'd looked at the same spot from the safety of the sidewalk. Her stomach shifted uneasily, a hollowness settling in as she glanced down. The air seemed thinner up here, and the sudden rush of nerves prickled along her arms. This was probably not wise. But it was decidedly too late to reconsider how to go about this.

Her foot scrabbled against the brick outside, the smooth stockings proving of no help. She winced as the abrasive surface scraped her toes. Her ears caught the faint murmur of voices from below, though the words were too distant to make sense. Wendy adjusted her grip on the window frame, her gaze dropping cautiously—and then she froze.

She only expected to see Stan.

Instead, there was Nick? Alfie? Andre? And *Felix*?

Her stomach clenched, a mix of panic and disbelief rushing through her in equal measure. What on earth were *all* of them doing there?

Her fingers tightened on the sill as her eyes darted from one familiar face to another. Nick's rigid posture radiated authority;

his arms crossed in a way that transformed his disapproval into a weapon. Beside him, Alfie appeared equally angry, though his expression was sharper, as if he were calculating exactly how much of his scorn she deserved for this spectacle. Andre stood closer to the wall, directly below her, his mouth twitching as if tempted to smile but too puzzled by her presence to do so. But it was Felix—Felix!—whose calm demeanor sent a fresh wave of mortification through her. He tilted his head slightly, observing her with an unruffled air, his lips pressed into a thin line of quiet judgment.

And then her eyes found Stan. The one person who shouldn't have been caught in the shadows of their fury. He was standing a little apart from the group, his shoulders taut and his face a portrait of guilty concern. Was he afraid to meet her gaze—or terrified of Nick? She couldn't decide, and the nervous energy bubbling inside her wasn't helping.

Wendy blinked rapidly, heat rushing to her cheeks. She'd prepared herself mentally for Stan's part in this chaos. She hadn't accounted for a full jury watching her, ready to tally her sins.

Andre came nearer until he was directly below her. Was he bracing himself? Oh dear, did he truly expect to catch her? She blinked down at him, then at Nick, who was gesticulating wildly and shouting, though she still couldn't quite hear him over her throbbing heartbeat. And Stan, her handsomely disheveled Stan, looked… helpless. He stared up at her as though he wanted to climb up himself but didn't quite trust the scenery.

Wendy opened her mouth to say something—anything, really—to ease the tension or, perhaps, to bolster her own resolve. But before she could, a firm hand shot out, grasping her wrist with enough strength to anchor her in place. She turned her head just in time to glimpse Felix stepping halfway into the room and rushing toward her, one hand gripping her arm, the other snatching the back of her gown like she was an unruly child caught at the edge of a pond.

"Wendy."

The voice carried nothing of the chaos from below. It was calm, decisive. And frustratingly familiar.

"What on earth are you doing?" she spluttered, trying to twist away. Her grip on the windowsill tightened to counterbalance the awkward tug. She didn't want to get caught, not by Nick, not Felix, not any of them. Just this once she wanted to speak to them about being a grown woman in love and not the little sister in need of protection.

"Saving your sorry, pretty face from plummeting to the gravel," Felix replied evenly, though his tone carried a distinct lack of patience.

"Don't!" *But, yes please!*

"Do you know what your face would look like after a fall from this height? Because I do. Teeth smashed, jaw tilted at an unnatural angle, a set of injuries that *I'd* be tasked with fixing, mind you."

Wendy froze at his words, the sting of their imagery rooting her in place for just a moment. She craned her neck to glance down again, her stomach flipping as the ground beneath her seemed to tilt precariously.

"It's not that high," she lied, her voice soft and doubtful even to her own ears.

Felix snorted. "It's high enough." Then, swiftly and unceremoniously, he pulled her back through the window, wrenching her balance loose before she had the presence of mind to protest. Her feet scraped along the wall, slipping in her stockings as Felix's arms locked around her, one beneath each of her arms. Without ceremony, he lifted her like he had when she was a little girl, planting her firmly on her bed.

Her heart pounded as she steadied herself, blinking up at Felix as he stood over her, panting just slightly but with the faintest trace of a frown between his brows.

"You almost fell," he said, the words so soft they held more weight than any of the shouting from below.

"I didn't," she corrected with a stubborn little spark. But even as she said it, her voice wavered, and she winced. Wendy looked at his face, his eyes warm despite their sternness, and she felt something unexpected—a pang she hadn't recognized in a long time. She was like that little girl again, the one who believed Felix could fix nearly any scrape.

"You fell, though, didn't you? The other kind of falling, I mean." His voice shifted, quieter now, the sharp edges softening. Felix crouched before her, his dark eyes searching hers as he took her hands in his much larger, steadier ones. His grip was light, but unwavering, as though to shield her from anything that might try to break her further.

Wendy's throat tightened. A knot formed slowly, climbing upward until her lips trembled and her vision blurred at the edges. "Very much," she admitted, the words unspooling faster than her mind had time to stop them. She sniffed and blinked a tear away stubbornly.

Felix exhaled and looked down for a brief moment, his head shaking just slightly. "You're in love with the prince," he said matter-of-factly. It wasn't a question. He lifted her hands a little, folding them together carefully between his palms as though he could somehow cradle her heart there along with them.

Wendy's lips parted to protest, but she knew that whatever she said she wouldn't believe herself. Instead of replying, she gazed at his face. He knew—he *always* knew—long before she did. It must be the prerogative of a man who once loved with body and soul, as he usually said, and then lost. And for all his frowning and lecturing, Felix was still here, holding her steady. His lost love was a cautionary tale, and Wendy knew in that moment that she wouldn't—*couldn't*—let Stan go.

Chapter Twenty-Eight

FOOTSTEPS POUNDED AGAINST the floorboards in the hallway, each stomp sending a jolt through Wendy's chest. Nick's voice, sharp as a razor and rising with purpose, grew louder. She clutched Felix's hands reflexively.

Felix didn't flinch. He didn't even look at the door. Instead, his eyes held hers like a lifeline. He gave her fingers a firm squeeze. "Whatever comes through that door," he said, his voice low but brimming with sincerity, "know this—I'm here for you. Always. Right by your side."

Those words pierced something in her. Wendy blinked, but it was useless; the first tear slid down her cheek as more threatened to follow. Felix reached up, brushing the trail away with his thumb with the gentleness of someone who had seen her grow from scraped knees to heartbreak.

"Listen to me, Wendy." He shifted closer, his broad shoulders framing her, shielding her from some unseen storm. "If you're truly in love—if this is the kind that only comes once in a life—you fight for it. Do you hear me? Fight for it with everything you have. Because if you don't..." His voice wavered just slightly, heavy with his own unspoken memories. "If you don't, the regret will be something you'll carry forever like me."

The weight of his words hit her like a crashing wave. He understood that sort of thing. He had loved and lost, and he never quite recovered.

The knot in her throat tightened, and Wendy had to bite her lip to stop the sob clawing its way up. Fight for it. Was she brave enough for that?

The footsteps grew louder—closer—until she saw the unmistakable grip of a hand rounding the banister outside. Nick. Wendy's heart climbed up to her throat.

But Felix didn't falter. He gave her hands one more heartfelt squeeze before standing, his frame towering over her. "Love, Wendy," he said, his voice a little softer now, "when it comes, it's yours. It's between a man and a woman, not society, countries, or anyone else who tries to meddle like List. Nobody else has the right to take it away from you. Don't forget that."

The door flew open further, crashing against the wall with enough force to rattle the glass in the windows. Nick came first, stepping through like a thunderstorm in human form, his brows furrowed, and his lips set tight enough to crack stone. Alfie and Andre followed seconds after, their faces split between bewilderment and something bordering on amusement. And Stan— Wendy's heart pitched at the sight of him. He lingered in the back as though that might somehow save him, his fingers twitching nervously at his sides, a prince momentarily dethroned in the wake of Nick's fury.

Nick's eyes locked on Wendy immediately, flicking briefly to Felix with what could only be called thinly veiled disdain. "Gwendolyn Folsham," he said, the words as sharp as a blade, "what do you call *this*?"

Wendy sucked in a breath, scrambling for something to say, but her entire body had gone traitorously still. Beside her, Felix gave the faintest shake of his head, a quiet warning not to panic.

"I'll tell you what it is," Felix said smoothly, his voice calm but crisp enough to cut through the tension. "It's a moment that calls for love and understanding, not scorn."

Nick crossed his arms, his gaze narrowing on Felix in that frightening way only big brothers could manage. "And you're the authority on that, are you?"

Felix smiled faintly, crossing his own arms as though Nick wasn't a tempest in human form.

"I'm the authority on her. I always have been." Wendy's pulse jumped. Nick's protectiveness could be suffocating—but it was love, unmistakable and fierce.

Felix's tone shifted then, quieter but firm enough to hold Nick in place. "And I can tell you this—it's not your anger she needs right now. It's your ear. Your patience. Because whatever's in her heart..." He glanced briefly at Wendy, then at Stan, and back to Wendy, his expression softening into something almost tender. "It's real. That much I can tell."

He was doing it again.

The room hung quiet for an agonizing beat, the only sound the faint whistle of wind through the slightly open window. Wendy blinked up at Felix, her heart swelling, her throat tightening as guilt and love and warmth tangled into one chaotic storm inside her chest. He had always been her anchor, her fiercest protector since that day Nick came home crying—the day their parents had died in the accident. Felix had been there, the only one who could hold her still when the world felt like it might crack wide open and swallow her into an abyss—and in that moment, she was infinitely grateful for him.

And now again.

Nick moved first, his weight shifting with slow deliberation as he stared at Wendy. "Is that true?" he asked, his tone a shade softer than before, though the question still brooked no nonsense.

Wendy opened her mouth to answer, but the words didn't come at first. Her eyes flicked to Stan in the back, who looked caught somewhere between terror and adoration. She sucked in a deep breath, straightened her shoulders, and summoned every ounce of Felix's words that still echoed within her chest.

"It is," she said, her words quiet but steady. "It is, Nick."

And though his frown didn't disappear entirely, there was a moment—a flicker in his gaze—that softened. Behind him, Alfie sighed audibly, and Andre glanced at the ceiling as if to consult the heavens.

Still, Felix didn't move from where he stood in front of her, unmoving, unflinching. Because he'd always been there when she needed him most, even the day when her parents died. And this moment, she knew, would be no different.

Stan's presence pulled at her like the irresistible tug of the tide. The room, crowded as it was with furious faces and Felix's unyielding calm, fell away as her gaze locked onto his. He stood frozen in the doorway, one hand gripping the frame as though to steady himself, his weight shifting nervously from foot to foot. He wasn't like the others—he wasn't storming, demanding, or scowling. He simply was there, and somehow that was enough to undo her completely.

Her breath hitched as her eyes drank him in—every detail vivid and devastating. The faint flush high on his cheekbones betrayed the battle inside him, though he tried to school his expression into something neutral. His golden-brown hair was tousled and he didn't seem as regal, more boyish. Vulnerable. But his eyes—oh, his eyes—were what unraveled her. They held hers in rapt attention, wide and searching, asking questions with no words. Questions she wasn't sure she could answer yet, but couldn't look away from.

And then it struck her, the cruel poetry of it all. Here he stood, at the edge of her chaos but entirely inside her heart, closer than anyone else despite the distance he kept. He hadn't moved toward her. He hadn't demanded anything of her. He was simply present, steady in a world that felt like it was tilting sideways. And he hadn't left. Not when it might've been easier. Not when it would've been safer for him, considering Nick's overprotective fury.

"I'm in love with him," she said. "I love Prince Stan."

STAN FROZE, HIS grip on the doorframe the only thing anchoring him to the spinning world. Her voice should not have sounded like that—not so soft, not so deliberate. Certainly not shaped around his name as if it carried every ounce of her heart.

His name.

That alone sent his chest into turmoil, but her eyes—those sharp, fiercely intelligent eyes—were fixed only on him. The weight of her gaze pinned him in place. He should have braced himself, prepared for whatever storm flew from her lips next. But he hadn't prepared for this.

Not for her words. Not for the way it felt.

Wendy loved him.

The thought landed hard in his chest, knocking the breath clean from his lungs. Wendy, the quick-witted, bold, maddening Wendy—a woman who could stare down her brothers' tempers, care for the sick with hands steadier than his own, and make him spin out of orbit with a single look—loved him?

His heart stammered against his ribs like it wanted to escape, but his feet refused to obey.

Her voice reached him again, trembling but sure. "You stayed."

It landed like a vow.

Nick, Alfie, Andre, and Felix turned toward him in unison, without a word, and yet there was shuffling in the room.

The words struck him, not a blow but a weight that shifted his footing in some irreversible way.

"Of course, I stayed." He might've been standing on the threshold now, practically wrapped in shadows while she stood framed by light, but his heart had long since crossed the divide to her side. It had done so quietly, without fanfare, yet…she had noticed. She *knew*.

He'd already told her how he felt.

How long he'd felt like that for her.

It seemed like forever for it was as though his heart had been made only for her.

His throat worked as he swallowed, but his voice—when he finally found it—emerged frayed and uneven. "I thought..." Another pause, the crack in his tone exposing the parts of himself he had always tried to keep hidden. He cleared his throat, but there was no salvaging this. "I thought maybe you'd need me." Her shoulders dropped, a fleeting but unmistakable sign of relief. It unraveled the last knot of doubt curling stubbornly in his gut. "You do, don't you?"

The question escaped before his mind could weigh it, his voice softer this time, slipping into uncharted waters of its own accord. Vulnerability. Hope. All of it bound together in one fragile plea.

Her answer came as an exhale, a single word so delicate it could've shattered in the air. "Yes."

Stan's pulse thundered as Wendy stepped toward him, her features haloed by the soft glow of golden light spilling from the room. Shadows danced across her face, but her beauty wasn't dimmed—it was sharpened, undeniable. His throat tightened at the shimmer of tears on her cheeks, the way they accentuated the quiet strength she radiated. She seemed like something out of a dream, otherworldly yet entirely real, heading straight for him. How could he do anything but hold his ground?

But the room, of course, refused to grant them peace.

"Wendy!" Nick barked, his voice cracking through the tension like the snap of a tree branch in winter. "This is absurd! You can't truly be considering this mad life of his! He's the target of the evil baron and if he doesn't catch the uncatchable man, he could be caught in a war."

Stan's jaw flexed. His temper simmered just below the surface, but he pressed it down. Nick's fury wasn't unexpected; in fact, he'd prepared for it... though it didn't mean it was less irritating. He squared his shoulders but didn't release Wendy's gaze, even as Nick approached, his boots landing emphatically.

"You think you can just waltz in here and sweep her away—" Nick nearly yelled.

"I don't think," Stan interjected, his voice cool, like tempered steel, "I know."

Nick glowered, arms crossing tightly. Alfie seized the charged silence that followed, his hands slashing the air. "What do you even propose to do about this, Stan? Now that you've... well... made a spectacle? Do you expect us to stand here and watch you take her away?"

There it was, the challenge that would have to be answered. Stan finally tore his eyes from Wendy long enough to meet Alfie's. "I intend to do the same thing you did," he said, speaking with a deliberate clarity that seemed to echo. "I'll marry her of course!"

A hum of reactions rippled through the room. Alfie muttered under his breath, and Nick's face turned a menacing shade of red.

"What?" Wendy whispered. Her surprise cut through the chaos, drawing Stan back to her. Her wide eyes searched his, and though they glistened with shock, she didn't pull away. That, at least, allowed some measure of calm to settle over his nerves.

"If you'll have me," Stan amended softly, his voice pitched low enough for only her to hear.

"You cannot be serious!" Nick exploded, practically vibrating with outrage. "Marry her? Do you think you're in a position to even ask for her hand? You don't have my permission!"

"No," Stan replied, his tone still and deadly, not a hint of hesitation. "Not yet. Because you haven't given me a chance to speak with her properly or even to state my case to you without everyone's voices running roughshod over her thoughts."

He turned to Wendy, drawing her hand into his full grasp now. Her skin was cold, but her grip was firm when she gave him a squeeze in return. He exhaled silently, tension bleeding away just from her silent assurance.

Nick groaned, dragging his hands down his face as though willing himself to muster a cooler head. "Wendy, you don't need to agree to this just because—just because—"

"Because what?" came her sharp reply, her voice startling in its strength. When Nick faltered, Alfie cleared his throat behind him, stepping forward hesitantly.

"Wendy, what we mean is that… if you would rather put this incident behind us, we all could simply… pretend we saw nothing," Alfie offered with a strained attempt at gentility.

"I don't," Wendy said with no hesitation, her tone wielding conviction like a blade.

Nick seemed wounded by the bluntness of her reply. "But Wendy—"

Stan seized his moment. "I would like to ask for your permission," he said, his head tilting toward Nick in a gesture of diplomacy—however fleeting. "The timing of it all could hardly be worse, but the sentiment is no less sincere. I've been thinking about it for a while."

"You have?" Wendy asked wide-eyed.

"Denied!" Nick fired back, the sheer vehemence leaving a stunned silence in its wake.

Stan felt Wendy stiffen beside him, and when he glanced at her, confusion mingled with defiance across her face. "I beg your pardon?" Wendy growled.

Nick's expression darkened, his shoulders stiff and his breathing sharp. "I'll never allow it! Never! Do you understand me? I won't stand for anyone dragging you away, out of *our* lives to *his* dangerous life—and away from me! You're *my* sister!"

The words snapped something taut in Wendy. She pulled back slightly, her gaze narrowing at her brother. "You'd deny me the man I love?" she asked heatedly, gesturing toward Stan. "A prince who says he loves me, and you'd deny me that?"

Neither Alfie nor Felix dared meet her gaze. Felix shifted awkwardly; his focus fixed firmly on the floor. He was the first to speak. "He's right, Wendy."

Stan felt Wendy recoil like the comment had struck her physically. Her voice trembled now, raw and hurt as she turned to Felix directly. "How could you say that? You told me to fight for love. You said those very words, Felix!"

Felix swallowed hard, his voice like gravel underfoot. "I said that because I believe in love. I didn't say it to see you pulled away from your family—to see you isolated in some foreign place where—"

"That's true," Andre said. "Stan has a dangerous life."

"Enough." Stan's voice, quiet but commanding, cut through. He turned his gaze to Andre, whose attempt at blending into the wallpaper had not gone unnoticed. "Andre. While we're speaking of overstepped bounds… care to explain what you discussed with my sister, Thea, in the hall the other day?"

Andre's demeanor shifted instantly. His jaw went rigid, his lips pressed into a thin, panicked line.

Stan raised an eyebrow. "Thought so," he said evenly, though his tone carried enough weight to have Andre fidgeting. "And I'm not done with that line of questioning."

"Neither am I," Nick growled, his frustration doubling anger with suspicion.

"It's still not the matter at hand!" Alfie interrupted desperately. "Stan, what will you do? What's your plan?"

Stan sighed sharply. "The same thing you did. I'll marry her." His tone softened as he turned back to Wendy, taking her hand again. "That's… if she'll accept me."

Wendy blinked at him in astonishment, though her hand made no move to leave his. If anything, he felt her grip tighten. And for a second, he thought the entire room might dissolve. Until…

"I don't want her dragged into your trouble. List is so close to waging war in Transylvania, and you want to take her away from her safe life and make her a target?" Felix said, cringing when Wendy's gaze was on him. "It's not safe."

"I'd never allow her to be at risk," Nick said.

"Never," Alfie added, and Andre nodded.

"Neither would I," Stan said suddenly, loud enough to reclaim every ounce of attention, his gaze sweeping the room with fierce determination. "I've no intention of putting her in harm's way. Nor would I take her from those she loves without caring for her safety. But I will love her. And what's more—I'll do right by her."

His voice was steady. And though his pulse raced, Wendy's calm fingers in his reassured him—it was enough.

Chapter Twenty-Nine

THE TENSION IN Wendy's old chamber was suffocating, a thick, invisible fog that clung to every surface and every silence. Wendy stood near Stan, her arms crossed tightly as though holding herself together was the only thing grounding her in that moment. Nick's glare burned a hole in Stan, and Alfie's disapproving frown seemed cut from the same cloth. Andre and Felix weren't much better, their expressions mirroring frustration, disappointment, and fear. And yet, even with the heavy weight of her brothers' judgments, it was Stan's stillness that unsettled her most. His face was set, his features schooled into calm, but his knuckles on the back of the armchair betrayed him, white and tight.

If Nick didn't give his permission, would Stan still marry her?

Would he leave London with or without her?

And would she truly leave the practice and her brother in England to follow Stan to Transylvania?

"Wendy," a cheerful voice interrupted, startling her from her thoughts. She turned toward the door where Pippa and Bea entered, wide smiles lighting their faces like the promise of a summer stroll. They looked so out of place in the oppressive gloom of the room, their bright gowns and laughing eyes unaware of the quiet storm brewing within its walls. The contrast was almost startling.

"Splendid, you're all here!" Bea chirped, gliding forward with the easy confidence of a newlywed, the glow of happiness still clinging to her. She tucked a loose curl back into place and grinned in Alfie's direction, whose mien instantly softened as he made his way to her and kissed her cheek with reverence. "Come, Wendy. We've come to whisk you away. We've much to plan, and Violet is expecting us."

But Pippa halted mid-step, her smile faltering for only a moment as her keen eyes darted between the figures in the room, each one radiating a tension she couldn't ignore. Only Stan was not glaring in her direction, though his lofty calm was arguably worse. She bowed her head, her brows raising in silent contemplation. Wendy didn't miss the fleeting glance Pippa exchanged with Bea.

"Whatever's amiss won't improve by standing about," Pippa declared, her voice a balm to the awkward silence yet commanding enough to head off any interference. Then she flicked her fan open and waved it dramatically. "Come along, Wendy. I didn't make the trek all the way to Harley Street just for you to say *no*."

Wendy swallowed hard, her gaze shifting from Pippa to Stan, whose brown eyes finally met hers. His voice was quiet when he spoke, but firm.

"Go with them," he said. "I'll… I'll speak to Nick." His jaw tightened almost imperceptibly, and while his words were steady, faint cracks lay beneath them—cracks only Wendy would notice. "It's better this way."

Better this way. Their fraught gazes lingered for a moment before Pippa seized Wendy's arm, too eager to pry her from the room where emotions simmered precariously. She tugged her toward the door, with Bea flitting along behind them, entirely unaware of Wendy's reluctance to leave.

Moments later, Wendy found herself in the carriage, bumping along London's cobbled streets. The warmth of sunlight filtered through the lace curtains, spilling onto Bea's rosy cheeks and Pippa's bubbly perfection. The air in the carriage should have been lighter, filled with Pippa's chatter and Bea's occasional exclamation, but Wendy felt weighted and disconnected, like an unwanted guest in her own life.

"You only just returned from your wedding and now there's the next ball?" Wendy's voice rasped out, her attempt at normalcy weak at best.

Bea nodded eagerly, her hands smoothing her skirts. "Violet is helping us prepare. It's to be held at Lady Anna Ashford's house." She clasped her hands together and sighed with drama only Bea could deliver. "The Ashfords, Wendy—can you imagine? This ball will be quite the spectacle. It's in honor of Princess Thea, so naturally, her brothers will both be in attendance."

Pippa, however, wasn't so easily distracted. Her sharp eyes softened as her gaze lingered on Wendy's face. "Did you cry?" The question was simple, direct, and impossibly keen.

Wendy nodded before she could stop herself, her throat growing tight as an unbidden tear escaped down her cheek. She turned away quickly, but the damage was done.

"What happened?" Bea asked, alarm replacing her cheerful tone. "What did I miss?"

For the first time since stepping into the carriage, Wendy conceded. Her lips quivered as she began to explain, her voice trembling under the weight of everything she had been struggling to understand herself. She recounted—not every detail but enough. Enough for her sisters-in-law to piece together the scandal, her heartbreak, her humiliation. The emotions spilled out like a dam finally bursting, leaving her raw and exposed under their watchful gazes.

"So, you saved his life?" Bea asked quietly when Wendy fell into silence.

Wendy shook her head, dabbing at her eyes with a trembling hand. "He got through the fever himself," she admitted, though her voice hinted at the bond that suffering together had forged. "It wasn't me."

"It was you," Bea said in awe.

"That's how you grew closer?" Pippa pressed gently.

Wendy nodded again, her fists curling against her lap. "And then they caught him climbing out of my room," she whispered, the shame of it rushing through her anew. A fresh tear rolled down her cheek, and she buried her face in her hands. "They think I'm compromised."

A beat of silence passed before Pippa spoke with a clarity that left no room for argument. "Well, nurses are always compromised, aren't they? It's expected because they see patients naked."

"Pippa!" Bea spat.

"It's true, isn't it?" Pippa said.

"No, not like—" Wendy's breath shuddered as her composure cracked further. "I'm not like either of you. I'm not in society properly. I can disappear into the periphery, but *you two* belong there. For you, this matters."

"It matters for you just as much," Bea said.

"I'm not a lady who's respected in society," Wendy said, accepting a handkerchief from Pippa. "How odd," she thought, "I'm usually the one carrying fresh towels. And now I need one."

"You're wrong," Pippa said, directing her words more at Bea than at Wendy.

Pippa and Bea exchanged a deliberate nod, one that spoke volumes in a single glance. Bea leaned forward, a smile tugging her lips. "But you will be."

"What do you mean?" Wendy asked wearily, unable to hide her confusion.

"Because tomorrow is the ball," Pippa replied in a conspiratorial tone. "Princess Thea will be introduced… and you could be, too."

"For what possible purpose?" Wendy's voice broke, and she shook her head fervently. "I can't be with Stan. You both know how dangerous everything is. If I am with him, it's…?"

"And things change, Wendy. You've outgrown being a nurse to the Ton. They may not see it yet, but we will show them—

Nick, Alfie, Andre, and Felix. You're elevating your status at the ball; trust us." Pippa received a nod of approval from Bea.

"There are two ways to rise in status: through marriage or respect," Bea held her hands out as if offering Wendy two imaginary platters. "If you try to do it through marriage, you could become Stan's princess."

"But that would be all," Pippa added.

Wendy furrowed her brows, momentarily forgetting to cry.

"So, there's the other way: respect. Which few people can earn." Bea glanced at her other palm as if the second imaginary platter contained all the answers.

"This is what you have already achieved, and it's why you've outgrown your role." Pippa placed a hand on her chest. "And oh, am I relieved. I should have seen it all along, and I'm so sorry I didn't. You're perfect for the position!" As the tears streamed silently, her lips couldn't form what came next, the impossible weight of it pressing the air from her chest.

Chapter Thirty

THE LANGLEY ESTATE was all warmth and elegance as Wendy stepped into its front hall, the muted tones of rich blues and cream wrapping around her like a soft blanket. The air inside smelled faintly of beeswax and lavender, the kind of comforting domesticity that made her glad she had come, even if her heart hadn't quite settled after leaving Harley Street. Pippa and Bea flanked her, their chatter bubbling ahead as a footman led them toward the drawing room.

Violet Langley, Countess of Langley, was already rising to greet them, her poised figure set against the backdrop of striking floor-to-ceiling window dressings. She wore a gown of soft pink. As Wendy expected, since she'd last seen her, the gentle swell of her belly was now unmistakable. She set her embroidery hoop aside with the efficiency of a woman who had better things to do than stitch apricot blossoms.

Bea rushed forward to kiss Violet's cheek. "Dearest Violet, how radiant you are!" Her glance swept downward. "And you're positively blooming."

"I'm not particularly radiant at five months along," Violet replied dryly, though her smile softened the words. She turned to Wendy, her warm hazel eyes crinkling with welcome. "Nurse Wendy, how kind of you to come. And as for you…" she aimed a kind teasing glance at Pippa. "I hardly dare guess what minor scandal has dragged you along."

"Scandal." Pippa snorted, brushing the accusation away with a flick of her wrist as she sank lazily into one of the rosewood chairs. "I'll have you know I've been outrageously tame... in the past week or so."

Wendy blushed and smiled despite herself, but her nurse's instincts kicked in as soon as Violet stepped closer, her hand delicately resting on her rounding belly. "And how are you feeling, my lady?" Wendy asked, her voice gentle but purposeful.

Violet chuckled softly and gestured for them to sit, though she herself remained standing, her energy betraying none of the fatigue so common to women in her condition. "Better than most expect, I think. The baby is quite active these past days. It's as if it heard of my plans to attend the ball and began rehearsing a dance." She smoothed her gown over her belly almost absently, a fondness softening the edges of her words. "And you, Nurse Wendy? I hope List's upheavals have not troubled you further. Dr. Felix Leafley postponed my husband's treatment for lack of material, which I know is due to List's intercepting of gold from Transylvania. I'm glad to hear you saved our prince's life. He's the only one who can stop List if anyone can at all."

Wendy stiffened. Not because Violet had spoken falsely—but because she had spoken too plainly.

The words "your prince" struck harder than they should. Wendy folded her hands more tightly in her lap, as if she could squeeze away the heat blooming in her chest. Violet couldn't know what those words implied. What they risked.

She longed to say she hadn't saved him—he had survived, yes, but not because of her. And even if she had, what did it matter if her presence near him might unravel everything else she had worked for?

Wendy opened her mouth to reply, but Bea, like an eager magpie, darted in. "We simply won't speak of upheavals. Violet dear," Bea's voice dropped to a conspiratorial whisper, "why are you not already in confinement? Surely, no ball is worth exposing yourself to the ton's prying eyes."

Violet arched an eyebrow, seemingly unimpressed. "No, thank you. This is no ordinary ball, Bea. You of all people should understand the importance." Violet fanned herself. "The nurse has no objections, and Langley himself trusts my judgment. After all, this is no small occasion. It would be a snub to Lady Anna Ashford, not to mention an embarrassment to my new friend, Princess Thea, if I were to feign timidity."

Wendy folded her hands on her lap, listening intently. She had always admired how the Countess of Langley could effortlessly wield logic and wit, delivering unassailable reasoning without crossing into frustration.

It was everything Wendy wasn't—assured, elegant, untouchable.

"And the introductions," Violet continued, crossing the room with the practiced grace of someone used to finding themselves the center of attention.

"It is a tremendous honor. Not one but three royal siblings to be presented at Lady Ashford's ball—Stan, Thea, and Alex." Her expression shifted slightly, warm but reflective as she named them. "Prince Alex should already be at Cloverdale House by now."

The mention of Stan's brother sent a ripple of dread through her.

Stan acted as though he wanted to stay with her, marry her even—but because of List and his duties, perhaps pressured further by his brother—perhaps he'd have to leave… Oh Wendy couldn't finish the thought. List's name alone lanced through the air, connected irreversibly to Stan, who was no doubt standing grim-faced at Cloverdale this instant. If Violet noticed Wendy's small shift in posture, she tactfully didn't acknowledge it.

Violet chuckled under her breath before crossing to a nearby cabinet. "Well, if you're all so concerned about me defying tradition by attending a ball, then perhaps this will help convince you." She invited them to join her upstairs, where she pulled open a smooth mahogany armoire and withdrew a dress, its fabric shimmering even in the filtered midmorning sunlight.

Wendy's curiosity stirred as Violet returned to them, holding the gown at arm's length for inspection. The rich emerald fabric caught the light like polished jewels, swirls of gold embroidery curling along the hem and bodice like creeping ivy.

"I had it made specifically for the ball," Violet said proudly, draping the dress over an empty chaise. "A pregnancy doesn't mean one can't make a statement."

"It's exquisite," Wendy found herself saying, despite her heart retreating to thoughts of Stan. "You'll certainly... make an impression."

"I should hope so." Violet smiled wryly, her eyelids fluttering closed for the briefest moment. But when she opened them, they focused not on the dress but on Wendy again. "And you, Nurse Wendy? Will you attend alongside your brother, Dr. Folsham? I am certain the doctors at Cloverdale have all been invited."

"But I am not a doctor," Wendy said, wringing her hands.

"I know, I know. You're far more important. I've seen you hand them everything they need—without you, the practice and Cloverdale would be like a fertile field without rain—nothing." Violet gave a self-assuring nod as if she'd merely stated the obvious.

Pippa and Bea turned curious, expectant faces toward her, and Wendy shifted uncomfortably against their stares. Her tongue fumbled before even a half-answer could take shape. How could they grasp what such a question implied? How could any of them see what her heart fought against at every moment?

To attend the ball would be to stand in the open, a nurse beside nobility, exposed before the very eyes she feared most. And if Stan so much as peeked at her—if anyone sensed what had passed between them—it would not be a pleasurable ball. It would be scandal.

For Violet, the ball was an honor, a confirmation of her role, her connections, her place in society. For Wendy, it was the cold acknowledgment of everything she could never have.

"In fact, Violet," Pippa said with a meaningful glance to Bea and back to Violet, "there's something we need to discuss with you. It's about Cloverdale House."

"And you," Pippa said with a smile.

"We've all been talking," Bea added, her tone gentler than usual. "About how you've carried the place these past months. Your work, your spirit… everyone sees it."

"We want to reward that," Pippa said, glancing from Violet to Wendy. "Celebrate it. But—"

But Wendy barely heard them. Her mind was already spiraling, caught in the impossible tug-of-war between love and duty. Stan was being pulled from London by threats and politics. She was anchored here, in her work, her purpose. How could they meet in the middle if the very ground kept splitting beneath them?

❦

Chapter Thirty-One

THE MORNING BEFORE the ball, Wendy knew Stan would move out of Cloverdale House for he'd been officially discharged. She missed him already, her chest aching with the weight of it, and yet anticipation prickled just beneath her skin—she'd see him again tonight. Thus, she headed for the morning room to check on an elderly patient when low voices from the parlor tugged at her attention. They weren't the ordinary tones of visitors or staff; the cadence was sharper, edged with urgency.

Her slippers whispered against the floorboards as she approached. The voices grew clearer. One of them, unmistakably, belonged to Stan. *Why was he still here?* She paused, her fingers lightly tracing the wall for balance as she leaned closer.

"No, Alex, I have not," Stan said, his voice controlled but tense. "And there's no need to remind me what's at stake. He'll cause a rift that will bring about war. I know it."

Wendy's brow furrowed as she turned her ear toward the door. Another man, then, replied, "So what have you been doing here? Why aren't you going back home? Why not appeal to the Emperor to send troops to protect our people?"

She dared a glance through the slightly ajar door, clutching the frame. There, beyond the parlor threshold, stood a man whose features startled her. He resembled Stan uncannily but with golden-blond hair, his face framed in sharper angles. He stood an inch or two shorter than Stan but wore a posture just as firm and unyielding. Prince Alex.

Stan's shoulders shifted as though bracing under an unseen weight. "Because I don't want to give up trying to use diplomacy with List."

"Diplomacy," Prince Alex repeated, incredulity dripping from the word. "He doesn't listen to reason." He paced two quick steps before halting abruptly. "I'll pen a note to the naval officers. We need to alert everyone back home."

"I'm not willing to leave England."

Wendy pressed a hand to the hollow at her throat, startled by the intensity in Stan's words. She hardly dared to breathe lest the sound betray her. Her breath hitched. He wasn't leaving. Not yet. But his brother wanted him gone—and for reasons Wendy had no power to touch.

"What's keeping you here?" Alex's voice dropped, sharp and pressing. "What could be so good that you'd stay even though List tried to have you *and* our sister killed?"

Stan hesitated, his gaze momentarily flicking toward the desk nearby, where the open letter from their parents lay. "Mother wrote that List is boasting again—that he'll begin by targeting the women who stand beside the men. That he'll erase them first, soften us, then strike."

Alex's breath caught. "That's how he plays it now?"

Stan nodded once, jaw clenched. "It's not just about politics anymore. It's personal. Tactical. Ruthless." Silence. "Brother, I'm afraid that Thea is not the only woman in my life whose loss,"—he paused—"would crush me."

The silence that followed made her ears ring. Her chest tightened as her breath grew shallow, desperate not to draw attention. Just then, her heel caught against the unsteady edge of a floorboard. The muffled creak echoed louder than a pistol's crack in the quiet corridor.

Wendy froze, her eyes squeezing shut as though the very act could render her invisible. She slid her back against the wall, trying to flatten herself into the intricate floral wallpaper.

She opened her eyes again only to find Stan standing just beyond the door, his dark, piercing gaze meeting hers.

"Wendy?" His tone was laced with a mixture of surprise and a tenderness that sent warmth creeping up her neck.

Alex followed, stepping into view, his expression shifting from curiosity to mild exasperation. Up close, the familial resemblance was even more striking, as though someone had composed an alternate version of Stan in lighter shades.

"Should I have asked *who*, then?" Alex straightened, raking a hand through his hair in a manner eerily similar to his brother's.

Stan turned toward him, his jaw set. "I know you don't think love is more important than duty, Alex. Spare me the lecture, for it is too late."

Love. The word seared through Wendy with equal parts thrill and dread. He had said it aloud.

He stepped closer to Wendy, who was certain the heat from her face could have melted ice. With a measured gesture, he reached for her hand. His touch was steady, grounding her, and reassuring her whatever storm churned in that room, he stood by her.

"Please meet Miss Gwendolyn Folsham," he said, his voice softer now. "Wendy, for short."

Alex surveyed her with narrowed eyes, one brow arched as though silently questioning his brother's judgment. Wendy felt a rush of self-awareness, her free hand instinctively smoothing her skirts under his scrutiny. Yet she did not flinch.

"Miss Folsham," Alex said finally, offering the faintest inclination of his head. His tone held the detached politeness of someone indulging a frivolity they didn't quite understand. "A pleasure, I'm sure."

"Your Royal Highness," Wendy replied, managing a curtsy even as her hand remained clasped in Stan's. Her voice cracked faintly, betrayed by the quickened beat of her heart.

"It isn't fair to her, you know," Alex muttered as he turned to his brother. "But then again, when has List cared for fair?"

Stan's hold tightened slightly against hers, his stillness speaking volumes more than words would. Whatever ground he stood on, he stood firm, but Wendy couldn't yet see the whole of it. Whatever war roiled beyond the walls of Cloverdale House, it wasn't just Stan's but hers, too.

STAN'S GRIP ON Wendy's hand remained steady, though the faintest tremor in her fingers sent an uneasy ripple down his spine. Alex's gaze flicked between them, his sharp blue eyes assessing, dissecting, unraveling every unspoken thread with that infuriating precision only a brother possessed. It was not the outburst Stan had anticipated, none of the scorn or fury he had braced for. Instead, Alex tilted his head, his expression as inscrutable as always.

Wendy shifted beside him, and Stan's focus sharpened. Her face, the delicate pink rising across her cheeks, struck him as both endearing and troubling. She sucked in her lower lip, trying to conceal that telltale blush, but it only sharpened his awareness of her discomfort. He couldn't blame her. None of this was fair—to her most of all. For all her strength, her courage in tending the sick here, she'd never been exposed to a world like his. A world thick with shadows, obligations, and danger. If she stayed by his side, how much would she have to remake herself to fit into it—a world of shadows and strategy, where loyalty could be fatal and love an exploitable weakness. A dart of guilt pricked at his conscience.

Then she shifted again, subtly at first, her fingers beginning to pull from his hand. He felt the movement instantly, like the first hint of a door slipping open in a storm. Instinct overrode thought. He tightened his grip, a silent command that she shouldn't leave his side now—not in front of Alex. He stepped closer, his other hand settling atop hers. The gesture demanded nothing, only offered her reassurance, a promise of stability when things seemed most precarious.

"Is this serious?" Alex finally asked, his voice even, but with an edge that cut through the quiet room. His gaze met Stan's, steady and unrelenting.

"Yes." The answer came from Stan's throat as firmly and easily as breathing.

His eyes lingered on Wendy, watching as her head dipped slightly. Her lashes swept down, her gaze averted. It stung to see her retreat into herself, though her stillness kept a tenuous thread between them unbroken.

There was no mistaking the flicker of reaction in Alex's eyes. His raised eyebrows conveyed more than his closed lips did. His mouth parted as if to say more, but before he could, Wendy gave a soft tug. It was nothing more than a gesture, an instinct to pull away and step back. But Stan caught it as if she'd yelled. He responded with urgency, as if her departure would tip everything out of balance. *I'm not letting you go.*

"So, you two…" Alex's words trailed into the stillness.

Wendy's nod was barely perceptible, the faintest angle of her chin downward. Her silence stung more than Stan expected, though he knew she was trying. She didn't look up at him, and yet she didn't try to free herself again. It was enough for him.

Alex exhaled loudly, the breaking of the moment startling Stan. "Then you need to protect her from List."

The words slammed into him, breaking the momentum of his thoughts. His spine straightened without him realizing, and his free hand flexed briefly. He hadn't prepared for this—for Alex to see Wendy as… as one of them. Someone who needed protection. He blinked, his mind stumbling through the consequences of that realization.

Alex didn't wait for an answer. "Don't look at me like that. You know I'm right. She'll be in as much danger as any member of our family now."

Stan forced himself to breathe, to catch the threads of this new, unexpected turn. His thumb shifted slightly over Wendy's fingers, grounding himself in the contact. "Of course," he said, though his voice betrayed him by faltering on the final word.

Wendy hesitated next to him, and he felt her withdrawing again. This time, she moved away fully, her fingers slipping from his grasp with all the grace and inevitability of sand slipping through his hand. His palm cooled where hers had been, the loss sending a pang straight to his chest. Her retreat felt purposeful, though there was nothing stiff in her walk as she stepped toward the hall. He kept his eyes on her for a moment longer than he should before turning back to Alex.

"You mean to help?" Stan asked, his tone wary. Alex had a way of turning help into something sharper, something heavier.

Alex sighed, shrugging with uncalled-for ease. "I mean that you've tied yourself to someone who will be a target—not later, but right now. You've made this more dangerous for her. And for you."

Stan squared his shoulders, locking his stance as though planting himself on solid ground. "I would never put her at risk."

"You wouldn't mean to," Alex cut in, irritation bristling beneath his otherwise calm voice. "But you love her, don't you?"

The question didn't require deliberation. The answer had nestled deeply within Stan long before Alex had asked it. "Yes."

The simplicity of the truth, spoken aloud, surprised even Stan. His pulse quickened slightly as the weight of the admission settled.

Alex's gaze softened, just a fraction, as the tiniest crease formed near the corner of his brow. He exhaled, shaking his head faintly. "More than I ever thought possible," Stan added, the truth folding out of him like a confession.

"I understand," Alex said eventually, his gaze steady as though willing Stan to believe him.

Stan tensed, leaning slightly forward. "You? Understand?" His lips curved faintly in disbelief before his brow furrowed, startled by the sincerity in Alex's voice.

Alex simply shrugged. "Why shouldn't I? I've sacrificed for far less, haven't I?"

Beyond the doorway, the faint echo of Wendy's soft footsteps disappeared down the corridor. Stan knew she hadn't heard Alex's answer, yet there was no doubt she carried something new away with her. The silence she left in her absence was not empty but charged.

Stan loved her. And that love now lived between them, unshakable as stone, a truth with teeth and consequence.

Chapter Thirty-Two

The night of the ball…

WENDY'S HEART SWELLED and sank all at once as she paced the quiet corridor. Stan's confession still echoed in her mind, impossibly sweet and utterly out of reach for a nurse bound by duty to London and her brother.

Wendy's gloved hand skimmed the smooth banister as she descended, her steps unhurried. The delicate rustle of her gown was an exquisite azure blue. Her heart fluttered in her chest, a mixture of nerves and anticipation heightening her senses. She hadn't seen Stan since he spoke to Nick and wanted to know what had happened.

The gown fit perfectly, hugging her waist, and flaring out in a cascade of silk that shimmered with each step. The neckline, modest enough to be proper, framed her collarbones, adorned with a simple lace trim. She had never felt quite so transformed. "Ready to grow up," Nick would say. The sense of it—the elegance and unfamiliarity—tightened her stomach, but not in an unpleasant way.

At the base of the staircase stood Nick straight and commanding with his hands linked behind his back. His dark coat, tailored impeccably, added to his natural aura of authority. By his side was Pippa, looking radiant in a sage-green gown, her face lit with an irrepressible smile. As Wendy came closer, Nick's eyes softened, revealing the kindness that lay beneath his sometimes stern, older-brotherly demeanor.

"Well now," Nick said, stepping forward to take in her appearance. His smile was warm, his tone brimming with admiration, though there was no teasing in it. "My not-so-little sister." He smiled wistfully, and there was that sparkle again she'd missed when he was distracted. "Tonight, you'll be the envy of the ball."

"But there's Princess Thea, Pippa, Bea; surely I won't be—"

"Admired for being a fiercely intelligent and thoroughly beautiful woman inside and out?" Pippa said, smiling at her with all the warmth of a big sister. "They will bite their knuckles and squeeze their fans with envy." Pippa winked at Nick and gently squeezed Wendy's hand as she added, "And I can't wait to watch them turn green with envy."

Wendy flushed, the words as sweet as they were surprising. She lowered her gaze briefly but couldn't suppress a small, pleased smile. "Thank you, Nick, for this dress. I hardly recognize myself."

"You shouldn't need a gown to know how remarkable you are," Nick replied simply, though the mischievous glint in his eye appeared a moment later. "But I'll admit, it's a fine choice. Too bad I can't take credit for it." He extended a hand to help her down the final step.

"Whatever do you mean?" Wendy asked.

"I merely carried the package with the dress to your chambers. Stan delivered it himself with these flowers." Nick gestured to the open door of the drawing room—the same one where Stan had given Wendy her very first lessons in the waltz. The drawing room table, one that could easily seat twelve people—since Nick and Pippa wanted to ensure there'd be room for all their friends from Harley Street—was covered in vases of the most luscious flowers.

Wendy stood frozen in the doorway, her breath catching as the scene before her unfolded like the pages of a dream too lovely to belong to this world. The drawing room—with its central crystal chandelier hanging over the mahogany table—had been utterly transformed, a sea of blossoms stretching the table's length, their lush abundance threatening to spill over the edges. Vases in every shape and size, from tall etched glass to simple porcelain, brimmed with blooms in a palette so rich it made her heart flutter.

Standing tall at the center in fluted vases were roses forming a cascade of deep crimson, the color of a whispered promise, mingling with creamy whites that seemed to glow in the soft evening light. Frilled carnations in blush pink and pale peach added playful charm, their scent faintly spicy, while stalks of lilies arched gracefully among the arrangements, their ivory trumpets sending forth an intoxicating perfume that filled the room, heady and sweet. At the edges trailed sweet violets between the larger blooms, their delicate purple heads nodding in shy, fragrant clusters, as though drawn straight from some sheltered wood.

Wendy stepped closer, her fingers trembling as she reached to brush the soft, velvet petals of a rose. Her touch was feather-light, yet the sensation rippled through her, a bloom stirred by the wind. The petals were impossibly smooth, their edges so perfect it made her chest ache. She dared to lean down, inhaling deeply, the familiar sweetness of the rose blending with the sharper tang of greenery and the faint earthiness of the violets. It was as if the very essence of spring had been bottled here, for her alone.

"He had these delivered with a message," Pippa said when Wendy caught her breath and turned back to her brother and sister-in-law.

Even though the flowers are as mismatched as our circumstances, I hope that you will see the beauty that comes from them together. Like us, they defy reason, logic, even expectation. Like us, they persist—bold, unashamed, and more beautiful because of what they shouldn't be, but somehow are. I hope that you will reserve all the dances on your card for me this evening.

Yours forever in love,

Most humbly,
Prince Ferdinand Constantin Maximilian Hohenzollern-Sigmaringen

"What does it say?" Pippa asked when Wendy clutched the note to her chest.

Thus, Wendy handed it to her, and Pippa gasped. Out of the corner of her eye, she saw Nick read the note, and he coughed. Pippa nudged him with her elbow, but then they exchanged that smitten look that made Wendy feel as though she'd become invisible.

But she wasn't, was she?

Her prince had found her.

But what if she couldn't keep him? What if loving her was the very thing that would undo him? Stan had choices—real ones. Options that didn't include staying in London under the weight of List's latest threat.

She'd overheard Nick speaking to Pippa earlier, and though he hadn't meant for her to hear, the words had landed with devastating clarity: "List has made it clear. He'll come after anyone tied to us, starting with the women."

Wendy pressed a hand to her chest, the truth unfurling with slow, terrifying clarity. List wasn't just a distant threat. He was a deliberate one, a calculated danger. She should step back to protect Stan, not merely because of her roots in London.

But how could she let him go? How could she simply watch him vanish from her life, when every flower in this room screamed his name as loudly as her heart?

She sank into the plush chair nearest the display, her cheeks warm, her hand fluttering uselessly to her heart. Prince Stan. No one else could have conjured such a dazzling spectacle. It wasn't merely the flowers—the sheer scale of it spoke of thought, care, and longing. How many hands had gathered these blooms, how many hours had they labored, and all for her? A dozen emotions tangled together within her—astonishment, gratitude, and something deeper, sweeter, that she hadn't yet been ready to act on until now.

For all the princely riches at his disposal, this spoke entirely of him—a man who hid romance in grand, wordless gestures, placing his heart among petals and stems for her to uncover.

"What did you say to him?" Wendy asked Nick, who instantly sucked his cheeks in and faced her like a deer caught at night under the bright light of a lantern.

Nick furrowed his brows and inhaled sharply. "In connection with what?"

Pippa nudged him again and flattened her lips. "Stop toying with her."

"I'm not toying with her. Stan and I discuss many things all the time. List. Cloverdale House. News. The weather…"

Wendy's gaze met Pippa's like two conspiring sisters who don't need words to express their displeasure with a rakish brother.

"What did he say about us getting caught?" Wendy asked.

Nick swallowed audibly. "He mentioned it."

Wendy's heart thrummed in her chest. She was waiting for Nick's response as if she'd been waiting to hear whether she'd passed an exam. Probably failed, though. Probably not qualified to be with the prince, was she?

"I told him the truth when he asked about you, Wendy," Nick said, rubbing the back of his neck.

"What did you say to him exactly?" Pippa asked.

"That I don't want to lose my little sister." Nick flinched at Pippa's gasp.

But Wendy remained solemn, as if she were being told how many questions she'd missed on that exam. For what were exams if not small tests of life?

"I told him—verbatim—that I only want to keep my little sister safe and see her happy."

"What does that mean?" Pippa asked, her eyes searching Wendy's. "Did he ask for her hand, and you declined? You didn't give your blessing?" Pippa's eyes were wide, but Wendy's heart plummeted.

Her gaze roamed over the table, drinking in every exquisite bloom. Speckled petals, intricate swirls of shades, blush-tinged edges—it seemed impossible that such beauty could be real. She cherished his presence here, in the quiet elegance of this gesture, in the soft echoes of the floral symphony he'd composed for her. And she'd have to remember this for the rest of her life since she was going to have to stay put. This fleeting glimpse into the adventures that Prince Stan could offer was all but a dream. And even though Nick didn't mean to hurt her, his words were shattering her heart.

Her lips curved into a trembling smile. "Thank you for hearing him out at least." She let her head hang.

"Well, I put a condition on my blessing," Nick said.

Her voice quivered, but as the words escaped her, it felt like a mighty dam breaking within her chest. A rush of warmth surged through her, unstoppable and fierce, flooding every corner of her being with a torrent of life and hope she hadn't dared to let bloom again.

"Oh, Nick!" Pippa hugged his arm, tugging at him with playful affection. Nick adjusted his stance, a faint, warm smile softening his features as he looked at Wendy.

"I wouldn't decline you anything that makes you happy, Wendy. And it's your decision—you're smarter than me, little sister," he said with quiet sincerity, his voice steady but warm.

Wendy felt her heart quicken, anticipation rising like the hush before an overture's first note. "So, what condition did you put?" she asked, her breath catching in her throat.

Nick hesitated for just a moment before admitting, "That he doesn't steal you away from my life. From our lives. Not just Pippa and me, but also Alfie, Andre, and Felix." For an instant, his voice broke—the familiar crack tugged at her memory, just as it did when he was almost still a boy, trying not to cry when they put flowers on their parents' grave before they left their childhood home so Nick could study medicine. That raw, boyish vulnerability unraveled something deep within her. "We'd miss you," he added softly.

And Wendy knew he couldn't bear to lose her as much as she couldn't bear to lose him.

She loved Stan though and wanted him in her life now. Forever. The thought struck her like sunlight piercing through a stormy sky, warming her from within. Tears blurred her vision as her chest tightened. Warmth coursed through her entire being, a rush of gratitude and love so intense it left her trembling. His unspoken longing, and the strength it took to voice it, struck her—and in that moment, she knew: she belonged. She wasn't just part of their lives; she was essential. The weight of that connection wrapped around her heart, unshakable and grounding her in the glow of the family she cherished as much as they cherished her.

"I have to go to him!" Wendy said, rushing to the door. "Let's go to the ball! Please!"

When she reached the door, he didn't release her hand immediately, clasping it gently as he continued to assess her. "Before we leave," he said, his voice softening, "Pippa has something for you."

Wendy glanced curiously at Pippa. The other woman's elation was poorly disguised, her bright eyes betraying that whatever this "something" was, it brought her great joy to deliver it.

"Come," Pippa said, motioning toward the small office tucked behind the main hall. Nick gently guided Wendy toward it, the steadying comfort of his presence lingering even as he released her hand at the door. Pippa moved toward the small writing desk by the window in the drawing room, where a neat stack of papers sat waiting. Turning back to Wendy, she extended them with careful purpose.

"What's this?" Wendy asked hesitantly, her fingers brushing the parchment as she took it.

Pippa folded her hands in front of her, her demeanor both serious and brimming with affection. "It's something I've been thinking about for quite some time," she began. "Nick and I have discussed it, and we both agree there's no one better suited to the task. And it kills two birds with one stone."

"But you love animals so much, you'd never hit them with stone. Not even in the proverbial meaning." Wendy laughed.

"True," Pippa beamed. "So, it's a task I'd like to give you."

"Task?" Wendy echoed, glancing at Nick for another hint, but he only offered her a small, reassuring smile.

Pippa stepped closer, her voice gentler now. "We've struggled to find someone who could be the beating heart of Cloverdale House. Nick and the other doctors can't commit the way the position demands, not when they have the practice and all the other patients who rely on them. But you…" Pippa's face glowed with sincerity. "You've already been that heart of the practice and do it with a flair that invites even more. We want you to lead Cloverdale House. Run it for us."

The words burrowed into Wendy's chest, lodging there with surprising weight. She looked down at the papers in her hands but didn't truly see them.

Deed of Appointment
Gwendolyn Folsham, Director of the Rehabilitation Center
Cloverdale House, Abbotsberry Road, London

Whereas: The Cloverdale House Rehabilitation Center, located at Abbotsberry Road, London, is established to provide necessary care, convalescence, and assistance for individuals seeking restoration of health and well-being, and is in need of an individual to oversee its governance, operations, and welfare.

Now Know Ye That I, Lady Philippa Folsham, acting as Trustee and Patroness of Cloverdale House, do hereby appoint Miss Gwendolyn Folsham to the position of Director of the Rehabilitation Center.

Hereafter Stated:

Position and Responsibilities
Miss Gwendolyn Folsham shall, in her capacity as Direc-
tor, have the full authority to oversee...

Wendy's eyes skimmed to the bottom of the page, and she saw that Pippa had signed her name.

"You mean... you want me as the director?" Her voice trembled slightly, the enormity of the proposition tightening her throat. "But I'm a woman! I'm just a nurse!"

Nick stepped forward, his broad form grounding her. "Yes, and you are the best," he said softly. "But this position suits you better. It's what you've been doing already in so many ways—organizing, caring for patients, handling what we can't. Wendy," he added, his voice full of warmth, "you are the force that drives our practice. I've watched you grow every step of the way, from a headstrong girl to the woman standing before me now. There's no one better suited. Alfie, Andre, and Felix agree too."

Pippa handed her another paper. "Here is their affidavit of support."

But Wendy couldn't read it; tears were forming, blurring her vision.

Wendy's hand shook slightly as she gripped the papers, the line between disbelief and elation blurring within her. "But—" Her words faltered, her throat tightening further. "But this would mean I'd need to live there. Full-time. Wouldn't it?"

Pippa, now smiling, gently took Wendy's hand in her own. "You don't have to leave us if you don't want to. Stay as long as you like, and if you wish to spend a night there, you'll have your own chambers. I've also arranged for an office to retreat to when life becomes—"

"Busy," Nick interjected, his grin evident beneath his composed exterior. "When life becomes busy," he corrected with a wink that made Pippa smile.

Wendy looked between them, her heart caught in her throat. The love and faith in their eyes—the belief that she could take on this role, that she was already capable—made her chest ache with overwhelming emotion. She'd never expected this, never imagined they would see her as more than the little girl thrust into their lives, the third wheel.

"I don't know what to say," she murmured, tears unwelcome but forming, nonetheless.

"It's a business proposal, of course," Nick said.

Ah, a proposal. Wendy sighed.

"A counter-offer to the life of Stan's wife?" she mumbled.

Nick swallowed and paused before he spoke. "I realize that I reacted rashly when Stan first offered for your hand."

He offered for me twice. Wendy's heart swelled with pride and something deeper that filled her chest and energized her body.

"If you need time to think," Pippa said softly, "take all the time you need. But Wendy, I'll ask you as a personal favor… consider it." Her eyes crinkled with mischief as she added, "Not that I'll accept no for an answer."

Wendy laughed quietly, a single tear slipping down her cheek. She met Nick's warm, steady gaze and found herself nodding before she could stop. "I'll think about it."

"Take your time," Nick replied, pride unmistakable in his voice. "But know this—whatever you choose, you will always have your place with us."

Wendy launched herself at Nick, her arms encircling him so tightly that it knocked the breath from his chest, her cheek pressed against the crisp fabric of his coat. Without letting go, she reached for Pippa, pulling her into the warmth of the embrace, their shared laughter muffled as it spilled into the folds of his coat.

"You're just not little anymore, little sis." Wendy squeezed Nick tighter when he said those words.

And with that, the weight of the papers in her heart wasn't quite so heavy anymore.

Chapter Thirty-Three

S TAN TRAVELED TO the ball with the Langleys. The carriage creaked to a stop in the circle drive, its wheels crunching faintly on the gravel. Stan tugged at his cuffs and shifted to allow Henry to exit first. The Earl's silhouette paused in the lamplight spilling from Lady Ashford's house as he turned back toward Violet.

"Are you certain about this?" Henry asked, his voice low but firm. His hand hovered protectively near Violet's forearm, his concern evident in the sharp tension of his posture.

"I am," Violet replied, her tone soft but unwavering. She lowered her gaze to her belly for a moment, brushing her gloved fingers across the fabric of her gown as though to reassure both herself and him. Then she looked directly at her husband, a small but determined smile tugging at the corners of her lips. "After tonight, I will yield to all your concerns and remain in confinement. But you know as well as I do—this evening is not one to miss."

Henry hesitated, then released a slow sigh, threading her hand through his arm. "Very well."

Stan stepped down from the carriage behind them, tugging his coat straight as he followed toward the glowing entrance. Ahead, liveried footmen opened the wide double doors, and the instant they entered, the grandeur inside caught him off guard.

He'd visited Thea at Lady Ashford's house when she'd moved in there a day ago but with the decorations of the ball, it looked even more splendid. Inside, the light from an enormous crystal chandelier spilled across the hall, casting a golden sheen over polished marble floors. An opulent staircase curved gracefully up to the next level, its balustrade gleaming with intricate carvings. The walls, covered with silk panels and adorned with heavy gilt frames, showcased portraits of ancestors whose expressions seemed to watch the evening unfold.

Nothing new.

Nothing out of the ordinary.

Yet, Stan's heart flip-flopped like a bird trying to take flight for the first time as he searched for Wendy but couldn't spot her among the guests.

Nick had promised they'd be there and yet Stan was restless with anticipation.

Voices hummed low, punctuated by bursts of laughter, and a quartet played softly from a side room, filling the air with a lilting waltz.

Violet turned her head slightly, her gaze wandering in quiet admiration. Stan tried to focus on the splendor as well, but his mind was elsewhere. He carefully scanned the crowd, searching for a familiar face—her face. Wendy. She wasn't here. Or at least, if she was, she remained tucked away from view. Disappointment prickled beneath his skin, but he ignored it. Nick and Pippa weren't visible either, suggesting they hadn't arrived yet.

Lady Anna Ashford's arrival pulled his attention forward. She stood poised under the chandelier, her gown a deep crimson that all but demanded attention. Thea stood beside her, the emerald of her dress accentuating her warm complexion. On Thea's other side, Alex shifted slightly, casting an uneasy glance toward the growing crowd.

"Have you seen him yet?" Alex asked, tilting his head sideways.

List.

Stan's heart sank.

"Who invited him?" Stan asked.

"Nobody," Alex said as he offered his arm to their sister. "Stay close."

Thea nodded with a regal gesture that was befitting of their mother, but Stan caught the flicker of fear in her gaze.

"It is time," Lady Ashford said and led them to the grand ballroom. "May I present Princess Theodora…"

But Stan didn't hear the rest of what Lady Ashford said. Her voice rose just enough to break through the muted noise of the ballroom, and Stan smiled at the guests respectfully as gazes turned in their direction.

He felt Thea's grip tighten on his arm—a silent plea for safety as she clung to both him and Alex.

The weight of curious, speculative glances pressed on him, but he kept his expression steady.

A stir of movement to the left caught his attention. Andre approached with effortless charm, his genuine smile accompanied by a slight bow. He murmured something to Thea, and though Stan couldn't catch the words, her warm response was unmistakable.

Then came another figure: List. His presence slithered into the scene like oil on water, where stagnation had no business moments ago. He wove through the cluster of attendees, his tailored coat cutting sharp lines against the candlelight.

"Baron von List," Henry greeted, his voice measured, his brow just barely lifting as he stepped slightly in front of Violet, adopting a subtly defensive stance.

"Henry," List replied with a bow that barely tipped at the waist, his smile too quick, his gaze too cold. "And you, Stan." It was uncanny that List always demanded the correct form of address and yet consistently chose to disrespect others by calling both an earl and a prince by their first names.

Stan shook his head, and Langley squared his shoulders.

"It's a surprise to see you here. I was unaware you were on

the guest list," Langley began.

"I didn't need to be to honor the evening with my presence," List retorted.

Langley quirked a brow in Stan's direction and Stan returned the look with a measured one of his own.

"Perhaps," Langley interjected, his tone as smooth as polished granite, "you would join me for a game of whist? It's quieter there and far more private."

List's response came too quickly. "Ah, the great Langley, luring me away already? Shall we discuss how our last game ended—or should we not? Surely the good prince recalls it better than I—for I've been poisoned?" List turned his sharp gaze to him, voice lined faintly with menace. Stan stared back evenly, tension coiling in his gut.

Could poison even kill a viper like List or would it nurture his venomous smugness?

Langley's eyes narrowed, and there was a pause heavy enough to silence a nearby murmur of voices. The air between them felt like a taut wire, drawn tight by the unexplained challenge in List's words. "Have you had... enough?" List added, his smile sharp.

Stan flexed his fingers inside his gloves, the soft creak of the leather grounding him as he glanced at Langley. Confusion mingled with unmistakable suspicion. Whatever List played at, it would not fester here. Not tonight.

Alex's posture stiffened first, alert and certain, before Stan turned his head to follow his brother's gaze. A young woman stood before Alex, her hand extended like she meant to bridge a gap neither sibling seemed aware of until now. She touched Alex's arm briefly, her movements tentative, almost shy. But then her expression shifted—a flicker of alarm or regret—and in moments, she turned sharply and walked away, her motions hurried, the crowd swallowing her up entirely.

Alex stood frozen for a beat, then darted after her, his stride purposeful and urgent. Stan watched his brother disappear into the throng, his own chest tightening. He couldn't help but wonder who she was, what it was Alex had failed to say—or what he had said too much of to scare her away.

Across the room, Thea stood near a cluster of Harley Street doctors, looking poised yet approachable, like she belonged in every corner of the world. Andre lingered closest to her, and though his attention was always amiably split between the crowd, Stan noticed how it returned to Thea time and again. He couldn't blame him, really. Everyone seemed to have someone to love, Stan thought, his chest aching with something undefinable. Happiness—that unrelenting desire to see his siblings find their joy—did little to soften his own sharp-edged longing.

He turned his gaze toward the sea of dancers, of ladies laughing into hands half-hidden by gloves, of gentlemen all overly eager to charm or impress. Somewhere beyond this whirl of movement, he had imagined Wendy would be there.

A soft, familiar sound broke through his haze. Violet. She cleared her throat delicately and touched his arm. Her fingers were steady, calm—a reminder. Her other hand held a glass sparkling beneath the chandelier.

"Stan," she began lightly, "you looked far too serious for a ball." She smiled gently as she raised the glass slightly.

He furrowed his brow as his gaze dropped to the cordial in her hand. The liquid inside appeared vibrant, a ruby hue that caught every flicker of light in the room. He tilted his head, suspicious but careful in his tone. "What is that?"

"Oh," she said, brushing it off with a quick glance at the drink. "One of the baroness's suggestions. Punch with something else, I believe. She handed it to me before asking all manner of questions about Thea. Quite interested in her, don't you think? Too much, though, considering she's just as bad as her husband." Violet sniffed delicately at the rim of the glass and grimaced slightly but followed it with a light laugh. "The smell is peculiar. I didn't want to refuse her outright."

Stan's gaze darted toward the punch table where he caught

sight of Sofia von List. Her head leaned toward her husband, her expression unreadable but her lips moving with precision, as though each whispered word was calculated to provoke him. It worked. List's smile spread slow and deliberate until the man practically oozed satisfaction.

That can't be good, Stan thought grimly, the unease settling deeper now. Sofia raised her gaze suddenly, and though her smile lingered, it didn't reach her eyes when they landed briefly on him.

Henry's voice cut through the moment, rich with affection as he addressed Violet. "If you truly plan to retire from these affairs after tonight, may I lay claim to a dance now?" He bowed slightly, his movement fluid, his smile reserved only for her.

Violet chuckled softly, her cheeks flushing. "It would be most ungenerous of me to deny you." She offered her free hand, and Henry then glanced toward Stan.

"I can hold this," Stan said, lifting the glass carefully from her grip before Henry led her toward the dance floor. Stan lingered momentarily, watching as the music swelled and Violet surrendered with graceful ease to Henry's arms. They swayed seamlessly among the other couples, and for a moment, the tension in the room seemed to dissolve.

But not for Stan. His hand tightened slightly around the glass as he turned, his gaze restless once more. The ballroom remained as it had—alive with motion, beauty, and decorum. Yet, it lacked her.

By now, Violet had entirely disappeared into the whirl of silk and music, her dress catching the motion of the floor as Henry spun her lightly. A nearby clock chimed faintly, and Stan checked the time. It was nearing nine. This kind of evening, he reminded himself, was still early. Yet the ache for Wendy, as sharp as it had been all those months ago, seeped into his chest like it had been born from years of waiting. She wasn't here—or not yet. Still, the moments stretched until it felt like a lifetime.

The scream was sharp and raw, slicing the air with a ferocity that silenced everything—the music, the laughter, even the sound of his own breath. It shattered the moment into jagged fragments that clattered to the marble floor.

Stan's shoulders stiffened, his pulse hammering in his ears as faces turned toward the dance floor, confusion giving way to dread. Slowly, the dancers peeled away, skirts brushing urgently against polished floors, their hurried movements forming a widening circle at the ballroom's center.

"Move," he murmured, his boots striking heavy against the marble as he pushed through the huddled onlookers. His heartbeat filled his chest, choking him, louder with every step he forced forward. He didn't realize he'd been holding his breath until the crowd dissolved completely, and he saw her.

※

THE CHILL OF the night air clung to Wendy's pelisse as she stepped into Lady Ashford's grand entryway, her hands instinctively brushing against the soft velvet trim. Nick and Pippa were in front of her, their careful steps barely making a sound against the marble floor. But it wasn't the usual hum of anticipation she felt at a ball. No music filtered through the house. No laughter or shuffle of dancers' feet. The silence was unnatural, pressing against her like a hand on her chest—ominous, too still, as if the house itself were holding its breath.

"Are we too late?" Pippa whispered, untying the navy ribbons of her cloak but hesitating to remove it completely.

It couldn't be, it was after nine o'clock at night.

Wendy's gaze darted to the sweeping staircase where Alfie and Bea rushed upward, their movements too hurried, too frantic to belong to the polished elegance of a Regency evening. Alfie's face was tight with worry, Bea clutching at his sleeve as though urging him to move faster. Wendy's stomach knotted. Something was terribly wrong.

Before she could fully take in the moment, Nick caught sight of Andre across the hall. "There." His voice came low but firm.

Andre appeared out of shadow and light, his cravat undone, his coat askew. He glanced back, his expression taut with urgency. "Oh, you're here!" he called out, relief flashing briefly across his face before he turned and bounded up the stairs two at a time, his coattails flying behind him. The knot in Wendy's stomach coiled tighter. She didn't need confirmation—something was very, very wrong.

The heavy slam of a door upstairs echoed through the house.

"What's happening?" Nick demanded, already moving after him.

Wendy didn't think. Her body moved on instinct, darting up the stairs behind Nick. Pippa's uncertain voice called after her, but Wendy pressed forward, her slippered feet sinking into the thick carpet as she took the steps quickly. Her heart raced harder with every muffled voice and cry ahead of her.

At the end of the corridor, she caught up to Nick, Andre, and the others. They had gathered outside a guest bedroom, the heavy oak door slightly ajar. From the other side came the unmistakable voice of the Earl of Langley. It cracked with emotion—fear.

"Violet!" he cried out. A loud thud followed, as if something had struck the door. "She locked me out!"

Wendy inhaled sharply, her focus narrowing. *Violet. Oh no!* Her pulse quickened as she pushed further, slipping past an uneasy Lady Ashford and an ashen-faced Stan. Princess Thea had just arrived in the hall, her skirts swishing faintly as she looked from face to face, wide-eyed.

The Earl stood near the doorway, his normally controlled demeanor breaking under strain. One gloved hand pressed hard against the doorframe, his other clenched uselessly at his side. "She locked herself in the bathroom!" His voice faltered, his frustration edging toward alarm.

Wendy's gaze shifted across the gathered group, her sharp senses cataloging every detail. Alfie hovered by the Earl, Bea gripping the edge of his sleeve. And then… Stan.

She'd seen him brave, composed, charming. But this? This was vulnerability. Real fear.

He stood in the corner, near the edge of the room. His hands trembled faintly at his sides; his usually composed stance fragmented. His face was pale, his jaw slack as though he couldn't reconcile the moment playing out before him. It hit her suddenly—he wasn't just shocked. He was afraid.

"What happened?" Wendy's voice cut through the tense room, even and calm, though her heart thundered in her chest. She strode toward Stan, her movements precise, her mind already turning ahead to assessment. "Stan?"

He blinked at her voice, his unfocused eyes snapping to hers. Then, raking both hands through his hair, he let out a shuddering breath. "I—I don't know," he admitted, his voice low and uneven. "One moment, she was fine. She spoke to me about—about the Lists. She even teased about the smell of the punch. And then, she danced with Langley. Everything seemed… normal. A moment later, she collapsed into his arms. He carried her here, and now…"

His words trailed off, a flicker of helpless frustration crossing his face.

"And now she won't open the door," Andre finished grimly, moving to knock firmly against the wood. "Langley, did she lose consciousness when you carried her here?" His voice was steady, probing for detail, though his expression betrayed his growing unease.

Langley nodded toward the door, his hand curving into a fist that rested against the panel. "No," he said hoarsely. "She came to as I brought her upstairs. Fought me, said no one was to follow her. And then…" He threw a helpless glance toward the door. "She bolted it."

Andre rapped again with more force. "Lady Langley. Violet," he called firmly. "It's Andre. Please, open the door."

But silence stretched thick and immovable from the other side.

Wendy's chest tightened, her mind racing through possibilities, discarding and grasping for explanations. Langley's panic was sharp and rising, and Andre's hands curled into tight fists against the frame, his steady composure cracking inch by inch. Wendy closed the distance, placing her hand lightly on Andre's arm.

Wendy stepped forward and rapped her knuckles firmly against the bathroom door. "Lady Violet," she said, her voice calm but edged with determination. "It's Nurse Wendy. Please, speak to me. I need to know you're all right."

Wendy pressed her ear against the door and heard a rustling of fabric.

Good, she was conscious.

Uncooperative, but alive.

Behind her, the Earl's ragged breathing cut through the silent room as he dug his fingers into the doorframe. "You are the only ones who can," he said hoarsely, his gaze fixed on Nick as if the weight of his words couldn't be borne alone. "I… I thought it would never happen. Years. Years of nothing, and then you helped me and then Violet… she told me… and now…" His voice cracked, and his hands trembled before he slammed a fist against the wall, his restraint snapping. "If something happens to the baby because of this—or to her!" He couldn't finish, his words swallowed by despair.

Nick placed a hand on his shoulder, steadying the man as Langley's composure threatened to unravel entirely. Wendy didn't turn, but her hands curled tightly over the doorknob, the Earl's grief pressing against the air like an invisible storm. The stillness from behind the door felt unbearable, every second stretching too long and too far for any of them to breathe normally.

She exhaled deliberately, grounding herself as she turned her attention back to the closed door. Whatever had happened to Violet—whatever had led her to lock herself away—Wendy knew one thing for certain.

They didn't have the luxury of waiting.

She could not let emotion cloud her. Not fear, not love, not the impossible decisions her heart begged her to make about Stan. Not now.

Duty first.

Always.

Chapter Thirty-Four

WENDY STEPPED FORWARD, her voice cutting through the murmurs like scissors through fabric. "Everybody out," she said, her words firm but calm. There was no room for hesitation. No room for debate. No time.

A ripple of murmured protests rose, uncertain and scattered. Wendy turned her gaze to Nick. His eyes met hers, steady and understanding. After a moment, he gave a brief nod. He understood. This was not for him—or any man for that matter. Not this.

Wendy's mind raced ahead, already cataloging what she might find on the other side of that door. She had to act now, before it was too late.

Pippa, Bea, and Thea hovered near the door to the room, their presence delicate and uncertain. They looked so young, so untouched by the harsh realities that Wendy feared could unfold here. She squared her shoulders, turning her attention to them. "Please," she said softly, her tone less commanding but still leaving no room for debate. "I need all of you to step out." The three exchanged nervous glances, but Pippa nodded first and gently coaxed the others toward the door. She saw his shoulders settle, just barely. Her voice had reached him, steadied him.

"Stan," Wendy said firmly before he could say a word. She leveled him with a look, the kind that left no room for arguments.

"Can you ensure everyone stays out?"

Stan hesitated, his jaw tightening, but at last, he gave a stiff nod and moved toward the door. The last trace of what had happened earlier was evident in the tension of his shoulders. He didn't like leaving, but even the prince obeyed Nurse Wendy.

Andre lingered, his gaze sharp with concern. He stepped closer, leaning toward her. "Are you sure you can handle this alone?" His voice was low, the question careful, as though he was half expecting her to say no.

Wendy met his eyes, her voice steady. "Yes. If I need more help, I'll call for you." Her confidence wasn't false bravado; it came from years of hard-won experience, from the quiet resolve of a woman who had faced worse than this and walked away stronger. They'd seen it before and knew what a miscarriage could entail. And Wendy knew that he'd be there if she needed his support. Andre hesitated only a moment longer before stepping back. His lips pressed into a thin line, but he didn't argue further. "I'll wait." He tilted his head as if to say "within earshot" but it was understood. After all these years of working together, the location, the ball downstairs, their impractical evening attire—none of it mattered. There was a life at stake and the doctors and their nurse from Harley Street would step in.

"I'm going to fetch some medicine," Alfie said from the doorway. He didn't ask; he simply stated it, as though seeking to keep some tangible connection to the moment, some action to take. Wendy gave him a brief, reassuring nod, and with that, he followed the others out.

The heavy oak door clicked shut, and Wendy exhaled, the sound seeming louder in the sudden quiet. Her gaze swept across the now-empty room. It was resplendent in its elegance, the softly buzzing gas light glinting off the lacquered furniture and pristine silk draperies. Normally, she might admire the beauty of such a space. But now, her attention fixed solely on the closed bathroom door.

Sliding her hands down her skirts to steady them, Wendy

reached the door and paused, resting her fingertips lightly on its surface.

She knocked once, her movements controlled. "It's just me now," she said, her voice even but gentle. "Violet, it's Wendy. Can I come in?" Silence stretched thin between them. Wendy leaned her ear close, listening for any hint of movement. Her pulse quickened as she waited, bracing herself.

"Please," she added softly after a moment. "It's just the two of us. I promise."

Then she heard the screech of the bolt and pushed the door gently open.

But even she didn't brace herself for what she found inside.

⟫⟫⟫⟪⟪⟪

STAN'S BOOTS STRUCK the floor in measured strides as he followed the others to the staircase, the tension tightening like a coil in the air. Langley gripped the railing, his hands white-knuckled as he leaned forward, scanning the scene below. None of them were in the mood for a ball anymore. Andre stood nearby, arms crossed, a deep crease cutting across his brow.

"Why do you think she collapsed?" Stan asked, his voice low but sharp.

Andre shook his head, his reply clipped. "Hard to say. Pregnant women can be unpredictable. But this feels... wrong."

"She seemed well earlier," Langley interjected, raking a hand through his hair. "She didn't seem ill, not even in the carriage."

Stan's chest tightened at the memory. "No, she seemed happy." He inhaled sharply. "But something changed at the ball."

Andre's jaw tightened. "Spoiled food, maybe?"

"No." Stan frowned, his mind racing. "I didn't see her eating anything." But then he blinked. "The punch." His tone sharpened. "It smelled... off. Like something acrid, almost metallic, and yet sweet."

Langley turned to him, his voice edged with alarm. "Poison?"

Stan nodded, the pieces fitting together in his mind. "She barely tasted it but handed me her glass. I set it down in the hall when we ran after her."

Langley swore under his breath and pushed off the railing, already moving. "If it's still there, Alfie can confirm. I'll find it." He dashed down the stairs, calling for the apothecary.

Stan exhaled, his pulse quickening as he met Andre's troubled stare. "If she's poisoned—what do we do? For her, for the baby?"

Before Andre could answer, Wendy's urgent voice rang from the chamber. "Andre!"

Stan's blood went cold, the sound slicing through him. He took an instinctive step toward the door, but Andre blocked him with a steady hand.

"This isn't for you, Stan. Not now," he said firmly, before striding toward the call.

Stan stood frozen, his fists clenched, every muscle taut as the weight of helplessness pressed down.

"If it's Wendy, it's always for me."

Chapter Thirty-Five

WENDY'S SKIRTS BRUSHED the tiled floor as she pushed the door into the dim bathroom, revealing Violet curled on the ground, her arms wrapped tightly around her knees. Her trembling was faint, nearly imperceptible, but the sight hit Wendy with the force of a blow.

The usually opinionated and energetic Countess of Langley was on the tiled floor, her face looked ashen, her lips dry, and her eyes were wide with horror.

"Violet," Wendy said softly, her voice calm despite the panic pressing at the edges of her mind. She crouched down, the layers of her gown shifting as she settled on the cold floor beside Violet. The chill of the tiles seeped through the fabric, a stark contrast to the warmth of Wendy's hand as she reached out, brushing a few damp strands of hair from Violet's face. "I'm here now."

Violet turned her head slightly, her lips parted as though to speak, but no sound came.

Flushed skin.

Clutching her stomach.

Wendy's fingers moved instinctively, pushing her pearl bracelet up and clasping Violet's thin wrist. She pressed two fingers to the pulse point, her practiced touch catching the weak and uneven thrum beneath Violet's skin. Her other hand pressed gently against Violet's cheek—clammy and far too cold. Wendy's jaw tightened.

The symptoms were…confusing.

"Oh, the baby. What about the baby?" Violet half whispered and half-cried.

"Breathe with me," Wendy murmured, her tone deliberate, soothing. "Can you do that? Nice and steady." But Violet's faint shaking continued, and Wendy's sharp eyes caught the faintest hint of greenish pallor beneath her jawline. Her mind hummed with focused energy, filing every detail, every clue.

"May I?" Wendy reached toward Violet's stomach to feel for the baby.

The muscles were tense, and the belly felt hard.

"Are you bleeding?" Wendy asked but Violet shook her head. *Good.*

Except that this meant something else was amiss. At five months, miscarriages were rare… unless the baby would come too early.

"Did you exert yourself too much dancing?" Wendy asked.

Violet shook her head again, covering her mouth with one hand. "Not even one whole dance."

As Violet exhaled, Wendy's stomach churned—a bitter, metallic scent tickled her senses. Her lips pressed together in a thin, firm line. No. This wasn't a mistake. This was intentional, methodical. *Poison.*

Wendy let go of Violet's wrist and she brushed the fabric of Violet's dress down to touch her stomach. Her calm expression did not falter, though her heart thudded with urgency when she realized how tense her stomach was.

Distress in pregnancy could harm the fetus.

Wendy helped Violet turn to her side, rested her hand gently over the small swell of her belly again. Often, the uterus relaxed sideways, and the baby would shift.

Nothing.

The child. Her thoughts steeled, cutting through any hesitation like a surgeon's blade.

"Violet," Wendy began, her firm yet soothing voice pulling Violet's glassy eyes toward her.

"What did you eat or drink?" Wendy asked.

Violet froze for an instant. She looked at Wendy but didn't seem to see her. And then, she grimaced, and began to cry.

"Tell me what happened!"

"Sofia von List… the punch… it smelled bad." Violet cried and curled back up, clutching her belly, and rocking back and forth. "Oh, Henry was so happy to have a child. Perhaps even an heir."

But Wendy didn't let her drop back on the floor.

Her next motions were brisk and decisive. She grabbed the bowl from the wash basin with one hand, poured the water into the bucket in the corner, and held the bowl in front of Violet.

"We've got to get the poison out before it reaches the baby." Wendy positioned herself behind Violet so that she could support her chest for the heaving she knew would come.

But Violet sobbed, barely holding her limp form up.

"Violet, we've got to do this now."

A heart-wrenching squeal escaped Violet as she cried even more, but nothing happened. She didn't cooperate.

"Andre?" Wendy called. "Andre!"

She heard footsteps. The door opened to reveal both Andre and Stan standing in the doorway.

"She's been poisoned."

Andre came to her side, placing one hand on Violet's belly and the other on her carotid artery. "Faint pulse. Tense abdomen."

"If it had reached the baby, the muscles would have relaxed. But the baby may still be alive." Wendy attempted to push Violet up, but she was too heavy for her. Then Stan caught her, lifting her gently yet swiftly and positioning her over the bowl.

Wendy's eyes were wide open when she watched the prince in all his finery hold her patient up, positioning her as if he'd done this before so they could get her to expel the poison.

"Military. I told you," Stan said and nodded as Andre took Violet's hand.

Then Andre explained what Violet had to do. She cried in protest, but Wendy couldn't let any more time go by. "Violet, your child's first breath depends on your strength right now—it's the only chance the baby may have to live."

Violet gave a faint nod, her trembling subsiding just enough for Wendy to note the flicker of trust in her weary gaze. Wendy didn't need words for what she saw there. It was enough. She gathered what she would need—a pitcher of water, linens to prepare for what lay ahead—and when Violet finally complied with Andre's instructions, Stan's hands were already steady, and Wendy pushed a wet cloth against Violet's forehead as they steadied her.

$$\sim$$

Chapter Thirty-Six

THE LIBRARY WAS dimly lit, the soft glow of a single lamp casting long shadows across the floor-to-ceiling shelves. The muffled sounds of the ball filtered through the walls, cheerful music and the occasional burst of laughter, a strange contrast to the hushed tension in the room. Stan closed the door behind him with a quiet click, the air heavy with the faint scents of old leather and ink. Around him, the others waited, Pippa, Nick, Felix, Alfie, and Alex. Their varied expressions mirroring the storm of emotions churning in his chest.

Pippa was the first to speak, her hands clasped tightly in front of her. "Will she be all right?" Her voice trembled, though she tried for a steadiness she clearly didn't possess. Her worry was written in every line of her face, her usual composure slipping just enough to show the raw concern beneath.

"She's with her husband and Wendy," Stan replied, his tone clipped, betraying the wariness he always carried in moments like these. "They'll have to wait now," Andre said. Andre had stepped away with Thea and Lady Ashford while the friends caught a breath before returning to the bustle of the ball.

Alex, standing with one shoulder leaning against the desk, straightened and reached into his coat. "I found this next to the potted fern in the entrance hall when you were all upstairs." He held out a small glass vial, empty, the faintest smear of residue inside catching the light. "List was gone already."

Stan's fingers closed around the cool glass, the chill biting into his skin like a mark of failure. His stomach dropped as he recognized the vial. For a moment, he could almost feel the slight weight of it as it had been slipped into his pocket days ago. By List. At the practice.

Nick stepped closer, taking the vial from him and raising it to his nose. His brows furrowed. "This is belladonna." His voice was calm but grim. "I noticed one of my vials missing."

Stan's jaw tightened, the suffocating guilt pressing hard against his chest. "He must have taken it the day he came to see you," he said, rubbing the back of his neck, his arms folding tightly as though bracing against a chill. "I should have seen this coming."

"You did see it coming," Alex said firmly. His eyes locked with Stan's, a touch of quiet reproach there. "But you couldn't have known where he'd strike as much as you can't tell where a cannon ball will land."

Stan inhaled sharply, like he was trying to breathe through ash. "This is all my fault."

Alfie, seated cross-legged on the carpet like a boy, waved the remark off with an exaggerated sweep of his hand. "It's not! Don't be absurd. I made the first poison in the first place."

Stan's head snapped up, anger flashing in his eyes—not at Alfie, but at himself. "No. You carefully dosed something that didn't put anyone at risk. He, in turn, chose to empty an entire vial of poison into Violet's drink. He tried to kill." His voice was taut, layered with frustration and held-back fury—not for the crime alone, but for failing to shield his friends from List's schemes.

"Stan," Alfie said, his tone softer now. "He's not merely targeting you, and yet you act as though you bear the brunt of responsibility for every despicable thing he's done. You're not alone in this." There was no censure in his words, only a quiet insistence that penetrated Stan's defenses.

"No one here is guilty of anything," Stan added, his voice catching on the anger bubbling within him. "Are you jesting? This group of people is the most upstanding, courageous, and trustworthy I've known." He hesitated for half a beat. "But I understand. If there's blame, I take my share just as much."

"List is dangerous. Father warned us," Alex said as if these three little words could encompass the viciousness that was List.

Stan opened his mouth, words poised on the cusp of an argument, but then he stilled, his voice faltering as his gaze dropped to the floor. "I wish I hadn't brought all this into your lives," he said slowly, almost haltingly. "If I left. If I went far away, luring him away…"

"You'll do no such thing." The cutting interruption came from Felix, who had entered unnoticed, his quiet presence taking up a sudden and immovable space in the room. His face betrayed little, but his eyes held a solemnity that stopped Stan cold. "He won't choose you over the rest of us. He hates too widely, and too deeply. And besides, you've already proven you're more than worthy of standing alongside us, not apart."

"We are stronger together," Nick said and Alfie nodded. Stan didn't reply, couldn't reply, as he took in the unwavering conviction in Felix's words. Nick stepped forward next. "And it's not just us who need you. You've proven invaluable to us. And if I may say it, you're the kind of royal who keeps things from fraying when tension is highest. You give us a voice against List."

Stan turned as Alex laid a hand on his arm. "What does this mean?" Alex asked hoarsely, searching Stan's face. "What are they saying?"

He looked at his brother for what felt an eternity. Somewhere, a decision crystallized as if it had been there all along. With them. Nick, Alfie, Andre, Felix, and especially Wendy.

"It means my place is here." His voice was steady, his decision certain. Stan turned to Pippa. "You've mentioned connecting the house to Cloverdale has been difficult. Do you think… might I work out an arrangement to take it on?"

Pippa didn't answer at first, merely dipping her head slowly, gracefully, an enigmatic smile tugging at her lips.

Nick's brow creased. "Why the house next to Cloverdale?"

"Because I'll need an embassy," Stan said simply. "Father will sign the documents. I'll remain in England as Transylvania's ambassador."

Alex straightened, his expression resolute, though his voice carried a quiet gravity. "Then we'll serve our home in different ways. You here, me in Vienna. But it will be strange, Stan, not having you at my side."

Stan met his brother's gaze, his own steady and unwavering. "It will. But this is how we make a difference, Alex. Together, even across Europe. You'll carry our name in Vienna, and I'll do the same here. We'll show the world what Transylvania stands for and that List shan't strike down what's good and right in the world."

"We'll stand against him." Alex nodded slowly, his jaw firm. "For our family. For our friends. For our people."

"And for each other," Stan added, his voice low but certain. "We'll always be brothers, Alex. No matter the distance."

A faint smile touched Alex's lips, though his eyes remained serious. "Then let's make them proud. Together."

"An ambassador of peace, justice, and fairness," Felix added quietly.

A murmur of agreement rippled through the room, but it was the shared looks, the deep resonance of unspoken unity filling the air, that stayed with Stan. The battle ahead seemed endless, but tonight, in the flicker of lamplight surrounded by determined faces, he felt the faint flicker of hope.

It was a miracle that he'd found his purpose among the Doctors on Harley Street that would shine a light on the path ahead—a fellowship born not of duty but of choice. They would stand against List.

Together.

AN HOUR LATER, Wendy remained by the hearth, her hands clasped tightly in front of her as she glanced at Langley, who was kneeling beside Violet. The fear of losing his beloved wife and their unborn child transformed this man, usually so strong and tall, causing Wendy's heart to shatter. His whispered words—soft and earnest—were meant only for his wife, yet Wendy couldn't help but overhear fragments.

Langley finally turned toward her, standing with a weariness that seemed to age him. "Miss Folsham," he said, the depth of his gratitude evident in his eyes, "without you, I… I don't know what might have happened tonight. You saved my family. You saved me."

Wendy's chest tightened, but she curtsied slightly, the movement awkward under such solemn words. "I only did what anyone would if something was to be done."

"Not anyone," Langley murmured. He glanced at Violet sleeping and put a hand on her forehead, his expression darkening. "List and his Baroness—poisoning her—it's despicable. He would see me without an heir, the title lost to the Crown. And with his scheming, blackmail, and criminal inclination, he'd have it placed neatly in his grasp." His fists clenched. "Wherever he steps, trouble follows. I should have known it would come to my family someday."

Wendy swallowed hard, the truth of Langley's words clear in her mind. Trouble had been von List's calling card since she first heard his name. Tonight was only further proof of how dangerous he was.

The door opened quietly, and Stan entered. His shirt was slightly rumpled, his coat carried under his arm and wet stained— he'd probably had a servant try to remove the stains after he held Violet when she tried to rid herself of the poison. He looked at Violet and Langley, his gaze somber before settling briefly on Wendy.

"How is she?" His voice was low, his usual commanding tone softened by grief.

Langley sighed. "Stable, for now. She had some chills earlier, but she's better now thanks to you and Miss Folsham."

"I didn't do much." Stan nodded, though the stiffness in his jaw betrayed no relief. He turned to Wendy. "And how are you?"

"I am well," she said, even as her exhaustion lingered in every part of her body. "It is the Countess who needs your concern."

He gave a short nod. "May I at least escort you home?"

The silence stretched as he took one last look at Violet. She exhaled shakily, a quiet melancholy settling over her as she stared at the flickering flames. The trouble wasn't finished. Not yet. Not with List still at large.

◆

Chapter Thirty-Seven

One week later...

THE DOOR TO his bedchamber closed with a quiet finality, the soft click resonating against the intimate glow of the oil lamp. Stan stood just inside the threshold, the scent of the room—a mix of fresh beeswax polish and the faint tang of linen—grounding him. Here, the burden of diplomacy and royal expectations loosened its vice grip. Tonight, it felt different. Tonight, it held Wendy.

"Please read this letter from my father," Stan said and handed it to her.

Stan,

Your appointment to ambassador is a solemn trust, requiring steadfast loyalty, prudence, and wisdom, all of which you have proven to possess in abundance. Consider this not only a duty but a privilege; to serve our people and uphold the honor of our House on foreign soil is among the noblest of callings.

Be assured that, as you fulfill this charge, my faith in your judgment and character is unwavering. May your efforts abroad bring distinction to our name and strength to our ties with England. You make me proud, son.

Prince Ferdinand

She moved further into the space, her skirts brushing against the polished wood floor with a faint rustle. Stan couldn't take his eyes off her as her eyes jumped and her brow furrowed. The glow of the lamp softened her, lighting the edges of her golden blonde hair and casting gentle shadows along the form of her neck. The chamber was too bland for her, yet she transformed it just by being here.

"You're staying in London?" she nearly croaked, swallowing visibly.

"Yes."

For a moment, she remained silent and so many expressions washed over her face that Stan thought he couldn't possibly follow the thoughts she had. But then, she smiled. It was one of those illuminating Wendy-smiles that could brighten the depths of the universe with her lovely glow alone.

"I imagined your bed differently," she said, eyeing the large four-post bed.

"How so?" He tried to keep his voice steady but felt it almost cracking from the nerves. Like a green boy. The urge to touch her, to keep her within reach, stirred with aching persistence.

"Smaller." She wrinkled her nose most adorably and looked around. "The walls are just white. The furniture is elegant but it's all so… practical."

"Clinical?"

"Yes!"

"And why is that a bad thing, *Nurse* Wendy? Clinical is your métier."

"Because this is your home. Your private space. It should be cozy." She crossed her arms and hugged herself.

"It's still new. I only moved in this week." Stan closed the distance to her. "I'm hoping you'll put your feminine touch on the room. You can choose any wallpaper, any lamp shades, anything you like as long you'll agree to make this cozy *with me*."

She paused. "But it's *your* home."

"I was hoping it would be ours. Our bedchamber. Our house."

"At the new embassy?"

"Yes, I'm the ambassador. It's mine." She furrowed her brows, but he didn't want to talk about the embassy this evening. "Wendy," he murmured, his voice catching slightly before he managed to steady it. "It'll be ours."

She turned, her gaze sweeping the understated elegance of his sanctuary one last time before it settled on him. Her lips parted, her cheeks pinkened—not with embarrassment but something unspoken that made his chest constrict. Slowly, he crossed the space between them, his boots sounding faintly against the floorboards until he stood mere inches away. Lifting his hands, he curved them around her waist, marveling for the hundredth time at how perfectly she fit there.

Her softness pressed into his palms, and when he gazed down at her, she was already looking up, her eyes brighter than any lamplight.

"You're looking at me like that again," she said. Her words were quiet, yet the way she spoke unmoored him entirely.

"How do I look at you, Wendy?" he asked, his voice low, savoring the shape of her name as it lingered in the space between them.

"Like you're trying to memorize me," she replied earnestly, her pink lips curling in the faintest smile. She inclined her head, her auburn lashes dark against her skin.

"I am," he admitted without hesitation. He moved a step closer, feeling the warmth of her body through the folds of her gown. "I want to remember everything about us."

Her gasp beckoned him closer. He lowered his head, brushing his lips to hers in a kiss so tentative that her sigh felt like a reward.

She welcomed him and the kiss deepened slowly, each movement reverent, a prayer pressed across her mouth. When her fingers slid up to touch the lapels of his coat, he dipped his head further, coaxing her closer against him as the sweetness of her scent clouded his senses.

Her hands did something to him. They were timid yet deliberate, gripping the edge of his coat before sliding the heavy fabric down his shoulders. It pooled at his feet, unheeded. His fingers worked on their own, finding the lace and buttons at the back of her gown, loosening each until the garment shifted, giving way under his touch. With each layer he removed, her breathing quickened—a soft, rhythmic reminder that she trusted him. When the last piece fell away, revealing her in nothing more than her simple chemise, he thought he might lose all his carefully tended composure.

Tonight would be special. It would set the tone for their future together.

Stan stepped back just a little, toeing off his Hessian boots as he straightened to meet her gaze once more. For the briefest moment, he hesitated, but one look at her—her flushed cheeks, the way her gaze trailed him shyly—was all the reassurance he needed. With deliberate precision, he pulled his shirt over his head, tossing it onto the growing pile of discarded clothes.

Her gasp filled the small room, and he felt a tightening satisfaction in his gut. She touched his arm and nudged him to turn around. He felt her gaze flickered to the scar on his shoulder, the pronounced mark cutting through his skin.

Slowly, she stepped around him, her bare toes whispering against the wooden floor. When her cool fingers brushed the scar, Stan froze, his breath halting. Her touch was gentle, even hesitant, but it reached deep into the parts of himself he had long thought impervious—except to her. Then, without warning, she leaned in and pressed her lips to the jagged line.

This was not what a nurse did to a patient.

They were just a man and a woman.

He closed his eyes, her slow kiss on his shoulder almost overwhelming him with its unexpected tenderness.

"It's healing well," she murmured, her voice soft against his skin. "Next, the redness will fade. All that'll be left will be a faint white line."

He swallowed, emotions too raw to disguise. "I'm alive because of you," he said, the words unfiltered and true.

She frowned slightly, and with that familiar independence, she shook her head. "You're young and strong. You could've recovered without me."

"No," he said, cupping her face so she had no choice but to look at him. "I know men who lost to fever. I've seen what it does—this slow, merciless assault on the body. I nearly succumbed, Wendy. I felt the darkness taking me. But your touch, your voice—you called me back."

Her throat worked as she swallowed, her eyes searching his. "It probably wasn't me." Modesty suited her, but it was misplaced in Stan's eyes as she continued, "Science surely has an explanation. There's so much I don't know. The human body is a marvel."

"There's much medicine can't explain, yes," he replied, his thumbs brushing her cheeks. "But there's much we do understand, too. And tonight, I want to show you some of the marvels we can be for each other."

The moment stretched as Stan's hands slid down her sides, settling firmly yet tenderly at her waist. Her gown's fabric was soft beneath his fingers, whisper-light compared to the warmth emanating from her body. Without a word, he lifted her, and placed her on the edge of the bed, her chemise brushing briefly against his thighs as she moved. The mattress dipped gently beneath her weight, and in the quiet, the faint creak of the wood seemed intimate, almost conspiratorial.

He leaned in, his lips capturing hers in a kiss that melted the air between them. His mouth moved slowly, deliberately, savoring her taste as if it were his last indulgence. Her lips, pliant and trembling, molded to his, and though her breathing hitched, her shoulders eased under the coaxing pressure of his hands. Stan fumbled with the ties of her chemise, the intricate knots proving stubborn in his haste. He forced himself to slow down, to savor the moment instead of rushing past it. The delicate material eventually gave way, parting to reveal the soft slope of her shoulder.

He paused to look at her, the glow of the oil lamp gilding her skin in shades of gold. She trembled beneath his hands, and as the chemise slipped further, his heart surged at the sight of her—bare, unguarded, divine. Each inch of her revealed sent a deeper, insistent heat sparking through him, yet it was her shyness, her quiet submission, that undid him entirely. Here, poised on the corner of the mattress, she was strong but also fragile, a contradiction he wanted to spend the rest of his life unraveling.

So, he leaned in again, his arms on either side of her. She didn't lie down but put a hand on his chest, still cool.

She must be nervous.

Her voice finally broke the charged silence. "You're so much… larger than me," she murmured, the uncertainty quivering in each syllable.

The corners of Stan's lips softened as he stilled, his thumb tracing a lazy circle along the curve just above her hip, where the chemise still clung. Her skin there was impossibly smooth, her body warm and alive beneath his touch. He wanted to reassure her, to banish every shred of doubt from her mind.

"We don't need to do anything more than this tonight if you don't want to," he said, his voice a steady, quiet promise. "May I just hold you, Wendy?"

⇶✕⇷

HER NAME ON his lips melted her restraint like ice under the warmth of his gaze—pooling and running away in rivulets from where his words had touched her. The rasp of his voice, rough and reverent, ignited a fire in her chest that she couldn't contain. She exhaled shakily, not daring to trust her voice as she gazed up at him. Everything about Stan—his sculpted shoulders, his unruly hair, his steady, smoldering eyes—unraveled her. He was so much more than she'd told herself she deserved. He was everything.

And she wanted all of him in ways she could barely understand.

"Help me," she plead. "I want you so deeply, it burns—" she gripped her chemise with one hand, and it wrinkled.

"My sweet Wendy," he said and supported her, gently easing her into his lap again, guiding her with such care as though she were something sacred. Her heart seemed to stop for a moment before it thundered back to life. The strength of his hands, the deliberate way they settled at her waist, sent an ache rolling deep through her. She felt small in his arms, but not fragile—cherished, held in place by his solid presence. She sank against him, nestling her cheek against the warm skin of his neck, unable to stop her lips from grazing the space just above his collarbone. How had she resisted this? Resisted him all this time?

She breathed him in deeply, that clean, masculine scent she already knew by heart. And when he kissed the crown of her head, his lips brushing softly as though marking her, it sent a shiver racing down her spine. Subtle yet electrifying. He made her want. Need.

She wanted more than safety and comfort. She wanted her prince—the unyielding force of nature who drove every doubt from her mind. Slowly, she shifted, sliding her legs over his thighs. The warmth of his body blanketed her, grounding her as she repositioned herself to face him. The hem of her chemise gathered high around her thighs, and the cool air only heightened her awareness of him—of every part of them touching. Soft linen against heated skin. Her knees brushing his hips. Her chest pressing lightly against his.

"Wendy," he murmured again, like he was savoring the resonance of her name. Like it belonged to him.

Her hands trembled slightly as she pressed them against his chest, feeling the hard planes of muscle beneath her fingertips. Her gaze darted to his lips—those lips that had driven her thoughts all evening—and before she could stop herself, she tilted her face upward, claiming them. At first, it was tentative, just a featherlight press, but her need swelled quickly, the restraint between them breaking like waves against the shore.

And while they kissed, he took her hand and guided her down to the hardness she'd not dared to touch.

He must have known or felt her hesitation, so he held her hand between both of his—his mouth never leaving hers, and he guided her to wrap her palm around his shaft.

Hard like stone but warm like the rest of him and covered in soft skin—a tantalizing and precious combination Wendy couldn't explain.

But she felt him.

And oh, how she did!

But his kisses confused her and distracted her from the exploration. His lips were warm and firm, and his kiss was intoxicating. She sighed softly as he deepened it, coaxing her response, and she gave him everything. Her fingers trailed to his shoulders, first tentative and then bolder, sliding into the soft, unruly strands of his hair. She tugged him closer, feeling the low, guttural sound he made under her hands—a sound that deepened the ache pooling low in her abdomen.

His hands roamed her sides, fingertips brushing the barest edge of her ribcage, each touch sending a spark through her. It wasn't just the way he kissed her—his lips coaxing hers and his tongue stroking with aching deliberation—but the way he held her to him like she was the most precious thing in his world. That thought alone had her gasping into his mouth, her breathing erratic as his lips left hers to trail along her jaw.

And somehow, she twitched on the inside.

When he grazed the sensitive hollow of her throat, her head fell back instinctively and she sank further onto his lap, giving him full access and relaxing her thighs. His breath ghosted over her skin, and then his lips followed—soft, deliberate presses that made her toes curl. She clung to his shoulders, consumed by a sensation so vivid she could hardly breathe.

"Stan," she managed, her voice trembling, slipping past her lips before she even knew she'd spoken. The way he stilled at the sound of his name—the reverence in his expression when his eyes met hers again—stole what little composure she had left. The intensity in his gaze made her feel utterly known, utterly seen. She cupped his face then, her palms framing the sharp angles of his jaw as she kissed him deeply once more. She wanted to tell him everything she couldn't say, to show him there was nothing of herself she wasn't ready to give. "Help me."

She held his member in her hand, close to her middle and even though she understood the mechanics, she was riddled by the sheer magnitude of what she couldn't wait for and feared at the same time.

His hands tightened at her hips, guiding her even closer, and her body obeyed without thought. She felt every inch where their bodies met, the heat of him searing through the thin chemise that still separated them. The sensation left her trembling, desire coursing through her as his kisses grew deeper, hungrier. His lips returned to hers, and her heart surged with each movement, each sigh he pulled from her lungs.

Nothing else mattered anymore. Not the worlds they came from or the obstacles that still waited for them. There was only Stan—the man she adored, the man she now knew she loved beyond reason—and the way his expression warmed like she was his whole world, too.

Chapter Thirty-Eight

WENDY'S HANDS WANDERED down his chest, slow and deliberate, her fingertips brushing against the edge of his exposed skin. Every nerve in Stan's body ignited at that soft, tentative touch; the faint pressure of her hands sent a storm of heat rolling through him. His breath hitched before he could control it, his chest tightening at the thought of how much more he wanted her to explore, how desperately he longed to give her every part of himself.

"Wendy," he murmured, rough and reverent, her name a force that tethered him amidst the chaos of his mounting desire. Yet, even as need coiled tight in his stomach, his hands on her waist remained steady—anchoring her, allowing her to take her time.

Her gaze lifted to his, the uncertainty melting into courage before his eyes, and it nearly undid him. The burn of her trust and that fragile boldness she willingly offered, left him humbled. She leaned in, no hesitation this time, no retreat. Their lips met again, and it was different now—sure, aching, and full of the silent promises neither had spoken.

The softness of her middle broke him apart. He pressed into her all while deepening the kiss, drawing her closer until there was no barrier between them, only her warmth enveloping him slowly. Every shift of her body against his felt deliberate, like she was learning him physically just as she knew his soul. And he wanted her to—yearned for her to know all of him, to feel each beat of his heart that thudded for her alone.

His hands moved, strong and careful, mapping the grace of her waist. The thin fabric of her chemise was no shield against the heat of her skin, so he tugged at the hem. She let go of his cock, stretched her spine, lifted her arms over her head, and he removed the last bit of fabric.

Her breasts sprang free and Stan cupped them. For a moment, he shuddered at their perfection but when she looked down at her perfect mounds in his palms, he wanted her to watch him take her nipples in his mouth. It was an act of control and submission at the same time. He couldn't help the way they puckered under his gentle tasting—every stroke slow, deliberate, as though committing her to an eternity he would guard fiercely.

"Wendy," he murmured again, his voice thicker now, laden with a rawness he couldn't hide. He heard nothing but her—felt nothing but her. She was everywhere—the press of her palms on his chest, her fingers tangling in his hair, her scent, that intoxicating sweetness of lavender and warmth. Her lips left him, only for a moment, and he couldn't stop himself from seeking the tilt of her jaw, tracing it with kisses that were soft but unrelenting.

Her head tipped back, granting him access to the tender line of her neck. Letting go of her breast—albeit vowing he'd return—he pressed his lips to the delicate hollow, her pulse beating beneath his mouth like a drum, pulling him deeper into the moment. Slowly, his hand traveled down, finding the smooth, firm curve of her thigh just at the edge of her folds. His palm settled there, finding her pearl as he pressed a little further.

She was so tight. *So precious.*

"Tell me to stop," he managed, though the words barely sounded like his own, gruff, and edged with longing. But he held firm, his hand still, his breath steady, waiting for her.

Her fingers tightened at his shoulders, and when she whispered, "I won't," the words threaded through him like fire and steel. He exhaled, a sharp but measured release, and pressed his forehead to hers, the closeness grounding him.

"If I push further, you will lose your virginity." It was a warning as much as a plea to let him push.

And she nodded. She was beautiful. Utterly, impossibly beautiful. Not merely in appearance but in the way she gave herself to him without reservation, her trust raw and unwavering. He cupped her face gently, the pad of his thumb brushing lightly over her cheek as he kissed her again. This time, it was languid and consuming, a devotion etched into every movement.

And he pushed a little, flexing his hips upward. She was on top of him and perhaps it was better, especially this first time. He didn't want to crush her delicate frame and didn't mind her riding him as hard as a wild stallion.

But she didn't know yet how, he could feel it.

Her tightness and then a barrier. Something extra tight.

"I think this is it." She mumbled and looked down.

And he just wanted to push on but not with her.

Never with Wendy.

She sucked her lips in, let go of him and used both hands to part her folds. Stan had to stabilize himself with both hands and gripped the covers, realizing he had never even offered her the comfort of the blanket.

And then it just happened.

She made a tiny noise like a sudden hiccup.

And he was buried to the hilt.

A second.

A minute.

He wasn't sure how long exactly they waited.

"No blood?" she asked, rubbing her fingers around the exact fusion of their bodies.

"There might be."

And to his utter surprise, she relaxed as if she had visibly melted into him.

And on the inside, she accommodated him as if they'd been

made to fit each other perfectly.

"Teach me," she whispered and let go. She wrapped her hands around his neck.

"It's my honor," Stan managed.

"Now, I'm not a virgin anymore," she said, curling the corners of her mouth downward.

"But you'll be my princess forever."

Stan couldn't stop his hands now, one sliding up the line of her back. The other remained at her thigh, his fingers splayed wide to feel the full warmth of her. Every inch of her pliant form against his drove him deeper into a place where only they existed—both untethered from duty, from reason, from time itself.

"I love you and will try to live up to the honor you give me," she said.

"You don't know what you do to me, Wendy," he mumbled softly against her lips, his voice raw with awe, the truth of his words stark in his every breath. "The honor is all mine. You're all mine now." She was all he wanted, all he needed, and he would spend forever proving it to her if she'd allow him.

Her response was wordless—a tilt of her head, the press of her lips trailing his jaw, the delicate curve of her body yielding to him perfectly. Each movement spoke louder than words, and Stan knew, with every steady beat of his heart, that this moment—this extraordinary, infinite moment—was his to cherish forever.

He'd waited for this. He'd wait forever.

He held on, barely. The curve of her body pressed against him, skin to skin. He couldn't ignore the feeling—soft, warm, effortless. Sliding a hand up her thigh, he whispered her name, his voice vibrating low in his chest.

"You've something boyish about you when you're unguarded," she said suddenly, fingers feathering along his jawline.

Stan laughed, his forehead resting briefly against her own. "I have only mischief in mind right now," he admitted softly, tilting her chin up. He caught her startled gasp with his mouth, kissing her deeply, until all that remained between them was pleasure and the soft hum of the oil lamp.

And as their laughter melted into the kiss, the world beyond the glow of the oil lamp faded, leaving only the promise of a future as boundless and bright as the love they had found in each other.

Epilogue

WENDY AWOKE AS the first golden light of dawn seeped softly into the room, filtering through the thin curtains and brushing her skin with warmth. She drew the shawl from last night's gown snug around her, her fingers grazing the silk threads that slid against the bare curve of her shoulder. Beneath the fabric, her body still hummed, alive with the memory of Stan's touch. She felt the goosebumps of his hand on her waist, the press of his lips at her neck. Each mark, each kiss lingered like an invisible thread tying the night to this very moment—the first day in the future they'd promised to one another.

The windowpane was cool beneath her fingertips as she gazed out over the sprawling garden. The lawn shimmered with dew, fragile and fleeting in the glow of the rising sun. She took a deep breath, tasting the wild sweetness of the earth mingling with the faint grassy air she loved so much. The tranquility stretched before her, vast and serene, and yet, her heart was full—not with peace, but with an ache so deep it bordered on joy.

Behind her, soft rustling and the creak of wood reached her ears. She turned her head slightly, and her heart gave the smallest flutter as she caught Stan shifting in the bed. His bare torso rose just above the crumpled sheets, his dark hair in wild disarray, his eyes half-lidded and dreamy as they sought her out. He stretched, the golden light painting him in warm hues, and when his gaze landed on her, the corners of his mouth turned upward into a lazy, lopsided grin.

"You didn't wake me," he murmured, his voice low and rough, still wrapped in the edges of sleep.

Wendy smirked softly, turning back to study the glass. "I thought you could use the rest. The night was… strenuous."

He laughed at that, deep and unrestrained, and she felt it wrap around her like the threads of her heart that would forever be bound to this handsome man. The bed creaked again as he stood, and she didn't need to look to know he was walking toward her. She could already feel his presence, breathlessly close yet still too far away.

Wendy turned her head, enough to glance at him over her shoulder. He stood bare behind her as if he were to bow and cut in, taking over her thoughts. He took another step forward, the low heat in his tone melting into something softer as his hands found her waist. He leaned forward, pressing his lips to the top of her shoulder, lingering there. Wendy closed her eyes for the briefest moment, letting the feel of his skin anchor her fully in the moment.

She opened them again and turned her gaze toward the garden. "Did you know," she said lightly, "that you can see directly into Cloverdale House from here? Right into the top-floor windows facing the garden."

Stan went still for half a beat before letting out a gruff hum. "I may have."

Wendy turned toward him fully now, the shawl slipping slightly, though she hardly cared. "Were you spying on me?" she asked, her voice archly accusing, though her eyes were alight with amusement.

"A little bit." Stan's grin didn't falter, not for a breath. Instead, he gathered her close, his arms enveloping her fully as his fingers skimmed under the fold of her shawl. He tucked a strand of her hair behind her ear before resting his forehead against hers. His voice dropped into a low confession, disarming and entirely his. "When I wasn't near you, I couldn't help but look. I just wanted to see you. To watch over you if I couldn't be right beside you."

The honesty of his words struck her, as did the depth in his gaze. Her heart clenched, pulling impossibly tighter in her chest. To her surprise, tears pricked the corners of her eyes, though she blinked them away, unwilling to surrender to them.

"Wendy," he began, his voice low and steady, though it trembled with emotion, "I once thought I couldn't let you get close to me. That my life was too complicated, too dangerous. That being with me would only drag you into the line of fire."

Her breath hitched, her heart pounding as his words wrapped around her like a warm embrace.

"But I was wrong," he continued, his voice softening as he leaned closer, his forehead resting against hers. "You've shown me that love isn't about keeping someone safe by pushing them away. It's about standing together, no matter the risks. You've made me stronger, braver, and more whole than I ever thought I could be. And now, I can't imagine a life without you in it."

"You can't keep me safe from everything, Stan," she whispered, her voice shaking slightly, unbidden. "You can't hold the whole world at bay."

"Maybe not," Stan said. "But I can hold you." He tilted her face up then and pressed his lips to hers. The kiss was unhurried and deep, reverent in its intensity, and for a fleeting moment, she forgot anything beyond this room, this man, this morning.

When they parted, they lingered there, close yet unwilling to break the fragile spell between them. Wendy glanced toward his desk then, a curious spark lighting her expression. "The empty frame," she said softly. "What's it for?"

Stan followed her gaze, a faint blush coloring his cheeks. Walking her toward it, he traced a finger over the polished wood before looking at her with a mix of pride and tenderness. "It's for you," he said simply. "For your appointment as director. You've earned this. Every bit of respect and admiration you command deserves a place like this in your new office."

"You knew about it?"

"Yes, Pippa and Nick spoke to me after I asked for Nick's permission." Stan took a step back and held both her hands in his.

"I sent a letter to my parents and asked them to come to our wedding. I'm afraid though that the ring I want to give you, an heirloom that's been in my family for over two hundred years, will arrive only when mother is here."

Wendy's breath caught, and this time she couldn't stop the tears spilling free. She laughed through them, her hand covering her lips as she shook her head. "Stan," she whispered, her voice shuddering with emotion.

"No," he said gently, cupping her face now as he kissed her tears away. "No words. You've already given me everything I could ask for. The least I could give you is the wedding you deserve, even if it will be winter before we can have it."

And as they stood there, bathed in the soft glow of morning, Stan took Wendy's hands as they stood in the middle of the grand chambers. Wendy's heart raced as Stan knelt before her, his dark eyes fixed on hers, his expression reverent.

"Wendy," he began, his voice steady though laden with emotion. "You are the healer of my soul, the light that found me in the dark. It would be my greatest honor if you would allow me to spend the rest of my life proving that you are my equal in every way. I don't just want you to be my princess—I want you to be my everything."

Wendy blinked, her breath catching. Princess. It hardly seemed real. She attempted to whisper but no sound came, just a squeal that made them both laugh even as tears rolled down her cheeks.

"I know you think you don't belong in palaces or castles, with kingdoms bowing in your presence," Stan said as he rose to his feet, lifting her hands to his lips. "But Wendy, I've already called them here. The court will come to you, and they will bear witness to what I've seen from the moment I met you—that you are better than any of us, my love. You are, and always will be."

Wendy's vision blurred with tears, but she refused to turn away. His words wrapped around her heart, filling every gap where doubt or fear once resided. She had spent so long protecting herself, believing that love, at least a love like this, was not hers to claim. And yet here he was, offering her the very world.

"Say yes," Stan murmured, so close now that she could feel his breath on her lips. His hands framed her face, holding her steady as if anchoring her to this moment. "Say yes, and I'll spend every day reminding you of just how deeply I love you."

"Yes," Wendy choked out, her voice breaking as she threw her arms around him, burying her face in his chest. His laughter, warm and rich, echoed through the vast room as he caught her, lifting her off the ground. She felt the strength in his arms, the heat of his love pulsing through her as though it could undo every sorrow life had dealt her before.

Their kiss was slow, deliberate, and when they finally pulled apart, Wendy rested her forehead against his, her heart thundering in her chest. "I never dreamed of this," she admitted softly. "Of something so… unreal."

"Oh, this is real," he said, threading his fingers through hers. "You've made the fairy tale real for me. You've saved me, Wendy. Now, allow me to give you everything."

For the first time, Wendy felt the grip of her doubts lifting. Where once she carried the burden of her shortcomings, she carried his love. It was here, with him as her prince, bringing not only his love but the world's recognition of what she'd always been to him.

Not just his equal. His everything. His princess.

Read about the royal wedding when Stan's family arrives for the snowy wedding in book 6, *Bring Me A Winter Miracle*.

The series continues with Felix's story in *The Taste of Gold*, book 5 of the Miracles on Harley Street series.

Author's Note

While crafting this story, I tried to balance the art of fiction with a dedication to historical accuracy. At times, I embraced artistic license to serve the narrative, but in other instances, I remained true to the realities of the Regency era, particularly when it came to the portrayal of diseases. What follows is a glimpse into the research that helped shape the world and characters within these pages.

Rickets:

At the beginning of the story, Wendy helps Andre prepare for the treatment of his young patients who suffer from rachitis. During the Regency era, rachitis—what we now know as rickets—was a distressingly common affliction, especially among children living in urban areas like London. At the time, it was poorly understood, often attributed to vague notions of poor parenting or even immorality. The term "rachitis" itself, derived from the Greek for "inflammation of the spine," reflected the limited medical knowledge of the period. The condition was also colloquially referred to as "the English disease," as it was particularly prevalent in England during a time when rapid urbanization and industrialization created overcrowded cities filled with air pollution and poor living conditions.

Treatment in 1818 was rudimentary at best. Physicians might have recommended wearing splints or braces to correct the characteristic bowing of the legs, but these methods addressed only the symptoms, not the root cause. Diet was often discussed in vague terms, but there was no understanding of the essential nutrients necessary for bone health. Families struggling with the economic hardships of the era had limited access to fresh food or adequate sunlight, which would have been helpful, though this was not yet known.

Fast forward to the 20th century, and we begin to see the unraveling of the mystery behind rickets. The discovery of vitamins in the early 1900s, particularly the identification of vitamin D and its critical role in calcium absorption, revolutionized our understanding of the disease. Researchers found that a deficiency of this vitamin caused rickets and that it could be prevented or cured with proper supplementation and exposure to sunlight. This knowledge led to the fortification of foods such as milk and cereals, a game-changing public health measure. These advancements, combined with improved sanitation, nutrition, and living conditions, have drastically reduced the prevalence of rickets in most developed countries.

The transformation in medical science and public health since the Regency era illustrates the remarkable progress we have made. What was once an affliction wrapped in mystery and stigma is now a treatable and, largely, preventable condition. While cases of rickets still arise in some parts of the world due to poverty or lack of education, our understanding of the disease gives us the tools to fight it effectively. The story of rachitis serves as a testament to the power of knowledge, innovation, and the ongoing quest to improve human health.

Sepsis:

Sepsis, a life-threatening condition caused by the body's overreaction to an infection, has a long and complex history. Even in ancient times, like the Roman era, healers observed the devastating effects of infections that spread throughout the body. While they lacked the tools to identify the specific causes, they recognized signs of what we now know as sepsis. Symptoms such as fever, chills, accelerated heart and breathing rates, pain, and confusion were well-documented, though their understanding was limited to the medical frameworks of the time.

During the Roman period, physicians like Galen attributed illnesses like sepsis to imbalances in the body's humors. This humoral theory suggested that health depended on a balance of blood, bile, phlegm, and black bile. They applied treatments such as bloodletting, an attempt to restore the body's equilibrium, but these methods, lacking any understanding of germs or infection, often fell short.

Centuries later, during the Regency era in early 19th-century England, the approach to sepsis had evolved little. Though symptoms such as fever and rapid decline were observed by physicians, the dominant theories still revolved around humors and miasmas—the idea that "bad air" caused disease. There was no knowledge of bacteria or germs, as germ theory was still decades away. A doctor encountering a feverish patient with rapid breathing or confusion might have turned to practices like purging or applying poultices, as antiseptic techniques and antibiotics were still unknown.

Fast forward to today, and sepsis is still a significant global health challenge. Its symptoms—fever, chills, rapid heartbeat, confusion, extreme fatigue, and clammy skin—are signs of the body's overactive response to infection. Modern medicine has advanced tremendously; we understand that bacteria, viruses, or fungi can trigger sepsis, and we have antibiotics, sterile surgical techniques, and supportive therapies like intravenous fluids. Yet, despite this progress, millions of people worldwide still fall victim to sepsis every year.

History reminds us that while our understanding of medicine has evolved, the fight against sepsis continues. From Roman times to the Regency period and into the modern era, the symptoms of this condition have been observed again and again. Although we now know its causes and have the tools to treat it, sepsis serves as a stark reminder of the importance of vigilance in combating infections and improving access to medical care worldwide. Through education and awareness, we can continue to shift the narrative on sepsis, ensuring fewer lives are lost to this ancient and persistent adversary.

Nurses:

While the period delights us with its elegance, it was also a time of stark contrasts, especially when it came to professions like nursing and medicine.

Before Florence Nightingale redefined nursing in the mid-19th century, the role of a nurse was an informal and often undervalued one. There were no standardized training programs, certifications, or nursing schools for talented women like Wendy like we know now. Instead, during the Regency-era, nursing was a skill picked up through practical experience. Women who took on this work often learned on the job, their knowledge passed down through observation, trial-and-error, or the guidance of more experienced caregivers, such as Nick and the other doctors in Wendy's case.

By contrast, doctors' education during this period offered a starkly different experience but it was reserved for men only. Aspiring physicians attended universities such as Oxford, Cambridge, or Edinburgh, or institutions like the Royal College of Surgeons. Their path involved rigorous study, including anatomy dissections, lectures, and apprenticeships under established doctors. This formal training culminated in earning a diploma or medical degree, conferring legitimacy and social respectability. Doctors, unlike nurses, were considered gentlemen of science, afforded status as professionals.

However, this divide wasn't merely about education. Medicine, as a whole, was dominated by men, and women were largely excluded from formal training or academia. For nurses, caregiving was seen as a natural extension of a woman's domestic role rather than a professional pursuit. Hospitals, often mistrusted by society, relied on these untrained women to administer care.

Particularly in the upper-crust households, it was not unusual for family members or trusted servants to assume nursing duties when necessary, as employing a professional nurse might be seen as improper, or even risky.

Yet, despite the lack of formal acknowledgment, these women forged ahead, offering care at the bedside armed with little more than determination and intuition. This was far removed from the structured, scientifically informed nursing model that would later emerge under Florence Nightingale's influence.

Through my story, I have tried to capture some of the quiet heroism and resilience of these early nurses. While their paths lacked the formal recognition afforded to their male doctor counterparts, their contributions were no less integral to the health and survival of many. I hope this glimpse into their world enriches your readers' experience and serves as a tribute to the unsung nurturing spirits of Regency England.

About the Author

Bestselling author Sara Adrien writes hot and heart-melting regency romance with a Jewish twist. As a law professor-turned-author, she writes about clandestine identities, whims of fate, and sizzling seduction. If you like unique and intelligent characters, deliciously sexy scenes, and the nostalgia of afternoon tea, then you'll adore Sara Adrien's tender tear-jerkers.

For more information and exclusive sneak peeks, new releases, and more, sign up for Sara Adrien's newsletter at www.Sara Adrien.com.

Catch up with Sara Adrien here:
linktr.ee/jewishregencyromance
saraadrien.com
instagram.com/jewishregencyromance
facebook.com/AuthorSaraAdrien
bookbub.com/authors/sara-adrien
goodreads.com/author/show/22249825.Sara_Adrien
youtube.com/channel/UCK9OLp1wN6IaGkXe7OugfHg

Also by Sara Adrien

Also by Sara Adrien and published by Dragonblade Books with the *Doctors on Harley Street*:

A Sight to Behold
(Nick and Pippa's story)

The Scent of Intuition
(Alfie and Bea's story)

A Touch of Charm
(Andre's story)

A Touch of Gold
(Felix's story)

Bring Me A Winter Miracle
(holiday special)

Lyon's Den books with *Doctors on Harley Street* by Sara Adrien:

Don't Wake A Sleeping Lyon
The Lyon's First Choice
The Lyon's Golden Touch
The Lyon's Legacy
and many more!

Find out more at www.SaraAdrien.com

ACKNOWLEDGMENTS

No writer creates a story alone, and I am no exception. This book would not have been possible without the remarkable people in my life who give me courage, inspiration, and hope every step of the way.

To my family, thank you for your endless support and unwavering belief in me. To my friends who graciously read and encouraged my work, Terri, Barbara, Janis, Rosie, Lyn, Emily, Andrea, and Dominique, your support and enthusiasm mean the world to me. A heartfelt thank you to Ariele and everyone at *Dragonblade* for your dedication and expertise in bringing this book to life.

And finally, to you, my wonderful readers. Your love for these stories is what makes this journey so special. I hope this book enchants you, makes you smile, and tempts you to share it with your friends. Reviews are the lifeblood of an author's work, so if you enjoyed the story, I'd be endlessly grateful if you left one. Most of all, I hope to see you return for the next adventure as the series continues.

With all my gratitude,
Sara Adrien

www.ingramcontent.com/pod-product-compliance
Lightning Source LLC
Chambersburg PA
CBHW071229300726
48975CB00002B/348